Cursed with a poor sense of direction and a propensity to read, **Annie Claydon** spent much of her childhood lost in books. A degree in English Literature followed by a career in computing didn't lead directly to her perfect job—writing romance for Mills & Boon—but she has no regrets in taking the scenic route. She lives in London: a city where getting lost can be a joy.

Rachel Dove is a tutor and romance/romcom author from West Yorkshire, in the UK. She lives with her husband and two sons, and dreams of a life where housework is done by fairies and she can have as many pets as she wants. When she is not writing or reading she can be found walking her American Cocker Oliver in the great outdoors, or dreaming of her next research trip away with the family.

Also by Annie Claydon

Festive Fling with the Single Dad
Best Friend to Royal Bride
Winning the Surgeon's Heart
A Rival to Steal Her Heart
Healing the Vet's Heart
The Best Man and the Bridesmaid
Greek Island Fling to Forever

Also by Rachel Dove

Fighting for the Trauma Doc's Heart

Discover more at millsandboon.co.uk.

FALLING FOR THE BROODING DOC

ANNIE CLAYDON

THE PARAMEDIC'S SECRET SON

RACHEL DOVE

MILLS & BOON

Published in Great Britain 2021
by Mills & Boon, an imprint of HarperCollins*Publishers* Ltd,
1 London Bridge Street, London, SE1 9GF

www.harpercollins.co.uk

HarperCollins*Publishers*
1st Floor, Watermarque Building,
Ringsend Road, Dublin 4, Ireland

ISBN: 978-0-263-29768-3

06/21

FSC
www.fsc.org
MIX
Paper from responsible sources
FSC C007454

This book is produced from independently certified FSC™ paper to ensure responsible forest management.
For more information visit www.harpercollins.co.uk/green.

Printed and bound in Spain
by CPI, Barcelona

FALLING FOR THE BROODING DOC

ANNIE CLAYDON

MILLS & BOON

To aspiring writers everywhere.
Wishing you many happy endings!

CHAPTER ONE

DR ROSS SUMMERBY stood at the window of his office, staring out. The Lake District afforded many beautiful views, but this was one that he never tired of, the lake stretching off into the distance to meet mountains shrouded in morning mist. He frowned at the one blot on the landscape, a tiny figure in a small rowing boat, cutting through the still waters.

A knock sounded behind him and as he turned the door opened. Sam Kovak was clearly far too frustrated to wait for him to invite her in.

'Have you seen her?'

Ross nodded. 'Yep. Sit down, Sam.'

Sitting down didn't improve Sam's mood. It didn't much improve Ross's either, but as head of the Lakeside Sports Injury Clinic, he reckoned that part of his job was to listen to what everyone had to say, and provide a few calming answers if necessary. Sam looked in need of calming answers, and he didn't blame her.

'I told her specifically. No rowing. I've given her exercises to do that will maintain her fitness, without putting too much stress on her hip. What's not to understand about that? She's a doctor, for goodness' sake.'

'Doctors generally make the worst patients.' Ross grinned at Sam. 'Unlike physiotherapists, of course.'

'That goes without saying.' Sam puffed out a breath. 'So, as a doctor, what would *you* prescribe for another doctor who won't listen to her physiotherapist?'

'It's not you, Sam. She just doesn't listen, full stop. That's why I put her in your care, because if your unremitting good humour can't wear her down then I doubt anything else can.'

The remark mollified Sam a little. 'So what am I going to do? I've tried sympathetic understanding…'

Ross chuckled. 'And how did that work?'

'It didn't. She just rolled her eyes at me. So I tried reminding her—because I shouldn't need to explain—that bursitis of the hip will only get worse over time if you don't make long-term efforts to bring down the inflammation and restore muscle balance. Not only will she end her sporting career, but the hip will gradually deteriorate…' Sam puffed out a frustrated breath.

'What did she say to that?'

'Nothing! She nodded, and I thought perhaps I'd got through to her. Then I arrive here this morning and what do I see?' Sam gestured towards the window. 'It's almost as if she's determined to self-destruct.'

'Yeah. That thought occurred to me too. Leave it with me, Sam.'

'What are you going to do?'

'I'm going to give up on her.'

Sam frowned. 'I thought we never gave up on anyone. That's one of the things I like about working here, so don't tell me you're changing your policy all of a sudden.'

'Nothing's changed, I'm just making an exception.

Maybe she's never had anyone give up on her before, and it's what she needs to make her face reality, eh?'

Ross had fetched them both a cup of tea, which was a way of calming his own mood as well as Sam's because Laurie Sullivan was beginning to get to him as well. A patient who had every chance of recovery but who seemed bent on destroying it seemed to mock all the people who'd fought against the odds here at the Lakeside Clinic.

As he walked out of the clinic, across the grass to the shore of the lake, he reminded himself that people came in all shapes and sizes. That no one should be dismissed because their actions seemed rash or not understandable. But Dr Sullivan was stubborn, and he was going to have to show her that he too could be inflexible when he wanted to.

He sat down on one of the wooden benches that were placed here for the purpose of enjoying the view. Laurie's rowing style was immaculate, as could be expected from a member of the England team, and Ross had noticed that there was a touch of grace about everything she did. It must have taken a great deal of work and determination to combine her impressive sporting achievements with a doctor's training, but somehow Laurie had managed it.

And now she seemed intent on throwing it all away. The one question in his mind was *why*? She was either too arrogant for words or there was something going on here that he had yet to fathom. This next conversation would settle that conundrum, at least.

It seemed that Laurie had exhibited enough defiance for one day, and she was pulling towards the small dock where the pleasure boats for those patients who *were* allowed on the water were moored. He'd wondered where she'd got the sleeker, sporting boat that she was using, and saw the flash of a boat rental company's logo at its prow. That must have taken a bit of planning as the boatyard was on the other side of the lake, a twenty-mile drive by road.

As she climbed out of the boat, Ross saw she was favouring her left leg. The stiffness in the right side of her hip hadn't been apparent when she'd been rowing, but that was no surprise. In his experience many sportspeople learned to work through pain to achieve excellence. Laurie caught sight of him and pulled off the blue woollen cap she was wearing to reveal her shock of red hair, cut short so that it wouldn't blow in her face when she was on the water.

She had the audacity to smile. There was a trace of mischief there, and somehow she managed to convey the idea that she expected him to understand that she may have bent the rules a little, but she'd done nothing wrong. As she walked towards him, she was clearly making an effort to hide the stiffness in her right leg.

She was perfect. Charming. And all this was about to stop.

'Lovely morning.' She stopped in front of him and Ross battled with the impulse to agree with her and allow her to go back to the clinic and get on with her day without any challenge.

'It is.' He motioned to the empty half of the long seat. That grace of hers, and her economy of movement, allowed her to disguise whatever pain she felt as she lowered herself onto the bench.

'Did you come out here to see me?' She scrunched

her nose slightly. Great nose. The freckles gave it a lot of charm.

'Yes, I did.' Ross tore his attention from her face and got down to business. 'I'm discharging you.'

That provoked a reaction. One that wasn't carefully controlled to stop anyone from divining what she was actually thinking. Her face fell, and he saw a flare of panic in her golden eyes.

'You can't. I'm supposed to stay for seven weeks, and I've only been here a week.'

Ross nodded. 'I think we've done just about all we can do for you.'

Laurie thought for a moment. 'But…the consultant I saw thinks I should be here. I'm all paid up for seven weeks…'

That was the crux of the matter. The consultant who had referred her had told Ross that he'd been unable to pass Laurie as fit for selection to the England team this year, and her stubborn refusal to allow anyone else to tell her what to do about her injury had rubbed a lot of people up the wrong way. She'd be out of the team for good if she couldn't show her commitment to addressing the injury that had been troubling her for months.

'We'll refund you, of course.'

Ross felt the sudden urge to smile as he watched her trying to maintain her composure. She was doing rather well, considering the ramifications of what he was suggesting.

'I'm not…' She swallowed, as if about to admit to having murdered someone. 'My hip isn't…at full strength yet.'

She wasn't better. Despite all its success with much more intransigent injuries than Laurie's, the clinic had failed her. And this was the only way forward that Ross could see.

'Perhaps *discharge* isn't the right word. I'm throwing you out.'

This was embarrassing, and Ross's good looks weren't helping. Dark hair and melting brown eyes had always pushed all her buttons and he had a body that was clearly at home with movement and action. And the fact that *he* was here to deliver this message, rather than Sam, had the worrying implication that Ross meant business.

He had to know what he was doing to her, and that this place was her last resort if she wanted to save her sporting career. She had been such a fool, ignoring well-intentioned advice and allowing the situation to escalate like this. But she'd always had a problem with authority…

Those long years of training under her father's watchful eye had seen to that. Laurie had borne his insults silently, determined that he shouldn't see her cry when he called her a failure. Keeping going was all she knew how to do, and now she'd been given an ultimatum. If Ross Summerby didn't sign off on her stay here, then she could kiss goodbye to any hope of getting back onto the selection list to compete for her country.

Why? Why had she gone out rowing, in direct contravention of Sam's advice? Laurie couldn't even remember now why she'd thought that was a good idea.

'You can't.' Blind panic was gripping her, and it was hard enough to keep her face expressionless, let alone think of something more persuasive to say.

'I think you'll find that I can.' He was watching her closely, and she felt a shiver run down her spine. 'My difficulty is that we have a waiting list full of patients, all of whom are committed to their recovery. I can let you stay on for another six weeks, and we can pretend to treat you for your own convenience, or I give your place here to someone who we can make a difference for. What would you do?'

That wasn't fair. The answer was obvious. Laurie hung her head, looking down at her feet, the way she had when she'd wanted to hide her emotions from her father.

'I'm sorry. It won't happen again, I'll do everything that Sam tells me…'

'Maybe you will, for a little while. I'd give it a week. Tops.'

If they made a bet on it, then Ross would probably win. She looked up at him and saw a trace of sadness in his face. Kindness, too, in his dark eyes. He didn't like this any more than she did, and it gave her one last chance.

'Okay. You're probably right. Is there anything… *anything*…that I can do to change your mind and let me stay? If you throw me out now, that effectively ruins my chances of getting back onto the England team.' Honesty was her final resort. And it seemed to work, because Ross smiled.

'There is one thing. You may not like it very much.'

Laurie had already reckoned on that. 'That's okay. I can live with not liking it.'

'We have a small apartment that we use for visiting specialists. In the old building.' He gestured towards the large residential property that stood a little way away from the modern clinic building. 'You can stay there and make use of any of the clinic's facilities you want to, the gym and the pool. You can even book a session with Sam, as long as you're not planning on wasting her time by ignoring what she tells you.'

That didn't sound so bad. It was the kind of freedom that Laurie had wanted all along.

'But there's something I need in return.'

Maybe she'd let down her guard and her smile had given her away. Laurie turned the corners of her mouth down. 'In my experience, there's always a catch…'

'No one here gets a free ride, and I want you to work here, part time, for four afternoons a week. You can choose what you want to do. There's a pile of filing in our basement that needs attention. Or you could make use of your doctor's training. I have some patients that I think may benefit from your particular experience.'

Seriously? Laurie had started to think that Ross had thought everything through, but this was the most bizarre thing she'd ever heard. Filing didn't sound all that appealing and working here as a doctor was madness.

'You want me…a completely unknown quantity… to work with your patients. You're sure about that, are you?'

His dark eyes softened suddenly. They were his greatest weapon, the one that made her heart pump ferociously and her instincts tell her that she could trust him. Her head was having trouble keeping all that under control.

'Sam tells me that a few of her patients have mentioned you've been encouraging them with their gym work and helping them pace themselves properly. Everyone here has some kind of stake in the clinic, and since you're no longer a patient then the only other option is employee.'

He let the thought float in the air between them. Ross clearly had few qualms about admitting his motives, but then he had nothing to lose.

'And it means you can keep an eye on me.' Laurie felt a trickle of embarrassment run up her spine.

'That thought did cross my mind. And I took the precaution of calling the director of the company that runs the chain of emergency GP clinics you work with this morning, and asking for a reference.'

'You did *what?* Thanks for that. Now I expect they think I'm about to leave. It's not easy to find a job in medicine that gives me the kind of time off that I need to train and compete…' Laurie bit her tongue.

'I imagine not. That's why I told her that I was considering asking you to help out here for the next six weeks, as part of your therapy, and that you'd be back with them after that. Adele thought it was a great idea and it would give you a chance to widen your experience a little. She put me through to your immediate boss and I'm sure you'll be pleased to hear that he gave you a shining reference.'

Laurie frowned. 'Adele. You know her, do you?'

'I know a lot of people. A clinic in an isolated location like this gets its referrals by going out and making itself known. And by being the best, of course.'

'You're sure about that? That you're the best?' Laurie knew that the Lakeside Clinic was the best of its kind, but she couldn't resist the dig.

'Yep. You're well acquainted with what it takes to be the best. Once you get there, you know it.' He leaned back in his seat, surveying the empty lake in front of him thoughtfully.

There was steel beneath that easygoing smile of his. He'd given Laurie exactly what she wanted and still she felt that he'd got exactly what *he* wanted out of the deal too.

'All right. Filing doesn't appeal all that much, but I have a good understanding of sports injuries and I think I can contribute something as part of your medical team. Are you going to pay me?' Maybe if the hours she worked came at a price, he wouldn't demand too much of her.

'Of course. I'm also going to be watching you, because our patients come first here. Always.'

That put her very firmly in her place. But Laurie could work with this. The ability to help others, along with the freedom to dictate her own regime, was what she'd always wanted. What she'd fought with her father for. If she disregarded Ross's watchful eyes, she could begin to persuade herself that this was going to be a piece of cake.

'You think I'd agree to work for you if you said anything different?'

'I wouldn't sign off on your working as a doctor here if *you* said anything different.' He gave her an innocent smile. 'Do we have a bargain?'

'You're saying that as if I have a choice. But, yes, it's a generous offer and it suits me.'

He shrugged. 'There's always a choice. I'm interested to know why you chose to row right past my window this morning when you could have quite easily gone in the other direction.'

Right. She should have expected that there was a

catch to this. Apparently he felt their arrangement allowed him to ask awkward questions that she didn't know the answers to.

'No idea.'

'Maybe that's something we could talk about sometime…' Ross's smile was altogether too knowing, and much too delicious for Laurie's liking. She got to her feet, trying to ignore the stiffness in her hip.

'You can talk about it if you want. I'll pass…' She threw the words over her shoulder as she walked away.

CHAPTER TWO

THAT HAD...WORKED? Ross wasn't entirely sure whether he'd done just what Laurie was hoping he'd do, or she'd done exactly as he'd hoped. It was difficult to tell, but when he told Sam about the arrangement she nodded, professing her approval.

'You gave her no choice, then.'

'That's the part that bothers me, to be honest. It all feels a bit too much like blackmail.'

Sam rolled her eyes. 'This isn't a hotel, it's a clinic. The one thing you've always asked of everyone is that they're part of the community here. If we're at the point where there's only one option you're prepared to accept, that's because Laurie's shut all the others down herself. If this doesn't work, I don't see what will.'

'If it doesn't then I'm out of ideas. I really *will* have to think about throwing her out.'

Sam smirked at him. 'Of course you won't. You don't give up that easily, Ross.'

Nice to hear. Although he suspected that even Sam underestimated the extent of the problem. Laurie was tough, determined and it was almost impossible to read her. There was obviously something going on beneath that poker-faced exterior, but for the life of him he couldn't think what, and Ross suspected that getting to the bottom of it was the one way to help her heal.

That made honesty his guiding principle. Laurie was a doctor and, even if only half of her reference was accurate, an exceptionally good one. There would be no skimming over facts that she wasn't ready to hear, and it was apparent from their latest conversation that there would be no hiding *his* thinking behind anything. That was fine, but his growing fascination with her made everything challenging.

She was no less fascinating when he called into her room at the clinic to see when she'd be ready to move. Laurie was strikingly attractive, but didn't have the kind of soft prettiness that some found so appealing. The set of her jaw was a little too determined, and the look in her eye a little too challenging. She was the kind of woman that Ross could admire endlessly.

And she was ferociously organised. Her bags were already packed and she was ready to go. When he reached for one of her suitcases she gave him a look that would have slain dragons and which sent tingles down his spine.

She fell into step next to him, wheeling both suitcases behind her, as they walked along the gravel path that led to the house. When Ross opened the main doors, she stepped into the entrance hall, looking around at the grand old staircase and the honey coloured oak panelling on the walls, which were in marked contrast to the clean lines and emphasis on light and space of the newer building that now housed the clinic.

'This is a bit different!'

Ross nodded. 'This is where the clinic started out.'

'Hmm.' She was taking in everything, the stained-glass panels in the doors, the flowers that Ross's mother kept in the hallway. 'When was that?'

'Thirty-two years ago. I was four, and my mother came here and started the practice, expanding it to a small clinic. We lived in an apartment on one side of the house and the clinic was on the other.'

'Thirty-six, then?' Laurie's half-smile told Ross that she was on a mission.

'I'll be thirty-six in a couple of months. September the fifth.' He threw the extra information in just to let her know that she could ask whatever she wanted about him. His life was an open book. Apart from a few pages that had got stuck together, but that was a long time ago now…

'And you were always destined to be a doctor? And come to work here?'

'Not really. I went through the usual cornucopia of career ambitions but in the end I decided that what I saw every day, the kind of good that my mother was doing, was what I really wanted. We'd never intended that I should join the practice, but she was ill for a while and I came back to help out. I found that this was where I wanted to be after all.'

'After all the time spent wanting to get away?' There was a hard edge to her tone suddenly.

'I wouldn't put it quite like that. I suppose you sometimes need to distance yourself from something for a while to realise it's what you really want. There's something to be said for feeling you have a choice.' Ross caught her gaze, and thought he saw a reaction in the fascinating depths of her eyes.

'Choices are what we make for ourselves.' She shrugged, looking around the hallway. 'You live here, then?'

'I have the apartment upstairs. My mother has the one downstairs, and the guest apartment is at the back.' Ross began to walk towards the double doors that led to the single-storey extension, holding one side open for Laurie to manoeuvre her suitcases through.

'You live on your own?'

'Yes.'

'No partner, then?' She raised one eyebrow, as if that was difficult to believe.

Maybe these questions were intended to divert him from asking any of her. If she thought they'd make him baulk, she could think again.

'No. You?'

She shook her head. 'I travel light.'

'Yes I can see that.' He motioned towards the two large suitcases and she cracked a smile.

'I travel light in all other respects.'

Ross opened the door to the guest apartment and she walked inside, looking around. It was small but comfortable enough for a six-week stay and Laurie walked across to the windows, pulling back the drapes to let light stream in.

'This is lovely. You're sure it's all right for me to stay here?'

'Yes, it's fine.' He took the front door key from his keyring, handing it to her. 'It's all yours for the next six weeks. There's a small kitchenette, but you can eat in the clinic's restaurant. The cleaner comes in twice a week, Tuesdays and Fridays.'

Laurie smiled. 'They won't have much to do. I don't make a lot of mess.'

Ross had noticed that. Her room in the clinic had been impeccably tidy, with none of the usual bits and pieces that people brought with them for a long stay.

'I don't make a lot of noise either. I won't be disturbing you or your mother…'

'My mother's away on holiday for the next couple of weeks, and my apartment's upstairs on the other side of the building. Unless you're planning a rave, you won't disturb me.'

She shook her head. 'I don't have enough friends for a rave. The ones I do have tend to go to bed early so they can be up to train in the morning.'

He watched as she walked over to the French doors, unlocking them and stepping out onto the small paved area outside.

'Nice view. Aren't you worried it'll be too much temptation for me?'

'No. As I said, what you decide to do about your own treatment is entirely up to you. Are *you* worried?'

'I'll manage.' Laurie gestured towards the spiral staircase that ran up to the balcony outside his apartment windows. 'Do I need to turn a blind eye if I see someone sneaking up to your place?'

'Such as…?' Ross pretended he didn't know what she meant.

'I don't know. If you had a thing going with one of the women at the clinic you might want to keep it quiet. Or one of the guys…'

Ross grinned. When Laurie pushed, she pushed. He was beginning to like pushing back.

'All my guests use the front door. And, no, I don't have *a thing* going with any of my staff, and I'm not gay. You?'

'I don't have a thing going with any of your staff either. And I'm not gay. I'll call the police if I see anyone sneaking up there at the dead of night.'

'I'd appreciate it. Always good to have someone keeping an eye out.'

Ross wondered whether she'd like to come upstairs to his flat and take a look through his wardrobes. If he hadn't had a full schedule this afternoon, he would have been tempted to invite her up. But Laurie had already turned to walk back inside.

'If you're free tomorrow, I'd like to sit down with you for a couple of hours. Just to talk through which patients you'll be responsible for.'

She nodded. 'That's fine. But I'm going to have to take a day trip back home before I start to work with them.'

Ross raised an eyebrow. Normally patients were encouraged to stay here at the clinic to promote a regular regime of rest and exercise. But then he'd just made it very clear that Laurie *wasn't* a patient any more, and he couldn't think of a reason why she should stay. Other than his growing curiosity, which wasn't anyone's business but his own.

'I need clothes.' She glanced down at the two large suitcases. 'Work clothes, that is.'

Right. Ross imagined that she would have noticed that the staff here often wore the same kind of casual sporting wear that he'd seen Laurie in for the last week. His own chinos and open-necked shirt were about as formal as things got. Perhaps there was another reason for her day trip, but he couldn't imagine what it could be.

'You'll be fine as you are.'

She shook her head. 'No, I have work clothes and sports clothes. The two don't overlap.'

It was a reason of sorts. And impossible to tell whether it disguised another motive.

'Okay, I've got to make a trip down to London the day after tomorrow to see some patients who've been referred to us. You want to join me?'

Laurie eyed him, a hint of amusement playing around her lips. 'Making sure I don't escape?'

Ross shook his head. 'You can leave any time you like, there's no need to escape. I'd just like to be the first to know if you do. Shall I book an extra train ticket?'

'Yes. Thanks.'

He'd either called her bluff or travelling down to London with him fitted in with her plans as well. Ross nodded his assent and turned, walking out of the guest apartment. He had no idea what Laurie was going to throw at him next, but he imagined that the next few weeks were going to be anything but dull.

What the blue blazes…? *Are you sleeping with someone at the clinic?* It was really none of her business. He could shapeshift into a vampire bat and hang upside down in the rafters all night if he wanted, it made no difference to what he did during the day as a doctor. Or as a boss. She supposed that Ross was her boss now.

One who had a very obvious interest in what drove her, and that was something that Laurie preferred to keep to herself because she wanted to forget about it. Her questions had started as a defence mechanism, a way of showing him how uncomfortable it was when someone else tried to pick your life apart, but he'd stubbornly refused to appear even slightly uneasy.

Then her own curiosity about him had taken over. Why someone like Ross didn't have potential partners queuing all the way up the steps of the fire escape. He had everything. Good looks, good job, a nice personality when he wasn't being so pushy. And even when he *was* being pushy he just oozed sex appeal. That wasn't her heart talking, it was a simple fact.

Laurie bent down to unzip one of her suitcases, feeling the stiffness catch in her hip. That was another thing. She'd fought so hard over the last months, trying to deny that anything serious was wrong, to both herself and everyone else. But Ross had taken that all away from her. He'd professed not to care whether she got well or not, although clearly he did. And then he'd put all the responsibility for her treatment squarely in her lap.

It was a case of being very careful what you wished for. Laurie had spent so many of her teenage years fighting for her freedom that it was a hard habit to break. She'd tried to free herself from being told what to do about her injury, and now she'd done it. It was a bitter victory, though, because she suddenly felt very alone.

Nonsense. That was nonsense. She'd feel better when she had work to do. In the meantime, she'd have to think about drawing up a therapy plan for herself…

At eight o' clock the following morning, Ross was sitting in his office, already working. Laurie wondered whether she should have come a little earlier.

Making a contest out of who could get up earliest

would have been just petty. Juvenile. Seriously tempting, though. Laurie tapped on the frame of the open door and he looked up, beckoning to her to come in. Those eyes made the idea of competing with him even more enticing.

'Have you thought any more about which patients you might take on?' It was phrased as a question, but the curve of Ross's lips left Laurie in little doubt that he reckoned she had.

'I'd like to know a little more about what you're expecting me to do first.' She refused to think of this as her counterattack. It was just a query.

He leaned back in his seat. Ross was every inch the boss, relaxed and assured, with an elusive air of being in charge. He might like to pretend that there were options, but in truth his word was law around here. She could leave, but then she wouldn't get what she wanted.

'What do you think?' He batted the question back.

Laurie took a breath. 'I think that I could contribute medically, and in helping to structure exercise regimes, but then you already have good doctors and physiotherapists on your staff, so I'd just be another pair of hands. What you don't have are any professional sportspeople.'

He nodded. 'Go on.'

'I think that's unique experience that I can bring. I understand the pressures and how injury can be a challenge.'

'I agree.' He grinned suddenly. 'We see eye to eye so far.'

Meeting Ross's gaze was becoming the biggest challenge in all of this. She wanted to enjoy the warm tingle of excitement that it brought and smile back at him, but Laurie had to remember that Ross held her future in his hands. One of the lessons she'd learned from a childhood that she was largely glad to have left behind was that showing her feelings to an authority figure wasn't a good idea.

'In that case… I suppose that the choice of which patients I can work with most effectively is clear cut.' Best not name any names. Best not give him the ammunition to slap her down, the way her father had.

'Yes and no. Pete Evans and Usha Khan are both professional athletes but…'

It was just as well she hadn't mentioned that Pete and Usha would be her first choice of patients to work with. It sounded as if Ross was about to rule them out. Laurie nodded and pushed two files across the desk towards her.

'I'd like to discuss two other patients with you. We're expecting Adam Hollier and Tamara Jones to join us within the next week, so you'd be able to take them on right from the start of their stay here.'

'That would be helpful.' Laurie reached for the folders. She'd never heard of either of them and wondered whether they were newcomers to their respective areas of sport. She flipped open the first file and ran her finger down the details for Tamara Jones.

'She's fifteen.' That was going to be a difficulty. In Laurie's own experience, fifteen meant traumatic choices and a lot of heartache.

'Yes. Tamara's a very promising young runner who lost the lower part of her leg in a car accident. She's had some problems with the fit of her prosthetic that have set her recovery back, and we're in the process of organising the adjustments. She's frustrated at the slow progress, though, and facing a crossroads in her life at the moment.'

'I can identify with that.' The words slipped out before Laurie could stop them.

'How's that?' Ross predictably picked up on every chance to ask her about herself.

'We're talking about Tamara. I can see that she's facing some enormous obstacles. How does she feel about the way forward?'

'The medical aspects of her rehab are just one part of the challenge. Tamara knows she wants to maintain her sporting activities, but the problems she's been having with her prosthetic have eroded her confidence.'

Laurie frowned. 'When you get that right she should find that she has a lot of options. Some runners who use blades are faster than those who don't.'

'In addition to what we can do for her medically, we'd like to help her explore all of those options. And help her get back to full fitness.'

Laurie closed the folder, clearing her throat. This young girl, trying to make the right choices in life, was uncomfortably close to home and tugging at her heart. She opened the next folder.

'Adam Hollier.' He was just a year older than Tamara.

'Adam's sustained a stress fracture to his foot…' Ross stopped suddenly, looking at her as she felt her cheeks flame. Did he somehow know about her father, and the way he'd pushed her? Was Ross actively *trying* to break her down?

'Over-training?' She managed to get the two words out.

'There's no indication of that. As with Tamara, we

need to address the medical issues, but also resolve how his injury has been caused. He's a bright kid and he knows that a susceptibility to this kind of injury may hamper him in the future, but he's so focussed on taking up sport as a profession that he can't see any alternatives.'

Laurie flipped the cover of the file shut. Slowly and deliberately, giving herself some time to think, she put the folders back onto Ross's desk. 'Can we take a break from this meeting? For a moment?'

'Sure. You want…coffee?' He took one look at Laurie's face and shrugged. Clearly he saw that she didn't.

'I want to ask you why you chose these two patients. Did you imagine that they'd be the most challenging for me? In which case, I think you should get your motives straight—you're here for them, not for me. We've already agreed that I'm going to take charge of my own treatment.'

He thought for a moment, obviously turning her words over in his mind. 'Honestly—'

Simmering anger came close to the boil. 'I find that being honest is always good. Particularly when you're dealing with a doctor-patient relationship and deciding whether the doctor in question has the resources to help a patient.'

'You're suggesting that this is all an experiment? That I've chosen a set of challenging patients for you and I'm going to stand back and see what happens?' His expression tightened into a dark frown. 'That couldn't be further from the truth. If you have issues that mean you're not able to help these kids, I expect you to say so.'

He'd boxed her into a corner. Or maybe Laurie had

done that all by herself, but however she'd managed to get here she had to move. As she got to her feet, she felt pain shoot from her hip down into her leg, and almost stumbled. Ross started forward and she glared him back down into his seat.

'I think…' She wasn't entirely sure what she thought, but pacing seemed to help. 'Did you know that I was over-trained by my father? Well past the point of exhaustion at times. That I had to go to court in order to go and live with an aunt when I was fifteen?' It wasn't exactly a secret, the facts were a matter of record, and she'd been questioned about it more than once at press conferences.

'No, I didn't know that.' Something that looked like tenderness bloomed in his eyes, and Laurie ignored it.

'Well, it caused a lot of problems for me. Kids generally come with families, and I don't have much of an interest in trying to work out that kind of relationship. It's not my thing.'

'Fair enough. I'm not asking you to be a family counsellor, we already have a partnership with a very good one.' He paused for a moment, as if waiting to see whether Laurie was interested in that kind of counselling herself, and she bit back the temptation to tell him that there was a lake outside and he was welcome to go and jump in it.

'So what makes me the obvious choice for these two patients?'

'In my experience, teenagers come equipped with accurate radar. They know who really understands what they're going through, and they know who'll fight for them as well.'

'You're not trying to make my life easy, are you?'

He had the temerity to smile. 'Why would I? And if you believe that you can't help these kids, for whatever reason, we'll take another look at the list…'

Ross laid his hand on the pile of folders, pulling them back across his desk. In that moment a fierce protective flame ignited in her chest. Adam and Tamara were both facing a difficult and uncertain future, and Laurie knew how much that hurt. She really wanted to help them, and if Ross thought that she could…

'I didn't say that.' She walked back to his desk, grabbing the folders. She had to pull a little before he'd let go of them. 'I'll take them.'

'The meeting's back on again? That's your official answer?' A flicker of I-told-you-so humour danced in his eyes.

'Yes, it's official. I'll read through their histories and come back to you with some ideas. And unofficially…' She planted her hand on his desk, leaning towards him. 'You have a lot of good ideas, Ross. But you could try not to be so darned smug about them.'

Laurie didn't wait for him to answer. She marched from the room, hearing the door bang behind her.

CHAPTER THREE

WHEN A TAP sounded on the door, Ross wondered if it was Laurie coming back to make peace with him, and decided it probably wasn't. He was pretty sure that when Laurie banged anything shut behind her, it stayed shut. Then Sam popped her head around the door and he motioned for her to come in.

'Have you decided on annoyance therapy?'

'Um… Not sure. Ask me another.' Whatever Sam asked him was unlikely to be as challenging as Laurie's questions, or to ignite any flames of confused feelings.

'How about I just saw Laurie coming out of your office, looking like thunder and clutching some patient files to her chest as if she was going to punch anyone who tried to take them away from her?'

Good. That was good. The way she'd pulled the files from his grasp had told Ross he'd made the right decision. Laurie had something to give these kids and she knew it.

'We had a full and frank discussion.' The upshot of which had left a nagging doubt. 'Do I come across as smug?'

Sam had the grace to laugh at the idea. But then

Sam always thought the best of everyone. 'Did Laurie say that?'

'She mentioned it.' The more Ross thought about it, the more it bothered him. He could take an insult, but Laurie had got under his skin and her opinion of him mattered rather more than it should.

'I've known you a long time, Ross. I remember when you were working to expand the clinic, and… dealing with other things.'

'You can say it, you know. I was there too, I know what happened.'

He'd come back here after qualifying as a doctor, newly married and with such hope for the future. Sam had been the clinic's first employee, taken on as the place had begun to grow, and it had been inevitable that she, Ross and Alice would all become friends.

Sam smiled. 'I saw how much you struggled when Alice left you. It was a hard blow for you, being told you'd never be able to have a family, and you worked through that disappointment. You built the clinic up, and made that your family instead.'

'Was it that obvious?' Ross *did* see the clinic as a replacement for the wife he'd lost and the children he couldn't have, but it still stung a bit when Sam said it.

'I knew what was going on because I knew both you and Alice. I don't think anyone else knew the details, but it wasn't so very difficult to see that you were in pain. If you seem a little…proud of yourself over the way the clinic's turned out, it's because there was a time when you had nothing else, and you put everything you had into it during those early years.'

Ross shot her a grin. 'Is that your way of saying that I *am* smug? Give it to me straight, Sam.'

'It's my way of saying that you could ease off a bit on Laurie. You're not her doctor any more and you don't need to pretend that your past has been all plain sailing. And, no, "smug" isn't the first word that comes to mind in describing you, Ross…'

Ross hadn't asked whether 'smug' was the second word that came to mind. Sam probably wouldn't have told him anyway as her approach generally consisted of dangling a few ideas and then allowing them to ferment. And this idea was fermenting at such speed he felt almost intoxicated by it.

He set aside the question of why this mattered to him so much. Why *Laurie* mattered to him. Why having her in the same room brought a tang of excitement, even if she was generally challenging him.

Ross had seen her from the window of the clinic, sitting in one of the wooden seats on the paved area outside the guest apartment, with a mess of papers on the table in front of her. He should go and make peace with her.

But there was no need. When he approached her, Laurie smiled. One of those radiant, mischievous smiles of hers, which couldn't possibly be anything other than genuine.

'May I sit?'

'Of course.' She waved him to a seat.

'I want to apologise.'

She wrinkled her nose. 'Really? I'd rather you didn't, because then I'd have to apologise back.'

He felt the muscles across his shoulders loosen suddenly. 'Then we'll put this morning behind us?'

She nodded. 'Since it's two o'clock, I think that goes without saying.'

Never let the sun go down on an argument. Ross dismissed the thoughts of all the nights he'd curled up on the couch when Alice had thrown something at him and shut him out of the bedroom. He should take Laurie's attitude for what it was and not make comparisons.

'I'd like to explain, though…' Laurie shook her head in a clear gesture that he didn't need to. Maybe not for her, but Ross wanted to for himself. 'Bear with me, eh?'

'If you want.'

'Setting this clinic up…was hard. I had to go out and find contacts who would refer patients here, and I was in the middle of a messy divorce. This place became my family and…if I'm a little too hands on at times that's something I probably need to work on.'

Her gaze searched his face. Laurie clearly wanted more, but Ross wouldn't give it. His decision to stay well clear of any potential romantic involvement had already taken a beating in the face of her golden eyes and indomitable spirit, and discussing the matter might only tempt him to change his mind.

'Maybe I'm a little hands off at times.' She gave him a grin that told him there was no *maybe* about it.

He wanted to tell her that she should never change. That her stubbornness was delightful when combined with her laughing honesty. But it was too great a step to take because it came from his heart, and his head told him that Laurie was still in danger of cutting off her nose to spite her face where her injury was concerned. *That* should be his one and only priority.

'Have you thought any more about your potential patients?'

'You mean the ones that you suggested, and who I'm

not reckoning on letting you take away from me?' She stuck her chin out in an obvious challenge.

'Yeah. Those. I'm planning on going to see Adam tomorrow afternoon in London. It would be great if you have time to come along.'

'It'll only take half an hour to pack. And I'd like to come, it'll give me a start on getting to know him.'

Ross nodded. 'Tamara will be arriving the day after tomorrow.'

'Good. Are just two patients going to be enough to fill my time for four afternoons a week?'

'I'm hoping you'll be spending quite a bit of time with each of them. And if you do find yourself at a loose end, there are plenty of clinic activities you can get involved with.'

'Ah. Those would be the ones I haven't had anything to do with over the last week.' She shot him a wry smile.

'Yes. Those.' Ross smiled back. 'There are a few outreach activities just for staff as well. We go to the Lakeside School sports day every year, that's a couple of weeks from now.'

'Okay… I've got to ask. What's your involvement with a school sports day?'

'We're part of a community here. We take an interest in what local schools and sports centres are doing and offer our advice and help on a pro bono basis, if they need it. The sports day is a good opportunity to go along and get to know people.'

Laurie nodded. 'That sounds like something I'd expect of you. Socially responsible.'

'It's actually a lot of fun. We dress up.' Ross had left

the part that he reckoned Laurie might find the most challenging till last.

She shot him a sceptical look. 'Dressing up isn't really my thing.'

'Okay. Well you don't *have* to dress up, you can just come along. You'll be missing out, though, we've built up a few good costumes over the years. I usually go as the Mad Hatter.' Ross backed off from the idea and the effect was almost immediate. Laurie's lip began to curl in an expression of mischief.

'Where are these costumes?'

'We have them stored in one of the basement rooms. I can let you have the key if you're interested.'

'I'll do you a deal. I'll come in fancy dress if you let me choose *your* costume. The Mad Hatter doesn't really suit you.'

That sounded like a challenge. And Laurie's challenges were rapidly becoming both awkward and delicious.

'Yeah. I could probably do with a change. Why not?'

I'll dress up if you let me choose your costume. Laurie rolled her eyes at her own terrible judgement. That had to be one of the worst ideas she'd had in ages.

She watched Ross's retreat. When he walked away from her, she could stare, without risking being caught. There was a lot to admire about him, even from the back.

He was sucking her in. Into the life here at the clinic, the way everyone looked after everyone else as if it *was* an extended family. Tempting her to depend on him, to accept his judgement as sound. All the things that felt so hazardous.

She'd escaped the sticky tendrils of her own family. Escaped her father's heavy-handed attempts to control every aspect of her life, her training and her career. She couldn't give anyone control over her life like that again. Particularly not Ross, because it was so darned tempting to let him.

So she challenged him. Every time, and at every turn. Even that seemed to bring out the warm mischief in his eyes, and Laurie suspected that he didn't much mind. That was just as well because she wasn't going to stop any time soon.

If that meant choosing the most embarrassing costume she could find for him then so be it. It might be classed as petty, but it was a lifebelt in stormy seas, something to buoy her up and allow her the self-determination she'd fought so hard to attain.

CHAPTER FOUR

ROSS HAD BEEN wondering what Laurie was doing ever since their train had arrived at London Euston Station and they'd gone their separate ways. Whether she would really just go home or whether she had another secret agenda. Ross told himself that Laurie could have as many agendas as she liked, as long as she did the job he was paying her for, and worked towards healing her own injury. *Secret* was far too emotive a word, everything else was her own business.

The minicab drew up outside the small block of flats in London's docklands, at ten to two. The driver opened a newspaper, nodding abstractedly when Ross told him he might be a little while.

Being ten minutes early was just a matter of the London traffic being lighter than usual, but if he'd thought that he might catch Laurie unawares then he would have been disappointed. She answered the door of her top floor flat wearing a pair of dark slacks and a white top, the neutral colours accentuating the vibrant red of her hair and her tawny eyes. It wasn't so very different from the attire he'd seen her in for the last week, but presumably this was what Laurie classed as her 'doctor clothes'.

It all became a little clearer when she beckoned him inside, asking him to wait in the living room while she checked that all the windows were closed before she left. There was an almost military neatness about the place, with none of the piles of books and mementos that adorned his own sitting room. Just space, and light, and everything in its own place. *This* was how she'd managed to juggle a career as a doctor with her sporting achievements, with the kind of ruthless organisation that made sense of having different clothes for her two different identities.

He walked over to the window. There was a magnificent view of St Katharine docks, with small boats moored by the old dockside and a couple of white sails scudding past in the distance.

'Tempting view, eh?' Her voice sounded close behind him, and Ross jumped.

'I can see why you like it. How long have you been here?' Ross wondered whether the tidiness might be just as the result of having just moved in.

'Six years. It's a very handy location as it's close to where I work, and my rowing club is nearby too.'

Ross nodded, trying not to scan the rest of the room for clues about Laurie's life. There wasn't much to be had from it anyway.

'You're ready to go, then?'

'Yes, all set.' She walked out into the hallway, grabbing her suitcase and ushering Ross out of the flat.

He'd deliberately not given Laurie any more details than the ones included in the file, wanting to see how she would handle her first meeting with Adam. The minicab drew up outside a comfortable semi-detached house and Laurie's suitcase was retrieved from the boot. Ross paid the driver and led the way up the front path.

'Dr Summerby. It's so nice of you to come.' Adam's mother, Ann, answered the door.

'Ross, please,' Ross reminded her as he stepped inside. 'This is Dr Sullivan, she'll be helping with Adam's treatment.'

'Also known as Laurie.' Laurie let go of her suitcase, leaning forward to shake Ann's hand. There was none of the suspicious caution that characterised all her interactions with the staff at the clinic, and the warmth of her smile left Ross in no doubt that it was genuine.

'Adam's in the conservatory.' Ann beckoned them to follow her. 'Still cultivating the grumpy teenager vibe, I'm afraid…' Ann lowered her voice.

Adam hadn't said much when Ross had seen him last, but he'd met grumpier teenagers. He heard Laurie chuckle.

'I'm told that grumpy teenagers of all ages are Ross's specialty.' She leaned towards Ann slightly as if confiding an important piece of information, then shot Ross a mischievous glance.

She was charming. Entrancing. And there was no doubt that her joke was partly aimed at herself.

'I've been known to have some success…' He glanced back at her, seeing a quirk of humour pull at her lips. Laurie was slowly picking his wits apart, leaving them in adoring shreds at her feet, and he made an effort to pull himself together.

'How does Adam feel about his injury?' Laurie turned her smile on Ann, who puffed out a despairing breath.

'It's difficult for him. He loves running and he's really good at it. Our other son is more academic, and this is the thing that Adam excels at.'

'You have a coach for him?'

'Yes, when he was little my husband read up on what you're supposed to do to encourage a child who's interested in sport and they used to go out for sessions together, but when Adam started getting really serious about his running, we enrolled him at the local athletics club and got him a proper coach.'

'And what's his coach's attitude to the injury?' It seemed that Laurie couldn't quite let go of the idea that Adam's coach had something to do with this. But it was a relevant question and Ross left Ann to answer.

'Sadie's been really supportive. I've shown her the diagnosis and she's done a lot to encourage Adam to follow all the advice that Ross has given. But Adam's pretty clued up about things and he says that no one can say whether this injury is the result of some weakness that will stop him from competing.'

'He's right.' Ross nodded. 'That's why we'd like to have him stay at the clinic for a couple of weeks, not just to help him recover but to help him work out how he's going to move forward from this.'

Ann nodded. 'We're so grateful you can take him. A cancellation, you said?'

'Yes, that's right.' Ross spoke quickly, before Laurie could react. He hadn't told her that Adam would be taking her place. 'I think that Laurie's own skill set, she's an athlete as well as a doctor, may be a good fit for Adam.'

'If he listens to anyone, he may well listen to you.' Ann gave Laurie a thoughtful look.

'I'll be doing my best for him.' The slight jut of her chin left no possibility of failure and that hurt unexpectedly. Ross had tried so hard to reach Laurie and she'd fought him all the way, but it seemed that Adam already merited her commitment.

When they walked into the conservatory, Adam was sitting in front of a large TV screen, obviously moved in there for that purpose, playing a computer game. His foot, encased in a supportive boot, was propped up in front of him. Ross hung back, holding a cautioning hand towards Ann. He wanted to see how Laurie would approach their patient.

'Hi, there. You're Adam? I'm Dr Laurie Sullivan, but I only answer to Laurie.'

Adam looked up at her, his concentration on the screen momentarily broken. Maybe he saw what Ross did, someone that he wanted to know better, because the controller slipped from his hand.

'Hi.'

'Switch that off, Adam…' Ann murmured the words, about to make for the screen, but Ross shook his head. Adam always did as he was told, but when Ross had last seen him he'd clearly not been enthused by the efforts being made on his behalf. He wanted to see if Laurie could change that.

'I'm working at the Lakeside Clinic for a while this summer.' Laurie's smile gave the impression that this was a bit of a holiday for her. 'I expect you'll be wanting to know why I think I can help you?'

It was different. Ross recognised the need to prove himself with each one of his patients, but he wasn't usually as forthright about it as Laurie was being now. But she seemed to have caught Adam's attention.

'Okay…'

'Right, then. Well… I'm a doctor, which you know already, of course. I'm also an athlete and I've had a few injuries in my time.'

Adam glanced at his right foot, looking away quickly as if it irked him. 'What injuries?'

'I broke my fingers once…' Laurie held up her hand, wiggling her two middle fingers. 'Got them caught in a rowlock. I made sure I didn't do that again. I couldn't hold an oar for ages afterwards.'

'You're a rower?'

'Yes, that's right.' Laurie's smile became even more luminous. 'I love it. I was at the World Championships last year.'

That got Adam's attention. 'What, rowing? For England?'

'I got silver in the women's single sculls.' She leaned forward towards Adam. 'It'll be gold next year…'

'I'd *love* to be able to compete at a national level…'

'Your sport's running?'

'Yeah, I was thinking of branching out a bit before I was injured.' Adam shrugged, as if that didn't matter any more.

Laurie nodded towards the game controller. 'Not the modern pentathlon? That was originally supposed to hone your battle skills…'

Adam got the joke, snorting with laughter. 'Nah. That's just a game. I was thinking more about the four hundred metres, instead of two…'

Adam and Laurie started to talk animatedly, and Ann finally smiled too.

'Looks as if you've brought your secret weapon along,' she murmured.

It did seem that way. Although Ross had had no idea that Laurie would manage to strike up such an instant rapport with the boy.

He dismissed the thought that everything she'd done so far seemed calculated to keep *him* at arm's length. That didn't matter. What mattered was that Laurie gave Adam what he needed, and in the process found healing herself. If Ross was to be consigned to the role of bystander, then so be it.

'You said that his teachers have sorted out some schoolwork for Adam to do while he's away. Perhaps we can go over the schedule together…?'

'Yes. Thanks. I'll make some tea.' Ann beckoned Ross into the kitchen.

It was hard to keep his mind from wandering away from what Ann was saying. Ross could hear Laurie laughing and talking, the note of enthusiasm dragging his attention away. Then silence, followed by the sound of the video game that Adam had been playing.

'Oh!' Ann looked up from the timetable in front of her, smiling. 'Is Laurie into video games?'

'Um… Not as far as I know.' Ross searched for any memory of a games console in her room at the clinic and came up blank. 'I'll admit it didn't occur to me to ask.'

'No, I dare say it's not the first thing you think of at a job interview. But Laurie certainly seems to be getting through to Adam, and these days that's a minor miracle.'

It was working. Ross had privately had his own reservations about the arrangement and Laurie had voiced hers in no uncertain terms. But if she saw what he did, then Laurie would have to come to the same conclusion that Ann had.

'Yes…gotcha!' He heard Laurie's voice from the other room. 'No! That was a sneaky move, Adam, how did you do that?'

He heard Adam laugh, explaining a bit more about the game to Laurie. Then the sound of electronic battle as they started to play again.

Ann was seeming a lot less worried about the prospect of her son being away from home for the next few weeks, and when they'd finalised the arrangements for Adam's schoolwork Ross accompanied her back into the conservatory.

'I'm sorry to drag you away…' He grinned at Laurie and she gave him a slightly sheepish look.

'Oh. Yes, of course.' She gave the games controller back to Adam and flashed him a smile. 'This isn't over, Adam. I'll get you next time…'

'In your dreams.' Adam was clearly looking forward to the next time, and since that would be at the clinic, Ross was all for it.

'There's a bus that runs past the end of the road and goes straight to the station. If you can manage with your bags?' Ann looked at her watch. 'The traffic won't be too bad at this time in the afternoon.'

'Thanks. We'll manage.' Ross decided that he should take at least part of the responsibility for Laurie's large suitcase, and surprisingly enough he received a nod of assent.

As soon as they were out on the pavement, and Ann had shut the front door, she glanced up at him. 'Sorry. About the video game.'

'Really?' Ross shot her a sceptical look.

'Well…no, probably not. Adam's a competitive kid.'

And Laurie had given him something to compete with her over. The boy couldn't have missed her own fierce will to win.

'You play video games?'

She shrugged. 'No, not really. Never, in fact. But Adam does, so I guess I can learn. He says I can get a costume upgrade after I've played a few more rounds. That'll be a relief, my avatar looks like an entrant in a beauty contest at the moment.'

'And what do you get after you'd played a bit more?' Ross couldn't help but ask.

'Body armour. And a large sword…'

'Right.' He couldn't fight back the smile that accompanied the mental image of Laurie in body armour, her hair glinting in the sun. Twirling a large sword over her head. 'As you seem to be getting on with him so well, I'd like you to draft an exercise programme for him.'

'Great, thanks.' Laurie's eagerness to get involved was obvious. 'But that won't put Sam's nose out of joint, will it? She's an outstanding physiotherapist…'

'Yeah, I know she is. Sam's just pleased that she doesn't have to put up with you undermining all her good advice. She'll be fine.'

Ross wondered whether that wouldn't be a little too much honesty, but Laurie shot him a wry smile. 'I don't blame her. I'd feel exactly the same.'

She knew. And she seemed more comfortable with Ross's direct approach than Sam's kindly tact. When the bus came, she passed her suitcase up to him with only a minimal amount of protest, allowing him to lift it on board and tuck it into the storage compartment under the stairs. They made the earlier train with enough time to get coffee for the journey from the kiosk at the station.

Ross waited until the passengers were all seated, then settled himself into the seat opposite Laurie's, and the train pulled out of the station and began gathering speed.

He'd done exactly as he'd intended today. Laurie was becoming involved with the work of the clinic, and that involvement seemed to be tempering her approach to her own injury. Adam seemed to be looking forward to his stay at the clinic now, which was a great deal more than he had been. Mission accomplished. So why did this feel like a hollow victory?

Ross had begun to enjoy the challenge that was woven into their relationship, believing that maybe it was the way that Laurie interacted with everyone. But now he'd seen her with Adam, he'd realised that she *could* reach out to someone. It had led him to the inescapable conclusion that she just didn't want to reach out to him.

That was fine. It was okay. Laurie could do whatever she wanted to. Ross needed to take responsibility for his own feelings, and ask himself why it irked him so much.

He just needed to take one look at Laurie for the answer. She'd taken a book from her bag and was concentrating on the pages, unaware of his gaze. He'd been the odd one out most of his life, the friend at school who lived too far from town to be included in trips to the cinema or parties. For a few brief years, when he and Alice had been together, he'd thought that he could finally belong, as part of a couple and then a family.

That hadn't worked out and now he was the odd man at dinner parties, the table carefully arranged so that it wasn't too obvious. The one who went home alone.

He'd reconciled himself to that, and made the best of it. But Laurie had awakened the yearning for more, and he wanted her to notice him. Maybe even be a little bit special to her.

Ross opened his laptop, switching it on. It shouldn't happen, and if all the little reminders that it wasn't going to happen stung, he'd better just get used to it.

'Did you follow up with Ann? About Adam's trainer?'

Ross looked up from the article he was reading on his laptop. Laurie was still holding her book in front of her, and the question had come straight out of the blue.

'I did, as a matter of fact, while we were in the kitchen. She's sure that overtraining isn't the cause of his injury, the trainer's a friend of the family and she shares Ann's view that Adam should enjoy his sport and have time for other things.'

Laurie nodded. 'Okay.'

This clearly wasn't the end of the matter. Ross closed his laptop. 'You're not satisfied?'

She shrugged. 'I don't know. Kids cover things up. An adult always has that implied authority, and if the trainer *is* pushing him too hard, he might not say anything.'

'Or it might be that the trainer isn't pushing him.'

Laurie glowered at him, folding her arms and letting the book slide onto her lap. Something told Ross that this wasn't over, and he swallowed down the familiar rush of excitement.

'All right. Say it. You may as well, I know you're

thinking it.' She was keeping her voice low so that other people in the carriage wouldn't hear her, but he was under no illusion that if they'd been alone she probably would have been on her feet and calling him out by now.

'I think that you may be looking for something that isn't there. Because of your own experience.' He murmured the words quietly.

'You might be right.' Laurie wrinkled her nose at the thought. 'And this is exactly *why* I thought that working with kids wasn't a good idea.'

'It's exactly why I think it is. You connected with Adam in a way I haven't managed to. And you care about him, enough to explore every avenue.'

'I can't...' She shook her head. 'I *do* care. Maybe a bit too much, because I can't be impartial.'

'Okay. Let *me* be impartial. You be his advocate. As long as we both know where we stand, that's fine.' Ross sucked in a breath, knowing he was about to take a chance. 'Or you could decide that I'm wrong about all of this and you'd rather do the filing.'

At least she was thinking about it, not just firing back a knee-jerk reaction. Laurie pursed her lips.

'All right. I can be his advocate. Can we put that in the job description because I won't be giving you an inch if I feel you're not addressing his issues.'

'Be my guest. Since you don't *have* a job description, you may as well write your own. Along with your own treatment plan...'

What *was* he doing? Ross had never suggested that anyone write their own job description or treatment plan, but he had an idea that if he gave Laurie a little room she might just come up with something that was both innovative and brilliant. Taking a chance on her didn't seem any risk, as long as he watched her carefully.

'You'll be wanting to see them, though.' She eyed him charily.

'The job description… Yeah. I'll be needing to see that. I made it clear that the treatment plan is entirely your own responsibility.'

'I'm still not quite sure why you'd do that.'

Ross took a breath. This was demanding and exhausting, and yet somehow exhilarating. A little bit like the best sex imaginable, but that was *not* on his agenda. He'd stick to Laurie's issues with the paperwork.

'Have you thought about that stunt with the boat? Why you did it?'

She gave him that incredible enigmatic smile of hers. 'I'm sure you have a theory.'

'I do.'

'Then the least you could do is share it.' She tilted her jaw just enough to let him know that she wasn't going to be letting him get away with anything.

'I think that you spent your childhood being pushed far too hard. You must have learned how to question your father's authority, because you left.'

Her smile solidified on her face. Ross saw a flash of pain in Laurie's eyes, hidden quickly. 'Go on.'

'Even now, you're defying anyone who tells you what to do. Your consultant, Sam. Me, for sure. But there's a part of you that knows you need to stop, and that's why you rowed straight past my window.'

'You're saying that I'm undermining myself? That's a pretty smart trick. I'm not entirely sure I'm that clever.'

'Then you don't give yourself enough credit. And I

think it's fair enough to say that most people have done exactly the same thing at some point in their lives.'

She nodded slowly. 'It's an interesting thought. Bit far-fetched, though, if you ask me.'

Sure it was. He'd seen the way that Laurie had reacted, and he'd touched a nerve. If she didn't want to admit it just yet, that was fine.

Before she could end the conversation, Ross pulled his laptop around, focussing on the screen. Out of the corner of his eye he saw her reach for her book again. Whatever she was thinking was hidden behind an impassive mask.

Why was he doing this? It was a great deal of trouble, and he'd have been perfectly justified in just discharging Laurie from the clinic, on the basis that she was refusing treatment. But there was no part of him that could let her go.

Not the lonely child who'd amused himself while his mother had worked all the hours she could to support them both after his father had left. Not the teenager, who'd spent much of his time alone, while his mother had worked. And not the husband, who had longed for a family of his own, but had been told that his chances of ever conceiving a child were somewhere south of one in a thousand.

His marriage hadn't survived, and he'd reconciled himself to the loss of his dreams, pouring all he had into the clinic. It had been his family when he'd been alone and hurting, and now it was Laurie's last chance. Ross wasn't going to let her lose it.

CHAPTER FIVE

SHE WAS BEGINNING to feel that Ross was far too perceptive. Deep down, Laurie had known that she was sabotaging herself when she manoeuvred right instead of left and had rowed straight past the windows of the clinic. But it had taken Ross to put that theory into words.

It was time to put her head down and work. Not to think about whether Ross was right or wrong, or any of the emotions he seemed to stir up so easily in her. She had aims. She wanted to get back to competitive fitness, and she wanted to help make a difference for Adam and Tamara. Ross wanted that, too, so where was the problem?

Wanting the same things as he did felt a little risky. She'd spent the last few days treating him as if he was the enemy, and if Laurie was honest she'd prefer it that he was. If he started wanting the same things as she did, they'd be tearing each other's clothes off before nightfall.

Not going to happen. Ross might seem to have his life sorted, but he'd dropped a few hints that had made her wonder whether he wasn't just as damaged as she was. And Laurie's own damage ran deep. Deep enough that she didn't want to re-create a family for herself when the one she'd had and left behind had almost crushed the soul out of her.

She got out of bed, almost stumbling as the morning stiffness robbed her hip and leg of their strength for a moment. A few stretches would sort that out, and then she'd go to the gym for her morning exercise routine. Then she'd concentrate on spending the whole day avoiding Ross as much as politely possible.

Stumbling block number one. When Laurie entered the gym she heard the muffled clank of weights from one of the machines. She reminded herself that there was no way that Ross could be checking up on her, because he'd been here first. Before she could bang the door closed behind her to alert him of her presence, he sat up, catching up a small towel and wiping his face.

Good definition. Really great definition. He wasn't muscle-bound but he was strong. Sweating. Laurie suppressed the urge to march over to him and ask him what he was doing here, because it really wasn't his fault that the male body held a particular allure for her when pumping weights.

'Hey. Just finishing up.' He got to his feet, obviously about to vacate the gym so that she could exercise alone.

'Don't rush away on my account.' She smiled, trying to inject a note of polite warmth into her tone that didn't sound too much like lust.

'I'm running a bit late anyway. I'll let you get on with...whatever you're about to do.'

His smile flashed an unmistakeable message. Ross had decided to back off. That was just as well, because when he passed her in the doorway she caught a hint of his scent. Raw sex, at its finest.

'Do you have a moment later? I've got a few questions about structuring the gym time for Adam.'

'Sure. Ten o' clock?' he called over his shoulder.

'That's great. Thanks.'

Stumbling block number two. How to stick to her routine when the clamour of pheromones was urging her to either fight or fly. Maybe some relaxation and breathing exercises were in order before she started on her morning workout.

It had been two days and Ross had kept his interactions with Laurie down to the bare minimum. She'd been working on her treatment plans for Adam and Tamara, and he'd left her to it. He'd skipped his morning workouts as well, so that there was no danger of his being there when Laurie went through her own exercise routine. He was aching with curiosity, and not sure how much longer he could keep this up.

But this morning she'd found her way to his office. The dark blue of her trousers matched her sleeveless top exactly, and she'd teamed that up with a pair of bright red sandals. He noticed that her fingernails were painted exactly the same shade as her shoes. He reminded himself that Laurie set store by dressing appropriately for any occasion, and that he was simply looking for clues, rather than appreciating the overall effect.

'Good morning. I was wondering if you had some time to see me today.'

Always. Particularly when she looked so good.

'Would now suit you? I was about to go and get some coffee. Would you like one?'

'Yes. Thanks.'

He fetched the coffee and found her waiting in his office, her laptop placed in front of her on his desk.

'What's your email address? I'll send my proposals through to you…' Clearly she just wanted to get down to business.

Ross reeled off his address and heard his computer chime. As he opened the document attached to his email a thought occurred to him.

'Have you chosen the costumes yet? Sports day is next Monday.'

'Ah, yes.' She smiled. 'I'm going as the chicken.'

The chicken costume was great. Covered in yellow feathers, and lots of fun. If Laurie had been looking for the most embarrassing costume in the clinic's collection, she'd chosen it for herself, but he imagined she'd carry it off beautifully.

'And me?' He tried to maintain an air of innocence.

'Not the Mad Hatter.' She glanced down at her hands. 'You're going as the egg. Or rather Humpty Dumpty.'

Right. As costumes went, the egg wasn't so bad. The kids had loved it last year when Mike had worn it, and it was difficult to feel awkward when you were almost entirely obscured from view inside a large papier-mâché egg. It was, however, a little difficult to go anywhere at a speed faster than walking pace, and the two eye-holes cut in the front didn't give a particularly wide field of vision. If Laurie had wanted to clip his wings, she'd done a fine job of it.

'Great. The chicken and the egg, then.' He refused to allow her to see his reservations. 'Who comes first?'

Laurie chuckled. 'We'll have to see about that, won't we?'

Three hours and two cups of coffee later, he'd been through Laurie's treatment strategies and they were very good. She'd obviously been talking more to Adam about his likes and dislikes and spoken to Tamara about what she wanted from her stay here. Ross had just one reservation.

'You've put a note here that you feel that Tamara might like to try rowing…'

'Yes.'

'What do you see as the specific benefits of that?'

'At the moment her prosthetic isn't fitting exactly right. I know you're doing something about that, but in the meantime it would be nice to get her moving.'

Ross thought hard. 'But rowing involves flexing your legs. Tamara's prosthetic hurts her when she puts too much pressure on it, and we need to correct the imbalance that's causing. Won't rowing make it worse?'

'Yes, competitive rowing. I was thinking more in terms of a Sunday afternoon scull around on the lake. Just put some oars in her hands and see how she does with them.'

'That's fair enough.' Ross wondered whether Laurie was actually capable of taking a Sunday afternoon scull anywhere. He supposed he'd find out soon enough.

'But how do you get out onto the lake in the first place? You'll have to row her, won't you.'

Laurie shot him an exasperated glance. 'Look, I know what your reservations are. You think I'd do anything to get back out on the water and from your perspective…well, I can see how you might come to that conclusion.'

'So convince me.' Ross decided to give her a little more rope.

'You have excellent physios and doctors here and there's nothing I can add to what they can do for these kids. So I tried to think about something I could bring. My own unique selling point, if you like.'

'Go on…'

'For Adam, I want to bring an understanding of how frustrating it is to be injured, and how it can eat away at your own belief in yourself. And for Tamara… I just want to give her the feeling of power and speed that she once had when she was running and that she will have again.'

It was a different way of looking at the problem. But this was why he'd asked Laurie to do these treatment plans.

'Okay. I'll buy it. We can take Tamara out this afternoon if that's something she'd like to do.'

'We?' Laurie raised her eyebrow and Ross nodded. It was time to step forward again and be a bit more hands on, because he needed to know that this was really right for Tamara.

'If I come along, you won't have to do any rowing.'

She looked at him thoughtfully and then nodded. Maybe this last two days had convinced her that he wasn't simply meddling in her life for the sake of doing so.

'Okay. Can you row?'

'Not as well as you, but I've lived next to a lake for most of my life.'

She gave him a bright smile. 'I'll go and ask Tamara if she'd like to do that then, and come back to you. What time's good for you?'

'About three?'

'Great. I'll let you know.' Laurie snapped her laptop shut, put it under her arm, and left his office without a backward glance. Ross was already looking forward to this afternoon, and hoping that Tamara would say yes.

He got to his feet, looking out at the lake. It had been his confidante as a boy, its ever-changing moods a source of endless fascination for him. When he'd come back here a newly qualified doctor, it had been the witness of bright new love, and then of disappointment and heartbreak. But now, staring out over the rippling expanse gave him no answers. Perhaps it had changed sides—those still waters knew that Laurie loved them and had allied themselves with her.

Nonsense. It was a large quantity of H2O, not a sentient being. He was on his own with the question of how he would convince Laurie that he really was on her side, and although he'd taken a first step, there was still a way to go.

Ross had voiced his reservations about this, but he hadn't turned the idea down flat. He seemed to be making an effort to give her some room and she appreciated that. She had asked Tamara about it carefully, not wanting to sway her with her own enthusiasm or her wish to show Ross that she was right. And Tamara had liked the idea and agreed. Laurie had lent her a windcheater and given the girl one of her favourite caps to wear, which bore the insignia of the England team.

They walked slowly down to the small jetty by the

side of the lake, Ross helping Tamara over the uneven ground. Then together they guided her into the sturdy boat that would carry three with ease, and Tamara sat down in the stern.

'Okay, so watch carefully, Tamara. Ross is going to row us out a bit and then you can have a go.'

'All right. We're not going to sink, are we?'

Ross grinned at Tamara. 'Nah, we've got a professional on our team. I'm going to be following Laurie's instructions to the letter.'

The chance would be a fine thing. The thought of having Ross do exactly as she told him shimmered through her imagination, starting off with the professional and then branching out into what she might ask him to do by candlelight. It was an intriguing thought but probably better left for later, when she was back on dry land.

'Let's hope so, eh?' Laurie shot Tamara a mischievous look and the girl laughed.

The lighter oars for Tamara were stored in the bottom of the boat, and Ross sat on the bench between the heavier pair, swinging them out into the water.

'This feels a bit different…'

'Yes, I adjusted the oar outriggers. You're tall so you need them a little higher.' Laurie turned to Tamara. 'See how the oars are mounted on those triangular shaped brackets that stick out from the sides of the boat. That gives Ross better leverage, so we go faster.'

'Yeah, gotcha.'

'Right, then.' Laurie settled herself on the bench next to Tamara. 'Off we go.'

He started to row the boat out from the jetty. Three strokes, and then he stopped.

'What? You're looking at me as if I'm doing this all wrong.'

'No! You're doing fine.' She probably shouldn't interfere.

'I know you have a few thoughts about how I could do better, though.'

Laurie shot him an apologetic look and slid forward. 'Maybe put your feet a little closer in, then you've got room to bend your knees a bit more.'

'Like this?'

'Bit more…' Laurie shifted closer, gripping his leg and putting it in the right spot. Good calves. Very good… 'Back a little straighter.'

Ross squared his shoulders. Nice. 'How's that? Comfortable?'

He nodded, taking another few strokes with the oars and then stopping again.

'What now?'

Her face must have betrayed her. 'That's a great deal better. Only the ends of the oars should go a little higher in the water. You're not stirring a Christmas pudding.'

'You getting all that, Tamara?' He grinned broadly.

Laurie heard Tamara giggle behind her. At least she was enjoying this. And Ross seemed to be as well, so it was just Laurie who felt unaccountably nervous. She shifted back again, resuming her place in the stern.

'All right, then. Give it a go… Great. Good rhythm…' Laurie bit her tongue. That sounded like innuendo, but neither Ross or Tamara seemed to notice. Maybe it was just because a pair of good shoulders in action always turned her on.

'What do we do?' Tamara nudged her.

'We could sit here and trail our fingers in the water.' Laurie grinned. 'Let Ross do all the work.'

'No! I want to have a go.'

Ross shot her a smile. That was obviously the reaction he'd hoped for as well.

'All right. Watch how Ross is doing it for a minute. If he had a sliding seat, then he'd be powering his strokes from his legs and back, but with a fixed seat like that he's using his shoulders more. So you shouldn't need to push with your legs.'

'Right. So the prosthetic won't hurt?' Tamara pressed her lips together. Laurie knew that every step she took was painful at the moment.

'It shouldn't do, but honestly I don't know. We're trying things out at the moment, and we may need to adjust your seat and the outriggers before we get it exactly right, okay?'

Tamara nodded. 'Okay. Let's do it.'

She was so brave. Willing to try new things and looking at what she could do, not what she couldn't. Laurie wondered again whether Ross had deliberately chosen these kids to make her feel ashamed of herself. If so, he'd succeeded.

She helped Tamara forward onto the seat in front of Ross's, carefully shifting her own weight so that the movement didn't rock the boat. Pulling her own rowing gloves from her pocket, she gave them to Tamara.

'Put these on, it'll stop the oars from rubbing your hands. We don't want you getting blisters.'

Tamara pulled the gloves on, and Laurie fastened them for her at the wrists. Then she lifted the oars up from the bottom of the boat and fitted them into the rowlocks, before sliding back into her own seat.

'Try the movement a couple of times without dipping the oars into the water. Forward…now back… Good. That's very good. Are you comfortable doing that?'

Tamara nodded. 'Yes, that's fine.'

'All right. Let's give it a go, shall we? Try just one stroke.'

Tamara repeated the motion, dipping the oars into the water this time. The boat moved forward a little and she turned the corners of her mouth down.

'We didn't go very far.'

Laurie grinned. 'That's because you haven't built up any momentum yet. We'll try it again, yes? A few strokes this time.' She caught Ross's eye and he nodded. As Tamara pulled on her oars, he replicated the movement.

'See, that's better. Keep going… No, don't look round at Ross. It's my job to make sure he's doing it right…'

Laurie called out the strokes, and Tamara started to get into the swing of it. Ross was following her, and the boat began to move a little faster. 'That's really good. Well done. You okay, Tamara?'

'Yes. This is great!' Tamara was grinning broadly.

'Okay, I'm going to pick the speed up. Follow my count. Keep your back straight, Tamara…'

The two of them were rowing in perfect synchronisation now. Ross was doing more than his share of the work, but Tamara would still be feeling the resistance of the water against her oars, and the sensation of pushing forward. The boat started to move faster and she whooped with delight.

'Yay! I like this…'

‘Keep your concentration… Good. Very good.’

They rowed in a more or less straight line, until they began to near the deeper waters at the middle of the lake. Laurie showed Tamara how to manoeuvre the boat around, and she managed it without too much help from Ross. When she began to look a little tired, they pulled for the shore.

‘What do you think?’ Laurie helped Tamara out of the boat.

‘It’s great. Can I do it again?’

Laurie glanced at Ross, and received a nod from him. ‘As long as your leg’s okay. Does it hurt?’

Tamara shook her head. ‘No, it doesn’t put any pressure on it.’

‘I’ll come and check on you later on, then. If everything’s still fine, we can go out again next week. And in the meantime you can concentrate on your exercises so you’ll be able to do a bit more.’

‘Cool. I’m hungry…’

Ross chuckled, holding out his arm to steady Tamara over the rough ground at the side of the lake. ‘We’ll go down to the kitchen, shall we? Get them to make you a sandwich.’

CHAPTER SIX

LAURIE WAS WAITING for him in one of the small clusters of armchairs that stood in the deep window bays throughout the clinic. He'd have to come this way on his route back from the kitchen to his office.

Ross smiled when he saw her and flopped down in one of the seats. 'You're waiting for me to say it, aren't you?'

'I'm waiting to hear how Tamara is doing.' And to hear him say it.

'All right. So you don't want me to tell you that you were absolutely right.'

'I didn't say I didn't want you to…' Laurie smiled at him. 'Thanks.'

He heaved a deep breath of contentment at a job done well. 'And Tamara's in great shape. She's demolishing a sandwich and telling the cook all about her trip out onto the lake. Seems you may have a rower on your hands after all.'

'Not necessarily. But while she can't run, it's good for her to have some goals. Ones that don't involve regaining what she had before. This is something different for her.'

'That's all?' He raised an eyebrow.

'I enjoyed it as well. Almost as much as if I'd been able to pull on the oars.'

'Maybe you will soon.'

Laurie puffed out a breath. 'You want *me* to say it?'

'Yeah. Go on. Since I shared first.' There was the hint of a tease in his tone.

'I've got an exercise regime and I'm sticking to it. Making sure I don't overdo things and stopping before I do too much. But then you knew that anyway, didn't you? Sam was in the gym the other day…' Laurie wondered how Ross would answer. She could understand it if he was keeping her under surveillance from afar.

'To be honest…?' Laurie nodded him on. 'No. I haven't asked and Sam hasn't mentioned it.'

She believed him. Maybe, after all the years spent looking over her shoulder, she wasn't so paranoid after all.

'My hip's feeling a little better.' Laurie turned down the corners of her mouth. 'Does Sam hate me?'

He let out an explosive laugh. 'Hate you? Sam doesn't hate anyone, she's one of the nicest people I know.'

'Yeah?' Laurie raised her eyebrows.

He rolled his eyes. 'What? I can't say something about one of my colleagues without you thinking I'm up to something? Sam's married with a three-year-old. Her husband's also one of the nicest people I know.'

'Sorry.' The inquisitiveness had gone too far. But Laurie had spent an inordinate amount of time wondering about Ross's love life. *You were right* had felt like a next step into intimacy with him, after long, battle-strewn foreplay. It didn't feel honest to engage in that if there was another woman in his life.

'That's okay. It's not as if the clinic's entirely immune to a bit of romance. Sam met Jamie here, he's an accountant and comes in to do the books for a couple of weeks every year.'

'That's…nice.' It sounded normal and happy and… all the things that Laurie's family wasn't.

Ross chuckled. 'Yeah, it is nice. They took one look at each other and suddenly Sam was interested in numbers. I think I gave her a pretty hard time about that, but she's forgiven me. Like I said, she's a good person.'

And life worked out for good people. What did that make Laurie? Despite all her efforts to regulate her existence, to keep everything under control, her life was a mess at the moment.

'I guess it's all a matter of finding out what you want.' Laurie shrugged.

Suddenly, Ross's brow darkened. 'You think so?'

This wasn't about Sam or her husband any more. 'I think… I'm a sportswoman. Focus and working hard were my ways of getting where I wanted to be.'

'I don't underestimate those things.' There was a hint of regret in his voice. 'But I don't think life takes much notice of them sometimes. It's not always on our side.'

'You mean Adam and Tamara?' Surely Ross couldn't be referring to himself. He could take anything he wanted from life.

The moment's hesitation before he replied was his real answer. The clinic, his life here was one dream. But there was another that he'd lost.

'Yeah. Yeah, that's what I mean.'

She could ask. Laurie had the feeling that if she did, she wouldn't receive the head-on, honest reply that he'd given to all her other inappropriate questions. Ross had his secrets, the same as everyone else. And she should let them alone, they weren't her business.

'I ought to apologise to Sam. I didn't give her much of a chance, did I?'

He smiled suddenly. 'No, you didn't. And an apology isn't necessary. Although I'm sure she'd appreciate it.'

'I'll go and see if I can find her.' Laurie got to her feet and Ross chuckled.

'Don't waste a second in making it so, will you.'

He was teasing again, but she didn't mind. He made no move to follow her and when she looked back he seemed deep in thought. Laurie wondered if he was taking a moment out for the things in his own life that he hadn't been able to make so.

Life was getting easier now, just as long as Laurie didn't think about it too much. She was working with Tamara and Adam, and working with herself to improve the condition of her hip. Ross didn't ask about her own progress, but demanded regular reports on that of the two teenagers. Fair enough. Laurie couldn't complain that Ross didn't fully trust her yet when she was still wondering if she could trust him.

A taxi pulled up outside the house just as Laurie was making her way back to the guest apartment, after a particularly gruelling session with Adam where he'd slaughtered her avatar twice. Laurie saw a woman get out and the taxi driver lifted two suitcases from the boot.

He might have stopped and helped her. But as soon as she'd paid him the driver got back into his car and drove away, leaving the woman standing at the bottom of the steep stone steps that led up to the front door. Laurie quickened her pace.

'Hi. Would you like a hand with those?'

'Ah, thank you. I thought I'd given him a big enough tip to encourage him to help me through the front door, but apparently not. I gave Ross a call from the car, though, and he'll be here in a minute.'

The woman smiled. Her dark hair was streaked with grey, but there was something about her eyes. Something about her wry humour, too, that reminded Laurie of Ross.

'Are you Dr Summerby?'

'I leave the Dr Summerby to Ross these days. I'm Maura.' The woman held out her hand giving Laurie's a firm shake.

'I'm Laurie… Laurie Sullivan.' This was awkward. Laurie wondered if Ross had told his mother that she was staying in their home.

'Ah, Laurie! Ross mentioned that you were our guest for a few weeks. How nice to meet you.' Maura looked around at the path that led from the clinic. 'Where is he? I brought far too much back from my holiday, and these suitcases are heavy…'

'That's okay.' Laurie decided to leave the question of what Ross had or hadn't told his mother about her for later. 'I'm sure I can manage to get them up the steps.'

'Perhaps I should wait. He does like to lift things.' Maura's smile had all the warmth and mischief of Ross's. 'You know how men can be…'

Ross might be a man, but Laurie was a world-class rower, albeit a little out of shape. The competitive urge that told her that she didn't need Ross for anything took over.

'He might be busy. I'm sure I can manage.' Laurie lifted one of the suitcases, finding that it wasn't too heavy. 'Can you get the door?'

Maura produced her keys from her handbag, opening the front door for Laurie, and she heaved the case up the steps and into the hallway. 'If you want to wheel it through, I'll bring the other one.'

'Only if you're sure…'

Laurie nodded in reply, and Maura extended the handle of the suitcase, walking towards her own front door. The next suitcase was heavier, but she could do this herself.

The case was slightly bigger as well, and difficult to manoeuvre. Laurie managed five of the six steps, but as she took the last, pain shot down her leg. She lost her footing, tumbling down the steps, her arms slung instinctively around her head and her injured hip hitting the gravel hard.

Get up. Get. Up.

She wasn't sure if they were her father's words or her own. They were just words that had been with her since her earliest memories. She took a breath and sat up. When she put her hand to the gravel to help her get to her feet, it stung like crazy, but further inspection showed just a graze.

Get. Up.

Okay! What did the annoying voice think she was doing! Laurie gritted her teeth and got to her feet. Her hip was throbbing and she could feel blood running down her leg, but that was probably just a graze as well. She looked up at the top of the steps and saw that the case had fallen forward into the doorway. Just as well, if Maura had packed anything breakable in there.

The steps seemed like a long and lonely climb, when what she really wanted to do was sit down for a moment and get over the shock of falling. The fear that she'd just undone all the work of the past few weeks and had really hurt herself this time. But as she slowly made her way to the top of the steps, her hip didn't complain too much.

Maura appeared in the hallway. That was the last thing she needed right now. Actually, the second to last, the last thing being Ross.

'You've fallen…?' Maura's manner was suddenly businesslike. 'Sit down and let me look.'

'I'm all right.' Laurie forced a smile. 'Just lost my balance. I hope there was nothing breakable in your suitcase.'

Maura rolled her eyes. 'If there had been, the baggage handlers at the airport would have made sure it was already in pieces. Sit down and let me take a look at your hand.'

There was no point in arguing, Maura had flipped from new acquaintance to doctor mode. And it was a little easier to accept *this* Dr Summerby's help. If Maura just looked at Laurie's hand, and didn't mention the fall to Ross, maybe this whole episode wouldn't be so acutely embarrassing.

Laurie sat on the wooden settle in the hall, holding out her hand. Maura took her glasses from her handbag, looking at it carefully and then flexing her wrist.

'You've got a nasty graze there, but your wrist seems okay.' Maura was gently applying pressure in all the right places, and Laurie managed to smile.

'None of that hurts. I haven't broken anything.'

Maura gave a wry laugh. 'I dare say you could have told me if you had, I gather you're a doctor yourself. Although sometimes the shock of a fall masks injuries.'

'That's just what I'd be saying to you, if the boot were on the other foot.' Laurie couldn't help liking Maura. Her manner was a lot like Ross's, but she didn't have the annoying habit of questioning every answer that Laurie gave.

'Did you bang your head?'

'No. I landed with my arms up around it.'

Maura nodded. 'Good instincts. Come with me, and I'll make you a cup of tea and find a pair of tweezers to get those pieces of gravel out of your hand.'

Laurie was just searching for a way to refuse the offer when a dark shadow appeared in the doorway. 'Mum?'

Maura's face lit up at the sound of his voice. 'Ross, darling. I didn't need you to help me after all. Laurie came to the rescue with the bags. But she's taken a bit of a tumble…'

Laurie swallowed hard. Maura was obviously bent on salvaging what little pride Laurie had left, but from the look on his face, Ross wasn't buying it.

'Are you all right?'

'Yes. Fine.' Laurie tried to keep the curtness out of her tone. 'Really, I'm all right. Three doctors for one grazed hand is overkill.'

Ross was shaking his head, but Maura chuckled. 'I suppose so. It doesn't do to fight over a graze. Ross, carry my bag through, will you?'

He picked up the bag with irritating ease, his gaze still on Laurie as she got to her feet. Maura held out her arm in an indication that Laurie should accompany them through to her apartment.

'I'm sure you have lots to talk about. I'm going to leave you to it.' She shot a pleading look at Maura. 'Really, I'd rather see to myself.'

Maura's gaze searched her face for a moment. 'All right. I'll call in later to see how you are, and if you need anything, you know where I am.'

'Thanks. I really appreciate it.'

Maura nodded, turning to follow Ross, who had already disappeared towards her front door with the suitcase. Laurie breathed a sigh of relief. Maura would keep Ross busy for a while, and by that time she'd be back in the guest apartment with the door closed behind her.

Some hope. Her hands were still shaking from the fall, and as she willed the key into the apartment door, she heard footsteps behind her.

'I reckon if you really *were* all right, you could have managed a quicker getaway.'

Laurie closed her eyes. Apparently it was far too much to hope that Ross would stay out of this.

'It's not a getaway, Ross. And I *am* all right. How many times do I have to say it?' She didn't turn to face him.

'A tip for next time. The less you say it the more believable it sounds. Getting up and walking away doesn't make you all right either.'

She tried to choke it back, but the blind anger swamped all reason. 'Get *off* my case, Ross. I'm not your patient any more.'

'No, you're not. I'm sorry that you don't give me enough credit to expect I might show a little concern for anyone who fell all the way down the front steps.' He spoke quietly, but when Laurie turned she saw a pulse beating at the side of his jaw.

'I didn't fall *all*—'

His gesture of exasperation silenced her. 'The case was at the top, and you have gravel in your hand. It doesn't take a genius to work that one out, Laurie.'

'I fell down, I got up. What more do you want from me?' Suddenly her father's demands seemed a lot less complicated. All he'd wanted was that she get up again when she fell. Ross wanted much, much more than that, and giving it went against everything she'd been taught.

He wouldn't push his way into the apartment, that much she knew, and shutting the door on him would end this conversation. Laurie turned, groaning as pain shot through her hip and the keys jangled onto the floor.

She went to bend down but he was already in the way. Frustration and the shock of the fall were almost choking her. Even picking a bunch of keys up for her seemed too much to bear at the moment.

'Get out of the way, Ross.'

'Will you stop being so pig-headed, Laurie?'

As he straightened up, she saw the hurt on his face. Suddenly this didn't seem fair and it occurred to Laurie that she was lashing out at the wrong person. Tears started to course down her face, and when he extended his arms she almost fell into them. He held her gently, silently, for what seemed like a long time.

'I'm sorry. I'm not angry with you.' Laurie felt his chest rise and then fall as she said the words.

'You should be. I haven't given you much room to breathe, have I?'

'It was my father that did that.'

'And then I made things worse. I knew that you had to stay here if you wanted to save your sporting career. It wasn't really a choice at all, you only had one option.'

'It was the right option.' Laurie wiped her face with her fingers, looking up at him.

He shook his head. 'I'm not entirely sure that makes any difference. I shouldn't have boxed you into a corner like that.'

'Make me a cup of tea, and you're forgiven. And give me a hug, because I fell right on my hip…' He knew what that meant. How scared she was.

His arms closed around her again, and she nestled against him. The first time anyone had ever hugged her when she'd fallen down. It was too short-lived, but maybe it was too much to ask for this one time to make up for all the others.

He opened the door, waiting for her to beckon him inside after her. Laurie fetched the first-aid kit from the kitchenette, putting it down on the coffee table and lowering herself onto the sofa.

'Tea first, eh?' Ross put the kettle on, watching as Laurie carefully rolled up the leg of her trousers. They hadn't ripped, but the force of the impact had left a red weal across her knee, which was oozing blood.

He brought the tea, and Laurie proffered her injured hand, knowing that he wouldn't ask to see the damage. Ross rotated her wrist, applying gentle pressure to all the same places that his mother had, but she let him do it. This was the beginning of trust, and it felt like a step away from the harsh regimes of her childhood. When he'd finished, she handed him the tweezers.

'Ow!'

'Sorry...' Each time he tweezed out one of the pieces of gravel that were embedded under her skin it seemed to hurt him more than it did her. 'That's the last one.'

'It's great. Thanks.' Laurie tried not to wince at the sting of the antiseptic as he gently cleaned her hand and then the weal on her leg.

'How's your hip feeling?'

'I'll have a bruise, but it doesn't feel too bad now. I don't think I've done any real damage.'

'Just had a bit of a fright.'

She nodded. 'Will you take a look?'

Ross smiled suddenly. 'I'm not your doctor, you know. Just an informed individual.'

'Maybe I'd just appreciate your opinion, eh?'

She rolled onto her side on the couch, feeling his touch through the thin fabric of her trousers, carefully working around the main areas of inflammation. 'I don't feel anything. In fact, there's a marked improvement on what I would have expected from your scans when you arrived.'

That was actually good to know. Her hip had been feeling better, but Laurie had been working blind, unable to examine it properly herself and loth to ask either Sam or Ross to do so.

'I may take a warm bath, just to ease everything a little.'

'Good idea. I'll go and let my mother know that you really are okay before she starts banging the door down to make sure.'

'Thanks. You'll come back?' Laurie didn't want him to go back to his own apartment just yet.

'Sure. It's fish and chips on the menu for tonight—

would you like me to go and get a takeaway from the kitchen?'

'Sounds good. Have they got any tomato sauce?'

He got to his feet, smiling. 'I'll bring some.'

This was comfortable and reassuring and…all of the things that you wanted if you were feeling a little low. Someone to just take care of you, without going into all the details of why it was your fault that you got hurt in the first place, and how getting straight back up again would be the best thing to do.

Laurie had just slid into a pair of loose sweatpants, still warm and relaxed from her bath, when Ross arrived back with two large portions of fish and chips, along with condiments and a roll of fabric under one arm. She fetched two plates from the kitchenette and set about unwrapping their food.

'That's pretty.' Ross had unrolled the fabric and she could see now that it was a quilt, the central portion of which was a stylised rendering of what looked very much like this house, complete with trees and the lake.

'Mum sent it. She has loads of these, she's always liked to sew when she sits down in the evening. She reckons that handmade quilts are the best medicine when you're not feeling so good, so she sent one over for you.' He shrugged diffidently. 'Not a lot of medical basis there…'

'What do you mean? It sounds like solid reasoning to me.' There was the element of care in it, which everyone needed from time to time. 'Are you telling me that your mum's quilts didn't see you through a few childhood illnesses?'

Ross grinned suddenly. 'More than a few. Some

of my adult ones as well, although I don't admit to it. Not really needed in this weather, though.' He was clearly being careful not to push any unwanted concern onto her.

But it wasn't unwanted. Unfamiliar maybe, and Laurie had rejected it up till now because she hadn't known quite what to do with it. But it made sense of the way that Ross ran the clinic as a nurturing community. He'd learned all this when he'd been a child.

'Nonsense. It was really sweet of her to send it.' Laurie sat down on the sofa, spreading the quilt across her legs. It was a little warm, but it felt comforting to tuck it around her.

They started to eat. She should say something… Thank him, or tell him how much all this meant. She didn't have the words. It wasn't until Ross had cleared the plates away that she plucked up the courage.

'I'm…not very used to being looked after like this.' Ross had probably already gathered that. No one looked after people who had the kind of attitude that Laurie did.

He nodded. 'I'd worked that one out. The courts don't usually allow kids to decide who they want to live with, unless there's a good reason.'

'I didn't… It wasn't my fault…' She could feel panic rising in her chest. 'My father said that I was making it all up, but I wasn't.'

The warmth in his gaze seemed to turn to fire as soon as it touched her skin. 'It never occurred to me that it *was* your fault. You want to tell me what really happened?'

Yes. Yes, she did.

'My father was a runner when he was young. He

reckoned he'd stopped because of an injury, but now I think he just wasn't good enough. He always said that he'd been robbed of a good career in athletics and he wasn't going to allow the same to happen to his kids. He was very determined.'

'Living out his own aspirations through you?'

Laurie nodded. 'I think so. We got to pick our sports, my brother chose tennis and I chose rowing because I liked the water. But there was no room for failure, and no room for anything else either. I wanted to succeed, but I wanted to be a doctor as well.'

'And he didn't approve of that?' Ross's tone was even, but the flash of derision in his face showed how he really felt.

'No. I was supposed to move to part-time schooling when I was sixteen so that I could concentrate on my training. There was no time for anything other than sport, and…' Laurie shrugged. 'My aunt was very different from him, and she said I could go and live with her and stay on at school. She was the one who fought him and helped me leave.'

'Your advocate.' Ross's lips curved into a smile.

'Yes. She was the one person who really cared about what I wanted. If I can be half as good an advocate for Adam and Tamara…' Laurie shrugged.

'You're doing just fine.'

'Sometimes I wonder. There's only so much that a person can do to change. I tell Aunt Suzy that she's responsible for the best in me, but that my father had me for fifteen years. When I fell just now, the only thing I heard was his voice, shouting at me to get up. That was always his thing, you fell down and you got straight up again.'

'Which is the most ridiculous thing I've ever heard.' Ross's disdain sounded loud and clear in his voice. 'Getting up again is a matter of giving someone the support to do so.'

'Which is what you do here.'

He nodded. 'I can see how you might feel that's overly intrusive.'

Ross understood. She'd reached out and found that he'd been there all along. Laurie's heart did a back-flip in her chest.

'You said you had a brother?'

Two actually. But Laurie never talked about her older brother. Even now, it was too painful and she didn't know what to say.

'You've heard of the tennis player Ben Sullivan?'

'Yes, of course. He retired a couple of years ago, didn't he?'

'Shattered knee. Due to over-training probably. He stayed on with my father as his trainer, even after he had the opportunity to find someone else. He's a year younger than me. I didn't see him for a long time, he testified against me at my court hearing.'

'That must have really hurt.'

Laurie shrugged. 'There was a time when I would have done the same kind of thing myself, I wanted my father's approval so badly. I didn't speak to Ben for years, but when he retired he got in touch. He's living with his girlfriend now, and seems to have found some sense of normality.'

'Came to the same conclusion as you?'

'I think so. We don't talk about it much, there's a lot of hurt there still.'

'Some wounds never really heal. We just cover them up and keep going.'

'You think?'

Ross didn't answer. His arm was slung on the cushions of the sofa, behind her back, and Laurie slid a little closer to him. That warmth wasn't so confronting now.

'This is a little out of my remit, too.' Clearly not too far, because Ross didn't move away.

'I think we're both very clear that you're not my doctor any more.'

He looked down at her, humour in his eyes. 'Yeah, we've covered that one very comprehensively. You do, however, work at the clinic.'

'And you're my boss.' Laurie pursed her lips. 'But I'm not on the clock at the moment. And this is nice.'

'Yeah.' He chuckled. 'Maybe we make an exception, then.'

She felt his arm around her shoulders and snuggled against him. No one could possibly have said for sure that this wasn't friendship and concern. If she disregarded her racing heartbeat and the cool scent of his body, Laurie might almost believe it herself.

CHAPTER SEVEN

IT HAD BEEN the first time in a very long time. Sitting, talking aimlessly, watching a bit of TV. Ross had almost forgotten what it felt like to have the warmth of a woman's body next to his. To feel cocooned in the quiet of the evening, knowing that someone else was there with him.

He'd been careful. Careful not to hug her goodnight or to kiss her although he'd wanted to do both very much. But something *had* happened last night. He'd known that Laurie's childhood must have been difficult, but not how much she'd been starved of the warmth that he took for granted. And in that understanding the first threads of trust had started to weave them together.

It wasn't enough. He couldn't allow himself to want more, because fate was both unpredictable and capricious in its cruelty. That was one thing he could never allow himself to trust.

She appeared in the doorway of his office the following morning. He beckoned her inside, watching her movements carefully as she sat down.

'You're looking better.'

'I'm a little stiff, but there's no real damage done. Thanks for being a friend last night.'

Unless he was very much mistaken, that was a statement of intent. Laurie couldn't be unaware of the chemistry that fizzed between them, but she'd settle for friendship. It seemed that was something they could both handle.

'What can I do for you?'

'Sam said you were going into town this afternoon. Can you give me a lift?'

'Sure. I've got to get some things for the new mother and toddler exercise group. It's Sam's project, but she's pretty busy right now so I said I'd take over for a while.'

'Sounds good. I've heard these groups are very beneficial.'

'You want to help out?' Ross reckoned that he knew the answer to that already.

'No. It's not really my thing.' She smiled sweetly at him. 'I can help you shop, though.'

'I'll be leaving after lunch. Two o' clock?'

Laurie nodded, getting out of her seat. Ross couldn't help noting that she managed it without a grimace. 'Sounds good. I'll meet you at the house at two.'

She was there, leaning against his car, waiting for him, when Ross walked across from the clinic at five to two. Laurie seemed more relaxed in his company than ever, talking and laughing as he drove into town. Last night really *had* changed things.

'I just need to pop into my bank and sort a few things out. Then we can tackle Sam's list.' She took it for granted that they wouldn't split up and go their separate ways when they reached the large shopping precinct.

'Okay.' Ross sat down on the edge of a high brick planter. 'I'll wait here.'

She reappeared from the bank ten minutes later, and Ross led the way to the large mother and baby store. 'We should be able to get everything here.' He handed Laurie the list and she studied it carefully.

'Nappies? What are you doing, having them to stay overnight?'

Ross chuckled. 'No, Sam says that it's a good idea to have some supplies, in case of any emergencies.'

'Right. Well it looks as if she's expecting a few…' Laurie pulled a trolley from the stack by the doorway. 'We might be needing two of these.'

They walked along the aisles, stopping every now and then to examine the toys on offer for Sam's toy box. Ross added a teddy bear to his trolley, which Laurie had picked up, and then a stuffed penguin.

'Oh, look!' She caught his arm. 'A baby gym. What do you reckon? We could phone Sam and ask…'

Ross walked over to the stack of boxes, running his fingers over the display model. 'It's well made, and it seems pretty sturdy.'

'But will they *like* it?'

'What, the mothers? Or the babies? Or Sam…?'

Laurie shrugged. 'I don't know. All of them. Perhaps we could ask someone.'

'Or we could make up our own minds.' That didn't seem so difficult. Ross came in here all the time to buy things for various godchildren and he always made his own decisions.

'Okay. You do that, because I'm not sure. I'll go and get some of the baby supplies, shall I?' Ross nodded, and handed her the list.

As he watched her walk away this seemed so different from all the other times he'd been in here, though. Laurie made all the difference. She was the woman he couldn't have, and here they were, buying supplies for babies that he couldn't have either. He stared at the baby gym. Suddenly it seemed to be mocking him.

He should pull himself together. But the pain was still as fresh as it had ever been. The moment he'd been told that he couldn't father a child. The times that Alice had thrown that into his face in anger, as if he could make any difference to the loss of all their hopes. The moment she'd walked out, saying that she was going to visit her parents, but taking six suitcases with her. He hadn't even had the chance to say goodbye properly, or to express his regret over what they'd both lost.

Laurie had stopped by the stacked shelves at the other end of the aisle, and was loading things into her trolley, consulting Sam's list as she did so. She was alone too, and maybe she could settle for a relationship that could never include any more than two people…

Maybe not. Laurie had made it clear that families weren't her thing, but people changed. It was a conflict that was impossible to resolve. His one great hope for Laurie was that one day she'd make peace with her own childhood and believe she could make a different kind of family. He couldn't hold onto that, and at the same time ask her to share a future with him that couldn't ever include a family.

He turned his attention back to the baby gym. He'd been over this in his head already, more than a thousand times. He should accept the way things were and get on with the matter at hand.

'Hey. What do you think?' He jumped when he

heard Laurie's voice. Goodness only knew how long he'd been standing here, staring blankly at the gym.

'Oh. Um…not sure, still.'

'Are you okay?' She peered at him.

Not really. But it was one of life's rich ironies that there were occasions when the only thing possible was to fall down and then get up again.

'Yeah. Fine. I was thinking about something I forgot to do… It's okay, it'll wait until tomorrow.'

'Maybe you need a break, Ross.'

What he really needed a break from was this place. 'I guess I can ask Sam and come back another time.'

'Or we could just text her.' Laurie's gaze was searching his face.

'Okay. Do you mind doing that? I'll go and pay for the first trolley load and take it out to the car.'

'Good idea. That'll save a bit of time.'

Something was up. It was as if an invisible hammer had knocked Ross for six, and he was trying to piece his wits back together again. Laurie watched him go and then decided that the best thing she could do was to hurry up and get this shopping trip out of the way.

She texted Sam, who seemed to know exactly what she was talking about, and texted a *yes* back almost straight away. Then she grabbed one of the boxes, along with a few more stuffed toys, and made for the checkout. By the time Ross arrived back from the car, she was already halfway through the queue.

Something was definitely the matter. He was smiling and affable, but the smile seemed pasted on. She wondered whether he'd seen that in her when she'd been trying to avoid his questions.

'Are you hungry?' Sam looked at her watch as they finished packing the rest of their purchases into the car. 'It'll be nearly five o' clock when we get back to the clinic, so we could stop off for something to eat. My treat, since you got me fish and chips last night.'

Warmth flickered in his eyes. Maybe he realised that she was trying really hard to cheer him up. 'Yeah. There's a nice pub about halfway between here and the clinic. They have a garden at the back which looks out over the lake. If that's not too much of a temptation for you...'

'You can throw as many lakes as you like at me, I'm a glutton for temptation these days.' Laurie smiled up at him. 'I might even buy you a pint, and then drive you home.'

Ross grinned suddenly. 'Now *that's* an offer I can't refuse.'

The pub served great food, and they sat outside to eat. Ross's mood had improved, and he seemed in no hurry to get back to the clinic so Laurie suggested they take a walk.

'It really is beautiful here.' They strolled together by the side of the lake.

'Everything a woman could possibly want? Big empty stretches of water...'

He was teasing. But Laurie was fast coming to the conclusion that there was something she wanted a bit more from her stay here.

'Someone to talk about things to.'

Ross nodded. 'I'm glad you think so.'

She had to ask. He'd been there for her, and she wanted to be there for him. She didn't believe for one moment that his sudden change of mood had been anything as trivial as something he'd forgotten to do at the clinic.

'One thing I've learned is that the things you feel that you can't say actually aren't so bad after all.'

'That's true.' He didn't take the bait.

'You've been here for me, Ross. I'd like to return the favour.'

He puffed out a breath. 'I'm sorry if I was a little short with you earlier. It's nothing…'

'I could throw your own words back at you, Ross, and remind you that the more you say that something's nothing, the less believable it sounds.'

'It's something.' Their pace had slowed to a crawl and he stopped suddenly, stuffing his hands into his pockets and gazing out over the water.

'Okay. That's all I wanted to know.'

She was lying, and Ross's sceptical glance told her that he was fully aware of that. Of course she wanted to know more, but pushing him wasn't going to help. He started to walk again, and she fell into step beside him. If he didn't want to talk, she should respect that. She'd fought hard enough to keep her own secrets. Just accept the afternoon for what it was and let him be.

He should let it go. Laurie didn't need to know about this, but he still wanted to tell her.

'I said that I was married. A long time ago…'

Laurie nodded.

'Alice and I met when I was at medical school. We got married and came back here, and then decided to stay. It was going to be the full turn of the circle for me. The lonely kid, who grew up and filled his house with children.'

'This seems like a good place to bring a family up.'

'Yeah, it seemed that way to us. We waited and nothing happened. After we'd been trying for a year we went for tests. It turned out that there is a one in a thousand chance of my ever becoming a father.'

She looked up at him, her eyes searching his face. Ross knew all the questions that were running through her mind, Laurie was a doctor, but she wasn't asking any of them.

'So I know you're wondering.' He turned the corners of his mouth down.

'Yes, I am. Sudden attack of tact.'

He couldn't help smiling, if only for a moment. 'There's nothing that medical science can do about it. I have a low sperm count that isn't linked to any other underlying conditions, it just means that I can't conceive a child.'

'And you were told a one in a thousand chance.' Laurie narrowed her eyes.

'Yeah. I explained to Alice that it's difficult for doctors to speak in certainties, and that one in a thousand was medical speak for *not going to happen*, but neither of us could stop thinking about that one chance. Each time it didn't happen, the disappointment got worse, but neither of us could bring ourselves to say 'never'. We tried IVF and that didn't work either. In the end she began to blame me for the loss that she felt. I guess that was fair enough, because it was my fault.'

'Your fault?' She was suddenly animated, and the fire in her eyes warmed him. 'I can't begin to understand what it might be like to be in that situation, but I do know that there's a difference between being the cause and being the culprit.'

'That's pretty hard to see when you're in the middle of it all.' He should give Alice the benefit of the doubt.

'I don't care if it's hard. It's the truth.'

He'd always known that Laurie spoke her mind, but Ross hadn't felt the full force of that before. It buoyed him up, relieving him of a little of the guilt that he felt.

'Sorry. That's just…what I think.'

'Don't be. I think it's what I needed to hear. Alice blamed me, and I just agreed with her.'

Laurie frowned. 'This is probably the wrong thing to ask, but…'

The weight lifted a little more. People generally didn't know what to say in the face of this kind of thing and so they backed off. Laurie was still there with him, and that was a precious thing.

'Ask it anyway.'

'Not everyone plans to have children.'

'May I ask *you* a personal question?'

Some of the tension left her brow. 'I really wish you would. At least I'll know what to say.'

The things left unsaid were the things that hurt the most. This was suddenly so very easy.

'What about you? Do you want children?'

Laurie gave the question some thought. 'My experience of families isn't one I'm keen to repeat, and if you'd asked me that a year ago I'd have said that I fought hard enough for my freedom and I'm not giving it up now. I still can't see it but…'

'But?'

'I guess never say never.' She looked up at him. 'Only you don't have that privilege, do you?'

She understood. 'No. I don't.'

Laurie took his arm 'I'm so sorry, Ross.'

The sudden hint of her scent, the feeling of her skin brushing his made Ross recoil. Just that small, friendly gesture made him want to forget all that he knew to be right, and to want more. Laurie jerked away from him, as if he'd burned her.

'I'm sorry. I didn't mean…' He could see the hurt look in her eyes and there was only one way to show her what he really did mean. He reached out for her, taking her into his arms.

'This is what you meant?' She smiled up at him.

'Yeah. This too.' He brushed a kiss against her cheek.

'Mmm. I like what you're saying.' She stretched up, kissing his cheek.

A whole conversation would have been better. They were alone here, by the shore of the lake, and no one would ever know. Ross could feel his body hardening at the thought and wondered if she felt that too.

Maybe she did. But it was okay because everything was suddenly okay between them. Everything apart from the misunderstandings and the vain attempts to keep each other at arm's length.

'Are you going to say it again?' Her eyes were amber in the sunlight, her hair flaming. She was the most beautiful woman he'd ever seen.

'I shouldn't…'

She heaved a mock sigh. 'Yes, I know. You don't mess with your staff. Does it make a difference that I'm only part time?'

Ross chuckled. 'I'm not sure. It might come under the category of splitting hairs.'

Laurie grinned. 'That's better than a straight-out *no*. And remember that I've been in denial for much of my adult life, so I'm very good at it—'

She gasped as he stopped her talking with a kiss. One of the sweetest—no, *the* sweetest—he'd ever experienced. He could feel her fingers clutching at his shoulders, her body pressed against his. Her mouth, and the softness of her skin. When she responded, everything seemed to just fall into place and a bright happiness washed over Ross.

He told her that she was beautiful, and she sighed. Felt her run her fingers across his shoulders, and was suddenly grateful for all those mornings spent in the gym, because Laurie told him that she approved. Ross kissed her again, knowing that this was the last time.

'Time to go back now?' When he drew away from her, Laurie understood his meaning.

'There are only so many rules that we can break, Laurie. Too many of them and we'll end up hurting each other.'

She nodded, holding her hand out to take his. 'Then maybe we'll just walk very slowly back to the car…'

She'd kissed him. Twice. That was a breach of the rules of more than double the severity.

Because…once might be classed as a mistake, but twice definitely wasn't. When Ross had kissed her the second time it had felt as if the limits that they'd put on their lives weren't just wobbling a little, they'd been truly crushed.

All the same, she didn't want to take it back. Laurie couldn't bring herself to regret it either. What she should do was stop it from happening again.

When they came within sight of the car, he let go of her hand. Started to walk a little further from her, the quirk of his lips showing his regret. They both knew that they couldn't take this any further.

'As relationships go…' she smiled up at him '…that might have been short, but it was very sweet.'

Ross chuckled. 'Are you telling me that you're breaking up with me? Already?'

'Afraid so. But I really hope we can still be friends. Not just civilised, let's do this properly friends. Real friends.'

His eyes softened. 'That would be my fondest wish.'

CHAPTER EIGHT

THIS REALLY SHOULDN'T have worked. Ross had told his secrets, and Laurie hers. They'd kissed and then broken up within the space of half an hour. But somehow it did work. They were building something, learning how to trust and how to work together. And Ross had just learned that no one…*no one*…could carry off bright yellow feathers in quite the way that Laurie could.

'Ready to go?' He tried to keep his face straight as he saw her walking out of the front door of the house in her costume for the Lakeside School sports day.

She pulled the beaked mask up, propping it on top of her head. 'Yes, I think so. The feathers are fighting back…' She flapped one arm and a feather drifted upwards then floated back down again, settling on the gravel at their feet. 'Are you sure we shouldn't go for different costumes? When I chose these, I was trying to make a point.'

'Yeah?' Ross feigned innocence. 'What point was that?'

'Don't ask. It was a really bad idea. You really don't need to go as an egg.'

'Too late now. I'm rather looking forward to it. It's nice that you didn't go for any of the safe options.'

'I just hope you don't mind feathers in your car.' She wriggled suddenly in discomfort and turned her back on him. Ross busied himself with looking the other way.

'Ah, gotcha.' She turned, to face him again, still buttoning the front of her costume, and held up a feather, a triumphant look on her face. 'They get everywhere.'

'If you need a hand…' He probably shouldn't allow himself to smile when he said that.

'Trust me. You really don't want to know where they're ending up.'

He probably did. Ross dismissed the thought as unworthy of someone who was going to be dressing up as an egg.

He drove the few miles to the school, with Laurie sitting in the back seat, steadying the egg to stop it from rolling around, and showering feathers in the process. When he parked in the school car park she got out and tried to brush some of the feathers off the seat, only managing to replace them with a new set.

'Don't worry about that. Best to get all of them in one hit with the vacuum cleaner when we get back.' He took pity on her frustrated expression. 'It's probably because it hasn't been worn before. All the feathers that are a bit loose are dropping at once, and it'll stop in a minute.'

'You reckon so?' She flapped her arms again in a remarkable impression of a chicken. 'You might be right, it doesn't seem to be shedding as many now. Will you do me a favour?'

'Sure.' Anything as long as it didn't involve feathers inside her costume. Ross didn't trust himself with that, and having it turn X-rated in a school car park wasn't the image they were trying to promote.

'If I ever, *ever,* say that I'm going to choose costumes again, lock me up immediately.'

Ever. Again. It had a ring of friendship about it that warmed his heart. It was a very fine second-best option.

'It's a deal.' He reached into the car, carefully manoeuvring the egg out. It had a shock of painted hair at the top, a wide smile, and a pair of arms folded across its wide stomach. Below that, the yellow and black check that matched his trousers.

Laurie lifted the egg over his head for him, and he secured the shoulder straps that held it in place. It wobbled a bit when he took a step, but he could see straight ahead of him through the eye-holes. Only Laurie had disappeared…

'You all right in there?' He felt something brush his knee, and a feathered head appeared, peering up at him from the base of the egg. He chuckled, giving her a thumbs up, and she disappeared again, reappearing in his line of sight and pulling down the chicken mask over the top of her face.

They walked slowly over to the crowd that had formed at one end of the school sports field. He could hear Laurie's voice, a little muffled, talking to the kids who ran up to her and they both posed for photographs. He saw Sam doing the same in her blue and white Alice in Wonderland dress, while Jamie looked after their son Timothy. Laurie seemed to be slowly working her way over to them.

Sam waved, and he heard Laurie complimenting

her on her costume. Then a blond head appeared at the bottom of the egg.

'Hey, there, Timothy.' He smiled down at his godson.

'Uncle Ross!' Timothy seemed to be intent on climbing up his legs, and there was just about enough room to lift him up in the confined space. The boy wriggled with glee at this amazing adventure, and Ross moved his head so that he could peer out of the eyeholes at his mother.

'Timothy!' He heard Sam's voice. 'Are you there?'

'Shh!' Ross pressed his finger against his lips and Timothy laughed loudly.

'Come out, come out wherever you are…' Sam's voice again, as she pretended to look around for her son, lifting the trailing tablecloth on the drinks table and looking underneath it.

'Where is he?' Laurie had joined in with the play-acting and was looking around as well. Thrilled with the idea of a talking chicken, Timothy shrieked, and Ross let him down so he could duck under the bottom of the egg.

'Here!' Timothy ran over to Laurie, and she squatted down, flapping her arms in a very good impression of a chicken. Sam was laughing, and Jamie rapped his knuckles on the side of the egg, shouting a hello.

The headmistress of the school, dressed in a nineteen-twenties flapper costume, came to welcome them, and the crowd of parents began to disperse towards the seating that was set up at one side of the large playing field. The children were shepherded by their teachers into groups, ready for the races to begin.

Laurie tapped on the side of his egg, presumably

to attract his attention, although in truth Ross's attention had never left her. That was one of the advantages of coming as an egg, no one could see him stare. She led him over to the seating, and just as Ross was wondering how she was expecting him to sit down, he felt the egg lift a little. He ducked out from under it, and Laurie placed it on a seat and sat down next to it, her arm around it. Ross sat down on the empty seat on the other side.

'This is fun.' She was grinning out over the sun-drenched sports field.

'Wait till you start getting the questions.'

She turned to him, pulling the chicken mask up onto the top of her head. 'What questions? You never told me there were going to be questions.'

'I thought I'd save that as a surprise. I always get one or two questions from parents who've decided their seven-year-old is going to be the next world champion.'

She winced. 'You're not going to tell them, are you?'

'What, that you're a bona fide champion? They'd be fascinated…' He paused for a moment for effect. 'Nah. Don't think so.'

She fanned her face with her hand with an expression of relief. 'Just tell them that the best way to make a champion is give them a happy, healthy childhood.' She seemed to be wrestling with her costume, and was shedding feathers again.

'What are you doing?'

'Trying to get to my purse. That chilled lemonade on the drinks stall looks really nice. You want one?'

'Yes, but that's okay. I think Jo's heading our way.' He gestured towards the headmistress, who was walking towards them with two glasses of lemonade.

'Would you like to help give out the medals?' Jo proffered the lemonade.

'We get to give out medals? Yes, please,' Laurie answered before Ross could, and then frowned at the egg. 'Although I'm not sure how Ross is going to manage with his costume.'

'That's okay. You give them out, and I'll just tag along.'

'And the obstacle race?' Jo eyed the egg.

'I'll have a go.' Ross brushed Jo's reservations aside.

'I'd like to.' Laurie craned around the egg to look at him. 'My hip's fine. I can manage something like that. What do you reckon?'

Ross decided to ignore the fact that Laurie had actually asked him what he thought, and answered for them both. 'Two for the obstacle race, Jo.'

'Righty. I'll call you when it's your turn.' Jo ticked the list on her clipboard and hurried away, brushing a yellow feather from her costume.

More feathers were dislodged during the course of the afternoon as Laurie got to her feet, cheering and clapping all the kids. All the children who competed got a medal, and when it was her turn to give them out, she presented each one of them as if it was a precious recognition of their achievement.

When she got to the little girl who was looking a little tearful, after having taken a tumble and come in last, Laurie presented her with her medal and then lifted her up in her arms. He turned to see Sam on her feet, cheering and clapping, and everyone else following suit.

'What did you tell her?' When Laurie helped him off with the egg, and they resumed their seats again, he saw the little girl run over to her parents, proudly showing off the medal that hung around her neck.

'I told her that it was a very special medal, because she'd been brave enough to get up and try again.'

Ross nodded. 'That's nice.'

And so unlike the woman who'd first walked into the clinic. She'd been quiet, self-contained and focussed. As if the only thing that mattered was winning, whatever she had to sacrifice in order to do it. Ross was proud of the fact that the clinic could work miracles, but this wasn't one of them. The Laurie who could give a child who'd come last in the race a medal and make her feel like a winner must have been there all the time. And entrancing as the old Laurie had been, this new one was downright irresistible.

CHAPTER NINE

LAURIE'S LITTLE JOKE had well and truly backfired on her. Two weeks ago she'd chosen the egg costume for Ross in an attempt to stop him from following her around to make sure she wasn't overdoing things. But so much had changed since then. And as it turned out, the yellow feathers were a bit more than she could handle, flying around everywhere and making her sneeze.

Ross glanced up and down the obstacle course, and then lifted the egg over his shoulders. Laurie put her chicken mask on, and they lined up with the others at the start of the course.

'What's he going to do about the skipping ropes?' Sam was in the next lane to Laurie.

'Goodness only knows. Improvise?'

Sam laughed. 'Yeah. We should finish as quickly as we can, so we can watch him.'

'Hey!' Ross's voice sounded from inside the egg. 'I heard that…'

Laurie rolled her eyes as the parent who had been given the starting pistol walked along the line to make sure everyone's toes were behind it. That was taking it all a bit too seriously. But as she looked down the course, she couldn't help feeling her heart beat a little faster. Couldn't help weighing up the opposition. Sam was the strongest of the bunch, and while Laurie was pretty confident she could beat her in normal circumstances, a chicken suit and a hip that shouldn't be overstressed would give Sam an advantage.

'Ready… Get set…' The starting pistol sounded and Laurie started to run. She and Sam got to the upturned gym benches, which were serving as balance beams, at the same time. Something was amusing the crowd, she could hear ripples of laughter.

'Oh, no!' She heard Sam's exclamation and looked round. Somehow the egg had got dislodged and Ross had become disorientated, veering blindly off course.

'I'll go and get him. You go.'

Sam hesitated.

'Go! You can still win. Honour of the clinic, eh?'

Sam grinned. 'Okay.' She jumped onto the beam, making her way adroitly along it, just as the man who had just passed them overbalanced and stepped off his.

Laurie started to run back towards Ross. She couldn't believe she was doing this. Laurie Sullivan. The most focussed, competitive member of any team. She flung her arms around the egg, and Ross stilled suddenly.

'Who's that?'

'Laurie. Come along, it's this way…' She tried to adjust the egg so that he could see through the eye holes, but it wouldn't go all the way. That would have to do.

They made their way over to the beams, and once Ross found his he made a good job of traversing it. Then she ran for the slalom, checking that he was still with her.

'Crawl tube's next.'

'You're joking, aren't you?' She heard him chuckle. 'You go…'

From inside the plastic tunnel she could hear the crowd's reaction. Ross was obviously playing this for laughs, and when she emerged from the other end she saw him bending over to mimic an egg-shaped crawl. The skipping ropes were out of the question as well, but as she picked hers up and started to skip, he copied the motion with his legs.

Her father would have been screaming his disapproval. All her life Laurie had been taught to compete, no matter what the context or whether the race was supposed to be fun. She'd left her father behind, but the guiding principle was so ingrained that it had turned into an instinctive reaction. Something she couldn't throw off.

But her father wasn't here. Ross was. There was a long straight run to the finish line, and she saw Sam at the other end, cheering and clapping. As Ross made his way at a slow canter, she ran behind him, stretching her arms out to make it look as if she was pushing him.

Everyone laughed. And the feeling was… Freedom. She felt free.

But as Ross made the finishing line, he tripped, staggering to one side and making a half-turn before he lost his balance completely. Laurie held out her hand to save him, but grabbing hold of a papier-mâché egg to stop the fall of a six-foot man was never going to work. He went down in a cloud of paper and dried glue, and Laurie only just managed to keep her footing.

'Ross! Are you okay?' She bent back the paper that was still covering his face.

'Yes. Yes, I'm fine. You didn't fall, did you?' The

tenderness in his eyes was all-consuming. People were crowding round, and she didn't even see them.

'No. Just managed to stop myself.'

'Coming through…' She heard Sam's voice. 'Coming *through*!'

A flash of blue satin on the grass beside her brought her to her senses. She could stay here on the grass with him for the rest of the afternoon, but that was sure to be remarked on by the teachers and the parents.

'Ross. Stay down.' Sam's put her hand out to stop him from sitting up and he ignored her completely.

'Too late.' Laurie shrugged. Ross was getting to his feet, brushing pieces of papier-mâché from his hair.

Sam puffed out a breath. 'Really, Ross. Laurie and I could have demonstrated all sorts of things to the kids. Neck braces, broken arms…'

'Dislocated shoulders.' Laurie grinned. She'd be very happy to inspect Ross thoroughly for bruises as well.

'Yes, dislocated shoulder.' Sam nodded sagely. 'That's a good one.'

'Sorry.' Ross chuckled. 'Looks as if the egg's the only casualty.'

'And the chicken.' Sam pulled the chicken mask out from under Laurie's knee, disturbing a small cloud of loose feathers as she did so. 'Think we'll get a gold medal for making the most mess?'

Ross nodded. 'Yeah. We came first on that one, at least.'

It was just as well that Laurie had thought to bring a pair of jeans along, in case she needed to change. Ross had fetched them from the car, along with his own change of clothes, and Laurie emerged from the changing tent with the remains of the chicken costume in a plastic rubbish bag, heartily glad to be rid of the feathers.

Ross was standing a few feet away, and the body language of the couple he was with screamed that now they had him in conversation, they weren't going to let him get away. He was nodding and listening, his smile fixed, and Laurie wondered whether she should go and rescue him. Then the man looked straight at her.

'Excuse me. Are you…?' He frowned, clicking his fingers as if he was trying to place her. 'The rower…'

No. She didn't want to be Laurie Sullivan the rower today. She'd been having too much fun. Ross turned and must have seen the dismay on her face.

'Laurie's on my medical team at the clinic.' He interjected quickly.

'Ah. I could have sworn…' The man frowned at her, and his wife shook her head.

'Don't, Brian.'

Okay. Maybe she *was* nothing like a winner today. Laurie gave a little shrug. 'It's okay. I get that a lot.'

'About your son…' Ross was steering the couple away now, and the thumbs-up gesture he made to Laurie behind his back told her that he had everything under control.

'All the usual questions, I see.' Laurie turned to find Jo, the headmistress, standing beside her.

'Usual questions?'

Jo nodded. 'Yes. Mr and Mrs Marshall have an older boy, nice lad, he's in the senior school now. He's very good at football, and when he was here they were very keen for me to get a special trainer along to the football club for him.'

'He's a little young for that, isn't he?' The children here were all aged from five to seven.

'I thought so. But they wouldn't listen so I called in my secret weapon.' Jo smiled, nodding towards Ross. 'Ross's reputation meant that they accepted his advice a bit more readily.'

'Not to be so pushy?' Laurie wondered what her own teachers had thought of her father. What might have happened if someone had shown the good sense that Jo had, and had called in someone like Ross. Nothing, probably. Her father didn't listen to anyone.

'Football's a very lucrative career.' Jo mused. 'But at this age, our aim is to give pupils a broad range of basic skills that they can carry forward and that gives them choices. Ross has helped us to structure a good sports programme, and he's worked with a number of our children who have special needs. And he's very good with the odd pushy parent.'

'He understands the issues?' Maybe Ross understood *her* better than she'd thought.

'Yes. And he's very committed to giving the children a good start.'

'I thought…' Laurie smiled. 'I thought we were here just for fun.'

Jo laughed. 'Well, you are. But it doesn't do any harm to let the parents meet him in a less formal setting. I liked your double act on the obstacle course.'

Double act? Laurie wondered if her growing friendship with Ross was that apparent. But that had just been a bit of fun, too.

'Miss… Miss…' A little girl was tugging at Jo's dress and she shot Laurie an apologetic look.

'What is it, Lisa? I'm talking…'

'But Josh has fallen up a tree!'

Jo mouthed an apology to Laurie and squatted on her heels next to the child. 'Which tree, Lisa? Has Josh fallen *down*?'

'No. Up! Over the stream.'

None of that made any sense to Laurie, but it clearly did to Jo. She straightened up suddenly, looking around and waving to a couple to catch their attention.

'Run to Mum and Dad, Lisa. Now, please.'

As Lisa scampered away, Jo's face took on a look of urgent concern. 'Would you fetch Ross, please, Laurie? I'm going to see what's happened.'

Jo hurried away as fast as her heels would allow her on the grass. Laurie ran towards Ross, catching his arm to drag his attention away from the Marshalls.

'Jo needs you. Something about a kid falling up a tree by the stream?'

'What?' Ross apparently knew what that meant too, and he set off at a run, leaving the Marshalls staring open-mouthed after him.

'Sorry.' Laurie shot them an apologetic look. 'We'll be back…'

She followed Ross. He'd overtaken Jo, who was now running barefoot, and Laurie set her gaze on his back and ran, feeling her hip complain as she picked up speed. That wasn't important right now. Ross and Jo's reactions had left no room for doubt that something was badly wrong, and that a child was in danger.

Ross skirted the corner of the school building and Laurie followed him. Up ahead she could see a small knot of children pressed against a plastic mesh fence that bordered the edge of the school playing field. And beyond that…

A little boy seemed to be hanging upside down from the branch of a huge tree that overhung a stream. He was screaming, a mixture of fear and pain in his voice.

Ross had already reached the fence and was clearing the children to one side, looking up at the plastic mesh, obviously wondering if he could clamber up it. But the fence was obviously designed to deter climbers and afforded no footholds. Laurie put on a spurt of speed, and as she reached him he was bending down to the children.

'How did he get in?'

One little boy's hand shot up. 'He crawled under it. There.'

Ross looked round, and Laurie saw that the fence had been cut at the bottom. She might be able to wriggle through, but she doubted it. She bent down to try, but the hole was too small.

'That's not going to work…'

Ross knelt down, digging with his hands at one side of the hole, and uncovering a steel spike that was driven into the ground, holding the bottom of the fence down. That would do it. If they could just free a bit more, they could get under. She started to dig on the other side of the hole.

'Steady. These are driven in pretty hard…' He gripped the curved top of the spike and heaved, expelling a grunt of effort as it came free.

His words didn't sting, the way they once would have. Laurie cleared the earth and found another spike, giving it a tentative pull. It was driven deep into the earth and it didn't move.

'Will you give this one a try?'

Ross grinned, but didn't say anything. He heaved the spike up, and Laurie set about uncovering a third one.

'Is that going to do it?'

Ross glanced at the fence. 'One more, on the other side. See if you can find it while I get this one up.'

Laurie cleared more earth while Ross concentrated on getting the spikes out of the ground. Jo had arrived, barefoot and gasping for breath, and was speaking into her phone as she herded the children away from the fence.

'Can you get under there?' Ross pulled the fence up as far as it would go, and Laurie wriggled underneath it. He was a tighter fit, and she had to put all her weight into pulling the edge of the fence out of the way.

The boy had seen them coming and was quieter now. Either that or he was beginning to suffer the effect of inversion asphyxia, but that would be unusual unless he'd been hanging there for hours. There was a tangle of ropes hanging from a large tree branch that hung over the river, and one of his feet was caught up in it. Ross was quickly taking in the situation.

'I'll wade out and see if I can reach him.'

'Yeah, okay. It looks as if I can get up the tree, but if the branch goes we're in a whole world of trouble.' The idea of the wide, heavy bough crashing down on top of both Ross and the boy didn't bear thinking about.

Ross nodded. 'I'll see what I can do from underneath first.'

He waded into the water, making his way towards the boy. The stream wasn't too deep, and he could reach the child's shoulders and support them, bringing his head up a little. But he couldn't reach his foot.

It was an easy scramble, up the sloping trunk of the tree. The huge branch that stretched out over the water was as steady as a rock, but she didn't put any weight on it. If the boy was okay where he was, it might be better to wait for the emergency services.

'What do you reckon, Ross? This branch isn't going to go anywhere.'

Ross's gaze flipped from the boy, lying listlessly in his arms, to the branch above his head. Laurie knew this was a difficult decision to make.

'We need to get him down now.'

'Okay. I'll slide out there.' She got down on her hands and knees to spread her weight a little, and crawled out. It was a journey of trust. Trust that Ross had read the situation right, and that they couldn't wait. His trust in her, that she'd take her weight off the branch if it seemed at all unstable.

The rope seemed to be caught in a complex arrangement of knots, and she couldn't see straight away which one would free the boy. But, stretching down, she could run her hand along the rope twisted around his ankle and find the right one. She tore at the knot, feeling her nails break and the warm, slipperiness of blood.

'Uh… Got it.' The knot unravelled and the tension of the ropes around the boy's ankle loosened, but his foot was still trapped.

'Can you get his shoe off, Ross?' Without the heavy, thick-soled trainers his foot would slip through the gap.

'Can't reach. Can you manage it?'

'I think so. You've got him?'

'Yeah, he won't fall.'

There was a second mess of ropes around the branch. Laurie tugged at them and they held, and she looped one around her leg.

Carefully she edged forward, reaching for the boy's foot. Tugging at the hook and loop fastenings on his shoe, she eased it off. The boy's foot slipped through the gap in the rope, leaving his sock behind. When Laurie looked down, she saw Ross making for dry land, with the boy cradled in his arms.

Now she just had to make sure *she* didn't end up suspended upside down. The rope was holding her, but she'd had to shift forward until most of her body weight was over the water. She puffed out a breath, inching sideways until she was lying along the branch again. A moment to let her muscles recover from the strain, and then she unwrapped the rope from her leg and slithered down the trunk of the tree to the ground.

Ross had laid the boy carefully down on the grass, and was trying to gently rouse him. His eyes fluttered open but he seemed disoriented.

That could be from shock, or the pain of his swollen ankle. Or it could be from some other injury as he'd fallen. Or from hanging upside down. Asphyxia caused by the internal organs pressing down on the lungs didn't usually happen this quickly but it was so unusual that there wasn't a lot written on the subject.

Ross was taking the most devastating of those possibilities first, and after checking his breathing, he pulled up the boy's T-shirt to see his back and chest and then applied gentle pressure to his ribs and stomach. No reaction. Laurie found the boy's pulse and nodded to him.

'No sign of internal bleeding.'

Laurie nodded. 'Let me check his hips and legs.'

Children of this age were more prone to dislocations than adults.

Ross shifted to one side, turning his attention once more to rousing the boy. Laurie ran her hands carefully around his hips and down each leg. Apart from the swelling in his ankle, she could find no evidence of anything wrong.

'Hey… Josh. Open your eyes…' Ross had found the boy's name stitched into the back of his T-shirt. 'That's good. Can you take a deep breath for me?'

Josh took a breath. So far so good. 'My leg hurts.'

'Yeah, I know. We're taking care of that. Anything else?'

Josh shook his head. He was looking much less red in the face now, and more alert. When Laurie checked his pulse it was pretty much normal, which was probably more than could be said about hers.

A clatter at the gates in the fence made her look up, and she saw Jo unlocking them. She hurried towards them, kneeling down next to Josh. 'How is he?'

'We can't find any serious injury. But he needs to be checked out.'

'Okay. We have a stretcher coming from the medical room.'

Ross nodded. 'And his parents?'

'His mother's here somewhere, we're looking for her. Ah…here's the stretcher.' Jo seemed to have everything well under control.

The young teacher who'd brought the stretcher hurried off to fetch Ross's medical bag from his car. Josh was transferred to the stretcher, complaining loudly about his ankle, and carried into the school building. His mother arrived, looking anxious, and Laurie did her best to reassure her, encouraging her to comfort her son.

Ross didn't do anything by halves. His medical bag contained pretty much anything a doctor might need, and his examination was very thorough. Finally he was satisfied.

'Josh seems fine, apart from his ankle, Mrs Spencer. He'll need to get that X-rayed, though. He may have broken one of the small bones in his foot. I can give you a lift down to the paediatric accident and emergency department.'

Ross was erring on the side of caution, and Laurie didn't blame him. Josh's listlessness earlier had worried them both, and no doubt Ross would be reporting on that and the circumstances of his accident to the doctor at the hospital.

'Everything okay?' Josh had been seen almost immediately and Laurie had gone to wait in the car while Ross spoke to the A&E doctor. Jo had followed them down to the hospital so that she could take Josh and his mother home again afterwards.

'Yes, the doctor's pretty clued up. He's going to run a few tests just to make sure, but he agrees with us. The only thing wrong with Josh seems to be his ankle.' Ross leaned forward, his hand on the ignition key. 'Home?'

'I think we should. So far today, the only real casualty's been an egg, and I'd like to keep it that way.'

Ross nodded. 'Me too. I won't be sorry to get into some dry clothes as well.' He indicated the damp patches on the legs of his jeans.

They drove in silence back to the clinic. Ross was

obviously tired, but when Laurie took off her seat belt and got out of the car he called her back.

'Hey. Hope you didn't have too horrible an afternoon.'

'I got attacked by feathers, helped smash an egg and came last in a race. Then I helped save a child from a tree. What's not to like?' Most of all she'd loved being one half of the Ross and Laurie double act, which seemed to work equally well for the fun things as well as the deadly serious endeavours.

'Joint last.' He grinned at her. 'But I imagine even that was a first for you?'

'I think it must be. Consider yourself part of a new experience.'

Laurie heard him chuckle as she walked away.

CHAPTER TEN

ROSS HAD TAKEN a long, hot bath, and then walked over to the clinic. He'd done his evening rounds of patients and staff, and no one seemed to need him for anything so he'd gone to his office.

Laurie was perfect. Unstoppable. His own dreams had been put aside and had slept soundly for a long time now, and he'd been able to tell himself that his life here was all he wanted. But then Laurie's sense of fun, her determination to face down every challenge, was enough to rouse anything from the deepest sleep. And now the dream was coiled around his heart again like a serpent, squeezing hard.

It was crazy. He knew he couldn't have what he wanted, but he was unable to set it aside. The idea that they could overcome every obstacle and get to know each other a little better. Take their time, and then learn to build a life. A family.

A family was the one thing he couldn't give her. And that would destroy any life they'd managed to build. No amount of thinking his way out of this situation would change hard facts, so there was no point in considering the matter any more. Ross opened the folder on his desk that contained the outstanding paperwork for the clinic. He was a little behind, and he could spend the evening catching up.

Four hours later, he was done for the evening. But it seemed that the evening wasn't done with him. He paced his apartment restlessly, before resorting to the only place he knew that conferred a measure of calm. Pouring a splash of Scotch into a glass, he walked down the steps from his balcony and headed out across the grass to the lake.

It seemed that he'd been sitting there a long time on the small dock, staring out into the distance, when he heard footsteps behind him. No need to turn, he knew who it was. And even now he wanted her company. Laurie sat down beside him, swinging her legs back and forth over the water.

'Hey.' He turned to see her face, shining in the moonlight. 'You want some of this?'

'What is it?' She took the glass, sniffing at its contents, and then took a sip. 'Mmm, that's good. Double malt. Not really enough for two, though.'

Ross shrugged. 'A little of the best is enough.'

'I guess so.' She took another sip and handed the glass back to him. When he brought it to his lips, he thought he could taste hers, but perhaps that was just his imagination.

They sat together quietly for a moment. It was nice. Companionable. Someone to share his thinking time with, if not his thoughts.

'So… I'm curious. Do you know what's going on with all the rope around that tree?'

'Um… Jo mentioned it to me the other day. The area of woodland is part of the school grounds, it's fenced off for safety reasons. Apparently there's some social media thing going on and they've had teenagers breaking in.'

'To wind rope around trees? I know that teenagers on social media have a mindset all of their own, but that sounds particularly odd.'

Ross handed the glass back to Laurie. 'It's a bit like bungee jumping. Only without the elasticity.'

'And they just hang there?'

'In pairs.' Ross was trying not to meet Laurie's gaze.

'What?' Laurie thought for a moment and then started to laugh. 'They hang from trees, making out together? Is *that* what you're saying?'

'Yes.' He was glad she'd put it into words so that he didn't have to. 'Jo said she found a few used condoms at the side of the river the other day. She's worried about it, of course. The school uses that land to teach the kids about wildlife and caring for woodlands, so they use it pretty regularly. I imagine they tried to cut the fence, where we found that hole, and discovered it was too tough so they got in another way. The hole wasn't big enough for an adult to get through, but a child could manage it.'

'Have you had anything like that on the clinic's land?'

'No, thank goodness. There's always someone wandering around, day or night, so they're a lot more likely to be seen. Or maybe we just don't have the right kind of tree.'

'Mmm. You'd need height and a really strong, unobstructed branch. Do you think the water's one of the essential requirements?'

'Don't…' Ross shook his head. 'Don't even try to work it out. You won't be able to un-think it later.'

'I half wish I could have done something a little crazy when I was a teenager.' Ross shot Laurie a questioning look and she grinned. 'Not *that* crazy. Just being allowed to have a boyfriend would have been nice.'

'Too busy training?'

She nodded. 'Yeah. Everything was about the training. Or maybe everything was just about my father, and he was all about the training. What about you? You must have found a few things to get up to around here. All this countryside and the lakes.'

Ross couldn't think of anything. 'Not really. A four-mile bike ride each way to the nearest town tends to put the lid on too much impromptu mischief-making. That's one of the disadvantages of living in such a secluded place. Although my mother might say it was an advantage.'

'So we were both lonely.' She took a sip from the glass and gave it back to him.

'I have the clinic. You have…' Laurie had a future, and he could see her moving forward to grasp it with both hands.

'A dodgy hip and a capacity for denial?' She chuckled.

'Your hip's on the mend. You're going to be back in a boat soon, and getting ready to win that gold medal.' Ross didn't want to think about all the other things that Laurie could do, because they wouldn't be with him.

'I have faith in you.' She turned suddenly to face him, her skin pale in the darkness.

Was that enough? He wanted it to be, but it wasn't.

'I have faith in you, too. I just don't have much faith in the future any more.'

Laurie's hand moved to the side of his face, her fingers resting lightly on his cheek. 'I wish you would, Ross. If you did, then maybe we—'

He laid his finger across her lips. Ross didn't want to hear about all the things that Laurie thought they could do together, because they were impossible.

'That's the difference between us, Laurie. You can change your future. I can't change mine.'

She flung her arms around his neck, as if she could somehow save him from something. Then suddenly she jumped away from him, her hand flying to her mouth.

'That's embarrassing, isn't it? Hugging the boss in front of everyone.'

'Look around. This happens to be the one place that isn't visible from any of the clinic windows.'

She looked, and then gave him a smile. 'I'm so glad you knew that. It smacks of a little healthy misbehaviour. You're beginning to seem quite human to me.'

'Thanks!' He feigned outrage. 'I didn't seem human before?'

'You're right a little too often for my liking.'

'I can be wrong…' He wanted so badly to be wrong. Wrong about everything, his sure knowledge that taking things further with Laurie would end in catastrophe.

And then there were those eyes. Dark and knowing. The hand that caressed the side of his face sending shivers down his spine. Ross leaned forward, planting a kiss on her cheek.

'What was it you said? A little of the best is enough?' She murmured the words. So close now that they were almost touching, and he could feel her breath on his cheek.

His fingertips grazed her arm. Her leg pressed against his. Each moment, each touch was precious and exquisite. And then one rush of emotion as he put his arms around her and kissed her. Her response matched his. Audacious and hungry, as if the past didn't exist and the future hadn't happened yet. Taking each moment, without fear or regret.

'That was undoubtedly the best thing that didn't happen to me today.' He held her close, knowing he'd have to let her go soon.

She reached up, running her thumb across his lips. 'I suppose if it never happened, then we could do it again…'

Laurie had asked for the day off today. That wasn't unexpected, she'd worked far more hours than she was being paid for over the last couple of weeks, and maybe she had other things to do. But Ross missed seeing her around the clinic.

When he'd popped into Adam's room, on his daily round of patients and staff, the boy had said that Laurie wouldn't be coming to play computer games with him today, even though she'd amassed enough points to give her avatar a complete change of wardrobe. She wasn't in the lounge, or walking by the side of the lake. And unless Ross was very much mistaken, she wouldn't be out in a boat somewhere.

Or would she? It had been almost three weeks since he'd seen her rowing past his window, and he knew that she missed it. Maybe that wayward spirit of hers had just had enough of the clinic's calm, ordered existence and she'd decided she needed to get back into a boat. He'd made it clear that he was no longer responsible for her treatment, but the thought still bothered him.

She hadn't taken one of the clinic's electric cars into town, and when Ross found an excuse to pop back to his flat for something, he noticed that the long curtains in the living room of the small apartment downstairs were drawn, even though it was nearly lunchtime. It was odd, because Laurie was such a creature of the light. She loved it and it loved her.

He'd told her that he trusted her, and he'd made a promise. He should keep it. She just wanted a day to herself and he shouldn't interrupt…

Ross arrived home late after an evening spent at the clinic, and opened the French doors that led out onto the balcony. As he stared out over the dark water of the lake, he saw a figure sitting on the bench at the water's edge. Laurie.

What was she doing down there? It was a warm evening, and the calm of the lake often drew him to that spot, but there was something about the way she was sitting, her shoulders hunched and her head bowed. Without even thinking about whether it was a good idea or not, he took the steps down from the balcony two at a time and walked down to the lake.

She must have heard his footsteps on the uneven ground because she turned her head towards him. He could see her face now, pale and impassive in the twilight, and she was nursing something on her lap.

'Hey…' Some instinct stopped him from remarking on the warmth of the evening. This didn't seem the right time for pleasantries.

'Hi, Ross.'

'May I join you?'

She nodded, as if she didn't much care either way, and Ross sat down on the bench. He could see now what she was holding—a small wooden model of a boat.

'What's going on?'

Laurie puffed out a breath. 'Nothing… Nothing. This seemed like a good idea but…' She shrugged. 'I'm not really feeling it.'

She looked as if she wasn't feeling anything, but Ross knew better. She'd learned to work through any pain by just pretending she didn't feel anything, and the more impassive her face, the more she was struggling.

'What's this for?' He reached out and brushed the model boat with his fingertips. As he did so, he saw that it was full of kindling, and that a box of matches lay on the bench beside her. Laurie was saying goodbye to something…someone.

'He's been gone a long time. Fifteen years ago today.' She turned, looking at him solemnly. 'I've spent almost as much time without him as I had with him.'

'And you thought you might send the boat out onto the water? As a remembrance for someone you've lost?'

'Yes, it's a model I had at home and… I put it into my case when we went down to London. I don't know whether it's the right thing now.'

'If you make it the right thing, then that's what it is.'

She looked at him thoughtfully. 'It won't make any difference.'

'No, it won't. Sometimes remembering someone and saying whatever you want to them makes a difference to you, though.'

She nodded. Ross wondered whether Laurie was so used to concealing her feelings that she wouldn't be able to break through her impassive mask now, but he knew one thing. She wanted to.

'I'll do you a deal. If you push your boat off from here it'll just float back to the shore. I have a pair of waders and I can take it out far enough to catch the current. You can say what you want to say and maybe that'll float away too.'

She thought for a moment and then nodded. Ross got to his feet, hurrying back to his apartment before Laurie changed her mind.

Laurie had been sitting here for over an hour, waiting for a moment that never seemed to come, when she could get in touch with her feelings and make some sense of them. All she could feel right now, on the anniversary of the death of her older brother, was overwhelming pain and terrible guilt.

Maybe she'd been waiting for Ross, to come out here and make sense of it all for her. That was rather too much to ask of anyone.

He was back before she could make any sense of wanting him here either, putting the waders onto the ground next to the bench and sitting down.

'Who's the boat for, Laurie?'

Good. Questions that were easy to answer.

'My older brother, Tom. He died when I was fifteen.'

'He must have been young.' Ross shook his head, understanding the terrible waste of a life that should have been just beginning.

'He was twenty-one.' Laurie puffed out a sigh and suddenly it became a little easier to talk. 'My father pushed all of us to strive for sporting careers. Tom was going to be the tennis player, but my younger brother Ben was always more talented. My father pushed and pushed and…he pushed Tom too hard.'

'What was he best at? The thing you'd most like to remember him for?'

No one asked that. Tom had been caught in a cycle of the wrong expectations and failure, and that was what defined his death as well as his life.

'He was kind, and very funny. He used to make me finger puppets when I was little and we'd make our own plays with them. Tom always came out with the best lines.' All the warmth came flooding back at the memory. Along with pain. But it was better than the emptiness that she'd been sitting here with.

'He sounds great.'

'He was really creative and he used to tell the best stories. For my tenth birthday, he made me a book about a dragon who made everyone around him do as he said…we both knew that was really my father. One day he had so much steam coming out of his ears that he exploded. It was…' Laurie choked suddenly, tears spilling down her face.

'Breathe.' Ross murmured the word, putting his arm lightly around her shoulders. 'Breathing helps.'

A great gasp of air *did* help. Somehow the tears were helping as well.

'My father wouldn't see that he wasn't cut out for sport, it wasn't what he wanted to do and he wasn't that good at it either. He just pushed and pushed, telling Tom he was a failure and that our younger brother was better than he was. Tom got hold of steroids from somewhere, in an attempt to make himself acceptable in my father's eyes, and…'

'The usual side effects?'

Laurie nodded. 'Yes, lack of impulse control and aggression. Combined with all the frustration and rejection he was already feeling. He was cycling home and…the lights were against him and he should have given way, but he didn't. He just rode at a lorry, expecting it to stop, and there was no way it could. I was fifteen, and it was then that I decided I had to get out.'

'So…he couldn't save himself, but…maybe he saved you?'

'I don't think he meant to. He was just influenced by the drugs.'

'Maybe. But it sounds as if he loved you very much. What would he say to you now, if he knew that you'd broken free of your father?'

More tears. But somehow the tightness in her chest seemed to be easing now that she was no longer struggling to keep them back.

'I think he'd say that he was happy about that. He'd probably write me a story.'

'Yeah? Then you've got something to thank him for.'

Tom's life seemed less like a catalogue of failure and missed opportunity now. 'Aunt Suze always used to say that it was all such a waste…'

'She's right, it was a waste of a young life. But what he was, the things he did will never be wasted as long as you remember him for them.'

Laurie wiped her face, picking the boat up from the bench beside her. This wasn't the brave face that she'd put on for her father. It was wanting to say the things she really wanted to, for Tom, and that felt very different.

'Let's do this.'

Ross nodded. 'Yeah. Let's do it.'

He pulled on the waders and they walked down to the water's edge. In the darkness, with Ross standing quietly beside her, Laurie said the things she wanted to say to Tom. Then he put the small boat onto the water and handed her the matches.

Her hands were trembling, and she broke the first two, trying to strike them against the side of the box. But the third flared brightly and she touched it against the kindling in the boat. It started to glow and then caught.

'You want me to take it out now?' Ross spoke quietly.

'Yes, please.' Laurie pressed her fingers against her lips, touching the kiss against the side of the boat, and Ross started to wade out, pushing the boat. The flames were spreading, now, and the fire that she'd carefully built was beginning to lick around the mast.

Suddenly, she had to be a part of this as well. Laurie waded out into the water and he turned, waiting for her.

No comments about how she'd ruin her sandals, or that the water was cold. When she reached him, he pushed the boat towards her and she gingerly took hold of it. They took a few steps more, Ross's hand around her waist steadying her against the pull of the current. This was what she needed to do, and she didn't want to do it alone. She wanted Ross to be with her.

Laurie said one last goodbye and pushed the boat out into the lake. It bobbed for a moment and then the current found it and it started to drift away, a speck of shining flame in the darkness.

She couldn't keep herself from crying again, but she didn't have to. Ross held her tight, the warmth of his body comforting her. Together they watched the boat float away, until finally the flames caught on the infrastructure and the light was extinguished.

Ross, the man who seemed to have an answer for everything, was as lost for words as she was. When she looked up at him, he was staring into the darkness, and Laurie thought she saw the glint of a tear in his eye. A tear for her beloved Tom that moved Laurie more than she could say.

'Thank you, Ross.'

He nodded, taking her hand, and they waded out of the water together. Silent in the darkness and yet so, so close. He watched as she walked awkwardly to the bench, her feet slipping in her wet sandals.

'I can't walk in these…' She sat down, taking them off. The rough ground between here and the cultivated lawn at the back of the house might be a little hard on her feet, but at least she wouldn't slip and fall.

'Want a piggy-back?' Ross was stripping off the waders and pulling on his sneakers.

Probably not the most elegant of ways to leave your brother's tribute, but Tom would have found it funny. And Ross seemed to know that Laurie would have felt awkward about being carried. She stood up on the bench, and climbed onto his back.

'Uh… You're a lot heavier than you look.' Ross didn't seem to be having any trouble carrying her, and was striding towards the house.

'That's because it's all muscle. Where's your knowledge of human anatomy, Ross?' Tom would have found the teasing funny, too.

'Next time I need a lift I'll know who to ask…'

'You think I couldn't?'

He shook his head. 'No. I'm horribly afraid that you could. Keep still, will you?'

Laurie wrapped her arms around his neck, snuggling against him. The warmth of his body penetrated through her wet jeans and his solidity was comforting and…

Maybe she shouldn't be feeling that. But Tom wouldn't have minded, he would have just laughed and told her to go for it. He would have understood the damage that her father had done, how she hadn't been able to consider the thought of a happy family or a relationship because all those things seemed like a prison to her. And maybe he'd understand how her feelings were beginning to change.

But, however much she trusted Ross, however much he trusted her, it still couldn't change anything. He didn't trust the future, and Laurie knew that he wouldn't go any further than a few kisses, which they could pretend hadn't happened.

He reached the patio and let her down gently from his back. She couldn't let him go now, and she caught hold of his hand, feeling his fingers wind around hers.

'Thank you, Ross. That was…everything I wanted it to be.'

He nodded. 'It was an honour to share it with you.'

Still she couldn't leave him. But Ross pulled his hand away from hers. 'You should get inside and get dry. Maybe take a shower to get rid of the Eau de Pondweed…'

'You don't like it?'

'It has a mysterious allure. You may want to check in

your pockets for fish, though. Why don't I make some hot chocolate? I'll meet you on the steps.' He gestured towards the spiral staircase that led up to his balcony.

'I've got hot chocolate. And plenty of milk.' She didn't want him to leave her for even a few minutes.

'Your place, then…' His grin made her shiver. Hot chocolate, your place or mine. That wasn't the way Ross did things. An invitation for drinks was just that, and your place or mine was a matter of which was more convenient.

She caught his hand, leading him into the small apartment. The drapes had been drawn all day, the light had hurt her eyes too much to let any of it in, but now she wanted to see the lake. She drew the curtains back, letting in the moonlight that reflected off the water.

He shooed her towards the bathroom, her jeans leaving a trail of water behind her. When she returned, he'd wiped the floor, plumped the cushions on the sofa, where she'd been sitting all day, and put the coffee cups into the sink. And there were two mugs steaming on the breakfast bar.

'This is nice. Thank you for this evening.' Laurie sat down next to him on the sofa, and he stretched his arm out on the cushions behind her. It was an open invitation for a hug, and she moved closer, taking him up on it.

CHAPTER ELEVEN

ROSS HAD BEEN thinking a lot about this. How right it seemed, and how very wrong he'd been. Laurie had changed. She'd learned how to trust the people around her, and that showing her feelings wasn't such a bad thing. She didn't need him any more, and it was time to let her go.

He waited until the day had run its course, knowing when he'd have an opportunity to find her alone. Laurie was a creature of habit, and she liked to go down to the lake after work and just sit for a while, watching the movement of the water. Maybe she saw something there that he didn't, currents that might shift a boat forward a little or impede its progress. Or maybe she just liked the view.

He said down next to her and she smiled. A *real* smile, open-faced and bright-eyed as if she was genuinely happy. It made Ross happy too, and rendered what he was about to do next all the more difficult.

'I have something for you.' He gave her the envelope he'd been carrying.

'Yes? What's this?' She opened the flap, taking out the sheet of paper and scanning it.

Significant progress...
Positive attitude...
Confident that Dr Sullivan is committed to improving her condition, and that she will continue to improve after she leaves...

'Leaves the clinic?' Laurie picked out the words that Ross had typed then deleted and retyped three times. 'What have I done *now*, Ross?'

'You've done nothing. Why would you think…?'

She waved the paper at him ferociously. 'Because this sounds a lot as if you're giving me the sack.'

Clearly she was in no mind to make this easy for him. 'I'm not giving you the sack. Read the letter, Laurie.'

'Yes, I'm reading it. It says lots of nice things about me, and how I don't need you any more.'

'You don't. You never did.'

'I needed you, Ross. I needed someone to give me a shake and make me realise what I was doing to myself. And this…' She flipped the letter with her finger. '*This* is how you give someone the sack. You give a really nice reference and then cut them loose. After you *promised* me that I could help these kids.'

Ross didn't recall actually promising anything of the kind. But she was right, he had told her that she could take charge of Adam and Tamara's treatment, and she'd made an excellent job of it. He expected all the staff at the clinic to know that his word was as good as a promise.

'It's the right thing—'

'No! It's *not* the right thing. If you want me to go you should just say so.'

He didn't want her to go. But that was the whole point of this. Somewhere, deep inside, her anger was making him want to reach out and hug her. More than just hug her.

'You're not understanding what I'm doing...'

'No, actually, I don't. Try explaining it to me. Words of one syllable, please.'

Ross took a breath. He'd worked all of this out in his head, and he was sure that he was doing the right thing. Only he'd hoped that Laurie might look at the letter and realise that this was the right thing to do, too, without the need for explanations.

'All right. Simmer down.'

'No, I will *not* simmer down, Ross. This is...too much.' She crumpled the paper in her hand, dropping it at her feet. The wind caught it, and it bounced across the grass, lodging against some stones at the water's edge.

'That's just a copy. I've already sent the original to your consultant.'

'Without telling me? Where do you get off manipulating me, Ross?'

That was exactly his point. It had to stop now.

'Look, Laurie. Three weeks ago I made you an offer it was impossible to refuse. I told you that the clinic wouldn't treat you any more, knowing full well that this place was your last chance.'

'That's right.' She shot him a fierce look.

'I didn't know then that you'd spent your whole childhood being forced into a mould, or that you'd lost your brother. But that's no excuse, I shouldn't have done it.'

Laurie crossed her arms, staring out over the lake

and refusing to meet his gaze. 'We've been through that, Ross. I've admitted that I was being unreasonable, and you stopped me from cutting off my nose to spite my face.'

'It doesn't mean that what I did was right.'

There was a sudden flash of warmth in her eyes. Angry warmth. 'So…what? You're feeling guilty because I got better? Perhaps you should think about taking up another career because doctor doesn't seem to suit you.'

She was deliberately missing the point and the words he'd wanted to say came out in a rush before he could stop them. 'I *care* for you, Laurie. More than I should… I want you to stay, which is what makes it so very wrong of me to compel you to do so.'

'So why on earth didn't you just say so?' The fire was back again. And Laurie's fire could so easily turn to passion.

'Because… If I could offer you more then I'd do it, right here and now. But that's not right for either of us, and you know it. This letter means you're free to go.'

Her eyes widened and she opened her mouth to protest, then closed it again. Laurie knew just as well as he did that a relationship couldn't work between them. There was really nothing more to say.

Standing up and turning his back on her was difficult. And the words she called after him hit him like a knife between his shoulder blades.

'Ross! Don't you walk away…'

He had no choice. This was the right thing to do but he was in imminent danger of taking it all back, just to see Laurie's smile again. When Ross reached the fire escape steps that led up to his apartment, he had the opportunity to turn and glance behind him.

Laurie had walked down to the shore of the lake and was bending to pick up the crumpled letter. That was something, at least. Maybe if she read it again, she'd understand.

A sleepless night brought no answers apart from the ones she didn't want to acknowledge. Three weeks ago, Laurie would have taken the letter and gone, without looking back. Ross couldn't have timed things any worse by giving it to her now, when all she wanted to do was stay.

The morning brought no knock on her door, and she didn't have the heart to knock on his. If this was what Ross really wanted, then she should leave. Laurie left a message for Sam, asking if she was free for lunch, and set to work. She didn't want to think about having to say goodbye to the friends she'd made here, or to Tamara and Adam, but she was going to have to.

Sam tapped on the French doors at lunchtime, looking a little worried. She proffered a couple of herbal teabags, which was a sure sign that she thought something was up.

'Mmm. That looks nice.' She perched herself on one of the stools at the breakfast bar and snagged a slice of tomato from the large mixed salad that Laurie took out of the fridge. 'What's going on?'

'I'm going to leave. Tomorrow, probably.'

'Leave?' Sam's eyes widened in surprise. 'But I thought you were staying for another three weeks.'

'Yeah. I was going to.' Laurie flipped the kettle on.

'So…' Sam puffed out a breath. 'You haven't had an argument with Ross, have you?'

'Has he said anything?' Laurie shouldn't ask, but her curiosity got the better of her.

'No. He actually hasn't said anything to anyone all morning. Something's bugging him.'

'He wrote me a letter.'

Sam stared at her. 'A letter?'

She should just tell Sam she had to go. Hand over her notes on Adam and Tamara and leave it at that. But the nagging hope that somehow there was a way that she could stop what was happening wouldn't let her.

'Help yourself.' Laurie pushed the salad bowl towards Sam. 'I'll show you.'

She fetched the letter, laying it on the counter. Sam took a sip of her tea and picked it up.

'Has this been through the washing machine or something?'

'No, I…um… I screwed it into a ball and threw it.'

'Oh. Feelings running high, then.' Sam smiled, as if that wasn't such a bad thing at all. Then she focussed on the letter, reading it through as she ate.

'I'll agree this sounds like something you'd write when someone's leaving. But isn't this what you wanted, Laurie? Ross has given you what you need to square things with your consultant.'

'He said it meant I was free to go. I'm assuming that's what he wants.'

Sam narrowed her eyes. 'You're sure about that? Let me read the letter again.'

There was no point in trying to eat. Laurie watched miserably while Sam re-read the letter.

'Well, I can't get inside his head.' Sam laid the paper

back down and took a swig of her tea. 'But I've known Ross for a while, and…when he decides that something's wrong he just can't let it go. It's admirable actually, but it can be annoying.'

'So…what do you think?'

'Ross didn't want to box you into a corner the way he did. If it's anyone's fault it's mine, because I told him that you weren't following my advice…' Sam turned the corners of her mouth down.

'You were right. I would have done the same. I was being unreasonable and I'm really sorry—'

'That's water under the bridge.' Sam grabbed Laurie's hand, squeezing it. 'I'm only bringing it up because I know that Ross wasn't happy about not giving you the choice, it's against everything he believes in. I don't know, but I think this may be all about that and nothing to do with wanting you to leave.'

'Too much of a gentleman, you mean?'

Sam snorted with laughter. 'Yes. It's not a bad thing, I suppose.'

'No. It's quite a nice thing really.'

There was a lot of sense in what Sam said, but Laurie had been too upset and disappointed to see it before. So afraid of rejection that she'd jumped to that conclusion far too quickly and not looked behind Ross's words.

'What are you going to do?' Sam was looking at her thoughtfully.

'I'm going to make it clear to him that I want to stay. I want to finish what I've started with Adam and Tamara, and I want to continue on here with my own exercise regime. This place gives me the framework that I need to get better.'

Sam nodded. 'Sounds good to me. If Ross has a problem with that, he'll say so.'

There *was* a problem, one that Laurie hadn't told Sam about. Ross had said he cared for her, and that he'd take things further if only he could. But maybe she could find a way for them both to do that as well.

Seduction. That was the way forward. If it didn't work, she could leave and put it down to experience. But Laurie had thought about this carefully, and it was what she wanted. It was what Ross had said he'd wanted, too.

The only problem was that she'd left the only really nice dress she had at home, along with the high-heeled sandals that went with it. That was a difficulty, but problems were there to be solved. Maybe a less obvious approach would be better anyway. If she made a joke of it, maybe they could laugh their way out of any embarrassment.

She slipped into a pair of thick black leggings, and dark-coloured trainers. A black polo-necked sweater she'd brought, in case the weather turned cold, was ideal and the dark blue woollen hat that she wore for rowing covered her hair.

Laurie slipped out of her apartment, looking up at the balcony. The French doors stood slightly open, as they did most nights, to let fresh air into his bedroom. Further along, a light in the sitting-room window told her where he was. She took the dark blue scarf she'd brought with her and tied it around her face, like a bandana.

Now or never. If she didn't do this now, she'd have to go tomorrow, because now she knew he wanted her, she couldn't take another day of wanting him without touching him. Laurie crept silently up the wrought-iron stairs to the balcony, slipping in through the French windows like a shadow.

The bedroom was deserted, as she'd expected. It had a masculine feel about it, with oatmeal-coloured walls and heavy oak furniture. In one corner, a solid free-standing mirror, the kind you saw in gentlemen's outfitters, and a mass of framed pictures and photographs on the wall. It was somehow cosy and…

It had a bed. That was the only thing that Laurie was really interested in. Maybe she'd find out whether the mattress was as soft as it looked, if things went her way this evening.

She heard footsteps in the hallway. She hadn't thought she'd made any noise and was wondering how best to attract Ross's attention, but it seemed he knew she was here. When he reached the open doorway, she saw his smile, and a stab of desire made her legs tremble.

'What do you want?'

He knew exactly what she wanted. The look on his face told Laurie that. But Ross would always test her, always make her say it. His gaze was fixed on her face and she pulled the bandana down. That had probably been a bad idea because she needed him to see her face and know that she was serious about this. Resolute.

'You told me that I was free to do as I wanted now. I know you believe that we don't have any future together and I respect that. But this is what I want, Ross. To be with you tonight.'

'To talk?' He took one step forward. Ross knew darned well that they'd done quite enough talking.

'No.' She flipped her finger towards the bed. 'I want you right there.'

Suddenly he grinned. That taste of mischief that made her heart thump in her chest and set her thinking about all the things that she and Ross could do together. Then he pulled his polo shirt over his head, letting it drop onto the carpet.

Beautiful. Ross had the kind of body that was made for pleasure, and a great deal of appreciation. She stepped forward, finding his arms, and then he kissed her.

It was like everything else between them. Two strong characters fighting for dominance, but both wanting the same thing. He left her in no doubt about what he wanted. When she caught her breath, pulling him closer, he smiled down at her and then kissed her again. He was going to make this night perfect.

Ross had been sitting in the pool of light around a lamp. Plenty of reading matter on the sofa beside him, along with the remote for the TV, but he couldn't set his mind to any of it. He hadn't seen Laurie for twenty-four hours, and it already felt as if she'd gone.

He heard a sound. The slight creak as the French windows next door opened and a corresponding one again as they closed. That wasn't the breeze. Someone was there, and there was only one person it could be.

He tried to walk slowly to the bedroom. Tried not to jump to conclusions about her presence here, but when he saw her there was only one conclusion. Laurie's sense of humour might be a little wry, but it corresponded with his own. He couldn't help smiling, because he got the joke. A thief in the night, taking what neither of them could commit to during the day.

And she wanted him. As much maybe as he wanted her. If her words hadn't made her purpose here indisputable, then her kiss would have convinced him. Taking everything he wanted to give her, and demanding more.

'You're sure about this…' He couldn't stop himself from asking. 'One night?'

'What makes you think I'm not? Although if you're really good it could be two or three.' She pushed him against the wall, pressing her hips against his and running her hand across his chest. Sheer desire almost made him fall to his knees.

'You want it all your own way, do you?'

Mischief lit in her beautiful eyes. Her hand moved down, unbuttoning the waist of his chinos. 'Try me. Maybe you'll like doing as you're told for once.'

Ross was sure that he would. Less sure that it was what Laurie wanted. They'd always confronted each other, and now that seemed like a complicated, drawn-out foreplay that would shape the night ahead.

'Maybe *you'll* like doing as you're told. You should try that.'

She kissed him, her lips hard and searching on his. 'If you want it, you're going to have to take it.'

Of course he was. Neither of them would have it any other way. She was strong, but his bulk was a match for her. He lifted her off her feet and carried her over to the mirror. Turning her as he set her down again, so that her back was pressed against his chest.

'Watch.'

'You are *such* a bad man. That's a nice surprise.'

Her obvious enjoyment gave him purpose. Pinning her against him, he removed the scarf around her neck with his free hand. Then pulled her sweater over her head, cupping her breast with one hand, holding her against him with the other. Laurie wriggled a bit, but made no effort to get free. The movement was just a little sweet friction, and looking over her shoulder into the mirror he could see that she liked that as much as he did.

'That feels nice.' She smiled at him in the mirror. 'Not nice enough…'

Ross unhooked her bra, letting it slip over her shoulders. 'Better?'

'Much…' She only just got the word out before his fingers reached her breast and she groaned.

He kissed her neck, his fingers exploring the way she wanted to be aroused. Keeping her gaze locked in his in the mirror, watching carefully for every emotion.

Ross told her everything, whispering in her ear. There would be no mistake about how much he wanted her, and no mistake about how beautiful she was. Flaming hair and a body that was so strong and yet so soft. When she reached behind her, her fingers searching for the zip of his jeans, he gasped. Seeing his own face and hers, their gazes locked together in binding passion, and feeling what she was doing to him was taking him way beyond anything he'd thought that sex might be able to offer them both.

Suddenly she turned in his arms, stretching up to kiss him. 'You don't get this all your own way, Ross. However much I might like it.'

Laurie backed him towards the bed, and he sat down suddenly when he felt the backs of his legs touch the mattress. He reached for her, but she batted his hands away, slipping her trainers off along with her leggings. Ross followed suit, sliding out of his chinos and shoes. Waiting…

She got up onto the bed, crouching over him, her eyes flickering with the fire that he loved so very much. Laurie was in control now, and the feeling of where that might take him was all-consuming and more delicious than he could ever have imagined.

This was…insanely wonderful. Crazily passionate and yet full of the trust they'd built up over the last few weeks. He was watching her every move, shifting back on the bed when she flipped her finger towards the pillows. When she moved his searching hands away from her body, he resisted just enough to allow her to push against him, but not enough to make any difference.

There was so much to admire about his body. When she did so with her tongue, running it across his chest and teasing his nipples, he groaned. This was payback time for all the delicious things he'd done to her. The way he'd held her in front of the mirror and made her watch, which made it all even more delicious because she could see the gentle mischief in his eyes.

'You're killing me, Laurie.' He choked out the words as her fingers gently worked their way downwards. Slowly, because she liked the response it prompted in him so much.

'You want me to stop?' She allowed her hand to brush lightly against his erection.

'No. I just want you to…' He groaned, his head snapping back as she went back again, this time with a more substantial caress.

'That?'

'Yeah. That.'

This was so much fun. Laurie had always reckoned that there were guys who were great friends and other guys who were great in bed. Ross was both, and they were just the same now as they always were. Pushing each other, challenging each other for control. Working it out, because he had the same sense of humour as she did, and he wasn't afraid to use it.

'Are you ready for me?' She grinned down at him.

'Are you quite mad? What do you think?'

'I think…not quite.' She bent down, kissing the overwhelming evidence that he *was* ready, hearing the sharp hiss of breath escaping his lungs.

'Uh… Yeah, you're right. Now I'm definitely ready.' He caught her hand as she slid away from him. 'Where are you going now?'

'Condoms. In my pocket.' Her leggings were… somewhere. Breaking away from him to find them was such a waste of those moments when she couldn't touch him. But she knew that it was important to Ross that the one in a thousand chance became no chance at all. He had to be free of those worries.

He reached out, flipping open the drawer of the cabinet beside the bed. 'There are some in there.'

Finding them was the ultimate pleasure, because Ross's hands on her body made her fight to keep from forgetting about the contents of the drawer. Tearing the packet open was an exercise in trying to focus while he caressed her breasts.

'Stop that, Ross. You know how many people rip holes in condoms in just this situation?' She gritted her teeth, trying to think about the article she'd read about that recently, and failing miserably.

'I couldn't give you an exact figure right now.'

He took the condom from her shaking fingers, and she watched as he rolled it into place. As she straddled him, lowering herself slowly down to take him inside her, his gaze held hers captive.

Two deep sighs, hers and his, which might have been one because they were simultaneous. When she twisted her hips, the feeling made her cry out and a groan escaped his lips. And when she bent to kiss him, he was ready and waiting with kisses of his own.

They were together. No more vying for control, each trying to please the other. Everything was shared, every pleasure she felt found its way onto his lips as well. She melted into his arms and he whispered her name, shifting her gently onto her back. When he slid inside her again, the idea that they were just having sex exploded into smithereens. This was making love.

He was so tender, so exquisitely passionate. Their bodies moved together in the same rhythm, making the very most of the intimate connection they shared. It was no longer a matter of holding back, making this last, but of relishing the feeling that was growing inside her. She could do nothing but allow him to take her, knowing that he too was in her thrall.

When she came, it was a long fall into mindless pleasure. She knew she was pulling him with her, and as aftershocks tingled through her body, his hardened suddenly. He let out a cry, and she held onto him, knowing that he needed her touch as much as she had needed his.

'That was...' What they'd done defied description.

'Crazy?' He grinned down at her, lifting his weight and rolling onto his side to hold her close.

'Complete madness.' She kissed him. If this was madness then every day could be this insane as far as Laurie was concerned.

'It was beautiful.' He murmured the words, tenderness in his face.

'Yes. Beautiful is the word I was searching for.'

CHAPTER TWELVE

THEY'D DOZED FOR a long time, happy to just be in each other's arms. Then Laurie felt Ross shift against her as he leaned around to kiss her.

'Are you really going to leave at dawn?' His finger caressed her shoulder.

'Yes.' If what they had together was going to survive, it needed to be separate. Away from the limitations that practicality put on their relationship. 'I'll see you later, though? At the clinic?'

Ross grinned. 'So you're not going very far.'

'Not so far that I can't come back again, tomorrow night. Or be at the clinic during the day. If that's okay with you.'

He shot her a reproachful look. 'I always wanted you to stay. Are you seriously in any doubt about that?'

'If I had been, I probably wouldn't have crept up the stairs onto your balcony. I'd have knocked on your front door in order to preserve deniability.'

He chuckled quietly. 'I prefer the balcony.' He rolled onto his back, putting his hands behind his head.

'Me too. Maybe I can try swarming up it dressed as a pirate. With a cutlass between my teeth.'

'Absolutely not. That's *my* fantasy, so you can keep your hands off it.'

'Your fantasy? Really? You mean finding me up here in one of those floaty nightgowns, and popping the buttons with the tip of your sword? I'd have to keep pretty still…'

'I'd anchor you to the spot with my dangerous gaze.' He chuckled. 'And then…' He leaned over, whispering into her ear, and Laurie started to shiver from the exquisite pictures he was planting in her imagination.

'Stop!' Finally she called a halt to it. 'Stop it, Ross. You're not allowed to say that to me unless you're willing to come up with the goods. Straight away.'

'I'm more than happy to do that.' He grinned at her.

'In that case…' She reached across him, hooking another condom out of the drawer and pressing it into his hand. 'I have a few fantasies of my own you might like. Only you don't get to hear them until you give me a bit of encouragement.'

He chuckled softly then tore the packet open.

'I'll give you all the encouragement you want…'

Ross was exhausted. The kind of exhaustion that came from staying awake half the night, talking and making love, and then being woken at four o'clock for one of the best good mornings he'd ever had. *The* best, actually.

He'd caught Laurie yawning as she'd got back into her clothes and had called after her as she'd slipped through the French doors. She'd nodded, agreeing that there was still time to get some sleep before they were due at work at nine.

Laurie had the best poker face he'd ever seen. He already knew that, but it was still a little unsettling. She greeted him with her usual smile, nothing in her face reflecting what they'd been doing together last night. He wondered if she'd somehow managed to forget, and decided that wasn't possible.

She knocked on his open office door at eleven, and he looked up and beckoned her in. Laurie closed the door behind her, which was the generally accepted signal that he was in conference with someone and not available. Maybe now her impressive composure would crack.

'I've got an idea. There's a games convention at a hotel thirty miles from here, and I want to take Adam. He really wants to go.'

'Right. Well, I'm sure it would be a nice day out for him.' Ross wondered how that was going to help Adam's foot.

'It's not just that, Ross. Adam's our model patient, you know that. He does all his exercises in the gym, he's made friends, he's eaten well and slept when he's supposed to.'

'But he's not getting out of the wheelchair, is he?' Ross had noticed that Adam spent most of his free time playing video games.

'No, he isn't. He isn't confident about his recovery, and it's as if he's putting off the bad news. That he'll get better and still not be able to run again.'

'And a games convention's going to solve that?' If Laurie thought it would then Ross was willing to give it a go.

'I want to try. I gave Ann a call and she thinks it's a really good idea, if we don't mind taking him. Will you come?'

'Okay. I can get Mum to pop in and cover for me and take a day out.'

'Thanks, Ross. I really think this might be a turning point for him.'

Ross leaned back in his chair. 'So how long are you going to be able to keep this up, then?'

She grinned at him suddenly, her cheeks flushing. The kind of look you gave a guy when you'd just spent the night with him, and Ross was surprised at how much it meant to him.

'Stop! I thought I was doing so well!'

'You were. *I'd* never have known what you were up to last night, and I was there. It's actually quite unnerving. I was beginning to wonder if you were suffering from a memory lapse.'

'That's my thing. Don't show what you're thinking. One of the things I learned from my father.'

It was the first time that Laurie had ever said it. Maybe that was the most solid piece of evidence that last night *had* happened. She was finally breaking out of the isolation that her troubled childhood had imposed on her life.

'It's not the way you have to be, Laurie. You can decide for yourself.'

She nodded. 'That's still under consideration. But it doesn't do any harm to keep this quiet. No one here needs to know that I slept with the boss, do they?'

'No, they don't. As long as *you* remember it…' Ross's words were only half in jest. He knew that their relationship couldn't last but he didn't want it to be swallowed up in her single-minded determination. Lost for ever behind her impassive eyes.

'I remember.' She laughed suddenly, scrunching a

loose piece of paper from her pad into a tight ball and throwing at him. Ross batted it away, smiling.

'How was your hip this morning?'

'Official answer?'

He nodded. 'If you like. Then I'll take the real one.'

'The official answer is that it's improving steadily. The real one is that I noticed you were careful last night, and…you were perfect. It doesn't hurt at all this morning.' The red of her cheeks deepened slightly. 'You were perfect in every other way as well.'

'You make me *want* to be perfect. It's what you deserve.'

He wasn't perfect, not by a very long way. He couldn't give Laurie a home or a family, because his home was the clinic, and that was the only family he'd ever have. It was a good life, but Laurie had a whole world out there and a whole life of her own. But that didn't mean they couldn't take a little time out of their lives for each other and move on a little richer for it.

'Would you like to come to me tonight?' She gave him an impish grin. 'Just so that I don't start to feel I'm stalking you.'

'I'll be there.'

Laurie nodded. There was a moment of shared warmth when her gaze caught his, and then she stood. No kiss but, then, it was a little inappropriate in this setting. Here they were just temporary colleagues, and they'd closeted themselves in his office to talk about their patients.

But tonight… When the sun began to go down, Ross took the bottle of champagne from the refrigerator, putting it into a shopping bag in case anyone should see him. But he was alone in the quiet warmth of the evening as he hurried down the steps from the balcony, tapping on the French doors of Laurie's apartment. She was waiting for him, unlatching the door and beckoning him in, and he stepped inside and took her into his arms.

'You're sure about this.' Ross looked around the foyer of the hotel.

'Positive. Ann's all for it.'

'Yeah, but…did she know about the costumes?'

'Of course she does. Everyone wears costumes to video game events.'

'I wasn't expecting them to be quite so revealing, though.' Ross nodded towards a young woman dressed up as some kind of warrior with a sword. Her body armour could only be described as skimpy.

'Oh! She's my avatar!'

'Really? You wander around on the screen dressed like that, do you?' He couldn't help grinning.

'Excuse me. I do *not* wander, I stalk. Anyway, she's wearing body paint.' Laurie narrowed her eyes. 'Let's hope it's non-allergenic or we'll be picking her up off the floor.'

'But Ann does know what *kind* of costumes….'

'She knows. She's taken Adam to these things before. He's sixteen.' She pursed her lips. 'You really did have a sheltered childhood, didn't you?'

'Yeah. Suppose I did.' Ross looked over to where Adam was sitting in his wheelchair, perusing the different programmes for the event. He seemed to be taking it all in his stride and had accepted a leaflet from the woman warrior without giving her a second glance.

He followed Laurie over to the stand, watching as

she took the standard programme out of Adam's hands and picked up the thicker collector's copy, passing a note from her purse over to the young man behind the counter.

'These are the ones I want to go to.' Adam flipped carefully through the pages of the programme.

'Okay.' Laurie looked over his shoulder. 'Yes, we have to go to that one, it's our game. Should we mark the ones you want?'

'No!' Adam looked at her as if she'd suggested defacing the Mona Lisa. 'If you have the collector's copy of the programme, the idea is that you get autographs from people on the pages. See, the paper's different, for signing.'

'Seems I've got a bit to learn. Shall we take one of those free ones for marking where we want to go, then?'

Adam nodded. 'Yes, that's a good idea. We should have one each.'

'Great plan. I definitely think Ross could do with one, he's got no idea what's going on.' She shot Ross a smile, as if expecting him to protest.

'You're right. Not a clue.' But he trusted Laurie. If she thought that this was going to work, he'd give it a shot. If it didn't work then at least it was a nice day out for Adam.

The stack of free programmes was at the end of the counter and Laurie waited a moment to see whether Adam would reach for them, before pushing the wheelchair a little closer. It was a good try, and if Ross knew Laurie she'd have a few more up her sleeve.

He pushed the wheelchair and Laurie walked by the side of it. They visited stands, got autographs and

Adam chatted to people in costumes about strange other worlds. The other visitors to the event were all good-humoured, if sometimes rather garishly dressed, and the enormous hall meant that the crowd wasn't too densely packed.

'This is so great. The one that Mum and I went to in London was really crowded and we could hardly see anything. Here you can get to the stalls and see stuff.'

'You'd see a bit more if you stood up.' Laurie floated the idea.

'No.' Adam shook his head quickly. 'It's fine, I can see. Thanks for bringing me.'

'I'm really enjoying myself. Ooh, look!' Laurie pointed to a large circular stand at the centre of the hall. 'There's our game. We have to go there.'

'Yeah. Look, there's your avatar.' Adam grinned. 'It would be really cool to get her signature, along with one from mine.'

Ross wheeled the chair over to the stand. Six steep steps led up to the central space where there was a landscape of trees with a backdrop showing an ancient castle, with various people in costumes engaged in swordfights. The woman he'd seen in the armour and body paint seemed to be making short work of her rather lumbering opponent.

'Just be a minute.' Laurie left Ross and Adam watching the fights, disappearing around the side of the stand. She reappeared again, smiling.

'What?' Ross murmured to her.

'No ramps. That means that Adam's going to have to walk up the steps. I know he can do it…' She turned the corners of her mouth down. 'Although I'll still be giving the organisers a piece of my mind. They should have made everything wheelchair accessible.'

'Yeah, I'll join you. Although we don't need to go up there, do we?' Adam had already collected the freebies that were available on other stalls from costumed characters who were wandering around the sides of the stall, and tucked them carefully into the backpack he'd brought.

'Photographs. I spotted them taking photographs up there a while ago. I think they're doing it between fights.'

'Has it occurred to you that they'll probably see the wheelchair and come down here? No one's going to let a kid in a wheelchair miss out.'

Laurie frowned. 'I'll think of something.'

When the fights finished, and people started to go up the steps to the podium, she left Adam's side, walking straight up to her avatar and speaking to her. The woman listened and nodded, then turned to Adam and waved. But she didn't come down the steps. Then Laurie re-joined them.

'They can't come down. Something to do with having their photos taken with the proper backdrops. We'll have to go up to them.'

Adam looked at the steps speculatively. If this didn't work, Ross wasn't sure what would.

'I'll help you, Adam. It'll be just like the way you do it in the gym.'

'I don't know…' Adam was looking up at the podium.

Ross felt a tap on his shoulder and turned to see a man dressed as an intergalactic warrior. 'Excuse me? I'll go and get my mates, and if the lad wants to go up there, we'll carry him. Bloody outrageous they don't have a ramp.'

'Thank you.' Ross ushered the man away from Adam so he couldn't hear the conversation. 'Thing is, this is his favourite video game and walking up there himself would mean a lot to him…'

He assured the man that his offer was much appreciated but that they didn't need any help, and agreed that they should complain that there was no ramp for wheelchairs. When he turned back towards the stall, he saw Laurie bending down to release the brakes on the wheelchair. She gave him a smile that clearly concealed disappointment.

'Let's go for some lunch, shall we?'

She was a little subdued as she filled the cafeteria tray with sandwiches and drinks, then led the way out into a large open-air seating area. Laurie found a table and sat down. Adam was leafing through his catalogue, the disappointment over the photos seemingly forgotten.

'Here's the thing, Adam.' Laurie gently caught his attention. 'I know exactly what you can and can't do. I know that you need a wheelchair to come here, because it's too much for you to walk around the exhibition. But I also know that you could make those steps, if you wanted to.'

Adam shrugged. 'It's okay. No big deal.'

'Well, it's a big deal to me, because I want to see you get better. I know that you wanted to go up and have your photo taken.'

Laurie had decided to confront Adam. She'd worked hard to make a relationship with the boy, and he trusted her. If she thought this was the right time, then it was.

'Suppose I fall.'

'You won't. Ross and I won't let you.'

'My foot...it isn't better yet.'

'No, it isn't, that's going to take a while. But you can do this, we've climbed steps in the gym together.'

Adam sat silently, shaking his head.

'I think I know why you won't.' Ross saw a glint of determination in Laurie's eye, which told him she wasn't giving up now.

'No, you really don't.' The boy reached for his drink, opening it and putting one of the straws from the tray into the bottle.

'I know how hard sport can be sometimes. But one thing I've learned is that you can't not try things because you might fail. If you can't run again, that's going to be difficult to deal with. But if you don't do the things you *can* do, it'll be even worse.'

Ross felt a tickle of embarrassment at the back of his neck. Was Laurie talking about him, too? He dismissed the thought. She knew how he felt and she accepted it.

'Let me tell you something. I came close to giving up at one point and ruining all my chances of ever getting back into competition rowing. But there's one thing I know for sure.'

The chatter of the seating area suddenly receded into the background. If Laurie didn't have Adam's attention, she had Ross's. She was using her own hopes and fears to reach the boy, and that took nerve and commitment.

'What?'

Laurie smiled, leaning towards Adam. 'I know that whatever I can and can't do in the future, I'll have tried for my dreams. If I fail, that's just as much a badge of courage as if I succeed.'

Ross swallowed down the lump in his throat. Maybe if someone had said something like that to him during the dark days after Alice had left, he might have felt a little better. Not great, he still would have felt the failure keenly. But somehow justified in having allowed himself to hope.

'I don't know what I'll do if I can't get back to running. I'm not much good at anything else.'

'You'll find something. I know a winner when I see one.' Laurie gave him a smile.

'Okay. We'll give it a go.'

'Great. Then you can sign *my* programme, eh?'

CHAPTER THIRTEEN

LAURIE HAD WHEELED Adam back to the podium, and he'd got unsteadily to his feet. Then something had happened that she clearly hadn't planned for. The woman playing her avatar strode over to the edge of the stage and held her sword aloft in a salute. The other characters had seen what she was doing and followed her lead.

'I've got to do it now.' Adam's brow creased.

'You've already done it, mate.' Ross grinned at him and the boy's back straightened a little.

Slowly, carefully they walked up the steps. Adam was holding onto his arm but he didn't need the support. Just the confidence. And his attention was all on the top of the steps, where the group of costumed performers was waiting for him.

As he reached the top, the woman knelt, holding the hilt of her sword out towards Adam. It was a little over-theatrical, but Adam flushed red with pleasure, looking up at Ross.

'I'd take it if she offered it to me,' Ross murmured to him.

'Wait!' Laurie was ahead of them, her phone in her hand, and when she rapped out the word the performers froze into warlike poses, used to people wanting photographs. It was perfect. Adam smiled, and Laurie took as many photographs as she could.

He took the sword. Leaning on Ross's arm, Adam was led around to the other side of the podium, which was a reconstruction of a scene inside a castle. Ross led him to the elaborate-looking throne and sat him down.

Then more photographs. Laurie was recording this all as the performers gathered around the throne, taking up different poses, all obviously rehearsed. Adam was grinning now.

As each of the performers took their turn to sign Adam's programme, Ross held out his hand to Laurie to take her phone. 'You go. He'll want a few of you both with your avatars.'

Laurie hesitated, and then nodded. 'He's having such a good time. I'm going to cry in a minute if I'm not careful…'

This meant so much to her. And Ross was so proud of her.

'I might join you. If you're not careful.'

She chuckled, wiping her hand vigorously across her face. 'Don't you dare. I'm relying on you to help me keep it all together.'

The performers seemed in no hurry and everyone else was standing back to give Adam more than his allotted time for photographs. And the customary bravado of a sixteen-year-old was looking as if it was going to crack at any moment.

'There are other people…' Adam gave the sword back to the woman warrior. She bent and kissed him on the cheek and Ross saw Adam's ears redden furiously.

'You have all the photos you want?' Her soft, Newcastle accent sounded slightly at odds with her warlike appearance.

'Yes. Thank you.' Adam watched her go, and then turned to Laurie. 'I want to go back now.'

'You're sure? Isn't there a bit more for us to see?'

'I've done everything I wanted to do. More…' Adam looked around the hall from his vantage point, perched on the throne.

'Okay. Just one more photo. Shift up a bit.' Laurie sat down on the wide seat, next to Adam, holding out her phone for a selfie. 'Smile, Adam. This is what winning feels like.'

'Who knew those conventions were so hard on the feet?' Laurie flopped down onto Ross's bed.

'Foot rub?'

'Oh, Ross. You say the nicest things. I don't suppose you could take your clothes off first, could you?'

He chuckled. 'No, I don't suppose I could. One thing at a time.'

'Really? I can do two things at once, I've been devouring you with my lustful gaze all day.'

'Have you?' Ross obviously liked the idea. 'I wish you'd mentioned that. I thought you were a hundred percent focussed on getting Adam out of that wheelchair. You did a fine job of it, by the way.'

Laurie smiled at the memory. 'It was so good of the people on that stand, wasn't it? All the sword-raising and the pictures.'

'It was great. And I was so proud of you. You have a real talent for inspiring these kids, you know.'

'I was thinking, I'd love to be able to do more of that kind of thing. Working at the emergency GP centre in

London is great, and it fits in well with my schedules, but I don't get to follow through on patients the way I have here.'

'Isn't that the problem, though?' Ross sat down on the bed, propping one of her feet up on his leg. 'Can you fit that kind of long-term care around your rowing schedule?'

He started to massage her foot and Laurie sighed. 'That's so nice. You have wonderful fingers, Ross. And, no, I'm not sure that kind of job would be possible during the rowing season. But I won't be competing for ever.'

Maybe she was crazy to think like this. To wonder if there was a place for her here with Ross, doing a job that she loved. To think that he even wanted her to stay, he was so sure that nothing could ever change, and that a new relationship would end as badly as his last.

'You're competing now. You'll have plenty of time when you retire and that might not be for another few years.'

'Yes. I guess so. I should just make the most of it while I can.'

'We both should. Every night and every day.' He laid her foot back down on the bed, shifting forward to kiss her.

If she could just make him believe that she would be happy without a family. But how could she do that when she didn't even know whether it was true? Things had changed so much, in such a short time, and she needed time to catch up. Maybe Ross was right, and letting go was the only way to save them both from pain.

'Every single night? Sure you can keep up the pace?' she teased him.

'Watch me. Sure *you* can?'

'I can only give it my best shot.' She pulled him close, feeling his weight pin her down on the bed. This was the way it was with her and Ross—the power of their lovemaking could chase away everything but the here and now. And he was right here, right now.

Ross watched as Tamara walked across the gravel drive from the entrance to the clinic. Her gait was so much better now that her prosthetic had been refitted, and she was gaining confidence with every day that passed. She was chatting to Laurie, who waved when she saw him sitting by himself on the cast-iron seat that was placed amongst the shrubbery at the front of the building. For all the world as if she wasn't expecting to see him there, and as if her and Tamara's arrival wasn't perfectly timed.

'Nice day.' Laurie grinned at him, plumping herself down on the seat.

'Yeah. I think it's going to be hotter today than yesterday.'

'I'd say you're right.'

That was probably enough said about the weather. Tamara had lowered herself down between them, and she might begin to suspect that something was up if they went into any more detail. Laurie had planned this so carefully for Tamara, and Ross was looking forward to it as much as she was.

The sound of an engine caught Tamara's attention. Well timed. Ross looked towards the entrance to the clinic's grounds and saw a minibus making its way towards them. In contrast to the vehicle's rather battered appearance, the trailer behind it carried three gleaming hulls.

Laurie was watching Tamara's face, as the minibus drew to a halt in front of them. A man got out, stretching his legs, and two women followed. The side doors of the bus opened, and three more men jumped down onto the gravel.

'They must be lost,' Tamara remarked, and Laurie shrugged. One of the men had detached himself from the group and was jogging towards them.

But Tamara couldn't take her eyes off the boats. It was obvious they were a very different kind of craft from the clinic's, and that their light frames and graceful curves were state-of-the-art water-going technology.

'Hi.' The man stopped in front of them. 'I'm looking for Tamara.'

Now *he* had all of Tamara's attention, and she was staring at him open-mouthed. Laurie nudged her, and she let out a breath.

'I'm Tamara.'

'Hey, there. My name's Grant Levelle. We heard you might be interested in coming rowing with us.'

'Yes! Please…' Tamara was on her feet before Ross could hold out his hand to help her.

'Great. Would you like to come and meet the others?' Grant was grinning from ear to ear. Tamara nodded, and he gave Laurie a nod before starting to amble with her at a slow pace towards the minibus.

'When's he going to tell her?' Ross was watching as the group crowded around Tamara, each one shaking her hand as they were introduced.

'Probably…right about now…' She smiled as Grant

bent down, pulling up the leg of his tracksuit trousers to reveal his own prosthetic.

Tamara was staring up at him, her eyes shining. Grant took her arm, guiding her out of the way as the rest of the group started to loosen the straps that fixed one of the boats securely to the trailer. He was obviously explaining everything that was happening, and Tamara was hanging on every word.

Laurie turned to him. 'Did you see her face?'

'Yeah. I think you've just made that young lady's day. Probably her whole year.' It was so nice to see Laurie's obvious glee. 'Why don't you go over?'

'I don't want to crowd her. This is her treat.' Laurie was watching the team just as intently as Tamara was as they unfastened the boats from the trailer. This was her life. Her teammates. She'd left them behind to come here, and Ross could see in her eyes how much she'd missed them.

He got to his feet. 'I should welcome them. And let them know where the sandwiches and drinks are.'

'Ah, yes. They'll definitely want to know about sandwiches.' Laurie jumped to her feet, leading him over to the group.

He welcomed each one of them, thanking them for coming and shaking their hands. Laurie hugged both of the women, exchanging jokes with the men and laughing at their suggestions that she'd been taking it easy for the last few weeks and they'd be seeing later how out of shape she was.

The feeling tugged at him like a long-lost memory. The one kid at school who wasn't part of a group because he lived too far from everyone else. He wasn't a part of this either.

Ross stuffed his hands into his pockets, making an excuse about having to go and see how things were going in the kitchen, and walked away. Laurie and Grant would look after Tamara, and he had other things to do.

Sam was standing inside the main doors of the clinic with a group of patients and staff, all watching what was going on. When she saw him, she fell into step beside him.

'She's in her element, isn't she?'

'Yes. Did you see Tamara's face when Grant showed her his prosthetic?' Ross would treasure that look. The moment that a teenager's future seemed to open up before her eyes.

'Yes, I did. Makes it all worthwhile…' Sam looked up at him thoughtfully. 'Actually, I was referring to Laurie.'

Something cold wound its way around Ross's heart. Sam was right, Laurie's face had lit up in just the same way as Tamara's had when she greeted her teammates. It was a stark reminder that her life wasn't here, with him.

'Yeah. It's a good day for Laurie as well.'

It was good to see everyone again, and to be around the everyday activity of people who took rowing seriously, the unloading of the boats from the trailer and setting them into the water. It was a temptation too. On a nice day like this, she wanted to stretch her shoulders and feel the pull of the oars. But Laurie contented herself with helping Grant make the adjustments needed to one of the sliding seats in the three-person scull, so that Tamara could give it a try.

'Who is that guy, and what's he done with Laurie Sullivan?' Grant joined her on the grass, watching as Ross double-checked Tamara's seat, talking to her and making sure that her position wouldn't put her leg under any strain that she wasn't ready for yet.

'He hasn't done anything with me.' Well…that wasn't entirely true. She and Ross had done a great deal with each other, but that wasn't what Grant meant.

'Someone has. The physio?' Grant nodded towards Sam, who was spending her lunch break making sure that anyone who wanted to come out on the grass and watch could do so.

'No. I made my own rule and I'm sticking to it. No rowing for another couple of weeks.'

'We can't tempt you?' Grant grinned.

'No, you can't. Don't even try. I need to get this hip properly sorted. Then I'll be back.'

'Fair enough.' Grant leaned back on his elbows. 'So you've taken to talent scouting in the meantime?'

Laurie rolled her eyes. 'No. Tamara's not committed to rowing, it's fun for her and something that she can do at the moment. I know that you know the value of that.'

Grant had made the same journey as Tamara was making, and he'd made his choice of sport. Laurie knew he was committed to helping others do the same if he could, and that was why she'd called him. The team was on its way down from Scotland and Grant had persuaded a few of them to stop off for the day with some of the practice boats.

'I know the value of it. I just never thought I'd hear *you* say it.' Grant's voice became a pitch higher in a bad impression of Laurie's. *'"Rowing's a bit of fun. I'm not going on the water until I'm fully fit."'*

'Well, that's a different side of me you haven't seen before, isn't it? I'm a doctor too...'

Grant nodded, appearing convinced. Laurie wasn't sure she shared the sentiment. She did feel different. She still wanted the water, the way she always had, but there were other things as well. Things that crowded into the box that she usually kept for rowing.

Maybe she was losing her edge. Maybe her father had been right, and too many other things in her life would blunt her resolve and damage her concentration. Even now, she was watching Ross, and not the boats that bobbed on the water.

'You've taken time out before.'

Grant nodded. 'You know I have.'

'Was it difficult? Getting back?' Laurie had convinced herself that this was just a delicious holiday. One full of sunshine, and this peaceful, optimistic place that Ross had built. And Ross himself, of course. She'd adroitly sidestepped the issue of getting back into competitive rowing again, because if she ever dreamed she'd lose that, she couldn't enjoy this.

'Nah. I came back better. Stronger, because I knew exactly what I wanted.'

'I think I will too.'

She obviously hadn't said that with enough conviction, because Grant raised an eyebrow. 'You're sure about that? Your hip *is* improving, isn't it? Not thinking of retiring?'

Laurie chuckled. 'Not while you're still out there for me to beat.'

'In your dreams.'

Ross had finished talking to Tamara and was strolling towards them. He sat down on the grass next to Laurie.

'Nice place you have here.' Grant smiled across at him. 'Good stretch of water.'

'You're always welcome to stop by if you're in the area. If you give me a call we'll find somewhere for you to sleep if you want to stay overnight.' Ross glanced at Laurie. Maybe that was an invitation particularly aimed at her.

'Thanks.' Grant answered before she could. 'Is Tamara ready?'

Ross nodded. 'Ready enough to explode if she doesn't get to go out soon.'

'Great.' Grant got to his feet, rubbing his hands together. 'Let's get her started, then.'

They watched as Tamara walked a few unsteady steps across the grass to meet Grant. He took her hand, tucking it into the crook of his arm and instead of glowering as she usually did when she needed help, Tamara grinned up at him, talking excitedly.

'Grant's made a friend for life.' Ross stated the obvious.

'Yeah. Grant's very committed to helping youngsters and he's so good with them.'

'It's just what she needed. Someone who can show her that she can do anything she wants. We can tell her that…' He turned to her suddenly. 'You were the one who helped her to really see it, though.'

'Just doing my job.'

'No, you weren't. You were doing far more than your job, Laurie.'

'I've been thinking about what we were talking

about the other night. You know, keeping on doing this kind of work.'

'Yeah?' Ross flopped down onto his back, staring up at the sky. 'Come to any conclusions?'

'Yes, I have. You're right, I can't be a proper mentor just yet, but I can start setting up a framework. Something that I can develop, with the aim of spending all my time on it later.'

'That would work. Something like a small charity, with lots of room to grow.'

'Yes, exactly. It would be a network, for teenagers. Maybe start with a website where they can find information about good trainers and good medical care. What they want would be the most important thing, not what other people want for them. We'd be entirely without any expectations of what the right answer for them might be.'

Ross turned to look at her. 'And you could ultimately provide a transition out of sport and into something else if that's what they really want to do with their lives? Or transitions into sport if that's what they wanted.'

'Yes, exactly. They come first, and we'd be advocates for them.'

'It's got a lot of potential.'

'I'd start small, getting contacts and setting things up. And when I do retire from rowing, I can devote more of my time to it on a regular basis.'

'You should talk to Sam about this. She'd be really interested in the idea, but she'd be the first to say that she doesn't have your killer instinct.'

'What?' Laurie aimed a play punch at his arm. 'You think I've got a killer instinct!'

'You know what I mean. You've got the audacity

to go out and push people out of their comfort zone to make something work. Sam's got a lighter touch, she's no less committed but she'll kill you with kindness rather than running at you with a battering ram. It takes all sorts, and together you might be unstoppable.'

This was what Ross did so well. Putting people together. Seeing how different approaches might work in harmony instead of tugging against each other.

'Could I count on your support?' She hardly dared ask him. It would be a way of keeping one thread of contact with Ross.

'Always. If the clinic can help you in any way, you only have to call.'

That wasn't what she meant. The clinic could certainly help her, but it was Ross himself that she really wanted. Laurie hardly dared ask.

'What about you, Ross? Will you help me?'

He pressed his lips together, and Laurie shivered in the afternoon sunshine.

'I can't. You know the reasons why, and that it's not that I don't want to. If you do this it has to be something for yourself and the kids you want to help.'

'I'm planning on setting up a charity, not a dating agency. You want to help these kids too, I know you do.'

The reply was only half a joke. If Ross thought that this was her way of keeping in contact with him... It wasn't, it was something that she wanted to do. But if one of the by-products was that she *did* keep Ross on her mailing list, and maybe in her life as well, it was an idea that suddenly appealed to Laurie a great deal.

He nodded, and for a brief moment she let herself bask in the idea that her future might contain Ross.

'I do. But I'm sorry, Laurie, we can't do it together.'

CHAPTER FOURTEEN

Ross stood in the doorway of the gym, watching as Sam and Laurie led the mother and toddler exercise class. Sam had brought Timothy in to help and being a little older than most of the other children in the class he was taking his responsibilities seriously, standing next to his mother and reproducing the exercises she was teaching. Clearly they'd been practising together.

Laurie was having fun, too. She moved amongst the group, helping those who needed help and quietly correcting the posture of anyone not keeping their back straight. A little girl started to fret, and Laurie spoke to her mother and then picked her up.

A month ago, Ross wouldn't have believed what he was seeing. Laurie, smiling at the child on her hip, entertaining her so that her mother could exercise in peace. She was good with her too, bringing a smile to the little girl's face with almost no effort at all.

'This one works better with two…' Sam raised her voice in a broad hint, but Laurie seemed intent on sorting through the toybox with her new friend. 'Laurie!'

'Oh. Sorry…' Laurie brought the little girl back to the group, pulling a dismayed face. Her mother took her, telling her daughter that she could go back and play with Laurie as soon as they'd accomplished this exercise together.

Ross turned away.

He'd been thinking a lot about what she'd said the other day. It had sounded like an invitation, a way that they could keep in touch and explore the idea of continuing their relationship. Maybe even take it further… Every time he thought about the prospect, he felt intense happiness, coupled with physical yearning that almost stopped him in his tracks.

But watching her now… Laurie was growing and reaching out. Who knew what the future would bring for her, or whether she'd be changing her mind about not wanting a family of her own?

He could stop wondering now. Trying to think of ways that he might share his life with her. Because the one thing he *didn't* want to share with Laurie was the grief and heartache of wanting their own child and not being able to conceive. She deserved better than that.

By the time he heard a sound at the balcony doors, Ross had resigned himself to keeping their arrangement exactly as it was. There were only a few days to go before she was due to leave, and although they hadn't discussed a date, Laurie had been reducing her work at the clinic. Taking her into his arms made that prospect a great deal easier to bear because it was then that Ross lost sight of everything other than the kiss that would so surely follow.

'I've been thinking.' She kissed him with the kind of passion that told Ross that whatever she *had* been thinking he was going to like it.

'Uh-huh? You should do more of it.' He nodded towards the bed. Dinner could wait.

'Not that.' She nudged his ribs with her elbow. 'Or I should probably say not *just* that.'

Ross chuckled, stepping back and holding up his arms in a gesture of surrender. 'Okay. So you've been thinking about sex and something else. I'll leave you to lead with whichever you reckon ought to go first.'

She walked into the kitchen, peering into the oven to see what was cooking and nodding her head in approval. Then she sat down at the kitchen table while Ross poured them each a glass of wine.

'I thought I'd just say it….' She grinned a little nervously and took a sip of her wine.

'That's always a plan.' Ross sat down opposite her, leaning across the table to take her hands between his. Whatever it was seemed to be bugging her, and a faint pulse of concern started to beat at his consciousness.

Laurie took a breath, which made the pulse beat louder. Then flashed him a smile that drove it away for a moment.

'I know you have concerns about continuing our relationship, Ross. But I want you to know that if you're up for giving it a try, that's what I'd really like to do.'

Warmth and pleasure drained from the moment as a challenging abyss opened up beneath him. Only Laurie could tip his world so completely. Ross's shock must have shown on his face because she was staring at him now.

'Say something. Please…'

He squeezed her fingers in what he hoped was a reassuring gesture. 'There's nothing I'd like more, sweetheart. But I don't think we can do that.'

Maybe she'd leave it there, and not make him go into details. And maybe not. Ross reminded himself that one of the things he adored about Laurie was her ability to say exactly what was on her mind.

'Why? Is this your way of telling me that you don't want me?'

Ross closed his eyes, rubbing his hands across his face. 'I don't think there'll ever be a time when I don't want you, Laurie. What I'm saying is that you and I can never have a family, and I won't ask you to give that possibility up for me.'

She reddened a little, her jaw setting in an adorably stubborn tilt. 'What if I don't care about that? What if I…' She hesitated briefly, before continuing in almost a whisper, 'What if I love you?'

Ross knew he loved her, too. It was the only thing that explained the deep sadness spreading through him at the thought of not spending his life with her. But he also knew it didn't matter. He could give Laurie his love, but she deserved so much more. Saying it would only draw out this agony.

'Do you even know what you'll be doing this time next year? What you'll care about? Because if we stay together, I'm not sure that I can let you go.'

Laurie sprang to her feet, pacing the kitchen. He loved her restless energy too…

'Then don't, Ross. Don't let me go.'

'Are you telling me that you can be happy with no prospect of ever having children?'

She stilled suddenly, pressing her lips together and staring at him. Ross could feel his heart hardening. It was the only way that he could bring himself to push Laurie away.

'Can't you just trust me, Ross? Can't you believe that I can accept that?'

'I trust you. Life's the thing I really don't trust…'

'Oh!' She flung her hands in the air in an expression of frustration. 'We're in control of our own lives, aren't we? Whatever happened to not giving up?'

'And whatever happened to facing facts?' Ross could feel his brow tightening into a frown. 'Or to making the best of what you have, for that matter?'

'Fine.' Anger flared in her beautiful eyes. 'You make the best of what you have, then. Don't give a second thought to anything else because it's just too much trouble to try for it.'

That stung. All the feelings about his marriage came flooding back. Alice's reproachful looks when she'd found that he'd failed her again that month.

'Grow up, Laurie. You might feel that you can push yourself and achieve all you want out of life, and maybe you're right. But none of that gives you the right to expect me to achieve the impossible.'

Her eyes widened in outrage. 'That's not what I'm saying, Ross. I'm telling you that we take what we have now and make something good from it.'

'And I'm telling you that we can't.'

Her lip began to quiver. If she cried, Ross wasn't sure that he'd be able to let her go, but Laurie pulled herself together suddenly, straightening her back and shooting him that blank look that denied him any access to her feelings.

'We're done, then.' She murmured the words, turning and walking out of the kitchen. Ross jumped as the front door of the apartment banged closed behind her.

* * *

It should have been an easy equation. Two suitcases in, two suitcases out. It was the way Laurie always travelled, never bringing home any more than she'd taken with her. The equation wasn't working this time.

There were her clothes. They weren't too much of a problem, although there were two T-shirts with the clinic logo on them and the fruits of a shopping trip with Ross, a pair of sandals that she'd bought to replace those she'd waterlogged, and a skirt she'd liked that he'd encouraged her to buy. They'd fit easily. The cork from the bottle of champagne that had been so much fun to drink, and which Ross had cut and inserted a coin into for luck, didn't take up much space either. Maybe she should just throw that away as it stirred up too many memories, but she couldn't bear to. She had so little of him to keep already.

There were so many other things, though. The comic strip that Adam had drawn for her. The two yellow feathers that had fluttered out of her T-shirt when she'd pulled it over her head on the evening of the school sports day, pressed carefully inside the programme like flowers between the leaves of a book. The rowing cap that Tamara had given her, which Laurie had promised to wear at her next competition, and the folder full of useful reading matter that Sam had presented her with when Laurie had suggested they collaborate on ideas for a new charity. Drawings from the kids at the mother and toddler class.

Then there were the books that Ross had taken from his shelves for her to read. They were a little easier. She'd only read a few of them, but she would leave them all behind, because there would be no opportunity to return them later.

'You know it's over when she starts to separate her books and music from yours...'

Grant had said that when one of the stream of girlfriends he'd had before he was married had left. The thought hit home now with a new appreciation of how incredibly sad the process of leaving someone was. She'd never let a relationship get far enough before now to exchange anything that needed to be returned.

She carried the books through to the sitting room, feeling tears prick at the sides of her eyes. Laurie wiped them away. This was a new kind of pain and it was hard to pretend she didn't feel it.

This was by no means the first time they'd argued, two strong characters who enjoyed the clash of wills and liked the ultimate reconciliation even better. But this time it was different. Ross was right, and at the same time a little bit wrong. He'd said he couldn't give her what she needed, but in truth it was Laurie who couldn't give him what he needed. She couldn't make him believe that stepping out into uncharted waters with her wasn't going to lead to disaster. Her love wasn't enough for that.

Now she could cry if the wanted to, and maybe it would ease the suffocating pressure in her chest. But clearly she didn't deserve the relief of tears, and they wouldn't come. She'd just helped destroy the best thing that had ever happened to her and there was no going back. Leaving might be the right thing to do, but it felt that this loss would overshadow everything from now on.

* * *

Ross had waited for the timer on the oven to ping, and tipped this evening's dinner straight into a freezer dish, abandoning it to cool. Slinging himself into an armchair, he glared at the wall.

Why hadn't he fallen on his knees and begged Laurie to stay?

Because it would have been wrong, that was why. There was no more talking to be done, no more making love and no goodbyes. This was the end, and going back now would only postpone the inevitable and make it worse. If the rest of his life was going to be lived without Laurie, he should accept it and get on with it.

But despite himself, Ross sat up late, brooding in the darkness and waking early the next morning to find his neck stiff and his leg numb from falling asleep on the sofa.

The sound of a car outside on the gravel drive took him over to the front window. Laurie had been waiting for the taxi, and the driver helped her load her suitcases into the boot.

Ross closed his eyes. This was the right thing to do, but he wouldn't watch her go. All the same, his lips formed the words.

Goodbye, my love. Be happy.

'Ross!'

There was only one person who could lend that note of exasperation to Sam's voice. An instinctive smile jumped to Ross's lips and then he remembered, yet again, that Laurie had gone. It had been almost a month now, and that hollow feeling of loss never seemed to get any better.

He took a breath, waving Sam to a seat and leaning back in his own office chair. Sam and Laurie had been working together on the new initiative for teenagers, and he'd helped Sam as much as he could. It hurt when Sam talked about Laurie but this was his only remaining thread of contact and he held onto it greedily.

'What's on your mind, Sam?'

'I so love that woman…'

Yeah. He could relate to that.

'…and she's driving me crazy.'

The chance would be a fine thing. Laurie could drive him crazy any time she liked, but Ross knew that she wouldn't be back.

'What's up?' He tried to focus on Sam.

'You know the swimmer, Phil Jacques? Of course you do, everyone does. Laurie's only gone and roped him in for a round-table discussion about sports training for teenagers.'

'That's good, isn't it? It's exactly what you need—a few household names on board.'

'It's fabulous. But you know when it is?'

'I reckon you're about to tell me.'

'Two weeks' time. At the conference in Birmingham that we were thinking of going to.'

'Okay…' Ross had been planning to spend a couple of days in Birmingham in two weeks to take in the conference and visit some prospective patients there. He wasn't quite sure how he felt about sharing a city with Laurie, but his heart knew how to react. It started to pump wildly.

'They're going to do it in front of an audience and

it'll be recorded for radio. Laurie's asked some other guests and she's going to use this as an opportunity to announce the new initiative. She's done all this in less than a month.'

That's my girl.

'You know there's no stopping her when she decides to do something. So…what's the problem? Aren't you pleased?'

'I'm delighted. Only…she wants me to chair the discussion.' Sam shot him an agonised look.

Sam was the best physiotherapist he knew, and she was great with her patients. She had more than enough knowledge to chair any discussion about the project that she and Laurie had been working on, and Ross guessed that this was Laurie's way of giving Sam the credit she deserved for all the hard work she'd done. The only trouble was that Laurie had underestimated how shy Sam was when it came to public speaking.

'I suppose…you couldn't focus on the fact that you deserve this, could you? Or that you're just the right person to do it, and you'd be great?'

'No. Ross, I really couldn't. In front of an auditorium full of people? Recorded for the radio?' Sam pressed her lips together, obviously trying not to think about it. 'You couldn't do it, could you?'

'You mean go along there and take all the credit for your work? I'm not entirely comfortable with that, no.' Ross wasn't comfortable with gatecrashing Laurie's discussion either. He wasn't sure which would be worse, finding himself in an argument with her or being on the receiving end of her blank, professional stare.

'But you've really helped us. You gave me that long

list of contacts and wrote introduction letters to all of them. You deserve a bit of credit for that.'

'I'm just helping out. You and Laurie are the ones steering this.'

'But Laurie can't do it. This whole thing is a fantastic opportunity for her to be able to speak about her own experience of the pressures that can face teenagers in sport, and she can't do that and chair the discussion at the same time. Please, Ross…'

He had to suggest something. 'All right. Let's break it down, Sam. What in particular are you most concerned about?'

Sam took a moment to think. 'Well, for starters, there's what to wear. Then what to say. When to say it, whether to ask questions or not, or whether I should just introduce people and let them get on with it…' She took a breath, and Ross used the opportunity to jump in.

'That'll do for starters. Can Jamie help with the what-to-wear-part? Go through your wardrobe with you?'

'Jamie? You're joking, of course. He says that I always look nice, so anything would do.'

'I'd be inclined to agree with him. That's no help, is it?'

'No, Ross. It's really no help at all.'

'All right. Well, moving on, have you asked Laurie what she wants you to say?'

'She said to steer the discussion. Get the best out of everyone.'

Ross was on firmer ground here. He knew exactly what Laurie meant. 'All right, so that's asking questions. We'll get a list of the guests and work out some questions for each of them, shall we?'

He was pretty sure that Sam knew which points needed to be emphasised, it was just a matter of sitting her down, somehow stopping her from panicking and getting the information out of her. If he and Jamie joined forces, that would be a piece of cake.

'Oh, would you? But when do I ask them?'

'We'll practise. We can get a few people from the clinic together, and we'll have some discussions. How about that?'

Sam nodded. 'Yes, that would be good too. But what on earth am I going to wear?'

Ross suspected that was Sam's biggest problem. If she could go in knowing that she looked like a million dollars, she'd be much more confident. Even if it *was* radio.

'I think I've got an idea. Remember Anita Lower?' Sam looked at him blankly. 'Compression of the third and fourth thoracic vertebrae.'

'Oh, yes I remember now. Nice lady. In such terrible pain. She's a friend of yours, isn't she?'

'Yes, and she always asks after you whenever I see her. She really appreciated all that you did for her. We're overdue a lunch together, and I want you to come along too. As you know, Anita works as an image consultant for a number of the big TV companies.'

Sam stared at him. 'Would she…? That's far too much to ask, Ross.'

'No, it's not. Anita's told me more than once that you turned her life around, and I know she'd be delighted to see you again. We'll go shopping and…' Ross waved his hand in the air to indicate that whatever it was that Anita did, she'd do it for Sam.

'Shopping!' Sam was all smiles now. 'Do you think I can do this?'

'My honest opinion… Yes, I think you'll ace it.'

'And Laurie's going to be there, of course.' A shadow fell over Sam's face suddenly. 'You'll come, won't you?'

He wanted to go, so badly. Just to see Laurie again, even if it was at a distance in the crowded auditorium of the hotel conference centre. To see her life moving forward, because that was the only thing he had to hold onto. That Laurie should be happy, because he couldn't imagine himself being truly happy again.

'I'll have to see.'

'See what? The same thing that Laurie was going to have to see when I suggested she invite you along? I know you two were close, Ross…' Sam turned the corners of her mouth down. 'You argued, didn't you?'

There was no point in denying it. Sam wasn't blind, and she was a good friend. She'd navigated a difficult situation with her customary ease, allowing Ross to support the initiative in many small ways, without ever asking why he did it through her and not by contacting Laurie himself.

'It's complicated, Sam.'

'I dare say it is. You know what's really ironic?'

A feeling of irony wasn't one of the emotions he'd experienced yet. He may as well, the others were a lot more draining.

'What's that?'

'I've known you a long time, but this is the first time that you've ever thought that *complicated* was a reason not to do something. Laurie's just the same. The more complicated and challenging something is, the better she likes it.'

He shouldn't ask. It wasn't fair to Sam, but he couldn't help it.

'How is she?'

Sam considered the question for a moment. 'I know you need to know, so I'll tell you. Just this once because I'm not going to be a go-between.' She paused, looking for Ross's assent, and he nodded.

'She's well. Her hip is in really good shape and she's getting back to full fitness now. She's working every waking hour, just as you are…' Sam shot him a knowing look. 'I see the same thing in both of you. Whatever happened between you broke both your hearts.'

Ross nodded. Sam was looking at him expectantly. Taking a deep breath, he said, 'She told me she loved me, that she wanted us to try to build a relationship together.'

Sam smiled sadly. 'And you said no.' It wasn't a question. He nodded again. 'Why?'

'Because I can't do it again, I can't be responsible for ruining someone else's dreams.'

'You weren't responsible for ruining Alice's dreams, Ross. She was wrong to put that on you. But you're wrong to push Laurie away. Clearly she knows about your fertility issue and yet she still wanted to be with you. You're denying yourself a chance at happiness—don't! Opportunities like this don't come along every day, when it's there in front of you, telling you you're loved and wanted? That's when you grab it with both hands. Now, the question is, what are you going to do about it?'

Ross stared dumbly at Sam, who was a little pink-cheeked now. Clearly this had been on her mind for a while, and now she'd put it into words Sam rose from her seat and walked out of his office.

He stood, looking out at the lake. It was the same view that usually helped him think through any difficulty that arose, but right now it wasn't helping.

He'd accepted what life had offered him and made the best he could of it. Now he had to go out on a limb to get what he really wanted.

CHAPTER FIFTEEN

LAURIE LOOKED WONDERFUL. She was wearing a cream, silky blouse with dark trousers, and the flaming red of her hair lifted the outfit from sensible to incredibly sexy.

She was nervous, though, Ross could see that. Even from this distance, right at the back of the auditorium, it was obvious that she was reading a prepared statement about the new initiative and she stumbled a couple of times. But Sam was magnificent. She gave Laurie an excited smile and asked the question that Ross had primed her with, the one he knew that Laurie would want to answer. Then Laurie started to loosen up a bit.

He mentally ticked off the points she made in his head. When she missed one, Sam came to the rescue and asked an appropriate question. All the work that he and Anita had done with Sam had been worth it.

The presentation finished to loud applause, and people began to crowd around Laurie. He should go. But Ross didn't move from his seat, wanting to see her at the centre of everyone's attention for just a little while longer.

He saw Sam scanning the audience as the lights in the auditorium went up. The look on her face and the impatient movement of her hand signified that he should be down on the stage, congratulating Laurie. Ross shook his head. Now wasn't the time.

But Laurie had turned, looking at Sam and then following her gaze. Her head tipped up towards him and for a moment they were the only two people in the crowded space. Then that cool, emotionless look that told Ross that Laurie was struggling with her emotions as much as he was.

He really did have to go now. He should leave her there, in the limelight, to do what she'd come here to do. Ross dragged his gaze away from the stage, looking for the nearest exit.

Ross was here. Laurie felt sick with excitement and then horrified that he'd got up from his seat and left the auditorium as soon as she'd seen him. It wasn't like him to turn away from a confrontation, however awkward, and Laurie tried not to go through all the reasons why he might have done and concentrate on the conversations she was having with the people around her.

It all took a while. There were questions, expressions of support, and a few pleas for help. The contact sheets they'd drawn up were filling fast, and that was exactly what she and Sam had hoped for. There was no way Laurie could have followed Ross, and even if she had, she didn't know what to say to him. Tell him about the pain of being apart from him? That she loved him? Or just lie to him and tell him that she'd succeeded without him and that she didn't need him?

Finally, it was just her and Sam, standing on the stage together, watching the outside broadcast team pack up their equipment. Laurie hugged Sam, and they walked back to the reception area of the hotel that was hosting the conference, where Jamie was waiting with Timothy. Laurie made a smiling excuse when Jamie asked her to join them for a spot of lunch and retreated to the lift, breathing a sigh of relief as the doors closed, leaving her alone.

She needed time to think. Ross was here and that *had* to mean something. Her hotel room on the fourteenth floor had the dual advantage of being somewhere to consider her next move and also somewhere that he could find her if he wanted to…

Laurie kicked off her shoes, deciding that she wouldn't explore the possibility that Ross would ask in Reception for her room number. He'd left the auditorium when she'd seen him, and he clearly wasn't in any hurry to see her. She dialled room service and ordered coffee.

'That was quick…' The knock had sounded after only a couple of minutes and Laurie had pulled the door open, expecting to see the room-service waiter outside.

Ross. Looking just as deliciously handsome as ever. More so. Laurie wasn't a connoisseur of men in suits, but he wore his very well. Darkly immaculate and thrillingly dangerous sprang to mind.

'You're waiting for someone?' The gesture of his hand indicated that he could go away and come back later.

'No! Well, yes, but it's only room service.' If she had to grab him and strong-arm him into the room, she was prepared to do it.

But that wasn't necessary. His gaze met hers, and that gorgeous synchronicity of movement that they'd always shared kicked in. She stepped back from the door at the same moment that Ross stepped forward. Nothing else mattered now, just that they were both breathing the same air.

'The presentation was great. Inspiring. You've worked hard.'

Was that what he'd come to say? Laurie swallowed down her disappointment. 'Thanks. Sam saved my life a couple of times. How long have you been here?'

'I arrived late last night.'

'And when were you thinking of leaving?'

'Not until I'd spoken to you.'

The whole world seemed suddenly bathed in light. And then she was in his arms. How that had happened wasn't entirely clear to Laurie, but she didn't care. She heard the door slam as Ross kicked it closed behind him, and snuggled into his embrace, breathing in his scent.

'Laurie… I've missed you so much.'

'Not as much as I missed you…'

'You want to make a competition out of it?' He smiled down at her and all the things that she wanted to say to him were lost in the gentle, flickering fire of his eyes.

'Yes. Let's do that.'

He kissed her, with all the passion and longing that she felt. Brilliant happiness robbed Laurie of anything other than the thought that he was here and holding her in his arms. And when she kissed him back she felt the sweet response of his body against hers.

Now all she could think of was the bed, and the few yards between them and it. Maybe they wouldn't even make it. Passion was clawing at her and Ross's kisses were driving everything else from her head. If she had only these moments with him, she would take them and deal with the consequences later.

She slipped his jacket from his shoulders, and Ross shrugged it off. Slowly, deliberately, she loosened his tie. Making him wait while the passion built between them, even more heady than it had ever been. He pulled her back against him, kissing her with a hunger that made her head spin.

Another knock on the door, and a voice announcing that this time it really *was* room service, made them spring apart guiltily. Laurie opened the door, feeling in her pocket for a tip, and then grabbed the tray, dumping it onto the credenza before she turned back to face Ross.

Gone. The moment was gone. She could see it in his face.

'Second thoughts?'

He pressed his lips together. 'It's not what I came for, Laurie. I came to talk.'

'Okay. I'll ask them to bring another cup…' She made for the door, wondering if the waiter had disappeared into the lift yet, but Ross caught her arm.

'I don't need coffee. What I *do* need is to tell you that I love you. If you can forgive me, and love me too, then we need to sit down and work out what we're going to do about that.'

There was only one cup. That didn't matter, she was just concentrating on irrelevant details because she couldn't get her head around the enormity of what Ross had just said. Laurie resisted the temptation to throw herself into his arms because he was right. They needed to talk about this. She poured the coffee with a shaking hand, taking a sip and then handing the cup to him.

'I love you, too. I'm sorry I left without saying goodbye.'

'Don't be. I drove you away, and…it was wrong of me. I couldn't see a way for us to be together and I thought it was for the best. I'm sorry.' Ross took a sip of coffee and handed the cup back to her, sitting down on the bed.

'Now we've got that over with…' Laurie sat down next to him, her heart thumping wildly. 'What are we going to do now?'

Everything depended on his answer. Laurie had thought about it and hadn't been able to find a plan that might work. She had to trust that Ross would be able to provide the answers that she couldn't, and suddenly that didn't seem so impossible.

'I know that I'm not a good prospect for anyone…' He stumbled over the words, and Laurie laid her hand on his.

'You just happen to be the one that I want. I've no desire to change that, even if I could.'

'I can't change it either. You're the only woman I'll ever want, and I love you with all my heart. The thought that you could love me too is what's given me the courage to come here and ask what I shouldn't of you…'

'Ask, Ross. I want to hear it.'

He nodded, taking the cup from her hands and laying it aside. Then he fell to one knee in front of her.

'Laurie, I want to take your hopes and dreams and make them happen for you. Everything you ever wanted, or will want, because they're more important than anything to me. Will you take mine, and hold them in trust for me?'

She saw it. Ross's way forward, a clear road that led to their future together. He might not be able to trust in life, but he knew that he could trust her.

'Give me your dreams. I'll take care of them and I won't let them hurt or disappoint you again. I'll give you mine, because I know that they're safe in your hands.'

'You're sure?' He blinked, as if he couldn't quite believe what he was hearing.

'Yes, I'm sure! Listen to what I'm saying to you for once, will you?'

Ross grinned. 'Okay. I'm listening. If I promise to always listen, always love you and try my best to make you happy, will you marry me?'

Tears filled her eyes and Laurie made no effort to brush them away. She didn't need to any more. Leaning forward, she flung her arms around his neck.

'Yes, Ross. I'll marry you.'

She felt his chest heave with emotion. Gently he disentangled himself from her arms. 'Close your eyes. I'm not letting you get away this time…'

She squeezed her eyes shut. There was a moment's pause and then Laurie felt him slip a ring on her finger. Then his lips were on hers as he kissed her. She kissed him back, holding onto him tightly.

'You can look at it now…' His lips brushed hers as he murmured the words.

'Is it nice?' She clasped her fingers together behind his neck. 'Feels heavy…'

Ross chuckled. 'I spent a while choosing it. Nothing was going to really be good enough for you, but I got the best I could find.'

'Then I love it. I'll look at it in a minute. Right now, I can't take my eyes off you, because it's been far too long since I've seen you.'

'Yeah. You're stuck with me now, that's not going to happen again.'

The world had shifted, and it was a different place now. Laurie stared at him, tears running down her cheeks, and Ross gently brushed them away, before folding her in his arms.

'Do you feel different?'

'Yeah, I feel different.' Ross chuckled quietly. 'It's everything, Laurie. Your love and mine, your dreams and mine. Nothing's going to stop us now.'

EPILOGUE

Four years later

THIS YEAR THEY'D picked Munich. The same hotel suite that Ross had booked for the World Championships three years ago. With the same hot tub to luxuriate in together, and the same stunning view over the city.

'How have I been doing as caretaker?' Ross handed Laurie a glass of champagne. It was the same question he asked every year, on the anniversary of the day they'd given their dreams to each other for safekeeping.

'Beautifully.' Laurie smiled up at him. 'Each year I wonder how you're going to surpass the last, but you always manage it.'

'More stamina than you expected?'

'A lot more.' She leaned into his arms, stretching to kiss him. 'I never thought anyone could love me so well. Or be such a great rowing coach.'

'I just cheered you on. Win or lose.'

'That's what made all the difference. And you made a very good job of cheering the last time we were here.' Ross had been hoarse for a week afterwards.

'It was worth it. I'll never forget the look on your face when you stepped up onto the podium and received your gold medal.' He bent to kiss her. 'Or the one when you made my dream come true and married me.'

'Hey! Are you pinching my dreams, Ross? A girl's wedding day is supposed to be *her* dream.'

Ross chuckled. 'Too bad. It was my dream as well. You can share, can't you?'

'With you? Everything.'

That was the way things were now. The new extension to the clinic, which was going to be a training centre for young athletes and house the charity that Sam and Laurie managed together, had been Laurie's idea, but Ross had put his heart into it as well. He'd taken care of her dreams and adopted them as his own.

A sound came from the bedroom and Ross looked round. 'Seems our favourite dream has woken up. I'll go and get her.'

Laurie never tired of watching him with their daughter. When she followed him to the doorway, she saw Ross lifting Penelope out of her cot, still wrapped in the baby quilt her grandmother had made for her. This was the best dream of all, the one in a thousand chance that had happened when they'd least expected it.

'Daddy…' Penelope knew just how to twist her father around her little finger. All it took was that one word.

'Hey, there, Penelope. You want to come and see what we're doing?'

'Daddy… Want play.'

Ross caught his breath. 'You want to play? With your bear?' He picked the stuffed bear up from beside the cot and Penelope pushed it away.

'Want play…'

'With me?' Ross made a funny face and Penelope laughed, her small fingers reaching for him.

'Did you hear that? Her first sentence. Almost…' His voice was a little hoarse, as if he had a lump in his throat.

'It sounded like a sentence to me.' Laurie allowed herself a smile. She'd been repeating the words to Penelope for a couple of weeks now, and finally the little girl had decided to use them herself. Her timing was impeccable.

'You haven't been teaching her to say that, have you?' Ross shot Laurie a suspicious look.

'Me? Would I do such a thing?'

He chuckled, holding out his hand to pull her close. 'You most definitely would. And I love you for it.'

'I love you, too, Ross. I have all my dreams right here.' She snuggled against him. The warm smell of his body, along with Penelope's gorgeous baby scent, enveloped her in a cocoon of happiness.

He kissed her cheek, a warm reminder of what tonight would hold after Penelope was asleep again. A crazy, unlikely thought began to form…

'Do you ever wonder? Whether a one in thousand chance might happen twice? We could try IVF this time…'

Ross chuckled 'Turning my world upside down *once* wasn't enough for you? You think I can survive a second time?'

'It was the first time I've ever seen you stunned into silence.' Those moments, when they'd stared at the pregnancy test together, and when she'd wiped tears from his eyes with shaking fingers, had been among the best of her life. They were enough, but Laurie had learned how to want more, in the face of knowing it might never happen.

'IVF's an option. Although I much prefer the traditional way.' A wicked grin hovered on his lips. 'Do you reckon that's one thousand times? Or one thousand full nights…?'

'I reckon nights. Statistically it could be a lot more.' Laurie shivered with pleasure at the thought. 'The journey's well worth it, even if we never get there.'

'My thoughts entirely.' He kissed her again, and she felt Penelope's small body wriggling between them.

'Daddy want… Want to play, Daddy.'

'You want *to* play, Penelope?' He chuckled. 'That's my girl. Unless I'm very much mistaken, she's just used an infinitive…'

'In that case, we'd better go and play with her immediately.' Laurie went to move, but Ross held her tight against him.

'I want to make another bargain with you. That we never stop dreaming.'

They'd always have more to do together, and Laurie couldn't wait to find out what would come next for them.

'It's a deal, Ross. Always.'

* * * * *

THE PARAMEDIC'S SECRET SON

RACHEL DOVE

MILLS & BOON

In memory of 'Aidy'—Adrian Rothwell.
Still dearly loved and missed by us all.

CHAPTER ONE

THE FIRST CALL came thirty-seven seconds into the early shift. A welcome distraction for Annabel, who had barely felt the coffee start to work after the morning she'd already had.

'Heathrow Airport, Terminal Two, fall after feeling faint. Incoming passenger from Finland, no history yet. Sixty-two-year-old male. Possible head injury from the fall.'

'Let's go.' Annabel grinned at her driving partner, turning on the sirens and strapping into the ambulance seat. 'I need to turn my crappy morning around. Saving a life might just do that.'

Tom, her long-running partner and work husband, pulled out of the ambulance station, Penny waving them off from the control desk as they pulled out into the slowly separating mid-morning traffic.

'Aidan?' he asked, flicking her a supportive best friend look. Tom was a gem. She couldn't help but open up to him whenever they were together. She rolled her eyes at him now, puffing a strand of dark hair out of her way with a blow of exasperated air.

'Who else? The builders are leaving stuff everywhere; the whole gaff is covered in dust. He's fed up, poor kid. Plus, he's doing some big project at school, and he keeps leaving little bits of paper everywhere, and going through Mum's old photos. I feel like I'm constantly just cleaning up all the time, and it still looks exactly the same. I'm about ready to pack us both off to a hotel with a pool for the weekend, just to get some peace. I would have already, but the builders are bleeding me dry. I swear, I've been saving to buy our forever home for years, but now it's here I wish I'd realised how much work it was going to be.'

Tom kept his eyes on the road, ever vigilant, but chuckled. 'It's your dream though! Just imagine what it's going to be like when it's all done. What's up with the little man, anyway?'

'Lord knows. Early hormones maybe? He's so moody lately,' she carried on, mentally checking the rig and the traffic as she talked about her frustration. They were going to be at the call soon, and then it would be all business.

Aidan was doing a project about family. She didn't tell Tom this, but she was pretty sure that the lack of names on Aidan's family tree had a little something to do with his current mood.

'It turned into a whole thing this morning. Apparently, I'm an utter dork and he hates living in the new house. I figured he'd forget about it a little once I'd explained that the work wouldn't take forever. And that I wasn't a dork. Obviously.'

'Obviously,' Tom chortled. 'Then what?'

'Then I dropped him off at breakfast club and…*ugh*. It was just tense, and I hate waving him off like that. He's not my biggest fan today.'

The station radioed, asking for an updated ETA,

and Annabel got to work, flashing him a rueful smile. She saw him clench his jaw, but he said nothing else, just put his foot down as soon as the traffic opened up.

'Nothing to say?' she probed once the cab fell silent once more, the sirens the only noise around them. Tom raised his brows, but still said nothing. Annabel huffed at him, but he smirked and ignored her. 'He is your godson.'

'Yep, and I'm not going to get involved. He still likes me.' Annabel's resulting scowl made him guffaw with laughter. 'Just cut him some slack. I know he's testing your limits, but it must be a lot for him too, right? It's not been the easiest of years for either of you. With his fall, and your big move? He's lived in one place his whole life, and so have you. It must be hard leaving your mother's flat; it's a connection to her that you've needed since she passed. I remember how upset you were when you started training. Your mother died, you started training to be a paramedic, then Har— Aidan came along. You haven't taken your foot off the accelerator for a long time. Once you get your house done, you need to enjoy life a little more, that's all.'

She huffed again, crossing her arms, but she knew he was right. It had been a busy time, and she knew how changes could affect a person better than most. She thought back to Aidan's fall. She'd been on shift when the call had come through from Aidan's school. He'd had a bad fall from the equipment in the gym. She hadn't taken the call, but she'd rushed straight to hospital as quickly as she could, to be by his side. Just thinking of her little boy, unconscious and covered in wires and tubes, it still made her shudder. Life could change in an instant. She owed it to both of them to relax a little, start to enjoy the little things a bit more.

'I know; you're right. This year has taught me to cherish the everyday a bit more. Aidan's probably picking up on my stress too.' She looked across at her friend, playfully tapping him on the arm. 'You're going to be a great dad, you know.'

Tom kept his eyes on the road but his face lit up.

'Oh, I know. Watching you all these years, I picked up a thing or two. We can't wait.'

'Another lamb to the slaughter,' Annabel muttered. 'I can't wait to see it either. I might even buy popcorn.'

They pulled into the airport in record time, heading for Terminal Two and their casualty. A small crowd of people were surrounding a shuttle bus pulled over at the side of the road, and Annabel pointed Tom their way. A couple of people from the crowd heard them coming and started to flag them down.

'Oh, thank goodness!' An ashen-faced woman wearing a bright floral summer dress half pulled Annabel out of the cab. 'It's my husband! He needs to go to hospital!'

Annabel felt the woman's shaky hand encase her gloved one, and she squeezed it gently. 'We're here to help, but I have to get my equipment quickly. I need my hand, okay?' She stressed that last part, knowing that the seconds were ticking away. The woman smiled through her panic and let her go. Within seconds, they were by the patient's side, but someone was already working on the man lying on the ground, a beach towel underneath him that cushioned him from the harsh surface beneath him.

'Sir, could you step aside, please?' Tom asked the man. 'Help's h—'

Annabel's gasp cut Tom off. Either that, or she didn't hear anything he said after her shock discovery. Her world had tilted sideways for a second, but she found she was still on her feet. She was suddenly years younger, sitting back on that airport bench, with waffle marks on her behind from the metal bench. And a broken, utterly shattered heart as she watched the man she loved walk out of her life forever. Her stomach recoiled at the memory.

Please, please, don't let me vomit in this damn airport again because of this man. It can't be him. She blinked hard. *I'm seeing things. What the heck was in that coffee?*

There was a man crouched over the patient, who was conscious and seemingly looking for someone, his head moving from side to side. His hands were reaching for someone as the man tried to settle him, speaking softly to him and trying to keep him from getting up. The wife pushed past the two ambulance personnel and knelt by his side. Tom started to talk to the Good Samaritan, asking curtly for details of what had happened, and Annabel walked towards the patient. Luckily, the professional part of her brain had switched to autopilot and she was focused on the job. The rest of her was in utter shock and wanted to turn the heck around and run for the hills. She knew she needed to run to the patient but her legs were uncooperative blobs of jelly. Just putting one floppy foot in front of the other was a herculean effort. All she could think about was the look on the Samaritan's face when he saw her: the look of utter disbelief at what he was seeing. She wondered what the expression on her own face might have told him. Did she look just as shocked as she felt?

He always could read me. It seems that some things never change. I need to focus! The patient. Dear God, why is he here now? Is it a coincidence? I need to work. Focus on work. I've wasted enough years wondering about what's going through that man's head, let alone his motivations. Get the job done and get the heck out of Dodge. It doesn't matter what he's doing here, as long as he's going. Maybe he's here to fly off again—he's good at that.

She took her chance as Tom distracted the man, to get to the patient lying on the floor.

She checked the vitals of the patient, talking to the man she now knew to be Frank Jessop, returning from a very busy holiday visiting family who'd moved to Finland. He'd overindulged on the flight, it seemed, and had a dip in blood pressure that sent his heart into overdrive. Lugging cases and sitting on a cramped, hot shuttle bus had been the last straw. Hitting the bus rail on the way down, he now had a fall to add to his misery.

Checking him over, Annabel was satisfied he had no obvious broken bones, but the pain in his back and knock to the head meant he needed to be transported safely to hospital to be checked over fully. His vitals were stable and holding steady. No blown pupils, and he tracked her finger with no issues. He had a headache, but nothing too concerning. He would be fine, but still needed to have a trip to hospital.

Now brought around by his Good Samaritan, however, Frank was eager to get up off the floor and on his way home. He was embarrassed and eager to forget about the whole thing. Annabel knew how he felt as she crouched down next to him on the ground. She could see that Tom was dealing with the small crowd, getting people on their way on the shuttle bus. Keeping *him* at arm's length from her, which she was grateful for.

Thank goodness she was working with Tom and not one of the others. The conversation Tom would want to have was going to be bad enough. She didn't want the rumour mill to start up again; she couldn't bear it. Especially not in her current role. She was the lead paramedic now; she didn't want to be the subject of whispers and awkward looks in the corridors again any time soon.

'I'm sorry, Frank, but we do need to take you in, get you checked over properly. You can't drive home, but you can make arrangements with your family to collect your car. Okay?' She could see the panic creep back onto the man's face, and she smiled at him gently. She had sounded a little robotic. She licked her lips, suddenly feeling parched. Exposed to the rays of the hot sun, and her own past. She kept her eyes focused on her patient's face.

'Don't worry, the car parking company have plans for this kind of thing. They'll get it all arranged till you can collect your car. Let's get you sorted, okay? My colleague will bring the stretcher.' She looked across to Tom, but he was already on his way over with the equipment they needed. The Samaritan was standing off to one side, near to Frank's wife. *How caring of him,* she thought childishly. She didn't look at the man as they got Frank strapped in and wrapped up, but she felt as if his eyes were boring into her cheek the whole time.

'Annabel?'

Hearing him say her name felt like an arrow right through the heart. How long had it been since she'd heard him speak her name? How many times had she spoken his, on the messages she'd left on his phone? The ones he had never answered. *'I'm sorry, Annie,'* were the last words he'd spoken to her, before walking through the security doors and leaving her standing there, in this very airport.

'Annie?' He said it again now, a little louder. She ignored him, but her whole body flinched, and she really had to stop her head from turning to the sound.

'Annabel,' he tried again. 'Please…'

'I'm working, sir,' she said as coldly as she could. She heard the break in her voice and hated herself for it. *Suck it up, Annie!* 'If you could just stand back and let us do our work.'

'I was first on scene…' he started, but she cut him off. She wouldn't compromise the patient, and she had done a thorough check-up on Frank. She and Tom had this, and she didn't want to be in *his* proximity a minute longer than she had to be. She felt as if her whole body were on fire, and she didn't like how out of control she felt.

'Thank you for that. If you have any pertinent information, my colleague can take it.' She risked looking at him now and felt so grateful that she'd managed to arrange her face into a professional, emotionless expression. It was one of the hardest things she'd ever done. Last week she'd abseiled halfway down a building to reach a casualty who was locked out on a balcony and unconscious. Thinking about it, that had actually been far easier than looking Harrison—Harry—Carter straight in the face without either breaking down, punching him right in his stupid girlfriend-abandoning face or running into his arms. She couldn't deal with him right now, or ever. She thought about the last time she had uttered his name, and she felt her cheeks flush at the memory.

He can't be here because of that though, right? If he is, he's a bit late. Six months late. Eight years late, for that matter. He's had plenty of chances to come back, and he's never taken any of them before.

She found herself staring deep into his eyes despite herself, trying to read him.

God, if only the frontiers of medicine could crack mind-reading. It would mean a lot fewer broken hearts. She wanted to know just what was going on in that beautiful head of his. His stupid, woman-leaving head.

'Why are you here?' she blurted, just as Tom arrived with the stretcher.

'I came to see you,' Harry said simply, and as Annabel's emotions did a double-take she felt Tom touch her arm, bringing her back to reality.

'You ready?' Tom was looking at Harry with a wary expression, as if he were waiting for him to explode and take the lot of them out with him. 'Annabel?'

'Yep, yep!' she yipped back like an overexcited terrier, turning away and looking at Tom. He nodded to her once before glaring back at Harry.

'You okay?' Tom said out of the corner of his mouth as they got the equipment ready. 'Did he really just say he'd come to see you?'

Out of the corner of her mouth, she shushed him.

'Tom! He'll hear you! And yes.'

'I can hear you just fine, dear,' Frank said as they lifted him off the ground. 'My hearing's fine. I really think I should just go home. I don't need all this fuss. You should be looking after someone who's sick.'

'Sorry, Frank you have a ride in the ambulance ahead of you. We need to get you checked over.'

Frank tutted, and Harry stepped forward. 'Can I help?'

'No,' Annabel said bluntly. 'Please, just step back and let us do our job.' She gave him a look that meant to maim. 'We don't need you here.' Harry raised his arms in surrender, his face a picture of hurt as he stepped back away from them. Annabel winced inwardly, but then thought back to being in that airport as her boyfriend told her he was going away without her, and her resolve strengthened.

Securing Frank to the gurney now, Annabel kept her head focused on the job. She just couldn't look at her friend. *Their friend, once upon a time.* One look right now at Tom and he would read her face and know her truth. She felt as if her secret was radiating out of her, and Tom had been suspicious enough over the years. One look, and he would work it out. She couldn't let that happen, especially with *him* right here. He was standing back from the small crowd now, alone, a suitcase at his feet.

Great. Anything else you want to throw at me today? A swarm of locusts, maybe?

She took him in once more as they pushed Frank to the ambulance, his wife following close behind, Tom talking to Frank, keeping a close eye on his vitals. She was looking at the details too—Frank, Tom and his attempts to catch her eye, and him. Harry. The man she'd once declared to be the love of her life. The one she'd also claimed, to everyone she knew, to be dead to her. He didn't look dead, of course. He looked positively glowing in fact. Tanned, well dressed, a little tired perhaps. She hoped that jet lag would bite him on the behind. He was due a bit of karma, surely? He was bronzed, his hair even lighter than she'd remembered. His sun-kissed skin was a perk of his fancy job, no doubt. Life must have been good in Dubai.

Well, la-di-dah. Good for you, Harry. Your new life without me obviously agrees with you.

He looked less of a boy now, of course, but she could still see him there underneath the day's worth of dark stubble. The angular jaw he kept flexing, tight-lipped as he looked right back at her. She saw that his legs were still strong and muscular, thicker set now than when she'd lain beside him, her limbs entwined with his. He still had the slightly floppy look to his blond hair, the nervous little twitch in the corner of his mouth. They got closer to him, and she watched as he collected his case and walked towards the car park. He didn't look back once. She swallowed to stop herself from calling his name impulsively. All she could hear in her head was his voice. *I came to see you.*

Looking back at Tom, she finally met his eye. They had a bit of a code, honed over the years of working together. It had been eight years since Harry had left, and Tom knew what seeing him again would do to her. He nodded once at her, their shorthand for checking the other was okay. She nodded back, her usual 'I'm fine' nod. Tom frowned but turned his focus fully back to the job. Reaching behind him for the door, he opened up the back and they got back to work. Before Annabel closed the ambulance double doors she looked around, but Harry was gone.

'As if I could ever expect anything else,' she muttered under her breath, before swinging the metal doors shut once more against her old, long thought buried pain.

Tom was the best friend a woman could ever ask for. He really was. Married to the job, and restaurant owner Lloyd, he was the ultimate paramedic partner. Not to mention the fact that he and Lloyd had taken her on some of the best nights out she'd ever had, they were great with their godson Aidan and they always, always had her back.

The week that Harry had left, the pair of them had declared him a scoundrel and vowed never to talk to him again. And they hadn't. No one had, truth be told. Not that Annabel had ever asked that of anyone. She'd pushed the other way even, in the early days. The truth was that for the first three weeks she'd wanted them to get in touch with him. She'd called him more than a few times, even called the hospital in Dubai he was supposed to be working in. All she'd got was a wall of silence. She'd wanted to know he was okay, as much as she'd hated herself for it. She wouldn't give him the satisfaction of begging him to come home or talk about how heartbroken she was without him, but it didn't mean that she could just turn her feelings off. As much as she'd tried to.

She'd been in shock for the longest time when he'd left. In the back of her mind she'd even hoped he would come back to her on his own. Get over there and miss her, realise he was still in love and come to get her back by his side. Hear one of her voicemails or read one of her texts and realise what he was doing.

But there'd been nothing, and she hadn't called him since those first few weeks after he'd left. She couldn't, not once she'd realised that he wasn't going to call back or come home and she would have to deal with everything he had left behind all alone. She'd vowed to herself that from then on she would never contact him again, and she'd stuck to it for years. Almost perfectly, till one day six months ago. Now look what had happened. He'd been there, in that airport of all places. Like the Ghost of Christmas Past, complete with sun-kissed skin and a look in his eyes she'd never seen before.

He'd looked so unruffled by seeing her, but he'd said he'd come to see her. What did he want? Why now? Had he been talking to someone in her life? Surely he hadn't hopped on a plane just to tell her that he still wasn't bothered about her. What she knew now, after seeing him, was that she was still bothered by him. When she'd passed by him she'd felt as if she was on fire. She'd wanted to talk to him even, hear what he had to say…but she didn't even want to know what he would say. It was too risky, and things were complicated enough. Would he still want to talk to her if he knew all the facts? Did he know all the facts?

All of these questions were making her head spin, and for the millionth time in the last eight years she doubted the decisions she had made since he'd left. She couldn't take them back now, and she wasn't ready to deal with them either. Burying her head in the sand had served her well up to now, or so she'd thought. The second she'd set eyes on Harry, her blood had turned to ice in her veins.

What had she done? What if he hated her?

For the longest time she'd felt as though she hated him, but the thought of him despising her knocked her off her feet even now.

Oh, heavens, it was pointless anyway. The whole thing was a mess, and now her morning was utterly ruined. She sighed and took a seat next to Frank's wife Janice, in the back.

'Ready, Tom,' she called and half a second later the vehicle was on the move, sirens on. Janice whimpered at the side of Annabel, and she put her hand on hers.

'Don't worry; it's just to get you there quicker. Traffic is a nightmare here this time of day.'

Janice nodded, the worry still evident on her face. 'Thank you. My daughter's on the way to pick the car up and the cases, so that's something. I do wish we hadn't troubled you. You must be so busy.'

Annabel waved her away, keen to help her feel settled in such a scary situation. 'No trouble at all. It's what we're here for. How long have you two been married?'

'Coming up to forty years now,' Frank replied, reaching for his wife with a shaky hand. 'It's why we went away, a little trip to see some family that moved abroad. My brother and his wife and their kids. We had such a lovely time, and now look.'

'Don't worry, you'll be fine, Frank. Don't let this spoil the memories of your trip. You got a lot of family?'

Janice reached into her handbag and pulled out a little book of photos. On the front cover, it read *Grand-*

parents Brag Book. 'Oh, yes! We have seven grandchildren, and our first great-grandchild on the way. Plus our two daughters.' She flipped through the book, and Annabel saw the pride on her face as she looked at each memory. People with smiling faces, babies sleeping in bouncers, birthday parties full of life and obvious love. 'You got any kids?'

'One,' she said. 'Aidan.' She reached into her pocket, unlocking the screen on her phone to show them both a photo of her son. He was dressed in his school uniform, standing in front of the front door of their old flat, beaming smile and book bag in hand. 'He's in primary school.'

'He's lovely.' Janice leaned in close to the screen. 'He looks like you.'

'I get that a lot.' Annabel smiled, checking on Frank as they chatted. 'It's just the two of us, so we're pretty close. He's a little whirlwind, keeps me on my toes.'

'He looks like butter wouldn't melt,' Frank muttered, wincing when he turned his head. 'Good age, by the looks. Enjoy it before the hormones kick in.'

Janice laughed. 'Oh, yes, wait till puberty hits. With our girls, I think we aged about ten years overnight.'

Frank groaned theatrically, and the two of them gave each other a knowing look. 'I used to beg my boss for overtime; it was easier than dealing with the moody twosome at home.'

Thinking about Aidan that morning, Annabel could relate. 'Kids, eh?' she laughed. 'Can't live with them, can't live without them.'

'Grandkids make up for it though. Plus, seeing your kids get a taste of their own medicine has given us a few laughs over the years. Best of all, you get to hand them back at the end of the day. You have any other family?'

She thought of her mother, feeling the familiar pang of loss stab at her, and nodded slowly. 'I have people in my corner. It takes a village, right?'

She thought of her station family, and the man at the airport. *He was my family once.*

'We do okay; it's always been just us. He has everything he needs.' She didn't know who she was trying to convince, but she squashed down the maelstrom of feelings pulsating through her.

We're just fine. Aren't we?

'How do you know the man who helped us?' Janice asked innocently. 'I saw you talking to him. We'd like to thank him too, if we could.'

It was said so innocently, but Annabel couldn't bring herself to answer at first. Quantifying Harry into a single sentence was impossible, but she tried anyway.

'I knew him a long time ago. Since the first year of primary school, actually. He moved away after we qualified; he used to be one of us.'

Janice nodded, seemingly satisfied. 'Are you still in touch? Could you thank him for us?'

She still had his number in her phone, despite having changed handsets over the years. It was a weakness of hers, so she pushed down the whirl of emotions running through her and gave Janice's hand a pat.

'I will,' she lied easily. 'I'll let him know.' One more thing to never tell Harry to add to the list. At least this one was small in comparison to the others.

'Annabel, are you going to talk about this, or are we going to be silent the whole shift?' In response, Annabel took a huge bite of her sandwich. Tom shook his head, taking a swig of his take-away coffee. They were sitting in the ambulance, having their break whilst parked in the grounds of the local community centre.

It was pretty quiet today, most of the classes and groups already having taken place earlier in the day. She'd been to a few of them herself over the years. Baby massage classes with Aidan, helping out at the coffee mornings to raise funds for new equipment. She'd even taught a few first aid courses here, helping out the centre by donating her time and expertise. There was a lot of social inequality in the area, and Annabel had seen enough of it to know that real change happened right at the root. It had helped her, back when she was still managing being a new single mum and keeping her career going. The memory made her smile, but she turned it off quickly. Tom was still staring at her as if she were a zoo exhibit.

'Stop staring, Tom, I'm fine. He's an ex; I was bound to see him some time. They don't go off and live on some remote island, you know. They do live on.'

'More's the pity,' Tom added. 'But this isn't just some ex; this is Harry. He also lives in another country, so seeing him again is not like bumping into him at the supermarket. And he isn't just some ex either; he's *the* ex. Wanting to talk to you. Harry. You know, your childhood sweetheart Harry. The man who left you alone to live a luxurious life in the opulence of the Middle East Harry. The man who broke your—'

'Trust in men—yeah, I got it. I don't want to talk to him. Whatever he has to say won't be good. He did me a favour, anyway. Jetting off to a dream paramedic job living in Dubai is all well and good, but I didn't even have a job to go to over there; I was just following him to his. I might not have even found a job, and then where would I have been? Sitting alone in some fancy place on my own while he carved out a career? I wouldn't have gone to work at the station or got my dream job with you guys. Looking back, it was all a huge gamble really. I didn't have a firm plan, and I worked hard to be a paramedic. It all worked out for the best.'

Wow, Annabel, that almost sounded like you believe your own fibs. You would have followed that man to the ends of the earth, and you know it.

Tom gave her a long sideways look before taking a bite of his own lunch. In between mouthfuls, he kept on at her. 'You would have landed a job in Dubai, and you know it. You're amazing at what you do. Not to contradict you either, but you trusted one man, remember? Long enough to make Aidan anyway. You could do it again, and Aidan won't be living at home for ever. You deserve to be happy, Annabel. Put the Harry thing to rest, finally. If he really is home to speak to you, hear him out.'

Annabel swallowed the piece of chicken from her wrap carefully before answering.

'No, I don't want to hear a word of what he has to say. And yes, I had a drunken one-night stand one time, after Harry left, and now I'm a single mum and—' She raised her finger at him when he tried to cut in. 'And I am happy with my lot. I don't want Harry to know about my life, and I mean any part of my life. I have the house now, and Aidan to raise. I don't need to see Harry to be reminded of that.'

He'd had his chance. Eight years ago, and six months

ago. He'd failed both times. When she'd seen him at the airport he had full use of his limbs. He could quite easily have picked up the phone, or even a pen to send a blinking postcard. *Leave me alone. Stop calling. I left you for someone else. I'm married. I'm the new James Bond.* Anything would have been better than nothing, than wondering what it was about her that had made him fall out of love and leave her sobbing in the departure lounge while he strode away from her, ready to fly away to a flash new life.

She heard Tom sigh at the side of her, a sure sign that he was holding his tongue and resenting the notion. They'd been here many times over the years, but Tom had never crossed the line. He respected her wishes, even though he didn't always agree with them.

She wound her window down, eager to feel the hot city sun on her face. 'I'm happy, Tom. I promise. Hear that, universe?' she half shouted out of the window. 'I'm happy, thanks, you can send him back now!'

Tom chortled beside her. 'Of course you are, you lunatic. But with your mum being…gone, and that big house to sort out, don't you think it might be nice to have another pair of hands around the place? I know you're used to looking after yourself by now, but it doesn't mean you have to.'

Annabel ripped into her wrap again with gusto, the adrenalin and shocks of the morning making her feel ravenous.

'My mum died when I was eighteen, Tom. Before I even started training. I've looked after myself for a long time now, and her for that matter. She was sick for a long time before the cancer finally took her. Besides, I have another pair of hands around the place. Abe's been helping out at the weekends, keeping Aidan occupied, and I've got some contractors doing the bulk of the work.' Tom raised his brows pointedly, and Annabel slapped her forehead when recognition hit. 'Oh, no—Abe! Do you think he knows? About Harry being back?'

Tom shrugged. 'I don't know, but Abe's his dad and he stopped talking to him too. Maybe Harry wants to make amends with more than just you. Do you think Abe would talk to him? Harry must be staying somewhere, right? Do you think he'd go to his dad's?'

Annabel sank into her seat. She'd never even thought of that.

'I don't know. When Harry chose to be a paramedic and not train to be a GP, Abe took it badly. They fought for years, and when Harry told him we were both leaving for Dubai, they had a huge fight. Abe's been my rock ever since, but Harry's his flesh and blood. I wouldn't want him to choose between his son and me. I'll give him a call later, try and suss out if he knows anything,' she said glumly.

Tom squeezed her shoulder. 'Don't worry; he's probably just visiting. He's got a life in Dubai, right? A job to go back to. Seeing him there at the airport was bad timing, sure, but he's officially come with a purpose. I'm sure he'll fly off again soon, once he's said his piece.'

Looking out of the window, she felt her head nod, but inside all she could think was how the thought of Harry leaving London again gave her a punch in her gut that she wasn't expecting to feel, and she knew that it wasn't going to be that easy. Not at all. God, she wished her mother were still here, so she could talk to her. Ask her what she thought.

It wasn't as if she hadn't said plenty when she was alive. Her mother being taken by cancer had robbed her of all those conversations. Something told her that things weren't going to be easy, and she felt a fresh wave of grief that she couldn't run to her mother, the one person who knew everything about her and Harry growing up, and always supported her. Even though her comments sometimes had stung a little. That was mothers though; they always wanted the best for their babies, and had strong opinions when they didn't agree with their offspring's life decisions. Her mother had been no different, but she would give anything to have her here right now, even if it was just to give her a swift kick on the behind. She wondered again what her mother would have made of Harry leaving her like that. How much she would have loved Aidan and being a grandmother. She hoped that, wherever she was, she was proud of them both.

As they finished their lunch and greened up their console indicating their ability to take a shout, ready for the rest of the shift, she packed up the rubbish. And her emotions. It was time to be a paramedic again. She focused on that. The rest would have to wait. It would all just have to wait.

Harry could hear his heartbeat pulsate like a jungle drum in his ears as he walked away from the scene, from Annabel. She'd taken his breath away, standing there. She was just like he'd imagined, bar the scowl and tired eyes. The look on her face when she'd seen him. The way she'd shut down his attempts to talk.

He'd played this moment over in his head so many times over the years. The fact that their first meeting had happened at the airport was awful. The place where he'd left her alone and jetted off to his new life.

He could still remember the confusion on her face that day. She'd met him at the airport, bags packed, all ready to come with him to their new life abroad. The look on her face when he told her he'd cancelled her plane ticket, that it wasn't working out. That he wanted to go alone, and wanted her to stay back in London, start over without him. He'd known this girl since they were snot-nosed kids in primary school, playing tag and growing up together. They'd gone through school together, trained together; their parents had been friends. He'd thought he was going to spend the rest of his life with her, but it wasn't to be and he'd ended up breaking her heart. The one thing he never thought he'd do. He'd been so excited and terrified to see her again, but seeing her there at the airport, tending to Frank, was the worst possible moment.

It was the last place he'd wanted to see her again. And he knew he would see her again and make her listen. He'd come this far, had waited so long to make his move, and he wasn't about to stop now. He'd hidden long enough, and he hated himself for being such a coward for so long. The younger Harry who had left her had been like a scared little boy, reeling from his own problems and not wanting to drag her along with it. Not after everything she had already been through. He was the one who was supposed to bring her joy, not sorrow.

Looking back, he wondered whether that was the right decision. He'd questioned it every day since. People had tried to get in touch with him. His friends, his father, and Annabel. He'd never replied to a single one, had deleted the text messages as soon as they came through. He couldn't bear to listen to the voicemails. They would only be full of anger and hurt anyway. The ones from Annabel he never read or listened to. He knew that if he heard her voice he would come undone and he just couldn't do that. He'd chosen his path and, as hard as it was, he had thought it easier in the long run. On her, if not both of them.

Moving home after eight and a bit years was never going to be easy, but he'd come with a purpose. To finally right the wrongs of the past and put down roots. He'd not announced to anyone that he was coming, and when Frank fell to the floor on that shuttle bus he'd acted instinctively. It hadn't even occurred to him that Annabel might be in the ambulance coming to help. And with Tom as her partner. You couldn't make it up, how odd life was.

Tom was their friend, back in the old days. They'd all gone through training together. Tom had been cool towards him too, but he expected nothing else, and Harry could tell that his shock had given way to wanting to protect Annabel, and he couldn't begrudge him for that. Tom was a good friend, and Harry had walked out on him too, in a way. Another person who'd called to check on him and got ignored. He'd dropped out of his life and never been back. Out of all their lives.

And now he had to go see his dad and tell him the good news. The prodigal son was home. Well, not home. He was going to book into a hotel. He wasn't that stupid. Once he got settled, he'd find somewhere more permanent. The fight they'd had before he'd left for Dubai was the last time they'd seen each other face to face, and he steeled himself for looking his dad in the face again. Abe had told him he was a disappointment years ago, and he didn't expect him to feel any differently now. Whatever Harry did to try to live his life and not hurt others, it never seemed to work out quite right. He hoped that now he was back in London he could break that curse. His thoughts led him to think of Annabel once more.

She'd looked at him as if he were a stranger. Less than a stranger. She'd looked at him with pure horror showing as plain as day on her features. He didn't expect anything less, of course, especially given the setting of their reunion. Harry knew that must have been brutal, and it was all down to him. He wished he could have told her that, that he was sorry she'd seen him there. Another Annabel conversation to torture himself with. Great. As if he didn't have enough of those already. Heading to the huts representing the numerous hire car companies, he steeled himself. London, Harrison Carter is coming home. I hope you're ready for this one.

Annabel drove the ambulance back into the station. They'd finished on time for once, and she and Tom were eager to get on with the rest of their day. Well, Tom was looking forward to a hot shower and a cold drink in a fancy wine bar with Lloyd. Annabel was looking forward to catching up on paperwork before picking Aidan up from his friend Finn's house. They'd had coding club after school, and then Finn's mum, Teri, was taking them out for tea. Teri was a nurse and the two single women had soon worked out that since their boys were such good friends, they could trade off on the childcare from time to time. It worked out brilliantly, and they got on great at work too. It made the two women's lives that much easier, and they always had each other's backs at work too.

Annabel frowned to herself when she thought of picking Aidan up from hers that night. How many lies she would have to tell—how much she would have to conceal about her day. Suddenly thankful for the list of jobs that needed her attention, she started to grab her things and head indoors to her office. Being the lead paramedic was great; it was what she had planned for her career for so long, and the bump in money was pretty nice too. Since things with Harry and moving to Dubai had fallen apart, taking the job she'd been offered at her old hospital—but had turned down in favour of Dubai—had made perfect sense.

Abe, Harry's dad, had held her together for the first few weeks, when she couldn't bear to go straight back to her flat with her tail between her legs to stare at four walls and wail. Thank goodness she'd not sold it before the planned move, or she would have been homeless to boot. Abe had even called the hospital, let the others know what had happened, and that she was tragically single and available for work. Dumped at the airport. She'd rocked up, cases in hand at Heathrow, and instead she had been dumped.

I'm going alone. It's not you, it's me. It would never work out there. Smell you later.

Everyone knew she'd got dumped by Harry and left to rot in her old life. Not that she saw it that way now. Things happened for a reason, and she knew that better than most. What had happened after, having Aidan, had kept her hands pretty full. She loved her job, had friends, a new home. She had been doing just fine, or she thought she had till she'd looked at Harry again. Felt the pull of him right in the pit of her stomach, just as strongly as before. Now she was back to feeling tired and wanting to hide away.

Heading into the ambulance station, she nodded to a few of the staff and motioned towards her office with a smile and a nod when they offered her some supper. She knew she probably should eat something, but she also knew that she'd only end up ordering pizza once Aidan was asleep in bed. She'd have the energy for little else.

Wading through her inbox, she noticed a new staff member form. Of course—Tom's replacement. They'd do a handover, and Tom would be gone. Off to pastures new, baby vomit and lack of sleep. If anyone could handle that, it was Tom. She was thrilled for both of them and couldn't wait to meet the new arrivals. Even if the little ones, not yet born, were the reason that she was losing the best work partner she'd ever had. Well, the second best. The pair of them were on standby, adoption process all done. They were just waiting for the call that the mother had delivered and they were parents.

She pulled out the staff form and laughed to herself softly. She was seeing things now. Imagining her ex's name in the square marked 'Employee Name'.

Rubbing at her tired eyes, she looked again. Blinked a half dozen times. It wasn't an optical illusion. A Mr Harrison Abraham Carter was due to start as her partner the very next day.

The words swam in front of her eyes as she slotted

the pieces together. HR had hired a new paramedic, and they'd told her that he was a previous employee. She'd never connected the dots. She'd never ever imagined that Harrison would even be in the UK, let alone in their neck of the woods. She'd stayed hands off, not wanting to seem pushy to the new girls in HR. They chose well normally; she had a crack team. *Damn it.* She realised that there was no option now. He'd forced her hand. She needed to speak to Harry after all. She couldn't let the dawn rise without at least a conversation. And what a conversation that was going to be.

Taking a moment to close the office door, she looked around first to see if she might be interrupted. She needed this to go well, with no distractions. Satisfied, she sat back down at her desk, took out her phone and looked for the number in her contacts. One she had called only once in the last few years, and never thought to be calling again. Not in her right mind, anyway.

Harry answered on the second ring, denying her any real opportunity to steel herself.

'Hello,' he said softly. She could hear the surprise in his voice. 'I'm so glad you called.'

'Hi,' she said shakily. 'It was you at the airport today then. I wasn't sure I hadn't had a small stroke and imagined the whole thing.'

He laughed, just once. 'Yeah, it was me. I'm sorry it happened that way. I wanted to speak to you properly, but I know it wasn't the best timing. How's Frank?'

She rolled her eyes, biting the skin on the inside of her mouth at her own stupid remark. To his credit, he didn't say anything else for a beat.

'It wasn't the best surprise,' she offered. 'He's fine. He got discharged.'

'That's good to hear. I didn't know you would be there though, truly. I was planning on telling you I was back in a better way.'

So he wasn't denying it then, or trying to play it down. He was telling the truth at least. Still, the job news was still ringing in her head. She needed to get control of this, get out in front of it. Before she clapped eyes on him again. There would be no running tomorrow. That was his forte, not hers. She wouldn't give him the satisfaction of seeing her squirm.

'Well, I would have guessed, given that you're due to start at the station tomorrow.'

Another pause.

He's wriggling like a worm on a hook.

She felt mean for thinking it, but she had feelings. Who knew? She was having all the feelings and being tired and exhausted after work wasn't helping. She needed to get this out. She needed to get off the phone, because even listening to his voice right now was too much. It was so much easier to pretend that she was over him when he wasn't around. Having him around was torture.

'It doesn't matter anyway. We worked together before. I suppose we can again.'

'I—' he started to cut in, but she couldn't let him. She'd lose the opportunity.

'Let me finish. When you left, I was in a bit of a state. Nice job, by the way. Waiting till the airport to tell me. Just lovely, really.'

She heard Harry suck in a sharp breath, and she kept talking.

'Five weeks after, I found out I was pregnant. I'd been on a few nights out with Tom and Lloyd, some of the nurses. I told them I'd had a one-night stand and—'

'You slept with someone straight after I left?' His voice was louder now, a tinge of anger running through his words. 'Is that what you're telling me? You got pregnant?'

'Shut up, please! No, I haven't slept with…anyone since you.'

Damn it. Don't talk about that.

'Not that it's any business of yours what I did after you left, but the baby was yours, Harrison.'

'Mine?' he echoed, his voice softer now.

'Yes. Is yours, in fact. My son, Aidan. He's seven, he lives with me. People think he was the result of a one-night stand because I told them that's what happened, but he's yours.'

She sighed heavily, sitting back in her chair. She felt lighter, light-headed even. She'd spoken her truth. The only other person she'd told wasn't here to tell her story. Her mother had taken that secret well, but telling a headstone was different from a living person. They couldn't give an opinion, for one thing. She figured the people around her had their suspicions, but she'd always shut them down. It was too hard to even think about Harry, let alone have people pitying her for choosing to have the child of the man who'd left her in the dust. Or telling him that she was having his baby. He'd ignored her calls, every one of them, and she hadn't called to tell him the baby news. Why should she? He'd gone and blocked them all.

She didn't want to co-parent a child with someone who lived in another country. She'd never had a dad, and she didn't want Aidan to grow up with a part-time dad. She'd protected her son. You couldn't miss what you'd never had, she figured. Though it was getting harder now Aidan was getting older. The questions had already started with gusto, and it was just easier to continue with her story. That his dad was someone she didn't have any contact with, that they didn't need him in their lives.

At the other end of the phone there was a resounding silence. She could hear him breathe, so she carried on.

'I just needed you to know, since you will probably meet him at work, or someone will say something, or mention him, so…that's it. That's why I called. Just so you had the facts.'

'Why didn't you tell me?'

She closed her eyes, listening to the hurt in his voice.

'What was I supposed to do, Harry, call you up and tell you? You left, remember? I tried for weeks to get you to talk to me. I called your work. They said you were unavailable; they wouldn't even tell me anything about you. What was I supposed to do, ship him off every once in a while to Dubai to a man he didn't know? I didn't even know if you would want to be his father. For all I knew, you had a wife and kids out there. You chose to leave, and I didn't want him not to have his father. I've had that myself, and it's not a nice feeling. Better no father than one who doesn't show up for his kid. We've done okay this far on our own. If you'd called me back, just once, I would have told you. But you didn't, Harry, and I made peace with it.'

Another lie, she told herself. It was only her pride that had stopped her calling when Aidan was born, and Lord knows she had wanted to. Giving birth without him had felt so wrong. Every time Aidan had done something amazing she'd wanted to pick up the phone. When he took his first steps, said his first word. Dada. Oh, how she had cried at that. Her gorgeous, perfect little boy saying that word had broken her heart all over again. By then it had been too hard to call him. What could she say? Our secret son said his first word today?

'I'm sorry, I wasn't attacking you. It's just…a lot. I didn't expect this. We need to meet.'

Annabel was already shaking her head, before she remembered he couldn't see her. Thank goodness he couldn't, because she had silent tears rolling down her face and her hands were shaking.

'I don't think so,' she said finally. 'I don't want to see you, Harry. You had your chance.'

Harry was sitting outside his father's house, the hum of the hire car's engine ringing in his ears. He was a father. *A father.* To a boy already half grown, no less.

A dad was something he had never thought he would be. Or could be. When he'd found a lump on his testicle a few weeks before Dubai, he'd known that the signs were bad. He'd been so tired lately, his health not what it was. He knew it was more than the intensity of the job, the stress of the planned move, and this was it— testicular cancer. When he'd burned his life back home to the ground and headed out to Dubai, determined to kick the cancer before getting Annabel back, he'd woken up that first morning in his new life with another lump to obsess over.

His new bosses had been amazing. He'd called to tell them he couldn't take the job, what he was facing, and they'd not only protected his job, they'd told him to come anyway and be treated at their world class centre. The second lump was more bad news, and it had taken the best expertise of the team he was supposed to be working with to keep him alive, and it had cost him his fertility.

The cancer was the reason he'd left Annabel behind. He'd seen what a toll her mother's cancer had taken on her and he couldn't bear the thought of her being his carer, all alone in a new country without her friends, nursing him with a cancer that the oncology department at the hospital in London didn't seem too optimistic about. He knew enough to know that the emergency scans they had done weren't good. He'd had a choice: stay home with a father who he didn't get on with, or go to his new life and fight to stay alive.

He'd been scared, but Annabel had been the deciding factor. He couldn't put her through that. He was Harrison Carter, strong, self-assured, always the first to run to a call. He didn't want Annabel to see him sick, or worse. She had been offered a job at the ambulance station where they'd trained. She was top of the class. She had a life to step into and he didn't want to ruin that for her. She'd wanted this her whole life and she was so close to getting it.

So he'd broken her heart, told her it wasn't working out, that he wanted to travel to Dubai on his own, and he'd left her there. Walking through the security gate, listening to her sob and call his name as he strode away from her. He didn't even look back, because he didn't want her to see his own tears.

As time had gone on and he'd found out he couldn't have children, going home had seemed an impossibility. What could he offer her, after all? What if the cancer came back, or she wanted children? He didn't want to derail her life all over again, so once more he'd chosen to protect her heart over his. Right then and there he knew he wouldn't go back to London. He couldn't get the all-clear and rock up at home with a ring. Not when it would only ever be the two of them. He knew that Annabel wanted children. They both did; they'd spoken of it often. An abstract vision for the future that they'd always assumed they would be able to fulfil when the time was right. Working abroad, saving up and seeing the world, then returning home to buy the house they'd always liked as kids and raising their little family.

Knowing that he would be returning home after so long with only the promise of the two of them together, he knew it wouldn't be fair. He'd broken her heart once and he didn't want to do it again. She could be happy with someone else, have the family she'd always wanted. He would just be a footnote in the story of her life. A bad, abandoning ex-boyfriend.

But now he knew that he should have come back all along. He should have flown home and fought harder. He was such a coward and look what it had cost them both. He'd ruined both their lives, and their son had been caught in the crossfire. Life was cruel but, thinking about Annabel's news, all he could feel was happiness right now. He had a child with the love of his life. That was something he'd never imagined post cancer. Hearing that he'd left her pregnant was just too cruel a twist of fate to comprehend right now. He felt as if the universe was laughing at him.

'I get why you don't want to meet, but I have so

many questions,' he said eventually, his throat feeling dry. 'Does he know about me?'

Annabel winced, stuttering a little. 'No. I told him I'd just met his father the once. The same as I told everyone.'

Harry could feel the shock wash over him, his nerve-endings tingling. 'You didn't tell anyone the truth? I can't believe it.'

'No, and I don't need your judgement. You'd just left, you weren't talking to any of us. I made up a story. People were mad enough at you, and I couldn't bear their judgement. I get that you're mad but—'

'No. Well, yes, I am, but…thank you.'

'Thank you? What the hell for?'

He closed his eyes in frustration. 'I just mean… thank you. I know that sounds stupid but thank you. I don't deserve it, any of it. I'm so sorry I didn't call. I'm sorry I put you in that position.'

'I did it for me,' Annabel said coldly. 'And Aidan. I didn't want him to know about you, that you left us both without a backward glance. You coming back has forced my hand.'

'I know, but I don't want to hurt you or him. That's the last thing I want. Listen, can I meet him? I'd like to meet him. I'm just outside Dad's at the minute, but—'

Abe... He had another conversation or twenty coming then. 'Sorry, I didn't mean to push. I just— How is he? How did you manage…?' His voice trailed off. 'Are you with anyone?'

She huffed out a breath. 'Since I admitted I hadn't slept with anyone since you left me for dust, barefoot and pregnant, I guess I don't need to answer that. Meeting

Aidan is another matter. I'll need to think on it. I have to think about him. He's gone through a lot recently.'

She sounded angry, guarded, and he couldn't blame her. He wanted to reply but he was too busy trying to get his size ten foot out of his mouth. He needed the next words to be clear, and to come out right.

'Annabel, I didn't mean it like that. I guess I'm just adjusting. I do have things to tell you though, a lot of things. Can we meet—just us, I mean? Without Aidan.' Just hearing him saying his name felt weird. 'Aidan.' He said it again. 'I like his name.'

'I don't think we should. Listen, you're working with me tomorrow; we'll have a lot to get through.' Harry heard a beep on the line, and Annabel spoke again. 'I have to go, I have another call. It's Aidan, I'm due to pick him up from his friend's house. I should go.'

'Wait…er…' He didn't know what he was going to say, but he had to get it out. 'You don't want me to see him, do you?'

Her hesitation made his heart stop. She didn't want him to meet her son. Their son. He'd really screwed everything up.

You're an idiot, Harry. What did you expect? The red carpet treatment? Two years of treatment and follow-ups, five years in remission, and almost a year to pack up his old life. All time away from his little family. All for nothing. He'd lost everything all over again. And more.

He held his breath, waiting for her next words.

'No,' she said eventually. 'I didn't tell you about Aidan expecting anything. You came back, so you needed the facts. That's it. Nothing more. We have a life, Harry. One that doesn't involve you. I told myself I would tell you the truth if I ever saw you again.'

She paused for a minute, trying and failing to keep her voice steady. She couldn't let him in now; she just couldn't bear the risk. She wouldn't survive another Harry heartbreak. 'You are my past, Harry, and I want you to stay that way. I'll see you in the morning, ready to work.'

She could feel herself start to cry again, and she ended the call before he could respond. There, she'd done it. She'd been true to her son, and herself.

When Aidan had been born, Tom was her birth partner. Her friends had been there for the whole pregnancy. Abe had been the parent she needed. Her shock about the baby and disappointment at Harry had been tangible, and she'd kept her distance from the deeper conversations. They'd all just circled each other: Annabel broken-hearted, reeling from the news that she was expecting, Abe helping her where he could in practical terms. He'd even told the station that she was in a position to take the job. To their credit, they'd pulled together as a team through her maternity leave, and when she was ready the job was hers to step back into. As hard as that was, with a baby to raise and a career to keep on track.

She'd almost folded and told Abe the truth so many times. Aidan was his grandson after all. He had played the role since Aidan was a baby bump, but she'd never told him they were blood. With her friends and colleagues, it had been slightly easier. She hated pity and that would have been one big party. Annabel herself had never thought that way, not once she'd held Aidan in her arms in that hospital room. Tom had gone home to rest, and he and Lloyd were coming to collect her and the baby later that afternoon. She had the support, the friends, the family.

Abe had scooped her up that day at the airport and had been steadfastly on her side ever since. If he had been speaking to Harry, that would be a different matter. She wouldn't have put Abe in that position, but they'd fallen out before Aidan left for Dubai. Abe was stubborn in many ways, and he had never hidden the fact that he'd wanted Harry to become a GP, take the practice on after his retirement.

She didn't know if they'd ever spoken after those first few months of getting radio silence, and she knew never to ask. It wasn't fair on Abe to do so. That was down to Harry too. He'd walked away from them all without a backwards glance. He'd never even told his friends.

When she'd looked at the newborn child in her arms, the child who looked so much like her now, she'd promised him that he would never be left behind. She'd promised herself that day in the maternity ward that if Harry ever surfaced again she would tell him about his son, but that would be it. He wouldn't be given any opportunities to wreck the boy's life as he had theirs. Not a chance. She knew what having a wayward father did to a child, she'd experienced it first-hand, and the toll it had taken on her mother. Aidan knew that his dad wasn't around, that his mummy loved him very much. All true. Till now.

The questions would get harder as he grew, she knew, and they had, but that was the promise she'd made that day, and even though she'd questioned her decision many times over the years, she'd stuck to it. She wasn't the one who didn't know how to treat people, or to honour the promises she made. Aidan knew he had a father. He just didn't know him. He was an abstract part of his life, and Annabel wasn't about to confuse him by telling him the truth.

Harry was back to work tomorrow at the station and work they would. Hell, she'd been through worse times lately. Like the night she'd called Harry and begged him to come home, almost confessing her love for him still. He'd ruined that second chance too.

CHAPTER TWO

Six months earlier...

ANNABEL TOOK ANOTHER swig of her drink and gripped the phone tight. She was more than tiddly now, and she was grateful for the numb sensation it provided. She never would have got the courage to call otherwise. Her inhibitions were well and truly lowered.

'Sometimes I despise you for leaving me here alone, to face all of this. When I'm tired, or on days like today. I needed you today, more than I ever have since you left. I really needed you and guess what, you weren't there!'

She flicked her glass around her, gesturing wildly and splashing some of the contents down herself. Aidan had been given the all-clear after his fall in the school gym, and Tom was staying with him that night in the hospital to give her the night off before he came home. His head injury had been terrifying, but with the fear and worry, adrenalin had kicked in. Once Aidan was in the clear and was due home, all that had left Annabel and instead of relief she'd felt sad. And angry. Both aimed at Harry.

When Aidan had hit his head, it had crossed her

mind that her son might die. She saw it all the time in her job. People took a little tumble and that was it. Lights out. Then she'd thought of Harry, miles away and utterly unaware that his son could have died. A son he didn't even know about. Instead of getting showered and going straight to bed, she'd opened a bottle of something strong instead, and the swirl of guilt had wrapped itself around her mind again. He should be here to see his son. She'd picked up the phone and dialled his number. She had a lot to say, even if it was into a voicemail void.

'Sometimes, you know, I have whole conversations with you in my head. I lie awake some nights, tearing a strip off you mentally. But what's the point, eh? You never hear me. You won't even get this. You probably didn't get any of the messages we sent. I doubt you even kept your old number. I don't even know why I bothered. Nostalgia, probably. It's been a funny kind of week. An awful, scary week. If you do ever get this, Harry—' Sigh. 'Come home. Just come home. You've missed out on so much already. You'll never know just how much. It could have been so different, you know? I—' Even in her haze, she stopped herself short of telling him about Aidan. It wasn't something she wanted to tell him in a message over the phone. The thought of never knowing whether he'd heard it would be too much for her to take and obsess over.

'Just please…come home. I still lo— I want you to come home. I don't want some phone call to say you're sorry. It means nothing. Just…just get here. Be here for the people that need you, Harry.'

Clicking the off button with an unsteady hand, she pushed the phone away from her on the table. Even in her drunken state, she knew that she'd just dropped the ball. Or, more like, an epic clanger. She'd meant every word, but she'd never gone as far as actually telling him that. She had never let herself get that low, that weak before. She felt as if she'd just rolled over and showed him her soft underbelly. The same spot that she usually kept covered with her daily applied armour. She hated herself a little for it. Thank God she was too drunk to call him again and take it all back. She'd shown enough weakness for one day.

Sitting in her flat, she wondered to herself how things had got so bad. How the girl standing in that airport wouldn't recognise the life she now had. And she couldn't one hundred per cent attest to the fact that the old her would have done things differently. Now, after almost losing her son to a stupid slip at school, she couldn't seem to be anything but mad. Mad that she was doing everything on her own. Dealing with the guilt she felt over her decision to keep the two people she cared about the most apart. Not all times were bad, after all. Many, if not most, of her happy memories pre-Aidan involved Harry, and Tom and some of the others on the team that had stuck around after qualifying.

She tortured herself wondering what Harry had been doing all this time. Was he even still in Dubai? For all she knew, he was married now. Had his own family to look after. How would Aidan fit into that? She didn't want another mother helping to raise her child. It was another one of the reasons she'd never told him. The more time that passed, the harder it might be.

Harry heard Annabel end the call, the line clicking off in his ear as he stood in the night. His father's house was right in front of him, his old estate car still sitting in the drive. Everything looked the same, if a little smaller. It felt smaller to him, but at this moment in time he didn't trust his eyes. He was still reeling from the bombshell that Annabel had dropped on him.

I have a baby son. No, he was nearly eight years old now. Hardly a baby. There'd been no sign that Annabel was pregnant before he'd left for Dubai. He knew she was telling the truth, but it didn't help him any. Now, instead of just feeling the shame and regret of walking out on his life, he also had to reconcile the fact that he'd missed out on meeting his son. Of course Annabel didn't want him to meet him. Why would she? He'd done nothing in the last near decade that would give her any reason or inclination to do so.

He'd walked away to protect Annabel, and that had meant cutting everyone else off too. It had been the only way. And now he was cowering outside his father's house, wondering what the hell he was going to walk into this time. What would his father say about this? He'd obviously kept his own call from Annabel too. Whether that was to protect her or his wayward son, he had no idea. He guessed he was about to find out.

Six months ago, he'd picked up the drunken message from Annabel. He'd been on shift, and when he checked his pocket and saw the missed call he could have wept. From fear or happiness, he didn't know. Then panic had set in. She'd stopped calling years ago—why call now? When he saw she'd left a voicemail he'd rung his father straight away, not wanting to listen to the news that she must have been calling about. Bad news from home. That must have been why she'd called. Given the fact that they'd both grown up for the most part with one parent and no other family other than the one they'd made for themselves, it was easy to make the connection. She was obviously just passing on some unavoidable item of news. Why else would she be calling, right?

When his dad had answered he'd felt more than relief. He'd also felt a sudden longing deep within him, a feeling that if he could have clicked his fingers to be transported back home, he would have. When his surprised dad had rung off, seemingly believing his son when he'd said he just wanted to say hello, that he'd been thinking about him, the feeling hadn't left him. He was healthy now. He was cancer free, all signed off. He'd built a life in Dubai. He had friends, even been on the odd date or two. It was a life but, hearing from the two ghosts from his past that still seemed to haunt him, he realised that he was done in Dubai. Infertility be damned. He wanted out. When he played the voicemail from Annabel, basically berating him for not being there, begging him to come home, he knew what he had to do. He'd called his dad back.

'Hello?'

'Hi, Dad. It's me again. Listen, I lied just now. Annabel called me.'

He heard the television being turned down in the background, and his father spoke again.

'Well, I didn't think you just rang to say hello after all this time of ignoring us. What did she say?'

'She told me off, basically.'

Abe chuckled. 'Sounds about right. What else?' he pressed.

'Nothing. She told me to come home. She said I should be there for the people I left behind.'

'She's got a point, son. Took you a while. Did she sound okay?'

'I think she might have been a little drunk, sad maybe. Everything okay back home?'

Abe sighed, a deep sigh that filled the silence between them. 'She's had better times, but it's not for me to say. What are you going to do? It's obviously rattled you. Are you okay?'

'Yeah, I'm okay. I stayed in Dubai. I don't know what to say. Is anything I say going to make up for what I did?'

'With me? Ah, son, I'm just glad to hear you're alive. You're not asking about me, though. What are you going to do about Annabel?'

'I'm going to listen to her, Dad. I'm going to get the next flight back.'

'No son, that's not a good idea. Not now. Not on impulse.'

'What do you mean, not now?'

Another sigh. His dad was being cagey, and about a thousand scenarios ran through Harry's mind.

'Is she getting married or something, is that what this is? Is she sick?' The big C word swam round his head. It had taken enough from their lives, but cancer didn't care how many times it took a bite out of a family.

'No, son, no. Nothing like that. Listen, you just dropping in for a flying visit is going to do more harm than good, believe me. I think you know that, if you're honest with yourself. Have you thought this through? She rang you for weeks, Harry, after you left her like that. You put that girl through hell. One call from her now and you're ready to come back. What's happened?'

Harry bit the corner of his lip. 'Nothing, Dad. Listen, back then…it was complicated. I was a different person. A stupid, scared and immature person. Don't you want me to come home?'

'I never wanted you to leave in the first place.' There was a snap in his tone.

'I know, Dad, I know that. Listen, can we not fight?'

Abe sighed. 'I don't want to fight, son. I regret that fight so much. I feel like I pushed you to go to Dubai, to get away from your old man.' He sighed heavily. 'I know I pushed you too hard, but it was only ever meant with love. Son, I want the best for you. And Annabel. You're still working, right? I assume you have a contract?'

Harry gripped the phone tight, looking around the locker room he was standing in. 'Yeah, I have a few months left on this one.'

'Well, then. You have obligations. You can't just up and leave. It's not the best time. Let things calm down a while, okay?'

'Dad, are you sure about this? Do I call her or what? Are you sure she's okay?'

'Yes, son, and I wouldn't call her. It's not the right time. Your first meeting can't be on the phone. There's too much to say. Trust me, I want to help you, but listen to me. Stay where you are. Let's talk again soon, okay?'

Harry sighed, the adrenalin from the call leaving him. 'Okay, Dad. Listen, I'd better go. I'm not finished on shift yet, and my break's nearly over.'

'Okay, son, you take care. Remember what I said. And Harry?'

'Yeah, Dad?'

'It's really nice to hear your voice, son. Don't leave it so long next time.'

Harry promised to call again soon, feeling homesick and torn in half with his emotions. This was why he'd never called before. Ignoring people's existence didn't make you want to hop on a flight home. Hearing his father's voice, and Annabel's, all in one night had torn down the defences he'd built up all these years. Denial and hiding were wonderful things, but it only took a small chink in the armour to show the cracks.

He'd stayed away for so many reasons, but he realised now he just had to take his shot. He had to go home, to put the past to bed if nothing else. He didn't want to be an old man full of regrets. He'd done the deathbed revelations. When the treatment had made him weak and scared, all he'd wanted was his family around him. He didn't want to be there again, years from now, with nothing but empty chairs around him.

The next day he gave notice on his job and made plans to come back to London. It was time. Annabel wanted him to come home, and he wanted to be there. He didn't tell his dad. With his notice period, he figured enough dust would have settled. He couldn't wait any more. He'd wasted enough time already. He had to take his shot, try to get the life he wanted back. He just didn't know at the time what that would look like. Certainly not discovering that he was a father—something he'd long given up on. He had to face his father too, which was an ordeal in itself. He felt weighed down more than usual with the guilt of disappointing the people he loved the most.

He was still standing on his father's front path when

he saw the curtains start to twitch in the neighbouring properties. Abe still lived in the house connected to his GP practice and he ran the place like a small village surgery, not like one of the many larger health centres in the big smoke. He was all about the people, and the care he could give to them. He lived and breathed their little community and had meant to keep it in the family. With a reluctant and unwilling son, that was never going to happen. They had had an uneasy relationship for years before Harry left. Made even more awkward by him leaving as he had.

They'd not spoken since the call home, but he had emailed his dad a couple of times. Just to say hello, nothing about coming home. He didn't want Abe to talk him out of it or tell Annabel. He had wanted to come home and see her for himself, but that had gone out of the window the second Frank Jessop had hit the deck.

Swallowing hard and trying not to look too suspicious to the neighbours, he started to walk up the path towards the main house. He was just about to knock when the door opened, and there was Abe. The two men eyed each other for a long moment and then Harry saw the handset in his father's hand. Lifting the receiver to his ear, he smiled for the person on the phone as he spoke, but the look he fixed his son with didn't convey any joy.

'I'd better let you go, love. No, no….' he placated the person on the phone, moving aside to allow his son to enter the house. The lamp in the hallway lit his way and Harry walked in, letting his father finish his conversation while he looked around the place. Abe didn't exactly keep office hours; some of his patients rang him to discuss soap operas, or to ask about their latest health niggle. Abe's door was always open. Ever the medical professional. Like father, like son in that respect, if not much else.

The house looked much the same. The decor had been changed, sure, but Abe's knick-knacks were all still there. The stack of books on his side table, science fiction and medical journals, mostly. The TV was on in the corner, a soap opera paused on the screen; the mug of tea on the coffee table was still steaming. It seemed Abe had already been interrupted from his quiet evening.

He could hear his father speaking in hushed tones in the kitchen, but Harry didn't try to listen. His attention had been distracted anyway, by a collection of photos that he hadn't seen before, all framed and in pride of place on the mantelpiece above the old coal fire. Another thing Abe was known for. His reluctance for change outside the world of medicine was legendary. The man would lick a yoghurt pot clean rather than waste a drop, and he hated technology in the home. He also wasn't one for photos, but his collection had grown by the looks of things.

Harry smiled to himself as he looked closer at the photo of the three of them on Brighton beach, years back when he was a young kid who'd dreamed of being a superhero in medical clothing. Abe, his mother and he were all huddled together, wrapped in a towel and wet from their dip in the sea. It was one of his favourite memories of his mother, of them together. Abe had been different back then too. Funnier, more at ease.

Perhaps Mum was the one that held us together too. Without her, we were both a bit lost.

He could hear Abe ending his call, talking about meeting up the next day.

Still just as committed.

Harry smiled to himself. Some things never changed. He went to put the photograph back on the mantelpiece and his gaze fell to the one sitting next to it. It was of Abe, holding a fishing rod and seemingly laughing his head off on the pier. A young boy was waggling a crab at him, no fear showing on his cute little face. It wasn't an old photo, and the boy wasn't him. They had done that over the years, but he didn't recognise the boy. He looked familiar somehow.

A voice behind him almost made him drop the frame. 'So, you came home then.'

Abe was standing in the doorway now, in his uniform of shirt and tie, the phone still in his hand. His expression was closed off, and he looked tired.

'Yeah, I did. I thought I'd come say hello.' He gave himself a moment. 'I'm starting at the old station in the morning. Permanently.'

To his credit, Abe didn't react. He didn't drop the phone or ask fifty-five questions about what Harry had been doing for the best part of the last decade. Or why in the last six months he hadn't bothered to mention that he was returning home. In fact, he didn't say much at all. He just stood there, staring at Harry as though he were a mirage.

'Nothing to say?' Harry tried, feeling the familiar sting of rejection. He wasn't a child any more, but it hurt that his relationship with his father was so stilted. With a pang, he realised that he had repeated the pattern, albeit unknowingly. His son was seven years old and he didn't even know his father.

Harry felt his head drop, the long flight and the events of the day catching up with him. His dad walked right up to him and pulled him into a hug. Harry was shocked for a moment, but wrapped his arms around him and hugged him tight. Abe was clinging onto him tightly, patting his back as the two men held each other. Pulling away, his dad smiled at him.

'I'm glad you're back, son. I really am.' He pulled him back in for another hug, and Harry felt the sting of tears.

'Me too, Dad.' Eventually, Abe released him, walking past him into the lounge. Instead of sitting back in his chair, he walked up to the liquor cabinet, putting the phone down and reaching for his best whisky. Harry didn't move till his father was holding out a full crystal glass tumbler in his direction. They both sat down, Abe in his chair and Harry on the couch. As he sat back, he felt something stab him. Something sharp. Reaching behind him, he pulled out a plastic dinosaur. He laughed, putting it on the arm of the sofa.

'Patients still coming in for a cuppa, eh? Someone's missing a Velociraptor.'

Abe sat back in his chair, taking a deep sip of his drink before eyeing his son again. He nodded to the photo Harry had just been looking at.

'It belongs to that little boy. He's mad on dinosaurs.' Another moment of awkward silence. 'So, you're staying for good? No fancy job to go back to?'

Harry felt like laughing as he considered his father's words. If only he knew how fancy it hadn't been at times. How he'd helped save lives in the sticky heat, after battling for his own life. It wasn't all sand and opulence. He'd worked hard, saved up, kept a low profile. He'd stuck to the plan, to create a career. Spent many nights in his bed, thinking of the woman he'd left behind. Wishing she was there, sleeping beside him. Smiling at him over the breakfast table. Dragging him to see the sights on their days off. She'd been a ghost in Dubai, always following him wherever he went.

No other woman compared to her. In his mind, he'd never completely left her. He'd just walked away from everything else. With the job and his cancer, it had been all he could take. All he could focus on. He hadn't wanted Annabel to deal with all that. He didn't want her to derail her life and end up as a nursemaid to him. Looking back, he realised that he hadn't been expecting to survive it. The thought of dying and leaving her out there all alone had seemed much worse than leaving her behind back then. Now it seemed, had he taken her with him, they would have been going through it with a pregnancy to worry about too.

He looked at the dinosaur on the edge of the couch, picking it up and running his thumbnail along its back.

'Nope, I'm back for good.'

'You got a place to live yet?' Ever the pushy father.

'No, Dad, not yet. I'm booked into one of the airport hotels till I find somewhere. It's been a bit of a day.' He turned the little brown figure around in his hand.

I wonder what Aidan likes to play with. I don't know a thing about him. Will I ever?

Saying it had been a bit of a day was downplaying things, just a bit.

'I bet it has. Too busy to call home first, give us a heads-up?'

Us? Who was that on the phone? Are the jungle drums already banging away?

'You don't need a hotel.' Abe motioned in the direction of the staircase with the glass in his hand. The ice tinkled against the tumbler. 'Your room's right there. Cancel the reservation, stay here.' He cleared his throat. 'You should be close for work, you know. It's fine, I have the room.'

He was trying to play it down now, but Harry was really touched by the sentiment. He kept fiddling with the dinosaur, his dad now pressing play on the television and settling back down in his chair. After the show had ended and they still hadn't said anything, Harry decided to talk.

'I came back because of Annabel's call, Dad. She told me I'd ducked out of life for long enough, and she was right. I know you said it wasn't good to come back then, but I waited. I worked my notice; I gave up my place. I'm back. I even got my old job back.'

Abe side-eyed him, his eyes narrowing to slits when he saw the little plastic toy in Harry's hand. 'Is that all you came back for? Don't go breaking that either. It belongs to Aidan.'

Harry's eyes snapped to his. His fist clenched around the dinosaur toy. 'What did you just say?'

Abe sighed and, shaking his head at his son, he dropped his head. 'Cut the crap, son. The dinosaur is Aidan's. The boy in the photo is Annabel's son. He calls me Granddad. Catch up.' Before Harry could even try to retort, Abe had turned the television up again.

Harry looked at him, aghast. Looking from his father to the mantelpiece, he studied the photo. It was Annabel staring back at him. He could see it now. The little boy had her hair, her look. He stood and picked up the photo, looking at the others and seeing Aidan there too. The photos were all of Aidan. Aidan and his mum. Aidan and Abe. Aidan in his first school uniform.

He recognised Annabel's flat in the background, the one she had once shared with her mother. It was all here, his life laid out. Somehow, Annabel had raised this child without him, without even telling anyone the truth. He felt a stirring of anger, but he knew deep down it was misplaced. How could he be mad at her after everything? He knew Annabel well enough to know that she would have made Aidan her priority. He couldn't hate her for that. He loved her for it.

He wanted to shout at his dad though, for not calling him. He'd known all along, judging from the photographs. The similarities were obvious. Why hadn't he picked up the phone? He had so many questions, but one shouted loudest in his head. Turning to his dad, he clenched his jaw.

'Why didn't you tell me?'

Abe jumped at his words, and the television was swiftly turned off. Turning to look at him, his face determined now, he walked over to his son and embraced him in another hug. Harry being so much bigger than he, Abe chose to wrap his arms around Harry's waist. He squeezed him tight.

'Annabel never told me, but I knew. I'm not stupid, I did the math. We weren't exactly on speaking terms, were we? She told everyone a story, and she had no one in her corner. I love that boy; Aidan is the best thing you ever did. It made losing you that bit more bearable, if I'm honest. I missed you, son. I regret so much of our time together. I'm so sorry I was so pushy. I should have been a better father, but being a grandfather is the best thing ever. I was there for him, and he knows about you. I've told him so many stories about you over the years. I wanted to tell you, but it wasn't my decision. Can you forgive me?'

Harry looked at his dad, and nodded slowly. 'I get it, Dad. I don't like it, but I get it. How can I make any of this right?'

'You ask that very question, son, you ask that very question.' Patting him on the back like he used to when he was a boy, Abe gripped his hand tight. 'Welcome home, son. We have some work to do.'

Annabel Sanders was a shadow of her former self the next morning as she walked into work. She'd barely got a wink of sleep, moving from side to side in the king-size bed she'd splurged on as a housewarming present to herself. Aidan's room was finished, the first room she'd tackled as soon as she'd got the keys to her dream house. It wasn't a shiny new-build on some labyrinth estate, but very much a fixer-upper. Maud, the old lady who'd lived there for many years, had passed the year before and with the life insurance her mother had left her and almost all her savings it was just about enough. She'd bought Elm House, the very house she'd walked and driven past growing up. The one she and Harry had once dreamed of buying together. That would be another awkward conversation.

I hope he doesn't read anything into it. We are definitely done. We were done the minute he boarded that plane. So what if he still makes my stomach flip? That's just chemistry. It will fizzle out.

She headed into Reception, using her key card to buzz through to the main ambulance station. As soon as she walked in she was switched on, all business.

She ran the handover, the meeting room full of incoming staff, ready to work. It had been a quiet night all in all, but there had been reports of some gang-related tensions in the area. Often this meant injuries, RTAs. They liaised with the police regularly and kept their eyes and ears open.

She was just addressing the team on the issue when the door at the back of the room opened and in slid Harry. A couple of people looked to the door to see who had entered, and a few more did a double-take. One of the nurses, Purdie, was one of them and the glance she flashed Annabel almost made her garble her words. She kept it short and professional, eager to both get on with the calls and get out of the spotlight. She looked at Harry, and he was watching her. He had a small smile on his face and when their eyes locked she felt her mouth go dry. It felt as if her tongue had doubled in size. She took a breath and dismissed her team.

'Let's get out there, guys. Stay vigilant, and let's have a good day.' People were just starting to leave when she spoke again. 'Carter.' She addressed him by his surname, as their colleagues often did in work hours, as a quick shorthand, looking at him and acknowledging him. 'You're with me. Ambulance seventeen.' She figured it was better to get off on the right foot. Show the people she worked with that Harry was just another staff member to her and she was still in control. Try to cut the gossip short before it engulfed her whole.

Harry pushed away from his leaning position against the wall, and it was then she noticed that he was in full uniform. She'd not even noticed it when he'd walked in; all she had focused on was his face. She swallowed down the wave of nostalgia as she kept her eyes on his. She couldn't read him, and it irritated her. Even after all the years that had separated them, she'd always thought that she would be able to read him.

What is he thinking, after our conversation? Is he going to let it drop?

'No problem, Sanders.' He said it easily, fitting back into his old role as easily as she did hers for the onlookers around them, even though their locked eyes said differently to each other. The room was full, thick with murmurs. Neither of them heard any of them. They just stared at each other.

Is he trying to read me too?

She returned his curt nod, and then the moment was broken. He was gone.

What is it about that man? I can't help but watch him leave. And wish he would come back.

People were on the move and he was swallowed by uniforms and the swish-swish of the doors. Annabel was still looking when they swished closed for the final time. With a sigh, she started to head out when she noticed Purdie was still in her seat. Purdie was the bones of this place, even more than Annabel was. She was one of the best, and she never missed a blessed trick. She'd run the admissions ward when she'd first started there and then the cancer ward floor, and her nurses all adored her. She covered A&E on her days off, attending the briefings when she was on her overtime shifts. They ran like a tight, happy little ship. If Purdie had been a mama bear, they would all have been her cubs. Whether they liked it or not.

Annabel kept an eye on the door, trying to stride

purposefully across the room on jelly legs, but Purdie stopped her as soon as she was in reach.

'Did you know he was coming?' she asked, straight to the point as ever.

'Did my shocked expression give me away?'

Purdie raised her dark eyebrows, reaching for Annabel's hand and pulling her down in the seat next to her.

'Thanks,' Annabel replied, her voice dull and flat. 'I think I'm about to keel over.'

'He's working here now, with you?'

Annabel could barely bring herself to nod. Her face felt numb, as if she couldn't control her expression any more.

'Well, I'll be... Takes a lot to shock me, but...' Purdie slapped her free hand on her thigh and covered her friend's hand with hers. 'Take a minute, catch your breath.'

The two women sat in silence, staring into space as they processed the news together.

'He looks good though, right? That tan, that hair?' She laughed a little, and Annabel snorted. 'Oh, come on, even you can admit he looks well. It's good to see. He's been in Dubai this whole time?'

Another numb-faced nod. 'I think so. Who knows?'

Purdie nodded. 'He's here alone?' Her voice was delicate now, measured.

'I don't know that either.' She hadn't even thought about it, but the phone call came screaming back to her. 'Yes, actually, I think he is.'

He came to talk to me, and I blindsided him with the news about Aidan. He didn't exactly give the impression that he had a wife and kids in tow. That's something to be grateful for. Because of how compli-

cated things are, she lied to herself. *Not that I care either way.*

'Not about the work then, eh? Well, that changes things.'

Annabel frowned. 'How?'

Purdie put her arm around Annabel's shoulder and drew her in. Annabel went willingly, resting her head on her friend's shoulder. She smelled like Purdie always did. Comforting. Motherly.

'Believe me, my girl, that boy is back with a purpose in that head of his. If he's here alone, he's come to find something, not leave it behind.'

'He came for a job. Tom's job.'

Purdie laughed louder this time, her whole body jiggling with mirth and making Annabel's frazzled head bounce on her shoulder.

'If you think that man came all this way just to work here, looking at you the way he just did, then I have a feeling that we'll be having lots more conversations like these.'

Annabel groaned, burying her head further into the nurse's shoulder, and Purdie's deep, rich laughter filled the empty room once more.

'Great, I can't wait,' she said sarcastically, and Purdie laughed again.

'Things happen for a reason, child. I keep telling you that. You'll see.'

Annabel had a feeling that whatever was going to happen, she wouldn't really have a chance to avoid it anyway. What a pair they were, both ostriches with their heads in the hot Dubai sand. She needed a minute before she started her awkward day, cramped up in the ambulance with her old childhood sweetheart, the air thick between them like London smog.

'I guess I will,' she muttered, burying deeper into her friend's embrace.

Sitting in the front of the ambulance with Harry felt like stepping into a time machine. She could smell his aftershave as she buckled herself in, and it took all her concentration to focus on putting on her seatbelt without giving away how much she was dreading their first shift back together. Her two worlds were starting to collide, and not only had she not seen it coming, she'd even pushed them together herself.

Telling Harry about Aidan was something she had tortured herself over for the longest time. Every time she saw Abe with Aidan, it was on the tip of her tongue to blurt out that Granddad wasn't just an honorary title, especially after all the support Abe had shown her since Harry left. It was a blood connection too. If Aidan had looked like a mini Harry the decision would have been made for her, but with him taking after her in the looks department she'd continued to lie. For a while there, she'd almost believed her own version of events. A one-night stand with a man who had vaporised into thin air. It was half true, so she'd made peace with it. Now Harry was back, and she had a feeling he was about to open a can of worms.

Her own feelings aside, she needed Aidan to be okay through all this. She needed to protect her son. That was the driving force behind the lie in the first place. After the time off school recovering from his injury, and the house move, the last thing the poor lad deserved was to get to know a person who wouldn't be around in a few months. She didn't know why Harry had come back, and that was keeping her up at night too. It had been six months since that disastrous phone call. He'd hardly thrown some clothes into a case and raced to the airport after her call, had he? She'd tossed and turned, thinking about the awkward day that lay ahead, and spent hours staring at the ceiling, worrying if she'd done the right thing by coming clean.

Aidan had been his usual full-of-beans self this morning, and she'd caught herself comparing him with the new Harry. The tanned stranger who had turned her life upside down for the second time. She'd never told anyone the truth about Aidan's parentage. She'd ridden out the stares and the whispered comments from those around her, judging her for sleeping with some stranger so soon after Harry had left. The obvious suspicions of those who knew her best. As her belly grew, more and more people asked questions, and she'd answered them all with a smile on her face. She knew the truth, and because people already blamed Harry for walking out she hadn't wanted the pity or stupid comments around her son.

She guessed, deep down, she hadn't wanted them to hate Harry any more either. Being in love with the man who'd left you pregnant and broken-hearted frankly sucked. She'd pitied herself enough; she didn't need any more from the people around her.

She didn't want to be that person ever again, feeling lost and out of control. It was directly at odds with her work persona. Over the years, the story had never changed from her lips, and gradually the questions stopped. Everyone at the station loved Aidan, and she was happy.

Am I? Today, I'm just not sure. I need sleep. That's it. It's the shock and the night of tossing the pillows on and off my bed.

She'd thought that Abe suspected something, back in those first few weeks when she did nothing but cry on his couch, her hormones making her heartbreak feel that much worse. He had never once asked about the father or told her that Aidan needed a father. He was the one person who had never shown anything but excitement and love for Aidan, and those things grew once Aidan was born. He had been a grandfather to Aidan from day one, and with him and her friends she'd muddled through those first sleep-deprived months, and had childcare backup when she went back to work. Once her friend Teri was on board, having just had her own son Finn, she had a little army of willing carers to enable her to navigate those first few years.

Annabel tried to shake off her strange mood, looking across at Harry. He was strapped in, his body turned away from her as he looked out of the window. He looked relaxed, his back against the seat, his hands in his lap. To anyone else, he would have looked positively serene, but Annabel still knew his tells. The hands on his lap weren't still; he was tapping his fingers together, an old sign that he was feeling the tension.

Good, she thought, her old resentment waking her up. *You should suffer, Harry.*

Abe had an old saying; he'd told her it often over the years. *What doesn't kill you builds character.* Well, she'd had enough character-building for one lifetime. She was happy, she'd made peace with the past, as much as you could when you got ghosted by the love of your life. She *was* happy, till the minute she'd set eyes on him. Now, everything seemed skewed, off-kilter. As if he'd come back from the dead and no one had batted an eyelid.

Even Tom had been quiet on the subject since. Although preparing to be new parents meant he and Lloyd were really busy. Her problems weren't theirs, after all. Life went on. With her job, she knew how fragile life could be, how short and cruel sometimes too. She wished her mother were here to talk to. To talk about Harry coming back. She swallowed down the pain she felt and turned her mind back to the job.

'Ready to green up?' she asked, her finger on the button that told the station they were ready to take calls. 'We have Hillingdon today but, given the nightshift, we might have to switch things around.'

Harry turned away from the window. His hands stilled in his lap. 'I'm good to go. It might take me a minute to get acclimatised again, but I'm good.'

'Anything you're rusty on, just shout. I'll be the lead today anyway.'

He pointed out of the window at the road beyond the car park. 'Oh, it's not the medicine, more the location. It might take me a second to navigate around the old place.'

Old place. Wow, that was like a bullet to the heart. Arrogant too. Not the old Harry.

'Well, luckily, I still know the streets like the back of my hand.' She pressed the button, pulling out of the station because she just couldn't stand sitting there any longer. 'And I don't need a co-pilot.'

'Ambulance seventeen, request for help, Hillingdon, on the estate.'

Annabel looked up to the sky when the address was read out. It was on the next street from her old flat, and she felt as if her dear old mum was messing with her from above. Their first meeting had been at the airport, and now this.

The patient was Phyllis, a new ambulance service regular. She was in early dementia; home care nurses came twice a day and her husband Jerry was well able to care for her. They only called for help when she fell, which was becoming more and more frequent as her condition worsened. Jerry couldn't lift her on his own, and falls in the elderly could be much more serious than they first looked. Picking up the radio handset, she radioed back that they were en route and flicked on the sirens and lights.

As they were heading towards the estate Annabel's new house loomed into view and she felt as if her heart might stop. The sold sign was still up out front, with no signs of life in the windows. The skip she'd hired for the building rubbish was sitting outside, half full. She saw Harry's head whip back to look as they sped past.

'The old house finally sold on, eh? Maud passed away? That's sad. Bless her.'

'Huh?' She turned the next corner, nodding to a driver who gave way to let them through. 'What house?' She felt as if her ears were on fire with the effort of acting dumb. Her whole face felt flushed. Catching sight of herself in the side mirror as she checked the traffic, all she saw were her own panicked eyes staring back at her.

'*The* house. From when we were kids—don't you remember?'

'Oh. Yeah, I remember. It might be better to concentrate on the job though.'

'Gotcha. All business.' He reached for the radio, telling the control desk that they had arrived at the address. As soon as she stopped the ambulance he was off into the back, pulling his kit on and grabbing the backboard. He didn't even acknowledge her, just headed to the door to the flats.

A worried-looking Jerry led the duo into the hallway of the flat, where Phyllis was now sitting up, smiling at Annabel.

'Hello!' she said jovially, giving them all a little wave. 'I can't get up.'

Jerry stepped to the side but stayed close by.

'I know, love. These are the paramedics, remember? They've come to help, and you remember Annabel.' Once upon a time, before she became ill, Phyllis had run the local nursery which Aidan had attended. She always seemed to remember her, even now. It helped, and when the calls came in they were usually given to Annabel if possible. It was easy to scare an already confused person just by being a stranger, especially one in uniform carrying scary-looking equipment.

'Annabel, how's the little fella doing?'

Annabel was standing right next to Harry, their shoulders brushed up against each other in the narrow space. She felt his body go rigid against her. As her brain scrambled for the right thing to say, she found herself wanting to tell him something about Aidan.

'He's great, Phyllis. He's loving his new bedroom and doing well at school. He says hello and sends his love.'

Phyllis beamed. 'He'll go far, that lad, I said, didn't I, Jerry? Footie still going well too?' Annabel was astonished at how good her memory was today. From Jerry's face, she could tell she wasn't the only one.

'Yeah, he's playing for the Hillingdon Wolves now, Under Eights.'

The same team his dad played for when they were kids. Harry had the chance to turn professional, but he'd chosen medicine.

'Is that true?' Harry whispered beside her, his nose tickling her ear accidentally as he leaned in. She couldn't suppress the shudder that he evoked, but she recovered herself quickly.

Work, Annabel, work.

'Yes,' she whispered back to him. 'I don't lie.'

She moved closer to her patient, offering her hand. 'Come on then, Phyllis, let's get you sorted and off that floor.'

It was almost lunchtime when they finished their latest job and clocked off to eat. A woman had cut herself in her kitchen. A slip of the knife and she was now in the hospital getting stitched up for a minor cut. The poor woman was more upset about messing up her planned wedding anniversary dinner. Her husband couldn't have cared less about the dinner; he had just arrived in A&E, suit crumpled, tie askew. He'd searched for her the second he'd walked through the doors and, seeing her, his face had relaxed and he'd dashed over, cursing the traffic that had kept him from her side and scooping her into his arms.

She and Harry had watched them for a little while, and then departed silently. Annabel had driven to the sandwich shop near the community centre, and they were now sitting in the car park, hot coffees in their hands, food in paper bags on their laps.

'Annie, can we talk?'

She swallowed down her coffee rather gracefully, considering he'd spoken just as she was taking a mouthful of Americano.

'It's Annabel these days, and yes, we can talk.'

'When I left, I—'

Annabel felt the blood leave her face. She couldn't talk about that, not yet. She didn't want to feel the sting of rejection again. Not till she had recovered from his return at least.

'No, not about that. I thought you meant about Aidan, or the job.' She risked looking at him now, and he was looking back at her. He looked wounded, and she hated herself for it.

'It's relevant to Aidan.' His jaw flexed and he took a long time to take his next drink of coffee. 'Why did you tell me about him if you don't want to talk about anything?'

'I didn't say I wanted to talk about the past, that's all. Can I not have a bit of time? I told you about Aidan because I always told myself if I saw you again, if you ever came back to London, I would tell you about him. You told me not to contact you, remember? You ignored me for weeks. You asked me to let you go. So I let go.' She bit her lip, mad at herself for breaking her own ruddy rule.

'You did contact me again though. Six months ago. You called me and told me to come home.' Annabel's sharp intake of breath caused his brow to furrow. 'I handed in my notice, but it took time.' He paused, as if to add something else, but shook his head as though dislodging the words from his throat. 'I was on a lengthy contract by then. I came home as soon as I could, Annie. I want to talk, about all of this. I'm staying with Dad now. I'm not far away.'

The last remark sent Annabel's eyebrows up to her hairline. 'Abe's letting you stay? Wow.'

Harry chuckled, but it died in his throat. 'Yeah, I was a bit surprised too.'

'He does know then.' She spoke her thoughts out loud, not able to stop them. 'About Aidan. He would have been straight on the phone if it was news to him.'

Harry nodded slowly. 'Yeah, he knows. I didn't tell him though. We spent half the night and his liquor cabinet last night talking about it.'

Annabel tried to speak but she felt as if someone had sat on her chest. 'Oh, what a mess,' was all she could croak out.

'You okay?'

He placed his hand on her arm but as soon as his fingertips touched her clothing, she pulled away infinitesimally.

'Is he…is he mad?' she choked out. 'I didn't want to keep it from him, but it was just easier at the time. I always thought that he just kind of knew. He's dealt with enough pregnant women to work out a due date.'

'No, of course he isn't. He loves being a granddad. He told me loads of stories about Aidan, when he was little. He could never be mad at you for giving him a grandchild. You should call him; he's not mad at all. He's pretty pleased, to be honest.'

'He's the best granddad,' she said, smiling now at the thought. 'Aidan adores him.'

Harry's face softened and he reached for her hand this time. She moved it away, taking out a sandwich to cover her snub. Harry clenched his fist for a second, and then reached for his own lunch.

'He knows why you did it. I understand too, though I don't like it. I also hate the thought that you were with someone else, even if he was imaginary. Was there really never a guy?'

The look of relief on his face when she shook her head made her stomach flip.

Don't start this game, missy. There's too much at stake to let him play with your emotions. You can bet the farm that he didn't spend his nights in bed, pining alone for the other half of himself.

'I won't ask the same about you,' she countered.

Another flex of the jaw from him.

'I had other things on my mind for a long time,' was all he gave her. 'And then I was busy with work. I went on a couple of dates, but it never came to anything. I wasn't looking. When I got your call, all I could think about was finishing my contract and getting back here. I just didn't expect this. I do want to see him though. I've seen photos of him at Dad's. He looks just like you.'

Annabel smiled, as she always did when someone mentioned her boy.

'Yeah, he does. He's got your stubborn streak though.' She laughed despite herself. It was so hard to be angry at him all the time. Just being around him made her head spin from annoyed to elated that this moment had come. She'd thought of telling him about Aidan so many times over the years, played the scenes out in her head. Not all of them were filled with recriminations and anger. Some ended with them running off into the sunset together.

He came back because I asked him to. The day our son was nearly lost.

'Aidan had an accident at school. He fell off some gym equipment. It was pretty bad for a few days; he had a head injury, swelling on the brain. The day I called you, it was the day I found out he was going to be okay.'

His face fell, and this time his hand wrapped around hers with hesitation. She let him be.

'He's okay now though?'

Annabel nodded, shocked to see how pale Harry had gone.

'Yes, he's fine. Fully recovered, thanks to the guys at the hospital. It just made me think, that's all. About if he'd died.' She stopped and clenched her teeth to stop herself from crying. 'I felt so guilty over the years, and I realised that he could have died without ever knowing about you, and you would never have known him.'

'Dad never told me a thing; I guess it wasn't his place. I'm so sorry, Annabel, that must have been awful. That's why you called me?'

'I'd had a little to drink. I guess I was a bit of a mess once the adrenalin wore off. I wanted you there.' She pressed her lips together.

'You wanted me there?' he echoed. His grip on her hand tightened. 'I'm sorry. It must have been hard. I wish I had been there. For all of it. I can't imagine how scary it must have been for you.'

She looked across at Harry, and he was white, his face a picture of pain.

'Hey, it's okay. It was tough, but we got through it. I guess I had a bit of latent rage afterwards, and I had a drink or five when I got home—'

'Rage?'

He was looking right at her now, his lips almost bloodless.

'Yeah, you know. Life's a cruel mistress, and I think I got mad. At myself more than anything. I couldn't help him and I felt powerless. Even with everything we do in this job, I couldn't do much but just be there.'

'I bet that was more than enough for Aidan. It's just what I would have wanted.'

She gave him a little smile and looked away. 'I was just so glad he came through it. You'd never know it happened now, to look at him. It's like a bad dream.'

She was downplaying it; he knew she would. He'd known as soon as he'd heard her voice on that voice-mail that she was in pain, that something was wrong with his girl. He'd almost called her back so many times, but he knew a phone call just wouldn't cut it, and for once he'd listened to his dad. He could tell she'd been drinking, and he didn't want her to take those words back. He'd wanted to be in front of her, even if it was only for her to take it back and tell him to leave again. He needed to be there, explain things. The truth was, since being cancer-free and getting the all-clear, he'd just been…waiting. For what he didn't know, until he'd got that call. Just hearing her voice told him to return home, and he wasn't done yet.

Now just wasn't the time to blindside her with a confession of his own. He couldn't tell her now; he couldn't risk shutting her down when she was finally starting to open up. He thought about the time when he was sick. When he'd wanted nothing more than her by his side, as selfish as he thought that notion was. Now, he saw that his actions had released her from caring for him, from derailing her life, but it had robbed them of so much time together. Time together that they might never have had. Still might never have, given her mistrust of him. The thought added another band of guilt around his heart. He'd believed he was setting her free to live her life, but he'd just missed out on being a family instead.

'I'm sorry about not being there, and I understand the rage you felt.'

Cancer was a silent stealer of many, many things. It might not have taken his life, but it had changed it forever in so many ways.

He took another bite of his lunch, wanting to choose his words as best he could. 'If I had known about Aidan, I would never have wanted to leave him. Leave either of you.'

'I know,' she retorted, surprising him. 'That's why I didn't tell you when I found out. You wanted that new life, and I didn't want to interfere with that. I want to listen to what you have to say, Harry, I just don't have the strength quite yet. And I might get mad and punch you in the face. It would make it awkward at work.' She flashed him a rueful grin, and his heart almost popped out of his chest.

Ah, Annie. You can never be mean for long. Not without feeling the need to cushion the blow. If someone robbed your purse in the street, you would find a way to give him a backstory. A reason why that person needed your money more than you did.

'So you covered for me, had our child, looked after my dad, and then got mad at me years later after a Chardonnay?'

She looked at him for a long moment and then

started to laugh. A slightly manic laugh that made Harry's heart swell.

'I missed that laugh.'

'It was whisky, not some chick drink, and yeah, you missed a lot.' The laughter stopped then, and her smile faded. She was already checking her watch, but Harry didn't want the moment to pass.

'I know I did, but I came back. I'm here for good now.' He flashed her his very best Harry smile, the one that she never could resist. Till now, it seemed, judging from her unamused facial expression. 'I know that we're not in a good place, but I think with me being back we can—'

He wanted to keep talking, to tell her that he'd come back for her, unable to think about anything else since she'd called, but she was already shaking her head.

'There is no "we", Harry. I know I told you about Aidan, but I'm not about to uproot our lives for you when you might not even be here in a few months.'

'The job's permanent, Annie.'

She flinched at his use of her shortened name, but he kept going.

She is my Annie.

'I came here to stay. I'm looking for a place. Hell, if I'd been here any sooner I would have bought our dream house. I've left Dubai for good, Annabel, and I do want to see Aidan. We have a lot to talk about. I'll wait till you're ready, but I mean what I say. I'm here. For good. For you both.'

She banged on the side window in frustration, and he fell silent. He'd pushed too far. He steeled himself for the punch in the face she'd joked about. Hell, he would take it if it meant getting closer to her.

'I don't think so, Harry. Can you imagine how upsetting it will be for him? I can't do it to the poor boy. He doesn't have much family; I can't risk it. He's still getting back into school, into his routine.' She almost blurted out about the move but stopped herself just in time.

'You don't have to risk anything. I'm his dad; I would never hurt him.'

Annabel snorted, throwing the rest of her sandwich back into her bag and sanitising her hands. 'You don't even know him, Harry! He doesn't know you're his dad!'

'Whose fault is that?'

'Yours! You left me there like an idiot that day. What was I supposed to do—hop on a plane with a baby bump and surprise you?'

'That would have been better than how I found out, yes, but no, I—'

'This is pointless,' she snapped at him, so hard she almost showed him her teeth like a cornered animal. 'You don't think I feel guilty enough, lying to everyone all this time? Lying to my son? Lunch is over anyway. You ready?'

Harry felt his eyes roll back in his head. 'I don't want to fall out.'

'Really? Well, you could have fooled me, Harrison.'

Damn it. She full-named me again. A sure-fire sign that she's mightily hacked off with me.

'We have to work together and that's hard enough, okay? I can't deal with anything else right now. I have a lot on, and I don't want Aidan upset.'

Harry stared straight ahead as she took the wrappers and walked out of the ambulance to put them in the nearby waste bin. She'd looked as if she wanted to take the door off with the slam she gave it, and he watched her as she stomped back over, her lips constantly moving. She was talking to herself, as she always used to when she was worked up. He knew this girl—this woman—so well, and being near her after all these years felt like torture. He just wanted to take her into his arms, tell her his truth. Not that he could now, not after the conversation they'd just shared. He could tell that reliving that memory had affected her, and he wanted to pick a better moment than when they'd just fought.

He'd give anything to see her light up again. Light up when she saw him. The smile she used to give him when he walked into a room never failed to floor him, make him want to thank his lucky stars that she loved him. Instead, she got back into the cab and, without even looking his way, she put them back on work duty. A call came in seconds later, and they were off. By the time the last call came in, any chance to restart their conversation seemed lost.

'Ambulance seventeen, you're the closest to this call. Woman, thirty-six, chest pains.'

Harry took down the details and Annabel threw on the sirens and lights and they raced to the scene.

'Any history on this patient?' Harry asked, building up the best picture they could before arriving on scene.

'No, fit and healthy otherwise. The patient has been suffering stress of late and be aware she has an infant with her. No family to call.'

'Got it,' Harry replied. 'Two minutes ETA.'

They pulled up outside the neat house, where a woman was sitting on the doorstep, slumped over, the front door behind her wide open. They could hear crying, and next to where the woman was sitting on the front step there was a pram which was moving from side to side with the exertions of the screaming baby inside.

'Go!' Annabel shouted the second they pulled up, turning off the engine and yanking the handbrake up. She and Harry ran to the patient, kit bags on their backs. Annabel ran straight to the woman, who was now unconscious and blue. 'She's not breathing, Harry!' They laid the woman down on the hallway carpet, calling out to any occupants in the house, even though they knew she was alone, hoping that someone might just have come to the woman's aid. The baby was screaming in the pram, and Annabel found no pulse. 'She's not breathing. I think it's a heart attack.' She checked the patient's airway, loosening her clothing and supporting her head. 'Starting CPR!'

Harry rushed to bring the pram indoors, the outside temperature dropping now. Checking at lightning speed, he ascertained that the baby was no more than six months old, was well looked after, just hungry and a little cold. He parked the pram at the bottom of the stairs and watched as Annabel pumped the mother's chest. Checking for a pulse again, she shook her head. 'Defibrillator!'

Harry ran to get what they needed, Annabel pulling off the clothing and getting ready to shock the patient. Harry updated the station on the patient, taking the baby in his arms to stop her crying. She snuggled into the warmth of his body, stopping crying almost immediately.

'Come on, Diane,' Annabel said to the woman as

she got everything ready, her hands moving with precise speed. 'Don't you die in front of your beautiful daughter. Come on! Clear!'

She pressed the paddles to the woman's chest, and her body jerked up with the movement. Annabel checked her pulse again, putting the paddles aside.

'We have a pulse!' Diane gasped for air, coughing and murmuring as she came to. 'Diane, Diane, it's okay. We're from the ambulance service. We're here to help; we need to get you to hospital.' Harry had already laid the baby back down in the pram and was racing to get a stretcher. They hooked her up to monitor her heart, and Annabel made her lie back down when she tried to get up.

'Izzy?' she asked. 'Where's my Izzy?'

'She's right here,' Harry said from behind her. They lifted her onto the stretcher and strapped her in, Harry picking up the baby and letting her mother see her. 'Do you have milk in the changing bag?' Diane nodded weakly, and Harry picked it up off the back of the pram. 'Let's get you both in. Do you have anyone who could look after the baby?'

Diane shook her head, crying now. Annabel gave her some pain medication, and she settled a little. 'No,' Diane said weakly. 'My husband left me. He's selling the house. He left me for someone else. I've been so stressed. What happened?'

Annabel took the woman's hand in her gloved one, leaning in so Diane would stay settled. 'We think you had a mild heart attack, Diane, but we have some of the best doctors in the country waiting to help you. We'll take Izzy with us, okay?' The woman nodded, crying again now. Checking the monitors, both paramedics were happy to see that her stats were coming back up. She was out of the woods for now, but they needed to act fast.

'I just felt a bit ill. I thought it was heartburn. How did I have a heart attack?'

Harry, leading the stretcher out of the house, the baby quiet and settled in his arms, gave Diane a comforting smile while Annabel checked the house over quickly and locked up. She put the keys in the changing bag on Harry's shoulder and within minutes they were heading off. Harry offered to drive, and Annabel was glad. She didn't want to leave the poor woman alone. She'd grabbed the detachable car seat from the pram, and she strapped the baby into the seat in the back of the cab, wrapping a blanket around her. She was now starting to stir, reminded of her hungry belly.

'Do you want to call your husband? Anyone?'

'I only have Izzy. It was just the three of us. I thought it would always be that way. Don't call him, please.'

Diane shook her head, and Annabel didn't press the matter. Harry closed the doors, but not before he squeezed Annabel's shoulder.

'Good job there,' he told her.

'Back at you,' she said, meaning every word. 'Drive fast.'

Harry winked at her before he closed the doors, and she turned her attention back to the woman. They'd got there in time, but she knew that the image of the new mother, slumped and alone, the baby crying next to her, wouldn't leave her for a long time. She had people, but once she locked her doors in the evening it was just her and Aidan. The thought of something happening to her was something she tried not to dwell on, but it was there just the same. Seeing Harry hold the baby girl in his strong arms hadn't helped either. He'd never held Aidan like that, and she felt the pain of moments lost once more, and the crushing guilt of her decision. She'd taken things away from him too. Moments they would never get to have. They blue lighted it all the way to the hospital, and they didn't leave till the social worker turned up to help with the baby. Diane was going to be fine, but she had a long hard road ahead and she would need help to get there.

When they both got back into the ambulance some time later, they sat for a moment.

'I hope they'll be okay. She looked terrified.'

'She's a new mum going through a lot already. Hopefully the dad will come through for her.'

Aidan's jaw tightened, and she patted his leg. He reached for her hand and held it there, under his.

'If you ever need me like that, you'd call, right?'

She looked across at him, his features shadowed in the fast fading light outside.

'Of course,' she replied. 'It's one of my biggest fears. Not being well enough to take care of him. If I needed you, I'd call.'

He lifted her hand to his mouth and kissed it once. The shivers that ran down her arm could have been from the cold of the evening, but she knew it was more than that.

'Thank you,' he said. 'I'll always be here. Let's get signed off, eh? It's been a day.' He didn't let go of her hand the whole time, and for once she didn't object to his attentions.

They pulled into the station, sorted their jobs out and went in to clock off. Harry waved to some familiar faces, most of whom looked back at him open-mouthed. Word had spread about his return. He had expected as much.

Annabel went on ahead, her shoulders hunched. She'd probably seen the looks he was getting too. It was hardly likely to get her to let her guard down. He wanted to tell them all to mind their own business.

'God, I wish they wouldn't gawp,' she said at the side of him, while his face set into an irritated scowl. 'I'd better get my paperwork done.' He watched her leave. He could almost hear her defences clanging back up into place. Looking back down the corridor, he made a point of staring the onlookers out. Most of them had the good sense to look away, scattering like autumn leaves in the wind. Spotting a friendly familiar face, he started to smile.

'Purdie!' he said out loud, loud enough for everyone to hear. 'You are a sight for sore eyes.'

Purdie came running over, enveloping him in a perfume-soaked hug. Harry was taken aback for a second but wrapped his arms around his old friend. Their old friend.

'So,' she said when she finally released him. 'Finally saw sense and came home, eh? Good to be back?'

Annabel's office door slammed behind them, and the remaining onlookers moved on. Purdie raised a thick dark brow at him, nodding towards the door. 'That well, eh?' She pulled him in for another hug and as he leaned in she whispered in his ear, 'Give her time, Harry; it's been a bit of a year for her.'

He opened his mouth in shock. 'How do you know what I'm thinking?'

Purdie slapped him on the arm as they pulled away

from each other. She straightened his uniform like a proud mother hen. 'I know you kids, remember? You're made for each other. Just give her space.'

Harry pulled a face. 'I sort of think that was the issue in the first place.'

He got another slap for that one.

'I know, and you upset a lot of people around here, but some things just need to be done. I know you meant well. Life's messy, Harrison Carter.' She gave him her sternest look as she turned to go home, bag and coat in hand. 'It's time to clear up that mess, once and for all. You good, all healed?' She said this more softly, and he frowned at her question. Purdie was one of the few people who knew about his earlier diagnosis—she'd been working in Oncology at the time.

Was he all healed? Physically, sure, but the heart took a little longer to mend. Especially when a huge piece of it was missing.

'I'm good,' he said eventually, and she left happy. Harry found himself alone in the corridor, staring at Annabel's office door as though it was the entrance to heaven and he'd been hell-raising half his life. He could walk through that door right now, tell her the whole truth about why he'd left, convince her that he *was* here to stay. Make her believe him, that his running days were over for good. That finding out about Aidan had made him so happy, so utterly happy.

His childhood sweetheart had loved him enough, even after what he did, to raise his child and keep his name out of it. She could have done a million different things to strike back at him, and understandably so, but she hadn't. She'd even looked after his dad when his own son had never really known how. He knew he didn't deserve her, but he wanted her to look at him the way she used to. As if the sun and moon rose and fell with him. The way that he still looked at her. When she wasn't looking, anyway.

He stopped in front of the door, his hand raised in a fist, ready to knock. He could hear her moving about inside; she was so close now, just at the other side of the wood. He wanted to tell her how he felt, why he'd left—everything. Earlier it hadn't been the right moment, but he had to make one. He couldn't keep it inside him any longer. He wanted her to know the real reason he'd left. That leaving had torn him apart just as much as it had her. He wanted to meet his son too, but he understood why she was reluctant to let him. He'd destroyed her life back then, and he couldn't blame her for wanting to avoid that all over again. She was still there though, under her new tougher exterior. He knew she was still there; he just needed her to trust him again.

Pushing his hands into his pockets to stop himself from banging on the door and declaring his intentions, he summoned the energy to walk away. He needed her to see that he wasn't going anywhere. He needed to prove to his family that he was back, and he wasn't going anywhere again. Which reminded him; he had something to take care of himself. After he'd told his father about his cancer, Abe had implored him to get checked over now he was in the UK. Ever the GP, but he had a point. He needed to make sure he stayed well, so he could finally, after so long, claim his life back. He just hoped that Annabel would be interested in his plans. He couldn't help but get the feeling that it might just be too late.

He had almost reached his rental car when his phone

buzzed with a text. *Annabel.* His heart thudded loud and hard in his ears as he opened it up.

Aidan is due a visit to Abe's. If you are there at seven tonight, you can meet him. My terms. He doesn't know, and I want it kept that way, for now at least. You get one chance, Harry. Don't blow it.

Harry didn't even remember the drive home. When he walked into his dad's house later that evening, his face flushed with happiness, arms filled with shopping bags, Abe just raised a brow at him from his easy chair.

'You got a date?' The television was on in the background, a steaming mug of tea by his side. It felt as if he'd just come home from school; the wave of nostalgia hit Harry as soon as he walked in.

'Annabel said that I could meet Aidan, not as his dad yet, but still. I got a few things on the way home, snacks and a few games.'

Abe chuckled. 'We have food, you know, and games.' He looked as if he was enjoying all this.

'I know, but I wanted to make an effort, you know. They'll be here soon. What do you normally do?'

'Well, we eat and watch a bit of television. If it's nice we have a walk. Aidan generally takes the lead. He's a good kid. You make that appointment yet?' Their liquor cabinet talk had really been a bare-all for the two Carter men. His dad had cried and held his son close. It had thawed them a little, but now the doctor in him was getting bossy already.

'Not yet, but I will, I promise. Time got away from

me today. Dad, has Aidan never asked you if you were his real grandfather, or asked about his father?'

Abe looked away then, muttering something about changing the subject and asking silly questions, and Harry knew why. 'I get it—I left. I just wondered, that's all. I'll just put all this away. Is Annabel staying too?'

He'd realised, walking around the aisles in the shop, that she hadn't said in her text whether it was just Aidan who was visiting. That had sent him into a spiral as he'd considered where she could be going. A date, maybe? He didn't dwell on that for too long; he didn't want to think about another man raising his son or loving his girl. She'd given no indication that she even was dating. He knew he had no real rights here, but the second Annabel had told him about their son, before even, he hadn't been able to stop the fire he felt inside him. The same fire he'd felt when he'd received that voicemail. He just needed to find a way to stoke the embers in Annabel's heart. If enough still remained. He'd told her he'd been on a few dates, which was true, but he wanted her to know that no one had measured up to her. Not that he'd been looking. He'd always just felt as if he was hers, in a weird way.

'Nope,' Abe said easily, his focus already back on his TV show. 'She's got a lot of work to do at the house.'

'The house?' Aidan checked. 'You mean her mum's old place?'

Abe looked over the top of his glasses at his son.

'No. She bought the dream house, Harry. You two really need to talk.'

Harry remembered them passing that house today,

seeing the sold sign out front. Another cog clicked into place. She'd brushed him off when he'd spoken about it. He'd assumed it was too painful to think of. He realised now she'd been avoiding the truth.

'She never said.'

Abe's glasses bumped up his nose, taken along for the ride by his raised brows.

'I wonder why. Not exactly an open book these days, is she? It's a bit of a shack, to be honest; she has her work cut out for her. Especially working full-time, and with Aidan. But that's Annabel, right? She's never shied away from anything.'

Harry's shoulders slumped and he headed to the kitchen to get ready for Aidan's arrival. 'I get it, Dad,' he said half to himself, half to the occupant of the other room. 'She's amazing and I screwed up. I get it.' He pulled out one of the board games he'd bought, one he'd enjoyed as a kid. 'I don't have a clue what I'm doing. I'm not a father. You don't need to fill me in. I'm all up to speed on my failings.'

'I didn't mean it like that. Don't be such a prickly pear. I get why you left now, you know that. You think I had it all figured out when you came along?' Abe was in the kitchen doorway now, and Harry sat down on one of the breakfast bar stools. He felt so damn tired. 'When your mum passed, I had no clue. I regret a lot of things, son, but never you. I don't always understand you, but I know you loved Annabel back then.' He walked over, patting Harry's hand as he took a seat. 'And now, I'm betting. She hasn't exactly been busy on the man front either, not for lack of her friends trying over the years. Don't beat yourself up for not being a father. You didn't know, and you can't be mad at Annabel for that either. You're a brand-new dad. It's up to you now what sort of father you are.'

'I'm not mad at her.' Harry felt the need to defend Annabel even now. 'I left you all. She did what she thought was best.' He thought of how he might have taken the news if she had called back then. He'd been living in another country, not working at saving lives but fighting for his own. He wouldn't have been much help, and knowing his family were so far away would have killed him harder than the cancer wanted to. He'd won that battle, and now he needed to fight for his life once more. The one he'd never wanted to leave behind in the first place. He just had even more to fight for than he'd thought, and it made him all the more determined to do it.

Abe nodded in agreement. 'She did, and keeping that secret cost her a lot. You know how people talk. They love a bit of dirty laundry, a juicy bit of gossip. She tarnished her own reputation a little, so as not to take any more shine off yours. She's loyal to a fault. If you really want her back, son, you need to prove it to her. And Aidan.'

'No pressure then.'

Abe laughed, patting his hand again. 'You can do it, Harry. I'll help.' Reaching his arm across, he hugged his son to him and dropped a kiss on the top of his head. 'I'm glad you came home.'

Harry hugged his father to him, marvelling at the change in him. Maybe time and distance, along with the truth, had healed some of their old niggles. An ointment on old wounds.

'Me too, Dad,' Harry said honestly. 'Me too. Let's get ready for the little guy.'

CHAPTER THREE

Annabel parked her car outside Abe's house and looked out of the window, a deep sigh leaving her as she steeled herself for this momentous event.

'What's wrong, Mummy?' Aidan, sitting in the back seat with a pair of headphones half hanging off his ears, took off his seatbelt and wrapped his little arm around her shoulder. She could hear his favourite anime cartoons playing through the ear buds attached to his tablet. She turned and gave him her best 'everything's okay' smile.

'Nothing, kiddo, just a long day. You know I can't stay tonight, right? I have a guy coming to the house to look at the back garden.' She wanted to get it overhauled. It had been a lovely garden once, but it had got too much for the previous owner. Annabel had big plans. A patio so her station family could come for barbecues while the kids played on the play equipment she knew Aidan would love. She wanted a little vegetable patch so she and Aidan could grow their own food, something to do together. Her mother had always wanted one, and the balcony of their old flat had always had something growing, every bit of space used cleverly for home-grown fruit and vegetables. Doing it together, like she used to do with her own mum, would be family time well spent.

Aidan was so proud of his mum for the job she did; he was a great kid. Their quality time meant a lot, and having a garden was a huge plus to the house. The landscape gardener had been kind enough to meet her after work, though the timing could have been better. Leaving Aidan with Abe and Harry was so weird; she couldn't get her head around it. After the call today though, with Diane and baby Izzy, she figured Aidan knowing Harry might be a good thing after all.

'Listen, Granddad has someone living with him at the moment. Remember the photos of his son that you see around the house?'

Aidan nodded at her slowly, his eyes wide. 'He came home from far away? Really?'

'He did, so he's going to be there tonight. That okay?' She brushed his fringe away from his little face, the freckles across his nose matching her own. 'He's nice, and he works with me now, so you might be seeing him around for a bit.'

'Because Uncle Tom is getting me some cousins?'

Aidan had always loved being around people. He'd asked for a baby brother or sister for the last three Christmases. She was hoping that once the house was done she could get him a pet, stop the awkward questions. Tom and Lloyd having babies around would be great too, and she was looking forward to babysitting for them. She'd loved being a mum to Aidan right from the start, even though it was hard and lonely at times.

She felt the old feelings of resentment towards Harry creep into her thoughts, and she pushed them away. The last thing she wanted was for Aidan to pick up on any tension, and she found that the anger wasn't as strong as before. It helped that he'd told her he had only been on a couple of dates, but was that true? She had always wondered whether he had met someone over there. It had been a long time, and he was a hot single man. She could see what a catch he would have been over there, single and available. Was it really just a few dates?

'That's right, so Harry has come to work with me now, in Tom's job.'

Aidan gave her a little side look. 'Is he your best friend? Where has he been? What does he look like? Does he have a girlfriend? Is he staying forever?'

Annabel laughed, getting out of the car and opening Aidan's door. 'Wow, what's with all the questions today? Let's get you inside, I'm going to be late at this rate. I won't be too long, and I'm on a day off soon. We can do something. Cinema, maybe?'

Aidan nodded distractedly, already running through the flowerbeds to Abe's front door.

'Hey, wait up!'

The door opened just as he reached it, and Aidan crashed straight into Harry's legs.

'Hey, hello!' Harry caught him and righted him on his feet. 'You must be Aidan. I'm Harry.'

Annabel saw the shake in Harry's hand as he held it out to her son. *Their son.* Aidan stood frozen for a long minute before putting his hand into Harry's. Annabel felt as if she was going to pass out, but she held it together. Aidan turned and beamed at her. She tried not to catch Harry's eye, but they met anyway. She had half expected to see anger there, or fear, but all she saw was his happiness. He mouthed 'Thank you' to her, but she didn't respond. She felt as though she was rooted to the spot.

'Aidan, be good, okay? I'll be back soon.'

'Bye, Mum. Granddad, I'm here!' He was off indoors, leaving the pair of them standing at opposite ends of the path.

'Thanks for bringing him. Do you want some supper saving? I think we went a little overboard on the food.'

She opened her mouth to say no, but stopped herself. She needed to get on with him. She needed to squash down her feelings from the past, all of them. Good and bad.

'You know what, that would actually be great. I haven't eaten since lunch. I won't be more than a couple of hours.'

Harry nodded, his lopsided grin making him look like the boy she'd once known. 'Great. See you soon.' She was about to open her car door when he called out to her, 'Annie?'

She turned, leaning against her car door to face him. In the faded daylight, he was framed by the light coming from inside the house. She squashed down the feelings of attraction that stirred within her.

Why does he have to be so darned cute? I'm pretty sure that there should be some kind of rule for this kind of thing. Once someone stomps on your heart, they should suddenly lose all charm for the person who was left. He had to come back all put together and hot. Why can't he be fat, or balding? An extra chin or two wouldn't go amiss.

'Will you meet me tomorrow? We're both off shift.'

The fact that he now knew her timetable should have irked her, but they were working partners now, needing to be on the same shifts while his probationary period was ongoing. Annabel was torn over it. Did she want him to stay after? Would he want to stay after? It was exhausting trying to work out how she felt, to guess what the future might hold. So she did what she did best. She protected her heart.

'I have a bit of a full day, Harry; you know what time off is like. I have a ton of stuff to do—'

'At the dream house?' He said it softly. Not an accusation, a soft question. Annabel felt her whole body deflate. She leaned against her car for a moment, steadying herself.

'I don't want to fight, Harry.'

'You said you would listen to me. I just want to talk.'

He was heading down the path towards her before she could react, pulling the door shut behind him. He stopped right in front of her. The proximity of him made her heart flutter in her chest. She could just reach out and touch him, right now. Her hands tingled with the urge to touch her fingers to his chest. She used to love to run her fingers through his hair before pulling his mouth down to hers. She crossed her arms for lack of anything else to do with them. In the same moment, he shifted from one foot to the other and pushed his hands into his back pockets.

Was he feeling it too? It felt like a lot more than muscle memory.

She ached to bridge the gap between them, but it wasn't her who had put it there in the first place.

'I don't want to fight either. You asked me to come home, remember?'

'Six months ago, when I was tipsy and upset! Where were you then? Breaking some other girl's heart?'

Wow, where did that come from? Aidan's girlfriend question had obviously stuck in her mind.

'What? No! I had a contract, I told you. I worked my notice and left the same day. I came back. We've been over this. I told you the truth. I didn't want to do this over the phone. Why are you mad again?' He ran his hand through his hair, pulling at it a little in frustration. 'We need to talk about it all, about why I left.'

Annabel almost relented right there and then. He was offering to tell her why he'd left her that day, to raise his secret son alone and pick up the pieces of her life. She knew he hadn't known about the baby—hell, she was a trained paramedic and she hadn't even realised she was pregnant herself. She'd lain awake for so many nights, gazing down at her ever-expanding belly and wondering what Harry would have done if he'd known back then. If she'd called him on any of those nights.

The fact was, though, it was in the past. Some things you couldn't just take back. She was glad he knew now. The knot in the pit of her stomach had almost fossilised over the last eight years, and now the secret was out she felt lighter. Stronger too. She wasn't quite that panicked, worried mother she'd been six months ago. It had been a moment of weakness and, no matter what he said, she had spent all of Aidan's life believing Harry to be an utter cad. Nothing he told her would change that, and it was yet another reason to keep him at arm's length. She didn't want to betray that girl at the airport, the sacrifices they had all had to make since. It was painful enough to remember those early days. She had blocked a lot of them out. She would never have survived otherwise. It had just been the three of them for so long. Her, Abe and Aidan. While Harry had lived it up on the other side of the world as a ghost to those who loved him, a breaker of hearts.

'Tell me something first,' she said quietly. He leaned in a little, and she found herself leaning further away from him, pushing herself against her car. He made her head swim even now, but she needed to get this out.

'Anything,' he breathed. She clenched her teeth and looked him square in the eye.

'I did want to listen to what you have to say. I do. But answer this one thing for me. Whatever you have to tell me, will it erase what you did that day? Leaving me standing there like an idiot with my suitcases, and walking away from me? Making everyone we know wonder what they had done wrong.'

He reeled as though her words had slapped him across his chiselled features. 'Well, no, but if you j—'

'Then I don't need to know. Aidan is your son, you wanted to meet him—well, here he is.' She gestured with her hand towards the house, and spotted Abe watching them from behind the curtain. When he saw her looking he melted away and the curtains were pulled shut. 'Go meet him. He's a great kid. He will probably have a million questions for you. He's always wanted to go and see other countries. With one thing and another, we've not had a lot of time for holidays.' He winced, and she pushed down her sarcasm once more. 'I'm sorry, I really have to go.'

'To the dream house, yeah? You never answered me before.'

Great. Was everything about her life on show now, for him to comment on? She could tell he wasn't about to let this drop.

'Yes, the dream house. It's part of a different dream now, though. One for me and Aidan. I'll see you at work, okay?'

She left him standing by the kerb, hands on his hips. As she drove away, she willed herself not to look back at him in the mirror, but she found herself watching him as she drove away. When he was out of sight she brushed a tear away from her cheek and willed herself to pull it together. The way he'd looked at her was killing her.

Not for the first time, she found herself wondering if he would stay. What would London have to offer over Dubai for a man like him? Abe wasn't sick; he was still as fit as a fiddle and as sharp as a drawer full of knives. He'd not come back through obligation.

He said he'd come back because of her, but whenever she thought about thawing enough to speak to him properly, to hash out the last few years, Aidan's little face popped into her head. The way she'd felt in that airport. The years of people asking her about her son's father. All the times she had covered for him, making herself look worse in order for the people in their lives not to hate Harry, to tell him about his son. Any one of them could have got in touch with Harry to tell him about Aidan, to berate him for leaving them both. She had never wanted that, nor had she wanted to be a charity case either. She knew him well enough to know that he would have come home to do the right thing. The right thing by her, the woman he said he loved—but not enough to treat her better in the first place.

She'd chosen her path, and even though Aidan had had tears over the years about not having a dad like most of his school friends, they'd done just fine. She wasn't about to change that. Not on the strength of a few days, or because she knew how nostalgic she felt when Harry was around her. The thought of Aidan getting to know his father and then getting an airport goodbye like she did was enough to keep her driving away from him, and not driving back into his arms. What if he had run back home to hide from another woman he had left, back in Dubai? Could she trust him, really?

She had felt her resolve weakening when he was there right in front of her, but their compatibility had never been the problem. Him leaving her high and dry was the issue, and she just knew that she would never survive that again. When he told her the reason he'd left, and she knew he would, it would either make her hate him forever or make it that bit harder not to fall completely back in love with him. Given his eagerness to tell her and the way he'd looked at her, she was guessing it would be the latter. She needed a minute to prepare at least. She wasn't a young girl any more. She had other people to consider.

By the time she pulled up outside her house, giving a wave to the waiting gardener, all her tears had been shed and she had composed herself once more. Yet another piece of gauze wrapped around her shattered heart.

She wanted to know.

As Harry watched the love of his life drive away he thought his heart would snap in two. She still didn't fully trust him, and that thought was one that he could barely bear. Slapping his hand to his forehead the second her car turned out of sight, he kept his back to the house and willed himself to pull it together. He ran his hands down his face, surprised when they came away wet with his tears. He felt lower than a snake's belly and, after the day he'd left her, he didn't think it was possible to feel any worse. The light had gone out of his Annie, and he was the reason.

Pulling himself together, he turned back to the house. It was time to get to know his son and prove to his mother that he was still the man she'd once adored. He knew it would be a battle, but Harrison Carter was ready to stand and fight with everything he had.

'Hey,' he called when he walked back into the house. Aidan was playing a board game with Abe, rolling the dice as if his little life depended on it. Abe looked at him expectantly, and Harry shook his head. Abe scowled, his shoulders sagging.

'Stubborn,' he said to no one in particular. Harry's mouth twitched.

'Mum says I'm stubborn too.' Aidan was looking straight at Harry now, and Abe stood up from his seat.

'I'll put the kettle on. I bought extra marshmallows for the hot chocolate too.'

'Did she now?' Harry went to sit on the couch next to his son, taking the opportunity to continue the conversation.

'Yep. Are you really stubborn too?'

Grinning, Harry nodded, taking in every little detail of the child in front of him. 'I've been told that before, so yes, I'm stubborn.'

Aidan grinned. 'I knew it. Want to play?'

He offered Harry the dice, and he took them gratefully. 'There's nothing I'd like better.'

CHAPTER FOUR

DRIVING BACK HOME the next day after the hectic rush of the morning school run, Annabel played back the previous evening in her head. Aidan had crashed out on the couch at Abe's house, which meant that she took her supper to go, wanting to get Aidan into his own bed. Harry had carried him out to the car and not pressed for anything else. He'd closed the car door, leaned in and brushed his lips against her cheek, then simply walked back inside. She'd been left leaning against her car door, feeling as if her face was on fire from the touch of his lips, and confused about his sudden mood change. Had he given up already?

This morning Aidan had been full of Harry talk, about how awesome he was, how much Granddad had laughed, how rubbish Harry was at Scrabble. She had a feeling they'd had a lot of fun and she wished she could have seen them together. Seeing Harry striding across Abe's front path, their sleeping son in his arms, could quite easily have been her favourite calendar photo for the next, oh, ten years. He was so natural with him, and when he'd leant in close and kissed her on the cheek she'd almost turned and sought his lips. By the time she'd argued with herself about the merits of leaving or grabbing his face and kissing the life out of him, he'd turned and left, leaving her shell-shocked and standing on the front lawn, clinging to her car like a shipwrecked sailor clinging to a piece of driftwood. She thanked her lucky stars it was their day off and she could recover. Maybe even take a cold shower.

Pulling up in front of her house, she frowned when she noticed a car parked outside. She wasn't expecting any workmen today, and the landscape gardener wasn't due to start for a few days. She thought the car looked familiar on the second look, and when she parked up and the car door opened she knew why.

'Morning!' Harry was standing there, dressed in a pair of jeans and a white T-shirt that made his tanned skin look all the more alluring. She could make out the contours of his muscular body under the thin white cotton. His hair was neat and styled and he was holding two coffees in his hands and a rather large brown paper bag. 'Aidan let slip that you were decorating your lounge today, so I thought I'd come to help.'

In contrast to the well put together Adonis before her, Annabel felt like fresh roadkill. She'd scraped her hair back into a messy bun that morning, she had pancake batter down her hooded sweatshirt from making Aidan breakfast and she was currently wearing her paint-splattered decorating joggers. She wanted the ground to swallow her up.

'I…er…' She could smell the coffee now as they gravitated towards each other. She scrambled for a response that would make him leave but gave in when her stomach rumbled. She thought back to last night and smiled at him. His face lit up when he saw it and broke out in a sexy grin.

Oh, Harry.

'It depends. What's in the bag?'

'Bacon rolls with red sauce,' he teased, raising his eyebrows. 'You eaten?'

She threw him a grin of her own. 'I'm starved.'

He gestured towards the house. 'Breakfast for a tour? I brought some dust sheets from Dad too; he said you might need some.'

They walked up to the house together and Annabel watched him take it in as she unlocked the door and motioned for him to come inside.

'It looks so different. I can't believe you bought the place.'

Annabel laughed, thinking of the time warp she had sunk every penny into. 'I could hardly keep the old decor of the place as it was. Maud was lovely, but she didn't really bother with interior design. I found newspapers under the floorboards older than my grandfather. It's taken a lot of work to even get to this stage.'

They were standing next to each other in the hallway, and once more she felt the pull of him. They were here, in the house they'd always sworn they'd buy together, where they'd raise a family while saving the world one patient at a time. They were here, and so were the details, but the reality was far different.

I know he feels this too.

One look at him, and she knew. He was feeling everything she was, including the urge to just reach for the other and breathe them in. She felt so thirsty for him, and he was the one man that she couldn't drink in. It would never be just a sip, and then she'd be lost forever.

Not forever. He'll probably be gone by Christmas.

Annabel wasn't sure whether it was her voice she heard in her head or her mother's.

She saw his gaze fall on a photo of her and Aidan, taken at Aidan's last birthday party. It was sitting in the hallway on top of a box of stuff she couldn't unpack yet.

'I bet,' he replied, moving through the hallway and into the lounge. The builders had knocked through to the dining room and freshly plastered; it looked huge now. Annabel pinched herself every time she walked through the door. It was awful living in a building site, but the space was well worth it. Every week she saw her house come together, and it was worth all the dust and the hassle. She couldn't wait to just come home and enjoy her time off with Aidan. Barbecues in the garden with his friends coming around, Abe coming for Sunday dinner. Maybe she would even invite Harry too, if he was still around.

'Annabel, did you hear me?'

She realised that Harry was talking to her, and she followed him through to the lounge.

'Sorry, I was miles away. What?'

He was looking at the paint tins and rollers that were sitting off to one side. 'This is what you're doing today?' He looked at the light grey paint colour on the side of one of the cans. 'Nice colour.'

'Thanks, yeah. I was hoping to get it done but, looking at it...' That was the only problem with a big space; it meant more work.

Harry sat down on the floor and patted the floor beside him. 'We'll get it done. Eat first though, yeah?'

'We? Really?'

Harry shook his head at her. ‘Annabel, this is getting old now. I’m here. For you, for Aidan. I’m not going anywhere. Just let me help, okay?’

Annabel sighed, taking a seat next to him.

‘What, no rebuttal?’ he asked, amusement clear in his voice and the twitch in his lip.

‘What can I say?’ she countered, holding out her hand for him to shake. ‘A girl will do anything for bacon.’

After they’d demolished everything he’d brought they got to work. Well, Harry just started opening the paint cans and laying out the dust sheets and Annabel followed his lead. She flicked on the radio and, before too long, the pair of them were rollering the walls and singing along to the music. They kept to the small talk, nothing too taxing and nothing about the past. He told her some stories from his job in Dubai, some of the best and worst cases he’d had, and she found herself telling him hers, about their colleagues and the things that had happened to the station family over the years.

‘Purdie still working at the hospital then?’ Harry was wiggling his bum to a Diana Ross track, his brush making precise neat strokes along the top of the freshly fitted skirting boards. ‘I thought she’d have retired by now, gone home to her family.’

Annabel rolled her eyes at him. ‘Not quite, not from lack of trying though. I think she’s always too worried about letting her patients down; she talks about it, but then never quite follows it through. I think she might soon though; her family has changed now, expanding. You don’t have anyone you miss, from Dubai?’

They ended up at the paint can at the same time,

their brushes banging into each other as they both went to dip the bristles into the paint. His other hand was on hers in a second.

'I had friends, yes, good friends. We'll stay in touch. You know I was telling the truth right, about not having anyone over there?'

'I did wonder.'

His jaw flexed. 'Yeah, well, you don't have to. There wasn't anyone. Even if I had been looking, no one would have come close to you.' His hand was still on hers, his grip tightening just a little.

She swallowed hard. 'I'm a tough act to follow,' she teased back, feeling as if her skin was on fire from his touch. He took the brush from her and crossed it with his across the top of the paint can.

'I don't really care what you thought. I can't blame you for wondering. It wasn't like I hadn't imagined you with someone else, someone else making you happy. I never looked at anyone else once I met you. I know you don't trust me, but you can trust that.'

'I do.' She squeezed his hand, rubbing her thumb along the back like she always did. They'd always had a thing about hand holding. In the car, on the couch watching TV, in bed as they fell asleep. 'I know that.' Their hands were having a little reunion of their own.

Harry moved, and his mouth was on hers before she even registered the movement. For a long, sweet, heart-pumping minute she kissed him back. She could feel his stubble on her cheek as he lowered his mouth to her neck, leaving a trail of hot salty caresses on her collarbone as he pulled her closer. He pushed the paint can to one side with his knee and lifted her up with him till their torsos touched. The feel of his body against hers ignited something in her, and she wrapped her arms around him, pulling him to her greedily. He pulled her to her feet, not once letting their lips or arms break contact. He walked her backwards towards the wall and, remembering at the last moment that it was wet with fresh paint, she pushed against him gently to stop him. He noticed and pulled away in an instant, his face pulled into a frown.

'Sorry, did I do something wrong? Do you want me to stop? I just couldn't help it. I've been wanting to kiss you since I saw you.'

She giggled, lifting a hand to smooth out his furrowed brow. 'Wet paint,' she reminded him. 'And me too.'

He smiled, his expression changing from stricken concern to happiness, and he moved his hands around her bottom, lifting her till she was straddling him, secure in his arms. They had just reached the hallway towards the bottom of the stairs when there was a loud knock at the door.

Harry had never been as upset to see a postman in his life. Annabel jumped away from him, running to the door to answer the intrusion into their moment together.

She kissed me back. She wanted me.

The thought made his heart soar and once she had returned to him, a few little parcels and envelopes in her arms, he went to her again.

'Wait...' She stopped him in his tracks. He could see her chest heaving, just like his own. They were both smeared with spots and trails of dove-grey paint, telltale signs of where their hands had just been on each other's bodies. 'Harry, we can't.'

He could feel his shoulders sag, and a pang in his heart at her words.

'Why not? You kissed me back, Annie.'

Her face was stricken and she touched her fingers to her lips. 'I know. I know I did but I shouldn't have. I got carried away. I think you should go.'

Harry did not want to leave. He never wanted to leave. 'No, please, Annie—'

'It's Annabel. I think you need to. We can't be alone.'

'But you said—'

'I know what I said, but it's just lust, Harry. Nostalgia. We're not those people any more; we have a son. Responsibilities.' She waggled a parcel in his direction and he saw Aidan's name on it. He had never hated the postal service before, but he sure did now, for shaking them out of the moment. He'd been so close.

'What about tomorrow, at work? We'll be alone in the ambulance. We need to talk; I have to tell you—'

'I don't want to hear that yet! You know that!'

'Why? What are you afraid of? That you'll have no reason not to be with me any more? To give this a try?' he shouted back at her, but she jumped at his tone. *Damn it.* He never wanted to make her feel like that. 'I'm sorry. I didn't mean to shout. I don't want to go.' He motioned around him at the half-finished room. 'We need to finish this. Let me go get some lunch; we can talk then.'

She gripped the contents of her arms to her tighter and looked around her at the room. 'I only have a few hours; my friend's on school pickup. Aidan will be coming.'

'That's fine. I can be gone by then, if that's what you want. He knows we work together. It's not that unusual that I would be here, surely?'

She kept her distance from him and although he wanted to grab the post and take her into his arms, he resisted the urge.

'I don't regret the kiss. Do you?'

It took her a while to answer, and Harry held his breath for every long second while he watched her process her emotions. Eventually, she slowly shook her head. 'No, I don't, but it's just so complicated, Harry.'

She wanted it too. That made his heart skip a beat.

'I know, but I'm not going anywhere, Annie. Never again.'

'How do I know that you mean that? I never thought you'd go in the first place. I couldn't go through that again if you left, or it didn't work out. You said it wasn't working before. That could happen again.'

Harry sighed hard, all the energy leaving him. 'I know I hurt you when I left, and I didn't ever expect to do that either, believe me. I was a mess, Annie, but I'm not that person any more. A lot has changed, and knowing about Aidan…' He couldn't help but smile at the thought of his little boy. The little boy that they had made out of so much love. His little miracle baby. Made before the cancer ravaged his fertility and took away what he'd thought was his chance of ever becoming a father. 'He's amazing, Annie, and I want to be his dad more than anything. I want you, both of you. You just have to let me prove that to you.' He slowly moved towards her now, and she didn't back away. Taking the parcels and envelopes from her, he put them to one side and took her hands in his. 'And I will prove it. That I'm the partner you had before, in work and out. Will you let me?'

He was saying all the right things. The feel of his hands in hers made her nerve-endings sing, and she was still reeling from that kiss.

God, that kiss. The physical side of things had always been great, and her body was still on fire from getting a taste of him after all this time.

If they hadn't been interrupted, she was pretty sure that she wouldn't have put a stop to things. She wanted to let him in, but her previous hurt was in her head the whole time. And then there was Aidan. The poor kid had always believed that his granddad was a friend of mummy's, and his father was out of the picture. And now Harry was back, he'd met Aidan, he was supposedly here to stay, and it would be so easy. She could just let him in, back into her life and everyone else's. Give Aidan the father he had always wanted and deserved. She knew what it was like not to have one. Did she really want that for Aidan? Wasn't it why she had always turned down any offers from suitors over the years? She just couldn't seem to find the words when it came to saying yes. That airport heartbreak had become a millstone around her neck. Every time she saved a life, did well at work, aced another week of single parenting, that was what always whispered in the back of her mind.

He left you there, without even a backward glance. Everything you did up to that point and beyond, the fact that you weren't enough was always there.

It was one of the reasons she'd never bothered with dating once she'd had Aidan. Her friends, and even Abe on occasion, had tried to set her up with dates, but she'd never pulled the trigger on any of the prospective new men in her life.

Sometimes, on her worst days, when Aidan was playing up, the chores were never ending and work was full-on, she went back to that day. Sometimes she felt like whatever she did, however independent she was, she would always be that girl who vomited in the middle of the airport lounge after being left high and dry by the man who was supposed to put her before all others. BAE, indeed. One of her so-called 'friends' from work had once joked that Harry had took it to mean, *Bye, Annabel. End of.* She'd never forgotten that.

'Annie? You there?' Harry's voice pulled her back into the room and she broke the physical contact with him and turned away, kneeling by the little stack of deliveries and starting to open them up.

'Yeah, I'm here. Ham on white for me, please. The old sandwich shop around the corner's still there. I'll sort these out.'

She felt him behind her, and his feet didn't move. She concentrated on opening the next cardboard box as if her life and sanity depended on it. She couldn't trust herself to look at him, so she did what she always did. She buried it deep in her heart, away from the harsh light of day. Opening parcels and painting she could do. Major life decisions would have to wait till another day.

'I won't be long,' Harry said eventually. She could hear the rejection in his dull tone, and she closed her eyes against the sting of tears that threatened to erupt.

The door closed, but when she looked up he was still standing there.

'Harry?'

'I had cancer, Annie. That's why I left. I know you don't want to hear this, but tough. A few weeks before we were due to go to Dubai, I got diagnosed. Testicular cancer. Aggressive. I didn't want you to wreck your life, give up on your dreams and nursemaid me instead. I was scared, Annie, and sick, and upset. I wasn't cheating on you or planning to. I didn't leave you, not like you thought. I loved you, Annie, so much. I just did what I thought was right. After your mum, I just couldn't put you through that again. It was bad, but my bosses in Dubai surprised me. They had a research centre over there, specialising in my illness. They offered to still take me, to keep my job on. I needed to earn, and I needed to get out of Dad's house. You know things were bad between us back then. I felt cornered, so I went. I just couldn't put you through that in a new country, all on your own. I got better, I got your call, and it gave me the hope I needed to come home, to try to win you back. And, as I keep saying, I'm back for good. Did you hear me, Annie? I didn't leave you because I wanted to, okay?'

She nodded, not trusting her voice to even make any coherent sound other than a strangled squeak. Everything he had just unloaded on her was swimming around in her head.

Cancer. He'd had cancer. He'd left her to spare her from going through it all again, and so he did it alone. He was just as alone as she was. More so. She felt her face redden as she played back in her head every time she'd nipped at him since he'd got back.

Harry spoke again, softer this time. He sounded so sad, but she couldn't get her head to lift to look at him. 'I'll go and get lunch, and when I get back we are going to talk about this.'

When the door closed and the sound of his footsteps disappeared, she stared at the wall, her grey matter trying to keep up with the flurry of information. *He was sick.* That was something she'd never considered on her list of reasons Harry had left. Not even once. Reaching for the phone in her pocket with paint-splattered fingers, she dialled Tom's number with shaky hands.

'Hey, girl! How's the painting coming along? We're just in the baby shop! I tell you, Lloyd is hammering the old plastic today! Will you tell him that a baby cosy toes is not essential for a pair of newborns? I swear, we need to do a Pinterest intervention at some point.'

Annabel broke down into racking sobs and when she tried to speak it came out as one big wail.

'Anna Banana, what's wrong? Lloyd, Annabel's upset, come here, quick.' She heard footsteps, the background noise of the busy shop die down, and then Tom and Lloyd's voices.

'You're on speakerphone, we're hiding in the disabled toilet. What's wrong?'

Where to start...?

'I kissed Harry! That's what's wrong! He showed up this morning with breakfast, and we were painting and...'

Lloyd, who was usually the calmer of the two, did a little whoop into the handset. 'Oh, wow, that's amazing! Why are you upset? I thought tha— Oof! Tom!'

She could hear the phone being wrestled from him, and Tom was the next to speak. 'Sorry about Mr Excited over here; he's been sniffing the baby talc. I have to say, though, I saw this coming.'

'What?' Annabel retorted crossly. 'I didn't. I didn't see any of this coming, and that's not all either. He had cancer, Tom. That's why he left. Not for some leggy blonde or because he didn't love me. Because he had cancer. He just told me, and then went out for sandwiches!' She sobbed again. Tom sighed, and she could hear him and Lloyd whispering to each other. 'Guys, help! I don't have long; he only went to get lunch. What the hell do I do? I've been awful to him since he got back, and he tried to tell me so many times. I'm evil, I didn't help him. I kept his son from him, I didn't listen to him. What the hell am I doing, Tom?'

The line was silent for what felt like forever.

'Tom?' she sniffed into the phone. 'You there? Please say you're there.'

'Sorry, it's just the shock. I'm processing. Poor Harry! I guess it makes sense, though, doesn't it? The Harry who left you wasn't the Harry we knew. I feel so bad now; I should have tried harder to reach him. He must have been really scared. I can't believe he just did that on his own. It must have been awful. But you kissed him though, right? So you didn't send him away after? Annabel, I've got to say, the writing was on the wall as soon as we saw him at the airport. You know the truth now; there's nothing holding you back, is there?'

'Yeah, and it's better than the writing on the wall in here. I mean, do they not teach spelling in school any more?' Lloyd's voice chipped in. Another muffled struggle, presumably Tom giving his husband another shove.

'Focus! What I mean is, well…you've hardly been happy since he left. I know you think you are, but you've never even looked at another man. We've tried to set you up with every straight man in a ten-mile radius, and you've never been bothered. Aidan's growing up now; what about you? Do you want to rattle around in that house like Miss Havisham in your retirement? I hated Harry for what he did, but he came back. He obviously went through something life-changing, but he still came back. I know it's crazy, but he obviously thought he was sparing you from going through what he faced. He knew your mum, what you both went through before you met us. He obviously never wanted to go. That means something, right?'

Annabel wiped her tears away with her free arm and nodded.

'Right?' Tom pressed.

'I'm nodding,' she retorted sulkily. 'He's only been back a short while though; why would he stay now? What's keeping him here, once the novelty fades? I can't go through that again. And then there's Aidan.'

'Exactly,' Lloyd spoke up. 'There is Aidan to think about. Don't you think he deserves a chance to be part of a family? We support all types of families, obviously, but you've done this alone for so long. It takes a village, right? Harry could be part of that village, honey.'

'He's Aidan's real father,' she blurted out. 'That changes everything.'

The line went quiet again, and Annabel held the phone away from her face to check that the call hadn't disconnected. 'Hello? You still there?'

'Give us a second. You keep dropping bombshells, and that's the first time you've admitted that to us.'

Now Annabel fell silent.

'Did she hang up? Call her back! Tom, call her back!' Lloyd's high-pitched tone made Annabel chuckle through her tears.

'I'm here. Nice return fire, by the way. Did you know Harry was Aidan's father the whole time?'

'Er...well...' Tom floundered.

'Yes, we did. Don't forget, we know you. The timing made sense, and we scraped you off your bedroom floor when he left. There's no way that you'd have entertained another man. Then or now. We took you out, remember? There was no man. Aside from the ones you brushed off, and the one you threatened to throat punch for getting handsy.'

Annabel cried again, half laughing, half wailing.

They'd never questioned her or judged her once. She loved them all the more for it.

'I wish you'd said something.'

'You never said anything either; you shut us down whenever we got near to asking. We figured you would in time, but you never did. We wanted to respect your wishes. We get it, Annabel. We already hated Harry.'

'Yeah, I feel sorry for that now; we need to send him a fruit basket or something.'

'Lloyd, shush! Has Harry met Aidan yet?' Tom asked.

'He's living with Abe, so yeah. Aidan doesn't know though.' A thought occurred to her and she felt as if ice water had been poured down her back. 'Does that mean everyone knows? Oh, no, I can't do this. He's working at the station—what am I going to do? I have to end this, now. There's too much at stake. I can't risk Aidan getting hurt; he's had such a tough time lately.'

She could hear footsteps on the path once more, and the whistle that Harry used to do, the one he always did when he was happy. He thought that there was a chance now. Maybe he was just feeling lighter now he'd spoken his truth. She'd done that. She'd messed up, muddied the waters. She needed to undo it.

'He's coming, I've got to go.'

'Wait, Annabel! Don't do what I think you're going to do. Stop being so scared! He told you why he left! This is what you want! Stop hiding!'

She ripped open the last of the packages at speed, her phone shoved between her chin and her shoulder. She didn't want him to think she'd been sitting there blubbing since he'd left, even though she had.

'I can't do it, Tom, it's too late. It's too complicated! I'll call you later, okay?' She ended the call, Lloyd and Tom's protestations ringing in her ears as she shoved the phone back into her back pocket. When Harry walked in a second later, a carrier bag swinging from one arm, she was sitting cross-legged, her face hidden by her hair as she stacked up the assortment of bits she'd bought for the house, and for Aidan.

'Hey,' he said, shutting the door and coming to sit beside her. 'I got some doughnuts too, and extra for Aidan after school.' His smile crumpled when she turned to look at him. 'Oh, God, I'm sorry. I shouldn't have just dropped all that on you and left. Are you okay?'

Annabel pushed the items to one side, and she reached for the sandwich he was proffering in his hand.

'I'm okay; it was just a shock.'

'Not like me, dropping bad news and running off. I'm glad you know, though. I've wanted to tell you forever. And the kiss was amazing. Just like before. Better even.'

She reached for his arm, pulling him down to sit next to her. 'Harry, that kiss was—'

'One of the three greatest things that has happened to me in the last year. The first being when you called me, and the second finding out you'd had our son.'

He gripped her hand in his and she pulled it away, putting her hands on the top of her knees to stop them doing their own thing and reaching for him. He looked at his empty hand, and then the floor.

'You still don't trust me, do you?'

'Why didn't you just tell me about the cancer? How bad was it? What treatment did you have?'

'It was bad enough. Stage two. I had three tumours, I had to have some lymph nodes removed. Intensive treatment. I was a cue ball up top for a while.' He swallowed hard, pushing his food away. 'I didn't tell you because you would have come with me. You'd have travelled to a different country and put your life on hold, and I didn't want that for you. I was terrified, Annie, and I couldn't put you through that. Not after all that you went through with your mum. I was there for that; I saw how bad it was.'

Annabel thought of her mother, the pain she'd gone through. She would have been by his side in a heartbeat.

'I would have liked to have been given the choice. You took that decision out of my hands. You made me feel like dirt, embarrassed me in front of everyone. I would have helped you, been there. What if you had died, Harry? How do you think that would have gone? How everyone back here would have taken that news?'

Harry came to her, and his hands were cupping her face. He touched his forehead to hers. 'I know. I was stupid,' he whispered. 'I've regretted it every day since I left, but at the time I was so sick and scared, I just thought it was the right thing. Then, after, I…'

'All that time though.' She shook her head, pulling away a little to look into his eyes. 'You pushed everyone away. How did you even cope, out there on your own? Why didn't you answer us when we called?' Her voice tapered off into a choked sob. 'You must have been so scared, so lonely. I can't bear it, Harry. What on earth were you thinking?' Once again, she was flip-flopping from feeling awful for him and wanting to slap him for being such a stubborn fool. He could have had everyone around him, and he could have had his son. She would have looked after them both; she knew she would. Just thinking about it made her upset all over again. She didn't like feeling out of control, and he hadn't even trusted her when she'd needed him most.

'I can't believe you didn't even tell anyone. You went through that all on your own, but you had me, Harry. You had me! You had all of us! I can't understand the lie you told us all.'

'I wasn't thinking straight. I was fresh out of training, young and terrified. I wasn't going to see the next year out. What about your lie?' he countered, sitting back on his haunches, away from her. 'You never told anyone about Aidan, not the truth. I'm his father. What about what you took from me? Don't you think I deserved to know? You stopped calling a couple of months after I left. No one told me about him, Annie, not even my own father. I missed out on my son's whole life because of you, and I didn't deserve that.'

Annabel reeled back. She'd been expecting this in the back of her mind, but it still felt like a slap in the face.

'You left me—what was I supposed to do? I didn't know you were sick, did I?'

'Oh, I don't know. Write me a letter, pick up the phone. Send me a sonogram, maybe! Anything would have been better. What if I'd never come back? You called me months ago to tell me to come home, and you knew what I'd be walking into.'

'Oh, yeah, that would have been a great phone call: *Harry, I hate you, but you left me a baby when you went.* How would you have taken that, mid treatment?'

'Forget about the treatment! Did you not think I had a right to know? I'm not the only one who lied here.' His eyes were shining with anger, and Annabel didn't have a retort.

He lied, I lied. So much wasted time. We can never come back from this. Anything I've been fantasising about just seems too hard now.

'I know. I have no room to talk. I have my own regrets, even more now I know the truth, but it's too late now. I wanted to protect myself, and Aidan. I nearly called, so many times.'

'Yeah? Well, I wish you had,' he spat back, his anger still evidently controlling him. 'I never got a choice in that decision either.'

He was so cold. It sent her barriers clanging right back up around her.

'Yeah, well, we can hash this out all day, can't we, but it just proves my point. We shouldn't be together,

Harry. There's enough water under our bridge to sink the whole thing.'

Harry's jaw flexed, and she looked away. She realised she'd been hoping for him to fight, deep down, but there were two deeply hurt people in the room now. He'd lied to her; she'd lied right back. Not exactly the basis for a loving relationship.

'We have Aidan to think about. Whatever this is, he has to be the priority.'

'I agree,' Harry said, his voice thick with sadness. 'That's it then. So no more kissing, right?'

'Right,' she agreed. 'I'm sorry, Harry. I really am. Are you well now? I know it's a bit late to ask now, but what happened? What was the prognosis?'

It took him a minute, and then he was opening his sandwich.

'I don't really want to talk about it right now. I'm fine, healthy as a horse. You know now; that's the main thing. We'd better get back to work. I don't want to fight any more.' He was looking straight at her, but all she could see on his face was disappointment. She could identify the emotion because she was pretty sure it was etched across her features. Tom and Lloyd were going to kill her. 'Let's get these eaten; we have a lot to do before school's out.'

She sneaked a few glances at him as they ate in the quiet of the house, but he didn't look her way again, and then they were back to work.

Harry was in the kitchen washing his hands free of grey paint when he heard hurried little footsteps heading towards the house. He looked across at Annabel, who was busy tidying away.

'Should I go?' he checked. They'd worked quietly for the rest of the day, apart from a few awkward 'Pass me the roller, please' or 'Another tea?'. He'd finally been able to tell her everything, but it had gone far from the way he'd wanted it to. They still weren't together, and the recriminations were thicker than the paint fumes in the room. It was a start, at least, but the afternoon had gone a little differently to the morning. The dancing, the kiss, the heat between them. The radio had been on low, but this time no one danced.

'No, it's fine,' she managed to reply before their son barrelled through the door. She gave him a little smile, and he flashed her one back. He was mad at her but he still loved her, more than ever. He wished he could go back and shake their younger selves, make them talk to each other.

'Mum, Mum! Guess what!'

She smiled at Harry, her face lighting up properly for the first time since lunch. 'I hope you're ready for this; he's a chatterbox after school.' She headed out to meet Aidan, and he met her in the kitchen doorway.

'We get to take someone to school for career day! I can't wait! Toby's dad is a pig farmer, and he's going to bring in a piglet!'

'Oh, really? That's so cool!' Harry said to him, and Aidan turned and noticed him for the first time. 'Your mother used to love piglets back when we were kids.'

He saw Annabel go rigid, and he replayed the words in his head.

'You knew my mum when she was little. I forgot!' Aidan exclaimed, all thoughts of the piglet forgotten as he looked from one adult to the other. 'What was she like? Granddad always says she was born with ants in her pants.'

Annabel laughed, leaning across to ruffle his hair. He brushed her hand off, smoothing it back down with a mini scowl on his mini-me face. 'Mum! Don't mess up my hair!'

This had Harry and Annabel both laughing. Harry knelt down, closer to Aidan's eye level. 'Mums do that, kiddo, and your mum was a little tornado when she was younger.' His gaze flicked to hers. 'She still is. Who are you taking to career day?'

Aidan gave his mum a sidelong look and moved a bit closer. 'Well, I was going to take Mum, but I don't know after today. Jade said her mum's an air stewardess, and she gets to go on aeroplanes for free. I was going to ask Granddad, but he's pretty old now.'

'Aidan!' Annabel chided softly. 'Abe isn't that old.'

Aidan rolled his eyes theatrically. 'He likes old things though, and Jamal's mum is a doctor too, so that would be super boring.'

'GPs *are* super boring,' Harry agreed, laughing. His heart was racing just being near his son. He wanted to scoop him up, give him a hug, but he was all too aware that Annabel was watching the pair of them as if she was waiting for a bomb to go off. He had a thought then. It was a risk, but one he was willing to take. A shot at one of the final lies that stood between them all, the elephant in the room. 'You know, I've been on a few aeroplanes myself, for work. How about me and your mum come together? Would that be better?'

Annabel's sharp gasp went unnoticed by Aidan, but Harry heard it loud and clear.

'If the station would let us have the time off, of

course.' He glanced at her now, trying his best to gauge her mood. She looked like a rabbit caught in the headlights. Aidan was bouncing on the spot between them.

'Really? Oh, Mum, that would be so cool. Can you both come?' He made a batting motion with his hands. 'That would knock the other kids out of the park!' He bounced over to his mother and pulled at her hands excitedly. 'Mum, come on, *please*!'

'Well, I'm sure that Harry has other things to do than come to your school, honey.'

'I really haven't,' Harry countered, pushing his luck now but still desperate to prove himself to them both. The thought of having an insight into Aidan's school life, his friends, and the world he inhabited was so appealing it was worth risking Annabel's wrath. He didn't enjoy her discomfort, but she had called him. She'd told him about Aidan and, despite their failed kiss and their fight, he still felt that the embers of hope had been stoked. He couldn't just shut his feelings off, even if he wanted to. He wanted to drain the water from under their bridge.

'If it's okay with the boss, I would love to come.'

Aidan's face lit up. 'Yes! Mum, can I go online now? I want to tell Finn and Josh!' He was already heading up the stairs at this point, and Annabel let him go.

'Just until your tea's ready, okay?'

'Yeah! Okay!' he shouted down the stairs, before his door slammed shut. Not long after, they could hear the *pew-pew* of the game and Aidan laughing and chatting excitedly with his friends.

'He loves that game,' Annabel said, walking past Harry to start tea. 'I've tried to play it loads of times, but I always die before I manage to land.'

* * *

Opening the freezer door, she took a second to gather her thoughts without Harry's gaze on her. The cold air helped to cool her face, which felt as if it was on fire. First today, and now this. She would be going into school with him, while every kid in the class hung on his word and stories of faraway adventures. She wanted to know about his life, so it would be good to hear, but all she could think about was the fact that she'd been left behind, and why. When she'd thought he was jet-setting and making his mark, she was raising a child, keeping his secret, and he was facing his own battle on his own.

She couldn't bear it. She hated the bitterness and bubbling fear that rose within her at inconvenient times; it kept her away from Harry as much as she wanted to let him in. The barb he had thrown at her regarding Aidan still smarted. He was right, but it was one more thing that they had between them. They could have the chance of being the family she'd always secretly wanted, and now she felt wretched at the thought of it never happening. She hated herself for being so weak, so wishy-washy in her decision-making, and her mother would have gone mad. She was almost glad that she wasn't here to see any of it. She'd died confident in the knowledge that her only child had Harry by her side.

'Listen, it's been a long day,' Harry said from behind her, and she knew he was close. 'Don't bother cooking for you and Aidan; I could get us a pizza or something, or we could go out to eat? I was hoping we could talk more. I need to clear the air.'

Grabbing a couple of steamed vegetable bags from the icy depths, she turned to him.

'We have a rule, no junk food in the week. I'm grateful for your help today, but I do need to crack on with getting things sorted. Once Aidan's in bed, I'm planning to crash myself. We have homework, the usual stuff to get through. I'll see you at work tomorrow.' She tried to be as sweet as possible, but she could tell by his face that he was disappointed. 'I have to keep things normal around here. Aidan's had a lot to deal with lately. I'll see you at the station, okay? It's been a bit of a revelation day; I'm having trouble processing things.'

Harry looked at her for a long moment, and slowly nodded. 'I overstepped.'

'You overstepped,' she echoed. 'Honestly, Harry, it's just a lot. I am trying. I'm sorry I never told you about him. I really am. I'm sorry for a lot of things.'

'I get it, Annie. I don't really have room to talk, do I?'

'I guess not, but I get it now. See you at work? I promise a ceasefire.'

He held his hands up in surrender, before tiptoeing forward on the lightest of feet and bending his head to hers. 'Me too,' he said softly, dropping the tiniest brush of his lips against her cheek and, before she could blink, he was heading to the hallway and out of the door.

She looked at the thawing bags of vegetables on the countertop and touched her hand to the spot where Harry's lips had touched her skin. Turning on the radio, she poured herself a glass of wine before attempting to turn her attention back to the daily chores. The lines between her real life and the life she'd always pictured were blurring, and it was getting harder and harder to see which one was the real one. Or which one she really wanted.

CHAPTER FIVE

HARRY WALKED INTO the station bright and early, eager to get the day going now he was finally getting settled back into work. Over the last few weeks he'd been spending time with Aidan and his dad, reconnecting with his father slowly and getting to know the amazing little boy who still didn't know he was his father.

Annabel had kept him at arm's length since the day at the house, and although she didn't flinch as much when he was around her any more, she wasn't letting her guard down either. There were no more barbed comments, but the atmosphere between them was still charged. They'd not spoken about their fight, neither seeming to want to rock the boat.

He caught her watching him sometimes, at work, when he was playing with Aidan or talking shop with his dad. They were together a lot, and she never stopped watching him. Sometimes, he wanted to ask her what she was thinking, what the frowns and worried expressions meant, but he was still scared of spooking her again. When he did finally ask her the question that burned deep in his heart, he wanted to be sure of the answer. Anything less would kill him.

He'd waited a long time to be back in her life, and

now that he was back, and had a real chance, he didn't want to risk blowing it again. Too much was at stake for all of them. They'd both kept secrets from each other, but now they were out there he saw a real chance for them, the three of them, if they could get over their past.

The school career day was coming up at the end of the month, and Aidan was still so excited about them both coming to present to his class; he'd spoken of nothing else. She hadn't stopped that, so he found himself wondering what his next move should be as he wandered into the staffroom to get a much-needed cup of coffee. The stuff Abe bought tasted like the bottom of a birdcage.

The moment he walked in he immediately regretted his caffeine addiction. It was full of people, and he was still tiptoeing around some of them. He decided to get what he needed and get out of there. Saying 'Hello' as he walked in, the room growing quieter in his presence, he filled his cup from the coffeemaker, taking a deep gulp of the hot black liquid before turning back to the door.

He bumped into Annabel, who was just coming into the room. 'Turn back around,' he said, taking her under the elbow and steering her away.

'What?' Annabel craned her neck over his shoulder. 'But I need coffee!'

He handed her his cup, walking them both to the room where they carried out the handovers.

'There you go. It's a full house in there.'

'Ugh.' She pulled a face and Harry sniggered. 'I wanted breakfast though!'

'I'll buy you a bacon roll when we hit the road. Why didn't you eat before you left?'

She rolled her eyes at him. 'That would be something. I'm all about getting Aidan up and out on a morning. I swear he's hitting his teens early.' She took the cup in both hands and took a drink as though she'd just emerged from the desert. 'Ahh, hello, my delicious dark lord.'

Harry laughed, and she elbowed him playfully.

'Knock it off, I'm having a moment here.'

'Oh, I know not to bother you before coffee.' They nodded to a couple of passing nurses as they neared their destination.

'You remember that, eh?' she teased, taking another sip.

'I remember everything. Every little detail,' he said, waggling his eyebrows. She blushed, and his heart skipped a beat. 'Come on and bring the dark lord. Let's get this show on the road. I can already smell the bacon.'

In the last few weeks they'd fallen into a sort of uneasy groove with each other. The tension at work had lessened, although she'd never quite managed to quell the butterflies that still fluttered in the pit of her stomach when Harry leaned in close in the ambulance, or when they witnessed a tender moment with one of their patients. She'd even cried on him when one of the calls had been a bad one, and he'd held her and let her sob her heart out on him without even a second's hesitation. Feeling his arms around her had made her feel so supported, and she knew he a hundred per cent had her back. Just as he had before. He was every bit the paramedic she was, and they had soon dropped back into their old shorthand way of communicating and working on the job. As she went to reach for something, he was already in the process of passing it to her, and vice versa. It made them the ultimate team, and the station had started to hum with the buzz of them being back together.

With the career day coming up, she no longer dreaded it as she had. In fact, she was rather looking forward to it. Not that she'd tell him that. She'd found herself watching him with their son, and when they were on the job together. She was imagining what he'd gone through with his cancer, worrying about how he had come through it. How he felt now. He and Abe were even different together. They laughed now, the recriminations of the past seemingly starting to resolve. She was so glad; she knew that Abe had been so upset about his son's disappearance. Having Aidan around him had helped, but it would never replace his son. She understood that because no one would ever take the place of Aidan in her own heart.

By watching Harry—her Harry—she knew without a shadow of a doubt that he was in there too, right next to Aidan in the beating organ in her chest, and she knew that really he had never left. Now all she needed to do was decide whether she followed the beat of her heart or her head. Her mind was flip-flopping on a daily basis, and she didn't quite know which one to trust. So she stayed in limbo. Looking for a sign, a concrete reason? She just didn't know. So she focused on what she did know. The daily grind, her job, her son. Everything else was just too confusing to see clearly.

With the handover done, the two of them were soon

on their way, a princely breakfast fuelling their busy day. And a busy day it turned out to be. Two calls for chest pains, four elderly falls, one woman going into labour at home alone, and more than a dozen slips, scrapes and work-related injuries.

'Wow, London is just full of poorly people today.' Harry arched his back, shifting in the passenger seat of ambulance seventeen.

Annabel drove through the city streets, focused on the traffic but flashing him a tired smile. 'I know, and not one camel in sight.'

'Ha-ha.' Harry stuck his tongue out at her. 'Funny. It's not all desert dust and camels, you know.'

The next call came in, and Harry took care of the details while Annabel put the lights and sirens on, following the quickest route to the casualty while Harry fed back their ETA to the control room.

'Eight-year-old child, male, difficulty breathing. Mother is very anxious. High temp overnight first controlled with paracetamol and ibuprofen, but now the fever is spiking and he is unable to speak more than a few words without difficulty. Query for a possible asthma attack.'

Annabel's lips pursed, and once the road opened up she put her foot down on the accelerator. They pulled up outside the house in no time and were greeted by a man standing at the garden gate. He had a cigarette in one hand and a can of strong lager in the other. Harry nodded at the man, and his eyes focused on Annabel's.

'You get the equipment; I'll go in first.' Annabel rolled her eyes at him, but something about the man made her follow his lead for once. Their priority was the little boy inside. Harry got out and approached the gate.

'Hello, sir—you called for assistance?'

Annabel worked quickly, Harry talking to the man, who was swaying and bumping into the gate.

'I didn't. Her indoors did. I told her, Ben's just trying it on. Coughing and wheezing all night. Kept us all up. He just doesn't want to go to school. You're wasting your time, mate, and your little woman here. Last thing I want is another panic-stricken female in the place.'

'Well, we're here now. Is Ben your son?' He didn't like the way the man was sneering at Annabel. He obviously had little respect for women.

'Stepson,' the man countered, not even looking at Annabel as she came to stand at the side of Harry. Neither of them missed the sneer on his face as he spoke. The man pointed a thumb behind him towards the house, showering ash from his cigarette over himself. 'She panders to him too much; it's only a cold.'

'Can we come past, please?' Harry said, his hand already on the gate. The man slowly and sluggishly moved aside, and Harry caught hold of Annabel's shirt sleeve, taking one of the kit bags from her and leading her into the property.

'Hello?' Annabel called into the hallway.

'Up here,' a panicked female voice said. 'Quickly, please! Second bedroom on the left.'

The house was neat and tidy, aside from a full ashtray and a few empty cans littering the coffee table. A sports channel was on in the background, and they could hear the weak murmurs of the boy as they ran up the stairs.

'I told you, you're wasting your time. Isn't there anyone else you could be helping? I've warned her not to push my buttons.' The man was shouting up the stairs now, but the paramedics were already focused on the boy laid on the top of a single bed, his mother looking hollow-eyed and utterly panicked.

'Hi, Ben,' Annabel said, walking into the room as slowly as she could without losing time or panicking the boy. 'We're here to help, okay?'

The little boy was red-faced and because he was bare-chested, wearing only character pyjama bottoms, she could tell from his torso that he was really struggling to breathe. The little mite nodded, and the pair of them got to work. They listened to his chest, put a monitor on his finger and took his blood pressure.

'Mum, is it?' Harry said softly, turning to the woman while Annabel hooked Ben up to the portable oxygen tank they had carried in.

'Julie, yeah. Is he going to be okay?'

'We're here to get him sorted; this oxygen will help him breathe better, get his stats back up,' he said smoothly. 'Has he had any difficulties like this before? Any asthma, or any history in the family?'

The worried mother shook her head, never taking her eyes off the boy. 'No, nothing like that. I don't think the smoke's been helping him though.' She looked at the doorway now, wide-eyed, as if her partner was standing there, but when Annabel looked, it was empty. The television channel had been changed downstairs, the noise blaring out. 'He started with a cold a couple of days ago. Nothing major, but after last night I just couldn't keep his temperature down for long, and now...'

She crumpled, dropping a kiss on her son's head and keeping him close.

'Oxygen's low, decreased breath sounds on both sides,' Annabel said quietly, and Harry nodded once.

'Julie, we need to pop Ben up to the hospital, get him checked over properly. Can you grab him what he needs, and we'll set off? It sounds like he's got a nasty chest infection. I'll go get a chair. Be ready to transport.'

He didn't want to be carrying Ben down the stairs, and he had a feeling that the man downstairs wouldn't be very pleased with the idea that the emergency services were 'entertaining' his stepson and his illness. He walked out of the room, running to the ambulance as soon as the boy was out of sight, heading upstairs with the chair as quickly and nimbly as he could.

'Hey!' The man got up from the couch as Harry got halfway up the stairs. 'What the hell are you doing? Woman, I warned you!'

Harry ignored him, entering the boy's room and closing the door behind him. He didn't hear anything further, but the television volume went up again. Harry clenched his jaw and focused on the job in hand. He wanted to get the boy out of this place, and the fact that Annabel was here was making him nervous. The urge to protect her was raging through his body. He couldn't bear the thought of her being hurt. Someone with a temper and a drink in them was not a good combination.

Not on my watch, he thought, and they got the boy out of there as fast as they could.

Much later, after Ben was settled in the care of the staff at A&E, Annabel followed Harry out to the ambulance.

'Well, I thought that might go south at one point. I thought we might need to call for police assistance.

He was a piece of work, wasn't he? I felt sorry for them both.'

Harry didn't reply, and when they'd got back into the ambulance she looked at him with concern.

'You need a minute? We have a little time, if you need it.'

'I'll never understand people like that. The poor boy was ill; she'd have called before if it wasn't for him, I'm sure. He could have got so much worse.'

'He didn't though; he's going to be fine. We got to him, got him help.'

Harry responded through gritted teeth. 'That's not the point, and you know it. The kid deserved a father to be there for him.'

'You don't know that he hasn't. Families split up; it doesn't always mean that the father isn't on the scene, or that he doesn't care.'

'I hate that Aidan never had that.' He looked away from her, gazing out at the hospital's comings and goings. 'I hate that he thinks his father isn't in his life.'

'It's not like that, and at the time I—'

'I'm not having a go; it's just hard, that's all. I don't blame you. I get your reasons. I hate them, but I get it. The thought of you getting hurt today… It tore me apart. I would have taken that guy's head off if he'd come near you.'

'You don't have to worry. I can look after myself.'

'That's not what I'm saying. I know you can, but I want to be the one who looks after you too.'

He grabbed for her hand, taking it into his and placing it in his lap.

'I don't blame you; I blame myself. For everything.'

Not knowing what to say, how to make it right, Annabel squeezed his hand and then pulled away, clicking on the console that they were available for another call.

'We've got another hour; let's shake that last call off.'

He didn't reply, pulling on his seatbelt and jamming it violently into the holder.

She looked at him thoughtfully. 'Listen, it's Friday, and it's been a week. You got plans for tonight?'

That turned his head in her direction. She gave him a little smile.

'I think Dad has his poker buddies coming round. I was just planning to stay out of the way. Sleep off the day.'

'Well, as good as *that* sounds, I was thinking I might have a night off from cooking and order Chinese food with Aidan, maybe watch a film.' He looked bemused, and she patted his hand. 'I was thinking you could come over, share some noodles?'

He still looked drawn, but the lines on his brow lessened as he gave her a grateful smile. 'Noodles and a movie sound great. What time?'

Annabel, fresh from the shower, listened to Aidan giggle downstairs as he watched one of his favourite TV shows, camped on the couch under his comfy throw. The canned laughter from the comedy show filtered upstairs, and she smiled to herself as she thought of her son, sitting in his pyjamas, waiting for Harry to arrive. He'd be here soon, and the minute they'd left each other in the hospital car park, the butterflies had started. She was looking forward to it so much, and Aidan's face when she'd told him had made her heart sing.

They did rattle around a bit in the new house. When

he was in bed fast asleep, she ended up going to bed early half the time, bored of sitting alone and looking at the newly decorated walls or the list of stuff she still wanted to get done. Tonight would be a welcome change, and she couldn't help but think of it as a trial run either. Which meant she found herself wanting to make the effort, just a little.

She turned to her wardrobe and the half dozen outfits she had picked out as possibilities for the evening. They verged from ballroom attire to full-on sex kitten, and she groaned at her choices.

'Get a grip on yourself,' she chided her reflection in the mirror. She put them all back into the wardrobe and, heading to her dresser drawer, she pulled out her comfy black jeans and a white T-shirt. There. Not too much, but she did look good. She made to head downstairs, but at the last minute she blow-dried her hair so it fell in waves around her face, and slicked on a little bit of pink lip gloss. 'There, nothing too much.'

She nodded at herself in the bedroom mirror and headed downstairs just in time to hear the knock at the door. She took a second to quell the frisson of nerves that fizzed through her body and, taking a deep breath, she stepped into the hall.

'Hi.' She opened the door to Harry, who looked stunning in a blue checked shirt, open at the neck, paired with dark blue jeans. She wanted to laugh as she took him in but held it back. They had both tried a little too hard to look casual, it seemed. 'Come in.'

'Hi.' Harry smiled, stepping into the hallway and looking around him. 'Wow, the builders really cracked on with the place. It's looking great.'

'Thanks. I'm still picking dust bunnies up but yeah, it's getting there now.'

Annabel motioned him to come into the kitchen, and she noticed for the first time that he was bearing gifts. One was a football, and the other a beautiful bunch of flowers. She'd been so focused on him, she'd never even registered what was in his arms. The lounge in the TV was still playing, and Aidan's laughter filtered through to them. He hadn't heard the door.

'Selective hearing,' she explained. 'His show finishes soon. Come through?'

Harry eyed the doorway to the lounge but followed her through with a nod. 'I brought you some housewarming gifts. Thanks for inviting me tonight; it's already getting rowdy at home.'

Annabel's heart warmed when she heard that he considered Abe's to be home. The pair of them were so similar, they'd always butted heads. Abe had seemingly let go of the GP father-son dream, and when Annabel saw the two of them these days they seemed to be rubbing along quite nicely together, rowdy card nights aside. It made her so happy, after all those years of them being at loggerheads. It was nice to see, and Abe was far happier and less grumpy to boot. Win-win. He hadn't even been angry at her for keeping the truth about Aidan a secret, which had surprised her too. Given their struggles over the years, it could have been a heck of a lot worse. Of course, Abe had kept his own counsel for years. He'd never let Annabel know that he'd worked it out. Like she'd said, they were so similar in many ways.

'No problem. Aidan's been looking forward to it. If he wasn't glued to his programme, he'd already be in here chewing your ear off.' She took the flowers from him, leaning in to smell the blooms. 'Calla lilies too, my favourite.' Her hair fell over her eye and Harry leaned in, brushing the strand away with his free hand.

'I know. I remember.' She shivered when his fingertips brushed down her cheek and, closing her eyes, she turned her face into his hand. His eyes went dark and he leaned in, just a fraction. The paper wrapping the flowers being squashed between them rustled as she followed his lead.

'Is that for me?'

Aidan bounded into the room, and the pair of them sprang apart. Harry threw her a look that made her pulse race and addressed his enthusiastic son.

'Of course it is! I thought, with your new garden being sorted, you could get some practice in.'

Harry whirled around on the balls of his feet, leaning down to show Aidan the football. Annabel knew it was a decent one; Harry had been eyeing it in the shop the other week when they'd been shopping for new boots.

'It's so cool! Thanks, Harry! Look, Mum!' Aidan took the ball from Harry's hands, showing her his gift.

'Oh, that's great! We'll have to get a football net for out back; you can show us some skills.'

Aidan's expression was so happy and, looking at Harry's flushed face, she could tell he was equally elated. His red cheeks also gave him away as feeling just as caught out by their son as she did. The two of them started to chat away, and she busied herself by finding a vase for the flowers. They really were beautiful. She couldn't remember the last time a man had bought her any. Harry had always been a romantic in the past.

This is a housewarming gift, though, not a declaration.

Even her own thoughts sounded unsure. If they hadn't been interrupted, she'd have kissed him again. Glancing back at Harry, who was looking at her over Aidan's shoulder, she felt certain that he knew it too.

'Another prawn toast?'

Aidan shook his head, groaning as he patted his little flat tummy. 'No, thanks, Mum, I'm stuffed!'

Harry sat back next to him on the couch, patting his own belly. 'Nor me, I can't do it.'

The feast was sitting out on the coffee table, the credits of the family film they had just finished watching rolling on screen.

'Well, more for me then. Waste not, want not!'

Annabel swooped in for the last piece, eating it in two bites.

Harry chuckled, a low rumble. 'You always were like a dustbin,' he teased.

'Hey!' She flicked out a foot from her sideways position on the armchair, trying to kick him. He didn't flinch, just grabbed her bare foot. His touch made her skin tingle, and he stroked the top of her foot and slowly let it go.

Aidan was giggling at the side of him 'He's right Mum; you always order too much and then eat your way through it.' He made a snorting pig sound, and Harry joined in. She pretended to glare at them both, and caught Aidan stifling a yawn.

'Well, piglet, I think that means it's time for you to go to bed.'

'Aww, no!' he tried to protest, but another yawn cut him off. 'Okay,' he said glumly. ''Night, Harry.' He flung himself into Harry's chest, hugging him tight.

Harry looked shocked for a half second, before wrapping his arms around him and kissing the top of his head. ''Night, kiddo, sleep tight. And hey, if you want a goalie, I'm in.'

'Cool. Can we, Mum?' He lifted his head to look at his mother, and she found herself a little too choked to speak, seeing the two of them cuddled up on the couch, so natural with each other. She nodded and smiled robotically, pointing a finger towards the hallway.

'I know, I know—brush my teeth. 'Night, Harry!' He held out a hand and Harry high-fived him back.

''Night, Aidan. Sleep tight.'

'I won't be long. Make yourself at home,' she said over her shoulder as she headed up the stairs after her son.

Once teeth were brushed and hands and face were washed, Aidan snuggled down under the covers. Annabel tucked him in, turning his dinosaur night light down to low so the room glowed with a dull hue. The light from the landing trickled in, showing Aidan's tired face over the covers.

'Harry's so cool, Mum. He played football when he worked away, you know. I want to do that when I grow up.'

'Did he?'

'Yeah, he played with the other doctors. You should start a team, Mum, at the ambulance station. Harry could be the striker.'

Annabel laughed, sitting down on the bed and smoothing a tuft of hair off his face. 'Well, I think the nurses might like that, but there's no way I'd be getting my lily-white legs out in front of my colleagues and showing them how rubbish at the game I am.'

Another giggle filled the room. 'Yeah, you're rubbish.'

'Hey! I was great at netball at school, I'll have you know.'

That just produced an eye roll of epic proportions.

'That's lame, Mum. Messi is way cooler than any netball player.'

'I'll give you that,' she said, dropping a kiss on the top of her beautiful son's head. Seeing Harry and Aidan together had made her realise just how alike they were in their mannerisms. The eye rolls, the mickey taking. Harry always had been cheeky, and Aidan was just the same. She wondered what else she had blocked out about the past. 'Straight to sleep now.'

He turned onto his side, facing Annabel and resting his head on the plump pillows beneath him.

Sleepily, his eyelids already hooded, his brow furrowed. 'I like Harry. Do you, Mum?'

'Yes, I like him. He's good to work with.'

'I think he likes you too.'

'What makes you say that?'

'He looks at you a lot. Like how Uncle Tom and Uncle Lloyd look at each other.'

'Well, your uncles are in love, so it's a bit different.'

'I think it's the same. I think he likes you, Mum. Do you like him?'

'Of course I like him. He's a good friend, and we work together a lot so that's a good thing.'

'That's not what I meant, Mum.'

Annabel smiled down at him, fighting to stay awake as his busy day started to take its toll.

'I know, love. It's grown-up stuff; sometimes it's a bit complicated.'

'I know,' he said, showing wisdom far beyond his years. 'I just think that people who love each other should always say it. That's what Granddad says, and he's really smart.'

Annabel said nothing, her throat not co-operating now. She played with his fringe, just like she'd done when he was little, dropping another kiss onto his little forehead and watching in silence as his long dark lashes fluttered as he fell asleep. She was halfway out of his bedroom door when his soft voice, thick with sleep, stilled her departure.

'Do you think he'll stay forever? I really hope he does. We need him now, don't we?'

She turned to ask him what he meant, but he was already fast asleep.

'Yes, kiddo,' she whispered into the half light of the room. 'I think we do.'

Heading downstairs, she walked into the lounge and saw it was empty. The coffee table had been cleared, the cushions plumped and the television turned off. Just as her heart was sinking at the thought that Harry had left, she heard humming coming from the kitchen.

'You didn't have to do that,' she said from the doorway, watching him wash up at the sink. He looked so at home in her kitchen, as though he had always been there. Here in this house, with her.

'I don't mind, the least I could do really. I had a great

night.' He turned to look at her as he placed another clean plate onto the dish rack. 'Aidan asleep already?'

'Yeah,' she said, crossing the room and taking a bottle of white wine from the fridge. 'He was exhausted.' The leftovers from their meal had been wrapped up and put into the fridge. 'You even saved me some snacks!'

He laughed, another low rumble. 'I couldn't find a trough, so I improvised.' He dried his hands on one of the towels from the rack and leaned back against the sink, his forearms flexing under his rolled-up shirt-sleeves.

'Carry on with the sow jokes, I dare you.' She waggled the wine bottle at him. 'Drink?'

'Sure. Dad send a text a few minutes ago, complaining that Leonard is cheating. He mentioned something about 1976, so I'm guessing it's not the first time they've butted heads. I'm in no hurry. Glasses?'

'Behind you, top cabinet.'

They took them through to the lounge, sitting next to each other on the couch. Annabel flicked on the television, some comedy sitcom on low.

'You feeling better, after the Ben call?' She'd wanted to ask him since the minute he'd walked in but hadn't wanted to spoil the mood.

'Not really, but I checked with A&E. He's in for the night for observation. Mum's staying with him.'

Annabel filled both their glasses, offering one to Harry. Their hands crossed on the stem, and he stroked his finger along hers before taking it.

'That's good. I checked with the social care team. They are in the system, so I flagged up today's call with them. They'll check in with mum before they leave the hospital.'

Harry's shoulders relaxed a little, and he took a deep gulp of the cold drink. 'Thanks. I had been thinking the same thing, to be honest.'

'No problem. I would have done it anyway; the family needs some help. The mother's always worked well with them, by all accounts.'

Harry nodded. 'I got that feel from her. She obviously loves him.'

They fell silent, watching the television for a while in comfortable silence.

'I'd rather die than see Aidan suffer like that,' he said eventually, turning towards her on the couch. She tucked her feet up behind her, their knees touching now.

'I know that. He thinks you're amazing.'

'As a friend of his mum's, sure,' he retorted, his jaw flexing. 'As some long-lost son of his granddad.'

This isn't going how I thought it would. He's...angry.

'I don't want to argue, please. We're doing okay, aren't we?'

Harry sighed, and the anger seemed to leave his features. 'Sure. I've loved getting to know him. Dad's been great too. It's weird—the old issues, they just don't seem to be an issue any more.'

'He missed you, a lot. He did try to contact you; they all did.'

'I know,' he acknowledged. 'I just wasn't in the right frame of mind to hear from them.' He looked her right in the eye. 'I would have answered when you called again. I was on shift. I wish I'd called.'

She was mid sip, the rim of the glass resting on her lips. She finished the action, allowing the wine to cool her throat and give her strength. She'd almost bitten down on the glass when he'd spoken, but she had nowhere to hide with him staring straight at her.

'I know,' was all she could summon to say. 'I wish you had too.'

'Did you miss me?'

Stupid question, Harry.

'That's not a fair question.'

'I know, but I'm asking it anyway. Answer it, please.'

Answer it, he says. Hell, I could write a book about it. What the heck do I say? Do I tell him the truth, that I missed him every day? That I sobbed at every sonogram appointment? That I once punched an advert on the wall of the Tube station because it had an advertisement for Dubai on it? No, no, no. Protect that underbelly, Sanders. Don't give everything away.

'Well, yes. Short answer, I did miss you, for a long time.'

For ever, in fact. You ruined me for all other men. No, not that either. You sound like an old maid.

She took another sip of her wine and started to talk. 'I vomited. In the airport. Did you know that? All over the airport lounge. Pregnancy joys, I guess, but I didn't know at the time.'

He shook his head, his expression giving nothing away. She waved him off with her hand.

'Of course you didn't. Sorry. It was after you'd gone. I threw up right there in the check-in hall, in front of everyone. The woman behind the counter got a shock, I can tell you.'

'I'm sorry for that.'

'I threw up because I was already pregnant with Aidan. I didn't know at the time, not till a few weeks after. I ignored the signs, I suppose, or more I didn't see them. The possibility didn't enter my head. Even with all my training, I didn't have a clue.'

Harry hung his head, a look she'd never seen before on his face. 'Sometimes, even the best training in the world can't make you see the signs that are right there in front of you. Not till the body takes over and makes you see it. None of this is your fault. Did you ever hate me?'

'Who says I don't now?' she quipped, but he didn't laugh. 'No, I never hated you. We had a child coming. I had no room in my heart for hate.'

'Did you miss me all the time?'

He was looking at her intently, his eyes focused on her. Her eyes, then her lips. She licked them without thinking, feeling suddenly parched. She took another sip of Dutch courage, and she could feel Harry tense at the side of her when she took too long to answer. As though doubt had crept into the silence and filled it for him.

'Sorry. Forget I asked. I didn't mean to push.'

'Yes,' she admitted finally. 'I missed you every day. I missed telling you about work, about the funny things that happened in the station. When Aidan took his first steps, I cried myself to sleep. When I was in labour, Tom at my side, I shouted for you to come. He told me after. I was delirious on gas and air, half out of my mind with pain and fear. I missed you Harry; we all did.' She turned back to the television and heard the clink of his wine glass on the coffee table. Felt him take her glass from her hand. She kept her eyes on the television, feeling as if every nerve- ending was on fire.

'Look at me, Annie. Please.' For once, hearing his

name for her didn't make her feel anything but cherished. She was still his Annie.

She took a breath and turned to him. He was closer now, his face inches from hers.

'I'm glad I told you why I left. I wanted you to know. To understand why I made the mistake of not taking you with me. I missed you too. I loved you so much, Annie. Every single day. Your face kept me going on my worst days. I threw up a lot too, when I was sick. I regret a lot in my life, but nothing quite so much as how much I hurt you. How I wrecked our little family before it had even begun. The thing is, I—'

'Do you still?'

Her question threw him off track, and he tried to stay on subject. Being so close to her after all this time was intoxicating. It made his head spin. Her lips were so close, her body turned to him as her face searched his for the answer she sought. He was trying to get his lips to work, to form the sounds he was desperate to get out there, but all the treacherous things wanted to do was meet with hers. He wanted to kiss her stupid, and they tingled with the sheer need. Damn his body; it had let him down at some of the most pivotal moments. You never learned that in any textbook.

'Do I still what?' He finally managed to get them back under control.

Looking at him now, she looked like the young girl he had fallen in love with. Strong, driven, but less sure of herself.

'Love me.'

That was the easiest question to answer. It had never been in doubt, all these years. It had never dulled. Not over time or the thousands of miles, or even when he'd been fighting against the bad cells that were within him, trying to take him away from her for good. Throughout all that, she had been the voice in his head, his reason for getting up and facing each day. Every day—from the day in the airport to this one. Till the day he finally left this earth.

'Yes, Annie. God, yes.' He took her hands in his, rubbing his thumbs along the soft skin he'd once thought he'd never get to touch again. 'I never stopped. Never.'

She closed the gap between them and he met her there. Their lips melded together as they poured every ounce of their love into their kiss. He lifted her into his arms and she straddled him on the sofa, her hair falling over them both as they explored each other's mouths. Harry could feel her heart pumping fast, every bit as fast as his.

She broke off the kiss to draw breath. 'I love you too, Harry. Damn you, but I love you too.'

CHAPTER SIX

THE IMPOSING BRICK building of the inner-city primary school loomed in Harry's windshield as they pulled into the car park. He'd driven the whole way from her house with her hand in his lap, his hand covering hers between every change of gear. He'd even grumbled about that, declaring his intention to take back his hire car the second he got the chance and buy a car with automatic gears, so he didn't have to let go of her hand.

Annabel couldn't argue with that. She loved every minute of the time they spent together—the minutes they were alone, away from prying eyes. Since the fateful movie night, they'd been meeting out of work whenever they got a chance, and a babysitter. He'd taken her to Chinatown and watched her demolish half the menu with a big daft grin on his face. They'd kissed in the cinema like a pair of teenagers, all thoughts of the action flick forgotten as they held each other in the dark.

They'd never taken it further than that, though it was getting harder to call time on their kissing. Without even discussing it, they'd both seemingly reached the same conclusion. They were taking their time, the pair of them seeing how fragile this new relationship was, how much was at stake. At work, they'd still been the same team, all thoughts of the past put to bed, or left unsaid. She knew that they'd never finished their conversation, that he had more to say, but at this moment in her life she was content to stay in their bubble.

Harry had spent time with Aidan too, at the house, but they'd told no one about the development in their relationship. They'd been careful around Aidan, but once he was in bed their couch kissing sessions made her feel like a young teenager in love all over again. And she was kissing the same boy, who was now the hottest man she'd ever laid eyes on. She could admit that to herself fully now she was done being mad at him. Not that she needed to. Her wandering hands were testament to that. She was surprised they hadn't set her new couch on fire with the intensity of their barely contained heat. Amazing what a kiss could do to wake a girl up from a deep sleep. She was well and truly awake now, and she felt beautiful. Seen.

Sometimes, when they were walking down the corridor at work towards each other, acting professional, he would give her a look, or she would feel him brush against her skin, and she felt so deliciously high, naughty even. As professional as they kept things, hiding the development in their relationship from everyone around them, she felt as if they were walking around in their own bubble. Whenever he was near her, she felt his presence. She glowed like a star in the night sky and, judging by his fumbling sometimes, the way he tripped over his words, she knew she wasn't the only one lighting up. She just didn't want anyone else to see it. Not yet.

They didn't need any opinions from those around them. They'd not even discussed where it was going.

Annabel wasn't going to be the one to push it. She wasn't even sure herself what they were doing, but it felt right. They'd spent their rare weekends off together at Annabel's house, cooking meals together and dancing in the kitchen. He'd rocked up one day with a football net for Aidan, and they'd barbecued outside in the newly finished garden, Harry being the goalie to Aidan's striker. She'd never laughed so much, and Aidan was thrilled with having a man around the house.

It could be like this all the time, she thought to herself for the millionth time. *If you just let go, let all the truths blow away with the wind, we could be happy. We could be a family.*

He was still the same tender, loving Harry he'd been before, better even, but there were times when he grew quiet. He avoided going into too much detail about his illness, how bad it had actually been. It must have changed him, and she wondered whether he was truly happy being back, especially when he seemed so far away in his own head at times. She wondered what he was thinking, whether he was longing for far-off shores again. Was he really as recovered as he said he was? She didn't want to rock the boat, but she had a million questions. It was such a nice time sailing through life with him, so she gave him time.

The murmurs around the station were still there; she caught the odd look when they walked in together, chatting away to each other, but she held her head high and pretended that she didn't. She was the head paramedic; her position was one of integrity, and they were doing nothing wrong. At work, other than the fizz in her belly, she was always on the ball. She would never let a patient down; neither of them ever would. Medicine and patient care meant far too much to both of them. Once she had a label for what they were, other than childhood sweethearts and secret co-parents, then that would be a different matter. Work would have to know. She was still in control of her career, and that would never change.

Harry turned off the engine and looked out at the school. 'It looks nice.'

Distracted, she glanced at the school and smiled.

'Yeah, he loves it here. He's got lots of friends too. He wants to be a paramedic, you know.'

Harry's eyebrows shot up to his hairline. 'Really? That's great! A chip off the old block, eh? Dad will be furious.'

They laughed together, thinking of Abe.

'I think we should tell him,' she said softly.

'Rather you than me; he's already talking about getting him a doctor play set for Christmas.'

'No, not Abe.' She pulled his hand to her mouth, kissing the back. 'Aidan. I think we should tell him that you're his father.'

Harry didn't reply for a moment, but his expression said everything. His eyes brimmed with tears and he blinked, seemingly to push them back.

'Are you sure?'

'Yes, I'm sure. We're all spending so much time together, and I feel so guilty for keeping it from him. You do everything a dad does, Harry. You play with him, look after him—you're in his life. He deserves a real father, not some abstract faraway idea of you. I've taken enough time from you both. Enough now—we can be a proper family. No more hiding.'

Harry was moving his head like a nodding dog now, his grip on her hand tight. 'When?'

'Today, after school. We can take him to the park, tell him then.' Annabel stroked his face, which was now rather pale. 'You freaking out?'

He silenced her with an enthusiastic kiss. 'Hell, no. I'm ready.' His features clouded again. 'Does this mean telling him about us too?'

'I hadn't thought that far, in all honesty, but yes, I think so. One thing at a time, maybe. Let's do this first. See how he copes.'

'He'll have questions. What do I tell him?'

'The truth, as much as we can. You went to help people, to save lives. He'll understand that. Every adult around him is a professional lifesaver. We can tell him everything when he's older. He's always coped okay, understood that his dad wasn't around.' That was true, though she had seen him get upset sometimes. Father's Day. Christmas. Seeing other dads at the school gates. She didn't tell Harry any of that. It didn't need to be said. It would only serve to torture them both. 'You're here now. Things are different.'

There it was again. That faraway look.

'I want that more than anything, but we need to talk too. Before we go any further. I have things to tell you. I know I don't talk about my cancer much, but I do have more things to say.'

'We should go in,' she said, checking her watch. 'It starts soon; he'll be waiting.'

'You're doing it again.'

'I'm not.'

I am. I'm scared. What if I don't like the answer? What if he gets sick again, like Mum?

'We need to get in there. Aidan's waiting.'

'I can't have children, Annie. The cancer treatment was really intense, and at the time they offered to freeze some of my semen, but I was just too upset. I never wanted a child once I'd lost you. Another stupid regret of mine. I should have stuck some of those little soldiers on ice.'

The statement hung in the air between them. She felt as if it had slapped her in the face. Hard.

'That's not funny.'

'Do you see me laughing?'

'We have Aidan though. I guessed that your cancer might have left you sterile. Hell, I've done enough research over the last few weeks, I'll admit. What are you saying?'

'Aidan is mine. I'm not questioning that. I'm saying that I can't have children.'

'I don't understand. I haven't mentioned having another child. Does it bother you?'

'You're not listening again. It's not about wanting another child. I love Aidan. You know that. I'm telling you that I can't father a child.'

Harry sighed, and she knew he'd seen her check her watch again. In truth, she wanted to jump out of the car, avoid the conversation altogether. Was he changing his mind about them?

'Okay, Miss Punctual. The short version is that treatment was pretty intensive. It was touch and go for a while. They asked me if I wanted to freeze my sperm at the time but, with losing you, I just didn't see the point. Another thing I wish I'd thought better of. The upshot is, I'm sterile. Have been for about six years now. I've been wanting to tell you since I got back. Since we got back together. I need you to know, before we tell Aidan anything. What if we become a family, and you want more kids? I can't give you that. Everything else, yes, God, yes, but not that. I couldn't lose you again.'

Annabel felt upset, but not for herself. More for him. He'd been carrying this a long time; she could see on his face that he was terrified of her reaction. She could at least calm him down on that score. She'd known he was hiding something, and her relief was palpable. She didn't care; she'd made peace with it since that day at the house. She'd known the treatments, the prognosis, the complications that often occurred. Since her mother got sick, cancer had become her specialist subject.

'I've never thought about having more children. I'm happy at work, Aidan is thriving. We have you. Why worry about something when we don't have to?'

'You say that now, but—'

'But nothing. I love Aidan with all of my heart, but he's enough. More than enough. Hell, I don't even think I could do that again. Does it bother you?'

'I've made peace with it. I guess you can't really miss what you don't have, and I didn't have you either. I always imagined us having a family. When I found out about Aidan, it felt surreal. In a good way.' He was rushing his words out now, and Annabel sat and listened. 'I never thought I'd be a father. Being a father to your child, Annie? It's everything. He's the cherry on the top of my coming home.'

Annabel smiled, taking his face between her hands and pulling him in for a lingering kiss. Out of the corner of her eye she saw movement through the window. Kids' heads bobbing up and down.

'We need to go, but you don't need to worry, Harry. We *are* a family. You coming home completed that for me. And besides, Aidan's been dropping hints about a dog. If we get broody we can expand that way.' She smirked at him, and his face finally relaxed.

'Okay, but we need to talk about this some more. It's a lot to ask of you.'

'Don't you always want to talk?' she deflected expertly, sticking her tongue out at him to lighten the mood. 'You're not asking anything of me, Harry. I have my family. I'm happy, finally.' She kissed him again. 'Come on, we have an audience to wow.'

Aidan's smile was so big that it filled his whole face as the two paramedics gave their talk, telling the children about their day-to-day duties. Leaving out the scary stuff, and telling a few stories about rescuing people from railings, helped by other emergency services, about how fast the ambulance went, how cool it was to help the people of London. Harry talked of Dubai, the people he'd met there, the way their medical systems ran differently to those in England. How sweaty it could get out there, what his days off looked like. The children were like little sponges, absorbing every word, and sticking their hands up to ask more questions. The other parents even asked a few of their own.

All too soon, though, the school bell went and the children all said goodbye to their parents and started to file out of the classroom. Mrs Shepherd, the class teacher, was left sitting at her desk, marking papers. Before long, it was just the four of them.

'Well, kiddo, I think that went well.' Annabel gave

Aidan a sneaky hug and, for once in a public setting, he allowed it.

'Are you kidding? It was amazing!' He threw his arms out wide, making a rainbow-shaped arc with his hands. 'Thank you, thank you, thank you!' He hugged Harry's legs tight.

Mrs Shepherd came across the room. 'Sorry to interrupt. Aidan, you need to get out to break now. You can show them to reception if you like, but then straight outside for some fresh air.' She gave Annabel a friendly nod. 'Nice to see you again.'

'You too. Come on then, kiddo, you're missing your football time.'

Aidan walked them both to reception, holding one hand of each of them, keeping up a constant stream of chatter all the way. Harry winked at Annabel over his head, and she winked back. She really felt as if things were falling into place. Even with his bombshell. They just needed tonight to go well, and another barrier would be broken down.

'Fancy the park tonight, after school? We have the day off; we could get ice-cream?'

'Harry too?' he asked, moving his hands from side to side, taking them along with him.

'Who do you think wants the ice-cream?' Harry laughed.

They reached reception and said goodbye to Aidan. His friend was just coming out of the toilets, and as Harry and Annabel signed out of the visitors book and waited for the school office to buzz them out of the secure entrance they heard the boys chatting.

'You coming out to play football, Aidy? Miss said we could use the top field.'

'Yeah, coming, Joey.' The boy he called Joey looked at the two adults, who were watching the receptionist finish up a call behind the glass screen. She'd given them 'one minute' with the raising of a finger.

'Who's that with your mum?' the boy asked, curiosity on his face.

'Oh, that's Harry,' Aidan said. 'He's a paramedic like Mum. They work together.'

The receptionist put down the receiver and the door buzzed. They were almost out of the door when they heard something else before the two boys ran off to the doors to the playground.

'That's so cool,' Joey said, a hint of wonder in his voice.

'I know,' Aidan replied, pride evident in his tone. 'And he's my dad too. He finally came home.'

Annabel and Harry didn't say a word until they were back in the car, and Harry was pulling away towards Abe's house, where they were due for lunch.

'Well,' Annabel said eventually, shock vibrating through her, 'I guess he'll take the news in his stride. Do they sell gin-flavoured ice-cream at the park?'

The late afternoon sun fell in shimmering spots along the grass as they sat on a bench together. The three of them were each holding cones of ice cream of different flavours—bubblegum for Aidan, rum and raisin for Harry and Annabel. The closest thing she could get to gin in ice-cream form. Aidan's lips were coated in blue sparkly dust, and a short distance away children whooped and shrieked in delight as they swung on metal swings and pushed each other around on the spinning roundabout.

Harry's phone rang and, after taking it out of his pocket to look at the screen, he silenced the call and shoved it back into his jacket. Annabel frowned, but said nothing. It wasn't the time, but she noticed that even since he'd told her about his fertility the clouds had not completely disappeared from over his head. Come to think of it, he'd had a couple of calls the last few days, with the same response and mood afterwards.

'Aidan, when we were leaving your school today, we heard you speaking to your friend Joey—do you remember?'

Aidan paused mid lick, his eyes going wide. Annabel could see his eyes dart from side to side, assessing their facial expressions.

'You're not in trouble; you know that, right?' She looked to Harry for support, but he was staring off into the distance, seemingly deep in thought. She frowned in his direction but focused back on Aidan. 'You said something to him, and we just wanted to know what you thought.'

'About Harry?' he said between licks of his cornet. He was a little less enthusiastic attacking the iced treat now. At the side of him, Harry seemed to come to at the sound of his name, and Annabel gave him a nod. She thought he should take the lead. He'd missed enough moments. This one should belong to him. He took the cue, and addressed the little boy sitting between them.

'You said that you thought I might be your father. Did that come from somewhere? Did you hear it somewhere?'

Aidan had stopped eating now, his head down, and Harry put his arm around him. His phone rang again in his pocket, and he cursed under his breath before shutting it off altogether. He never moved the arm that was wrapped around his son. Annabel caught him looking at him.

He's acting strange. Even in the current circumstances.

'Shall I go get us a drink from the stand?' she asked, giving him an opportunity to talk to Aidan alone if he needed it. And herself a minute to worry about the phone calls. Was it Dubai, wanting him back? He wouldn't go now, surely?

'In a minute, perhaps,' he said softly, touching her shoulder with the arm that hung around Aidan's sheepish form. 'Aidan?'

'I guessed,' Aidan said eventually. 'Mummy only has photos of you at home, none of my dad, and you went away to work. Saving people. I thought maybe that's why you couldn't be here, because you had to help people far away. Granddad isn't Mum's daddy, because he isn't here, so I guessed he might be your dad. When we did our family tree project at school, Miss Shepherd said something, and I thought that might make you my dad. I got to ask the teacher lots of questions. I came top of the class.'

The expression on both adults' features was one of shocked wonder.

'Have you known for a long time?' Annabel said, a tear dropping down her cheek when she thought of her little boy being so clever, searching for answers like a little detective.

Aidan wiped it away. 'Yes, I think so. You used to get all weird when you looked at his photos at Granddad's. Don't cry, Mum. My mates are over there. It's well embarrassing.'

She laughed through her sobs, trying to get a grip but only managing to reduce herself to a snotty mess. Harry produced a pack of tissues from his pocket and passed them across with a smile.

'I figured,' he quipped. Looking straight at Aidan, his face lit up.

'It's true, Aidan, I am your dad— Oof!'

He was cut off by Aidan flinging himself into his chest, wrapping his arms around him. A smear of blue ice-cream stained Harry's top, but he didn't even notice. He hugged Aidan back, before lifting his chin to meet his eyes.

'I am your dad, but I didn't know I was your dad when I went away. The thing is, something happened, and I didn't treat your mum very well. I broke her heart, and so she protected you from getting your heart broken too. I'm sorry for that, Aidan, but I'm here now and I want to make it right. Grown-ups aren't very smart sometimes. Not as smart as you, anyway.' Aidan grinned at that.

'I came back to mend what I broke, and when I found out about you I was so happy.' He was smiling now, his eyes glistening with tears of his own. 'I should have been there for you, Aidan, but I wasn't, and that breaks *my* heart. We wanted to tell you today, actually, right here, but you beat us to it.'

The two males mirrored each other with their lopsided grins, and Annabel sobbed again.

'Mum!'

'Annie! It's okay!'

Annabel groaned, trying to pull herself together.

'Sorry, sorry! I'll go get the drinks, okay?' She stood up off the bench, giving them both a watery-eyed wave before heading over to the small crowd of people at the refreshments stand.

The two of them were left alone now, listening to the chatter of people around them.

'Are you mad at Mum, for not telling you?' Aidan's voice was curious, and Harry marvelled at the little character he'd helped create.

Harry shook his head. 'When I left, I didn't make it easy on her. I could never be mad. I love her, just like you do. You shouldn't be mad at her either. It was your mum who asked me to come home, and she told me about you.'

'Are you going to go away again?' Aidan's ice-cream was nothing but a small cone of wafer in his hand now, his little fingers sticky and stained blue.

Harry thought of the phone calls he'd received earlier. He recognised the number; he knew that they wouldn't be calling unless they had something important to say. He took a deep breath and tipped the rest of his own cone into the bin next to the bench. He didn't want to lie to his son. He wanted to be the parent who was there, who showed up, who Aidan could trust. He chose his next words carefully.

'There's nowhere I'd rather be than with you and your mum, and that's the truth. I'm happy to be here.'

Annabel was slowly walking back towards them now, and he winked at her as she approached. He mouthed 'I love you' to her, and she said it back, her troubled expression relaxing as she came closer to the bench.

'Good,' Aidan said. 'Now we just have to make Mum let you move in. We have a big house now, and Mum's garbage at football. We could play every day!'

He dropped a kiss on the top of his son's head, chuckling. The phone calls could wait. He didn't want anything to spoil the day. He wanted to focus on claiming his family and shouting from the rooftops that he was the father of this wonderful boy. The son of the love of his life, past and present. It was the future that had a question mark over it, hanging like the reaper's scythe over his head. One thing Harry was sure of: he was used to fighting, and this would be no different.

CHAPTER SEVEN

ONCE AIDAN HAD digested their talk, and many talks after in the days that followed, and Abe was in the picture, they let the dust settle and enjoyed life in their new groove for a while, until they decided that today, finally, was the day.

In truth, Annabel had been the one to beg Harry to take the plunge professionally. For some reason, he'd still been a little quiet. A little too cautious. Their nights on the couch were always full of hot kisses and tender caresses, but Harry was steadfast in making them wait. A little voice inside her head had been asking questions she didn't like the sound of. Tiny dandelion seeds of doubt were threatening to blow over their new lives, which felt like sunny, cloudless days in the park. Till now, when he'd been the one to pick the day.

When they were both finished on shift and changed, they headed to HR to declare their relationship. It was just a formality, needed to cover against possible sexual harassment claims in the future. Things could turn sour in matters of the heart, and the hospital, as any other business, protected itself from any fallout.

It wasn't uncommon for staff to date each other; with their hours and shift patterns, their dating pool wasn't exactly swimming with fish. Being together in those high-pressure situations, you really got to know a person. Tonight, they were going to know each other even better.

'All done,' Annabel said, puffing out a sigh of relief as they headed out of the hospital. 'Are you sure Abe will be okay with having Aidan for the whole night on a school night? I could have arranged a sleepover at one of his friend's houses, I'm sure.'

'Don't be daft; they were thrilled. He's probably going to grill the teachers on what science lessons they're giving the kids on the morning drop-off.' Harry stopped her in the foyer, turning her to face him and taking her into his arms. She looked around her to check for onlookers. 'And stop doing that too. We're official now, remember? HR certified to hold each other in the corridors. And other things out of work.' His look was positively devilish, and she couldn't help but giggle.

'Down, boy.'

Harry seemed brighter today, the melancholy that settled over him sometimes seemingly gone. The phone calls had stopped too, but it worried her what that meant. Still, making things official was good.

What else can he possibly have to hide? Unless he is secretly James Bond, we're good now. Nothing can break us apart.

'Hey, it's been a long time. We've waited enough. I've been back a long time now. We have the entire night to go out, drink, eat some fast congealing buffet food, and act like a couple. In public. With an empty house and a huge bed to get back to.'

The butterflies in her stomach were doing back flips

off her ribcage now, and she had to shut her thoughts down. Till later anyway. She had changed her sheets and might just have had a wax. A girl had to prepare, after all.

'I'm going to miss Purdie though; she's been there from the beginning. It will be weird not seeing her on the wards.'

'I know. She's been a good friend to both of us. Especially since I got back.' His smile faded a little, but he soon recovered. 'The oncology department won't be the same without her.' He caught sight of the clock on the wall behind her, and steered them both in the direction of the car park.

'Come on, let's go. First tequila is on me.'

He was wearing a dark blue shirt, paired with a pair of jeans that made Annabel drag her feet just a little bit, so she could watch his gorgeous bum in action as they headed to the party for Purdie. She was retiring, and not just retiring to stay home and knit. Her daughters had returned to Barbados, and she was jetting off next week to be reunited with them. To enjoy her well-earned twilight years and sit in the sun, watching her grandchildren grow up. Annabel was nothing but happy for her. Family was everything in this life, which they all knew could be short, and cruel.

The bar was nothing fancy, Purdie's colleagues opting for a private room in the back so that Purdie would be centre stage for her going away party. They pulled up in the black cab, Harry passing the driver some notes and taking Annabel's hand as they stepped out into the London night. There was nothing like her home city when the sun went down. The atmosphere was always one of excitement, the bustle of people in suits heading for after dinner drinks, celebrating birthdays, promotions and big deals being done. She loved living here, even when the calls and the pressures of her job brought her to her exhausted knees. Now Harry was here, everything seemed that bit brighter.

The second they walked into the already lively events room, Harry's hand gripped hers.

'Are you ready for this?' she asked him gently. 'Our first night out of the medical supply closet?'

He chuckled, rubbing his thumb along her palm.

'Let's go get a drink,' Harry replied in her ear, making her shiver slightly.

Purdie was already there, looking lovely in a pretty dark red velvet dress. She was standing a little way away, chatting to some of their colleagues. She looked over, and Annabel gave her a wave. She waved back, but she looked distracted, her eyes flicking from Harry to hers. Annabel shook off the uneasy feeling it gave her. Something wasn't quite right; she could feel it. She let go of Harry's hand and caught the barman's attention. She needed a stiff drink to bolster her confidence.

'Everything okay?' Purdie walked over to them as they headed over to a vacant table. 'I see the nurses are on form tonight.' Some of the oncology nurses were sitting at a table, cackling loudly and thoroughly enjoying themselves.

'Work hard, play hard.' Harry laughed. Purdie laughed too, but it sounded forced in Annabel's ears. She eyed Harry, and something in that look had Annabel's Spidey sense tingling.

'You okay, Harrison?' Purdie asked him, her professional voice in full flow now.

'I'm fine,' Harry said shortly. 'You should be enjoying your party.'

'Oh, child, I intend to.' She looked at Annabel, who was watching them both like a tennis spectator. 'You two finally got your act together, didn't you! I'm so glad! I was planning on locking you in one of the offices before I left. You've wasted enough time.'

'Yes, you're right there,' Annabel said, laughing now. Harry spotted someone, frowning, and he made his apologies and left, leaving the two of them alone. She took advantage of the moment. 'He's Aidan's dad too. His biological father.'

Purdie laughed then, a loud, joyous laugh. 'Oh, I knew that! Come on, you think anything misses my attention around that hospital? Please.' She pulled Annabel in for a perfume-soaked hug. 'I'm so happy for you all. It makes my heart glad. You want a holiday, you come to Barbados. Aidan will play with my grandbabies, we can drink cocktails and watch them play.'

'Now that sounds like a plan.' Annabel laughed, noticing that Harry was speaking to the head of oncology. The way they were huddled together, serious expressions focused on each other, had everything in her switch to full panic mode. The phone calls, the way he'd been acting…

She strode over and caught the tail-end of the conversation before the two men realised that she was standing there.

Dr Geller was speaking. 'With that type of chemo, I'm afraid the prognosis is not good at all. I'm sorry, Harry.'

Annabel felt as if her heart had fallen out of her heels. The room swayed. She knew what the consultant meant. She'd seen it enough times in her career, had had to watch her full-of-life mother fade away to nearly nothing. Everything fell into place. The secretive phone calls. Harry's sombre moods. Delaying their intimacy this long. She looked at Harry, waiting for him to refute the jigsaw pieces that were slotting together in her mind, but he just looked at her, stricken.

'It's true, isn't it? You're sick again,' she said. 'Aren't you? It makes sense now. The phone calls, the moods.' Another thought slammed into her shocked thought pattern, scattering whatever control she had over her words. 'That's why you came back. Not for me at all. You came back because you got sick again.' She laughed, a hollow sound from deep in her gut, shock and terror rippling through her. The tears were already escaping. She looked at her surroundings, aware that she was with her subordinates and friends. The pain of her old humiliation reared its ugly head.

I am such an idiot. He didn't come back for me. He came back six months after my call. He came home to make amends before he died.

It seemed so surreal, but she'd heard Dr Geller's words.

'I can't do this. Not again.'

'You can't do what? Annie, let's go outside. I'll explain.' Dr Geller had melted into the crowd, obviously eager to avoid the scene that was about to happen. She was trying to calm down, but she just couldn't stop her mind from going to the worst, darkest places. Aidan loved him; they were together. He'd lied about his cancer all over again.

Oh, dear God. I'm going to lose him. For ever this time.

Harry was trying to reach for her hands, but she felt

her anger rise and she shoved him away from her, as hard as she could. His hands fell to his sides, defeated.

'Just listen, Annie, please. Let's go back to yours; we can talk.'

'I can't believe I fell for your lies again! I told Aidan about you! You let me love you again! Why would you do that? I watched my mother die! A horrible, painful death.' She was sobbing now, smearing her make-up as she tried to wipe away the tears that were blurring her vision. 'Aidan!' Her broken-hearted humiliation turned to white-hot rage. 'You want Aidan to go through that? You're a selfish bastard, Harry, I hate you. Why would you keep this from me again? Why don't you trust me?'

'No, Annie, I'm—'

'No, Harry, I'm done listening to you. Done. I never should have trusted you.'

He had tears in his eyes too now, his hands limp at his sides. 'Stop, Annie, this is so stupid.'

'Stupid, eh? Screw you, Harry.'

Before she was even aware of what she was doing, she was sitting in the back of a cab, heels in her shaking hand. Just as it pulled away, she saw Harry run out into the street after her, stopping traffic while Purdie stood in the doorway of the bar. Car horns honked, but Harry was oblivious.

'Annie!' she could hear him shout after her. 'Annie, please! Stop! I love you!'

The driver turned to her, slowing down. 'You Annie? You want me to stop?'

She reached for her bag, wanting to ring Abe, to warn him that she didn't want Harry around Aidan. She didn't want Abe to be left in the dark again either, but she knew if she turned up to collect Aidan like this, smelling of tequila and looking like a fan at an Alice Cooper concert, it would upset them both far more. She realised she'd left her bag behind, in her rush to escape. She heard Harry shout her name again, and she covered her ears.

She reeled off her address to the cab driver. She had cash at home to pay him at the other end.

'No, please, just drive. Can you step on it, please?'

The cab driver looked as if he wanted to ask more, but he just nodded and discreetly closed the glass partition between them. The lights of the city streets flickered through the windows as they joined the evening flow of London traffic.

She processed everything from the evening, the last few weeks even, through fresh eyes. Filtering through the past few weeks with the new information applied as an overlay.

Harry is sick. Cancer sick. Possibly dying sick.

Her gut twisted and she felt as if her heart, newly whole, was fighting to keep the blood pumping around her body. She thought of her mother, the vibrant, strong single parent who had raised her to be the woman she was today. In her final days, her mother had been unrecognisable from the strong woman she'd been. The fire had still been there, but stifled by the cancer, and the treatment that had ultimately failed to save her.

Annabel cried fresh tears as the long-forgotten memory burned in her brain. She thought of growing up, just the two of them together. She'd had a great childhood, but a lonely one at times. Could she deprive Aidan of that chance, even after everything that had happened? Even if the reality could be short, and painful? She thought of how Aidan would feel if he knew that she had kept him from those final moments with the father he had just found, however hard they might be. She didn't want him to miss another moment. And, truthfully, she didn't want to waste any more time either. She loved Harry, and she'd been apart from him for far too long already. They all had.

What was more, she had just been horrible to him. In her shock and pain, she'd never even thought about how scared he must be feeling, about how he had made the same mistake again, not telling her to protect her. He loved her so much, he didn't want to share the pain. She was the worst woman in the world. She'd left him there, humiliated him. Just like she had felt in that stupid airport. She was so disgusted with herself.

She pulled up to the house, which was in darkness apart from the light she'd left on in the hallway. It really was looking great now, everything she'd dreamed of for all these years. A family home.

She smiled at the driver. 'I'm sorry, I won't be a minute. I left my purse behind at the bar.'

The driver nodded, and she then realised that her keys were also in her bag. Thank God for the hidden key she'd kept for when she wasn't there and Aidan needed to get in with her friend Teri. She picked her heels up from the cab floor and went around the side of the house, picking up the plant pot of flowers that she kept it under. She was just coming out of the house, money in hand, when her taxi pulled away.

'Hey, wait! I have your money!'

'I paid it,' a voice said from the darkness of the street. She heard footsteps, and Harry stepped out from the shadows, lit by the nearby streetlight. 'I came to talk.'

She saw her purse in his hands. 'Oh, thank God, my whole life is in there.'

'Not quite,' he said, slowly walking up the path. She met him step for step. 'You were in a hurry.'

'I know. I am so sorry I did that. I feel awful. I was just going to call you, ask you to come over.'

He halted. 'Really?'

She kept walking towards him till they were standing in front of each other. He had hope etched across his drained features now, and she wanted to just take him into her arms and hold him. Heal him.

Oh, the irony.

He held her purse out to her, and she took it from him and dropped it to the side on the wet grass.

'Really, now let me get this out. I care that you lied, and that was the last time, Harry. If we're going to do this, and I mean really do this, then you need to be honest with me. One more half-truth, however small you think it is, I'm out. And so is Aidan. So help me God, I could kick your ass, but I understand why you didn't want to tell me.'

He went to speak, but she gently touched her palms to his chest. He felt warm to the touch, and she realised how cold she'd felt since leaving his side.

'It's my turn to speak. I love you, Harrison Abraham Carter. I love every hair on your stupid, stupid head. I love that we made our son together, and that you are the man in a storm at work, and at home. These last few months have been—'

'Challenging?' he offered. She nodded, a sliver of a smile passing across her features.

'Challenging, annoying, terrifying. All of those too, but I was going to say amazing. I love you; I've loved you since I was a green as grass medical student, not knowing one end of an IV from the other, and I love you now. I'm glad you came home. I've felt more alive since you returned than I have in years. I guess I blocked a lot out because it was just too difficult to face. I never let you speak, but I am listening.'

'Can I speak yet?'

'No.' She bent down on one knee, right there on the moonlit path, and looked up at him.

'Harrison Abraham Carter, I don't have a ring but take these words as my vow. Marry me. Be my husband, for however long we have. For ever, hopefully, but I'll settle for any days the big man upstairs can give us. Make this fight our fight and be by my side. In sickness and in health.'

Harry brushed away a tear and knelt down with her.

'Annie, I'm not sick. I got the all-clear a long time ago. I went for a check-up when I got back to London. After our talk, I went to get my fertility checked. Just so I had the full picture. It's what I thought. That's what Dr Geller was telling me. With my treatment, it was never likely, but I wanted to be sure before I told you. Truly, Annie, I'm going nowhere. Ever again.'

Annie's breaths came thick and fast, her lungs gasping for air as she looked at the man before her.

'Oh, my God, I'm such an idiot. I made such a scene. I don't care about having more children. I meant that when I said it before. We have Aidan, and each other. We can adopt a whole house full of kids if you want. I don't care, Harry. I just want to be a family. I always wanted that.'

He stood, taking her with him. 'That's all I want.' He dipped down, getting down on one knee himself now and pulling a ring box out of his pocket. 'I was planning to do this tonight anyway but, as usual, I can't get a word in.' He opened the box, and there sat a beautiful ring. It was stunning, the jewels shining in the moonlight. 'I bought this ring six months ago, in Dubai. When you called, and I was coming back to you, I saw this in a shop window and I knew that if I ever got the chance to be with you again I wouldn't wait a moment. I wanted to be ready. Annabel Sanders, will you please be my wife? My Annie, for ever?'

Annabel was crying, her whole body shaking as she nodded and put out her hand. He put the ring on her finger and kissed it.

'I love you, Annie.'

'I love you too, Harry. I'm so sorry that we missed out on so much. You missed out on being a father for so long, but from today we can put all this right. Be together.'

Harry stood and, taking her into his strong arms, he kissed her with everything he had. She kissed him right back, not quite believing she was in his arms again. 'Let's get inside.' He wrapped his arm around her and they headed to the light coming from the doorway. 'We have a lot of time to make up for.'

He flashed her a devilish grin, and she laughed as he took her into his arms, heading towards the open door. They were finally where they wanted to be. They were home.

EPILOGUE

'So, LOVE OF my life, how do you like Dubai?'

Harry's voice behind her only momentarily distracted her from the view. She couldn't quite believe her eyes; the photos that her new husband had shown her hadn't done the beauty of the land nearly enough justice. It felt worlds away from London and the home her little family all now lived in together. Standing out on the balcony of their hotel suite, Aidan asleep in the adjoining room, being watched over by Abe, she sighed happily.

'I can't quite believe we're here. Together.'

'I know.' His arms wrapped around her waist and she felt the stubble on his cheek graze her neck, making her shiver, even in the heat of the night. 'I'm so glad we got to come here. I thought about it a lot when I was here, away from you all.'

'Only took us a decade.' She laughed.

'Well, you kept me dangling on the engagement hook long enough!' he teased, an old running joke between them now.

'Hey!' She slapped gently at one of the hands around her, and he nuzzled his scruff in deeper, scraping it along her cheek, making her laugh and shiver with lust, all at the same time. 'I'll have you know I am a busy career woman with a very full schedule.'

He growled, turning her to face him and kissing her impulsively. 'That's it, keep talking. Tell me all about it; I love a strong woman.'

She giggled, wrapping her arms around the back of his head, running her fingers through his thick hair. They had music playing from the corner of the lavish room, and a familiar song came on. Slowly, they started to sway together, enjoying the solitude after their busy day out sightseeing.

They'd even been to the hospital where Harry had worked, and Abe, Aidan and Annie had all loved meeting Harry's friends and colleagues, seeing just how much he was loved, how he'd been missed. They could all relate to missing Harry. They'd even met the doctors and nurses who had helped treat him for the aggressive cancer he'd arrived with. Annie had cried then, hugging more than one of them a little too tightly, and thanking them over and over. They knew all about her, which was probably the most surprising thing of all. Looking at Harry's proud and slightly embarrassed face, she knew she'd fallen in love with him even more right then and there. Something she'd never thought possible since that day they had met again in the airport car park. Even then, her heart had come back to life. Even through the hurt, and the anger at his departure.

Their colleagues had all been amazing. They were all thrilled for them, and the news about Harry being Aidan's real father had been met with happiness too, and more than a few knowing looks. She loved them all even more for keeping their suspicions to themselves, making those early years easier to bear. There were no secrets now, and the station was a happier place for it.

Purdie was happy with the result too. She video called them often, and Aidan was getting to know her family right along with them. Barbados was next on the holiday list, and they had already done Spain and most of the British tourist attractions. The days out as a family had been amazing, filled with fun, and their house was filled with souvenirs and family photos.

Her mother's photos had pride of place on the mantelpiece and every day she thought of her. She would have been so happy with how things had turned out. Annabel liked to think that she was looking down on them, content and thrilled that Aidan had two parents who loved him dearly, a tribe of people who would all drop everything to come to his aid.

Tom and Lloyd were blissfully happy too, their dream of becoming a family finally a reality. They were back in London, no doubt run ragged by their very cute and very active twin boys, Jayden and Nathan. When they'd first gone round to see them at their house she'd caught Harry looking at her more than a few times, not that he didn't anyway. He was always finding excuses to touch her, always looking her way, as though he thought she might just vanish in a puff of smoke. This time was different though; these looks were ones of concern. She was rolling around on the floor, tickling the twins while Aidan pretended that the floor was lava, making them gurgle with delight. He needn't have worried though, and she'd told him as much that night. Whilst she loved being auntie to the gorgeous boys, she was just as glad to hand them back.

She remembered all too well how hard it had been

raising baby Aidan, and their lives together had so many more things in it. Travel, their jobs, watching their son grow into a fine young man. Harry had even persuaded her to buy a puppy and, given the space they now had at home, she had finally relented. They were picking a rescue puppy up from the local shelter on their return; they'd had a pregnant Labrador bitch come in and the pups would be ready for new homes a few days after they returned home from their trip. Aidan had no idea; she couldn't wait to see his face when they went to collect him. Another boy in the household to love.

The four of them were so happy together, Abe keeping well, still as moody as ever. He was getting ready to retire, his practice safe in the hands of a doctor he'd recruited and trained up. Well, doggedly nagged at more like. The man was nothing short of a stickler, but he was far less sour these days. Having his son back and his fractured family back together suited him well. Harry and he were closer than ever, always laughing and discussing medical journals and breakthroughs together. They saw the merits of each profession and regaled each other with stories of great saves and low moments. There wasn't anything they wouldn't do for the little man in their lives, and her. Abe had even joined the nagging train about the puppy too, even going as dirty as playing the cholesterol card on her. For weeks before she'd finally given in, he had taken to emailing her medical evidence of how pets helped cognitive function in developing adults, and helped the elderly feel less alone and vulnerable to ill health. The man would live to be a hundred, and he had more friends than Mark Zuckerberg, but she loved him for it. These Carter men were determined; she knew that only too well.

The three men in her life were about to become four, although she hoped that the four-legged new addition would give her less trouble than the first three. Secretly, she was looking forward to it herself now, and she had a whole army of dog walkers and sitters on hand for when they had to juggle their shifts. She still marvelled to herself at how her life had changed.

'You back?' Harry asked, twirling her around on the spot, pulling her out of her private world once more. 'Where do you go when you do that?' he asked, the love and adoration plain on his face as he pulled her close once more.

'Nowhere far,' she said, a teasing smile on her tired but happy face. 'Just thinking about how things turned out.'

'Hard to believe, isn't it?'

'You're telling me. I wanted to run you over in the car park when I first saw you. Tom saved your life that day, you know.'

Harry laughed as she rested her head on his chest, feeling his heartbeat quicken, the low rumble in his chest.

'I owe Tom a few more babysitting sessions then.'

Harry was a great uncle, equally as great as he was a doting father, son and husband. The three boys all loved him, and he them. It was great to see him with them, and she thanked her lucky stars every single morning she awoke in his arms.

'Ten at the very least; I'm an excellent driver.'

'I'm glad you didn't,' he said earnestly. 'And you're

not that great. Our fence post would disagree, I think you'll find.'

'Hey! There was a squirrel there, I told you!'

They laughed together, turning back towards the view and looking out at the landscape laid before them. They were in Dubai together, finally. And now it was all the more special. Because they had finally found each other again, and their family was complete. She couldn't wait to see what the next decade would bring. Something told Mrs Annabel Carter that she wouldn't want to miss one single second of it. Life was for living, and loving, and giving second chances. One call could change a life for ever, and no one knew that better than her.

As they headed to bed much later that evening, lying there in the dark, she sent up a silent prayer of thanks for everything she had.

'I love you,' Harry sighed, pulling her close as they let sleep claim them both.

'I love you too.' She smiled in the darkness, kissing him again. She never wanted to stop kissing this man. And she never did.

* * * * *

MILLS & BOON

Coming next month

ISLAND FLING WITH THE SURGEON
Ann McIntosh

"I'm going in," Zach said, after he'd arranged the cooler and towels to his specifications and adjusted the umbrella for maximum shade. When he pulled off his shirt, Gen bit back a groan of pleasure, seeing his bare torso in all its glory for the first time. "Are you coming?"

"Sure," Gen said, her heart going into overdrive as she stood up and unzipped her cover-up, aware of Zach standing just a step or two away, waiting for her.

Oh, she hoped he felt the same way looking at her as she did at the sight of those magnificent pecs and his firm, ridged abdomen.

She didn't look at him as she shrugged the sleeveless dress off her arms and stepped out of it, before bending to pick it up and fold it carefully.

Then, with the long strides she'd learned during her pageant days, she walked past him toward the surf.

He wasn't beside her as she ran the last few steps into the water before doing a shallow dive beneath an incoming wave.

When she came up and turned back toward the beach, wiping the salt water from her face, he was still standing where she'd left him. When their gazes collided, despite the distance between them a shiver of longing ran up her spine.

Then he was in motion, not running but following

her with decisive, intentional strides. He didn't dive into the water, but kept wading until he was standing just inches from where she was bobbing in the water.

"You're trying to drive me bonkers, aren't you?"

It was little better than a growl, and her nipples tightened at his tone, while her core turned molten and needy.

"Is it working?" she asked, holding his gaze, trying to figure out if the gleam there was anger, annoyance or something else entirely.

"Yes," he snapped. "But this…" He waved his hand between them. "This is supposed to be make-believe."

She shrugged lightly. "It doesn't have to be. I'm horribly attracted to you, so if you want to change the rules, we can negotiate."

"Consider this my opening bid," he said, pulling her close, placing his hands on either side of her face and kissing her as though he'd never stop.

Continue reading

ISLAND FLING WITH THE SURGEON

Ann McIntosh

Available next month

www.millsandboon.co.uk